His skin was W9-BOA-511
and not with fever . . .

"You promised you wouldn't leave me," she reminded him in a voice grown suddenly husky. Impulsively, she lifted his hand and pressed it against her uninjured cheek. His skin felt hard and hot and abrasive against the softness of her face.

"I've changed my mind." But he made no effort to pull his hand away from her cheek. Instead, she was almost certain that the long fingers made an abortive caressing movement before being abruptly stilled. "You don't know what you're asking for, Amanda." These last words were almost desperate.

"No I don't, do I?" Her eyes met his again, their expression soft and seductive beneath the long lashes that half-veiled them. "But you could teach me, Matt."

And she turned her mouth into his palm.

Books by Karen Robards

Amanda Rose
Loving Julia
Night Magic
To Love a Man
Wild Orchids

Published by
WARNER BOOKS

KAREN ROBARDS

AMANDA ROSE

WARNER BOOKS

A Time Warner Company

WARNER BOOKS EDITION

Copyright © 1984 by Karen Robards
All rights reserved.

Cover design by Diane Luger
Cover illustration by Michael Racz

Warner Books, Inc.
1271 Avenue of the Americas
New York, NY 10020

Ⓦ A Time Warner Company

Printed in the United States of America

First Printing: February, 1984

Reissued: June, 1995

10 9 8 7 6 5 4 3 2

TO:

My husband, Doug
Dr. Walter L. "Pete" Johnson
and my mother, Sally Skaggs Johnson,

with love and appreciation for their
help and support over the years

AMANDA ROSE

chapter one

It was a perfect day for everything except dying.

Matthew Grayson lifted his face to the bright April sunshine and sniffed the sweetness of the air, an automatic gesture born of years spent at sea at the helm of his own ship. In those days—were they only a few months ago?—he had thrived on storms and dangers and challenges of every sort, thrived on pitting his courage and skill against anything that sea or sky or man—or woman—could throw at them. Grappling with death had always exhilarated him, making his blood sing with the sheer joy of being alive. Only now, when death was a grim reality and not a faceless chimera, had the singing abruptly stopped.

His eyes flickered once in his otherwise carefully expressionless face as he thought briefly, longingly, of happier days. The first time his men had seen him

9

laughing at death—he had been hurling mocking defiance in the teeth of a killer hurricane that had sunk a hundred ships from one end of the Atlantic to the other—they had looked at one another in quaking disbelief, silently questioning his sanity. Then, when their own ship, the *Lucie Belle*, had emerged from the tempest unscathed, the more superstitious among them had stared fearfully at their black-haired, swarthy-skinned captain. His teeth were flashing white in an exultant grin as he worked with unflagging energy while the crew was ready to drop from the exhaustion of more than forty-eight hours spent battling the storm. And, one by one, they had crossed themselves. It was then that the whispers began: Matt Grayson had made a pact with the devil, had bartered his soul for his own and his ship's safety. The *Lucie Belle* was blessed or cursed, depending on the speaker's point of view.

It was a rumor that Matt did nothing to encourage, but he didn't discourage it, either, because from then on men lined up in droves to sail on his ship whenever she docked in her home port of New Orleans. For every vacancy there were twenty applicants, and Matt liked being able to pick and choose. He prided himself on having the best crew afloat, and, in turn, the men prided themselves on their captain's invincibility. It seemed that nothing could touch Matt Grayson—not storms, not bullets, not knives, not even the occasional jealous husband. Nothing, until the devil was ready to claim his own.

The less superstitious among his crew had another, simpler explanation for their captain's uncanny ability to bring them safely through the worst the sea could throw at them. "Those born to be hanged will never drown" was what they said of him when the ocean rose up in fury and threatened to crush the *Lucie Belle*'s hull like a giant, angry fist holding an eggshell, only to set her down again safely in calmer waters some hours later. The saying kept his men from despairing when the waves were thirty feet high and the sea and the sky met and seethed like a briny mixture from hell's blackest caldron. Matt, hearing the words passed like a talisman from man to man, would throw back his head and laugh in incredulous amazement that grown men, and hardened sea dogs at that, could take comfort in something so ridiculous.

But he was not laughing today—had not been laughing for some time now—because it looked as if he would, after all, meet the fate the men had prophesied for him. Three months ago, in a sequence of nightmarish events, he had been summarily arrested, tried, and found guilty of the grisly murders of Lord James Farringdon, Tory nephew of the prime minister, and his wife and children; today Queen Victoria's government meant to exact its vengeance on one who had removed a thorn from its side. Today they were going to hang him, Matthew Zacharias Grayson, by the neck until he was dead.

"Aw right, get on down there." Those words, uttered in a low growl by one of his three burly guards, brought him sharply back to the sorry present. So, too, did the nudge of a rifle butt in the small of his back with which the guard emphasized his command. Matt winced, stumbled, and would have fallen out of the back of the dirty farm cart, which had

11

just rumbled to a halt after conveying him to Tyburn from Newgate Prison, if another guard, perhaps more humane than his fellow, had not caught hold of the chain that linked his shackled wrists and jerked him back upright. Not so long ago Matt would have felt a murderous flash of rage at being so treated, but lately he had been unable to summon emotion of any sort. He felt nothing but a curious blackness, as if he were already dead. Inwardly he blessed that lack of feeling. They were determined to do their worst to him, determined to wring every last drop of pain and suffering from his battered flesh. But he was beyond pain at last, and nearly beyond their reach. For that reason alone he was ready to welcome death with open arms.

"G'wan, get down. We ain't got all day." The first guard prodded him again with the rifle, sounding impatient. Matt thought wryly that he must be keeping the man from something important, like his luncheon. Well, no matter. He was ready to go. They were determined that he would die, and if he did not walk to meet the death they had decreed for him, they would drag him to it. He preferred to spend his last moments on earth like a man, not a cringing dog. Clenching his teeth so hard that a little muscle jumped in the side of his jaw, he clambered awkwardly down from the cart, stumbling and nearly falling as the short, thick chain between the irons on his ankles tripped him up.

"Watch out there." Immediately the guards were around him. Afraid he might try to escape, Matt surmised, and would have laughed if he could have summoned the will to do so. He was, or had been, a strong man, big, nearly six feet four inches, with muscles that had earned him a healthy respect in ports from San Francisco to Africa's Barbary Coast. But the months in prison, without sufficient food or exercise and with frequent beatings and other tortures (they had hoped to wrest a confession from him; he took pride in the fact that they hadn't succeeded), had shrunk the flesh from his bones. He was a mere shell of what he had been, and he doubted that he had the strength to overpower a girl-child, much less three guards who had surely been chosen for their bullish physiques. But it seemed they were taking no chances. They closed ranks around him, hustling him the short distance from the cart to the foot of the gallows as if terrified that he might break away.

If he could have, he would have, Matt acknowledged silently, staring up dry-mouthed at the men who awaited him on the platform above. The first twinge of fear pierced the apathy with which he had armored himself as he recognized the black robes of a priest, and the hooded executioner. Matt cursed himself inwardly. He, who had never feared anyone or anything in his life, would not start now. He would meet death with his head up, his step unfaltering, and laugh in the faces of those who had come to hang him. They had taken from him all else that he valued; he would not surrender his pride.

Urged on by the guards, he mounted the rough wooden planks, his movements slow and awkward because of the confining chains. Over their clanking, he suddenly became aware of a swelling roar. Surprised, Matt looked around and down. A milling, unruly crowd stretched around the gallows like an endless expanse of sea around a tiny island. The sight stopped him in his tracks. He had not been aware of them before, wished he had not become aware of them now. They were staring up at him, a featureless blur made up of hundreds of faces, come to watch him die. Their mouths shouted obscenities; their eyes screamed hate.

"That's him. That's the one. Grayson—bloody *murderer.*"

Matt stared at them. Missiles thrown by the crowd began slicing through the air around him, rotten tomatoes and eggs and even rocks. The guards, as caught up in the maelstrom of refuse as he was, cursed viciously and hurried him up the stairs. Matt did nothing to hinder them. Every ounce of his concentration was suddenly focused on fighting down the terror that tiptoed icily up and down his spine. He scarcely felt the rock that bounced off his left temple, leaving a darkening bruise and a trickle of crimson in its wake.

The platform was long and narrow, just wide enough for perhaps four men to stand abreast. It stood a good fifteen feet off the ground—far enough so that there was at least an even chance that the drop would break the victim's neck. After all, England in the year 1842 was a humane country; no one wanted a man to meet his death twisting at the end of a rope and choking for as long as a full half hour. No matter that it happened like that more often than not; at least it was not *planned.* Thinking of the horrible, blackened face and gasping sounds of a man he had once seen hanged and who had died hard, Matt promised himself he would watch for the hangman's signal, then jump upward at the last moment so that he would fall through the trapdoor with a little extra force. All he asked now was that his finish be quick and clean. Being slowly strangled to death by a frayed piece of hemp was an end he preferred not to contemplate.

He was not the only man scheduled to die that day, he saw as soon as he set foot on the platform. Two other poor wretches were there, their irons already replaced by a single rope securing their hands behind their backs in the attitude in which they would soon meet their maker. Each had a man with a rifle standing behind and a little to the right of him. The Crown was clearly taking no chances, even at this late date. Three nooses instead of the one he had envisaged swung gently in the breeze. Two sets of eyes other than his own were viewing the soft beauty of a budding spring day for the last time. Matt took odd comfort in the presence of the two other condemned men. Only now did he realize how little he had relished the thought of dying alone.

"Over there." His guards—he rated three, whereas the others had only one apiece, which surely meant that he was considered the most dangerous, or perhaps notorious, of the prisoners—shoved him into place before the closest noose. Its twisted brown length seemed to mock and beckon at the same time. Matt wished sickly that it was all over. It was not death he feared so much as the act of dying, he realized. Dying scared him horribly. He could feel cold sweat breaking out under his armpits and along his spine. Desperately he hoped that his sudden weakness was not apparent to the men around him. Clenching his teeth, he unobtrusively straightened his shoulders and forced himself to concentrate on the here and now. Philosophizing about death paid no tolls; in any case, he would soon be solving its mysteries for himself.

From his position at the end of the platform, Matt realized that he would die last—or first. At this point he didn't know which he preferred. But when the priest stepped up to the prisoner at the opposite end and began administering the last rites, Matt felt a dizzying surge of relief. It seemed that his stubborn body was determined to hang onto life as long as it possibly could.

Down below, the crowd quieted as they realized that the first execution was imminent. Matt looked out over the sea of upturned faces, his lips curling with hatred and contempt as he felt the blood lust of those for whom his and his companions' doom was merely an excuse for a holiday. A hanging was an event, more respectable than a cockfight or a bearbaiting but just as exciting. Fine gentlemen and ladies in their curricles jockeyed for position to one side of the gallows under a clump of tall young oaks whose just-greening buds provided some protection from the bright spring sun. Shop clerks and merchants' apprentices, given the morning off by masters who were just as likely to be present, stood shoulder to shoulder with pink-cheeked scullery maids and prim seamstresses. Jammed almost underneath the platform itself were London's street people—the whores and thieves and drunks who haunted the city's byways at night. They were so close that they had to crane their necks uncomfortably to see the condemned men above them. But they were content: they were in the best possible position to hear the snap of a broken neck. Vendors made their way through the crowd, hawking meat pasties and hot chestnuts and lemon drinks. Overall hung an air of festivity, as if the citizenry had turned out to gawk at a carnival come to town.

Matt scarcely felt it as one guard ponderously began to remove his irons while another kept him firmly fixed in his rifle sights. He was too caught up in the horror of watching another man suffer the fate that soon would be his. The priest made the final sign of the cross over the condemned man—a small, stooped fellow with a bald head and fear-dulled eyes—and stepped back. The executioner, a black hood obscuring all but his eyes, stepped forward to jerk a hood similar to his own over the victim's face. Then, his movements quick and efficient, he grabbed the noose and pulled it over the man's head until it rested against his scrawny neck. The man jerked as he felt the rough hemp against his flesh; through the obscuring hood Matt saw his lips moving, in what he guessed was a prayer, as the hangman tightened the rope and positioned the knot judiciously. Then the executioner stepped back and the drumroll began. The condemned man gasped audibly. To Matt's horror and pity, he saw a wet stain spreading down the front of the fellow's ragged breeches; the man's fear had rendered him incontinent.

"May God have mercy on your soul," the priest intoned, and the doomed man gave a hoarse cry. Then the executioner lowered his hand in a sharp,

17

slicing motion while his assistant obediently pulled the lever that opened the trapdoor. The little man screamed just once as he felt the floor dropping out from beneath his feet and himself falling through it. Matt had no time to breathe the prayer hovering on his lips, so quickly was the man gone. The rope snapped taut. The scream choked off in mid-cry. There was a sharp crack, followed by a moment of silence. Then the crowd roared its approval. It had been a clean death.

"*No*. Oh, please God, *no*." The next man to die, a huge, redheaded fellow bigger than Matt, lost all pretense of composure as the priest approached him. Matt could almost smell the man's fear. The good father paid no attention to the man's attempts to cringe away from him, but quickly muttered the service while two guards rushed over to assist the original guard, who had abandoned his rifle to lock the weeping man in a bear hug and wrestle him back into place. Matt felt goose bumps break out along his arms as the priest, hastily making the sign of the cross before backing away from the prisoner's flailing legs, was replaced by the executioner. At the sight of that black-hooded figure, the man screamed horribly while tears rolled down his square yeoman's face. Matt, watching as the hood was forced into place over the head of this second man, clenched and unclenched his fists in impotent sympathy. Would he, too, be so overcome by fear when his turn came that he would lose every vestige of pride and human dignity? he wondered desperately as bile rose in his throat.

"You gonna cry for Mama, too, Grayson?" the

guard tying his wrists behind him taunted in an undertone. Matt glared at the man, feeling a burning rage that the oaf should mock the terror of a man in such dire circumstances. In that single instant before his eyes locked with those of the guard who was squatting behind him, he registered that his irons had been removed and that the guard who was supposed to be keeping him covered was instead watching with wide-eyed interest the frantic struggle going on just a few feet away. Even before his brain had properly recognized the opportunity, his body, made desperate by the situation, acted. Before he was conscious that he meant to do it, he swung around, jerking his wrists from the guard's hold, freeing them from the as-yet-untied rope in a single, violent movement that ended with his hands bunched into two fists that slammed into the astonished man's temples like twin anvils. The guard crumpled with a single grunt; the other guard, the one with the rifle, looked back just in time to see Matt going over the side of the platform in a low, fast dive. Automatically he jerked his rifle up and fired. Matt felt the stinging sensation of a bullet plowing through the side of his right hip, but he didn't slow down.

"Escape! Grayson's escaped!"

"Look out!"

"Get out of the way, you fools!"

The report of the rifle mingled with the screams of the crowd. They panicked at the sound of gunfire, taking to their heels like stampeding cattle. Matt ran with them, knowing it would be hard to spot him among so many fleeing bodies. Dirty and unkempt as he was, dressed in torn rags, he looked no different from many of London's army of the poor. A tremendous burst of strength surged through his veins; he felt suddenly vitally alive, reborn. He had escaped— he *would* escape. Spying a fat burgher astride a rearing horse just ahead of him and to his right, near the fringe of the crowd, Matt fought his way through the screaming, streaming mass of people to the man's side.

"Get down," he growled, and to make sure there was no possibility of mistake, he grabbed the frightened horse's bridle with one hand and the man's belt with the other. Before the perspiring burgher could do more than gape down at him, Matt had hauled him out of the saddle and vaulted up himself.

"My horse," the man cried. Then, with a note of horror, "It's *him*."

But Matt had already set his heels to the horse's sides. He sent the animal plunging toward the edge of the crowd, knocking down those who were slow to get out of his way. Curses and screams followed his progress. Another shot—from a pistol, by the sound of it—whistled frighteningly close to his head. This added to the crowd's panic, which aided him. He reached the road at last and crossed it quickly, too canny to travel on it in either direction. They would look for him first along the road...

Leaning low in the saddle, one hand pressed tight against his hip in an effort to stem the blood that ran warm and sticky down his side, he galloped across the field that ran at a right angle to the road. He had no idea whether they were after him yet; in his lightning glances back he had seen no one, no cavalry charge of soldiers brandishing rifles, no rush of guards on fat farm animals. Likely the crowd was hampering pursuit—not that it mattered. If they weren't hard on his heels now, they soon would be. They would search the four corners of the kingdom. for him if need be.

His escape would be a hideous black eye for Queen Victoria's government, and they would be tireless in their quest for vengeance. The odds were high that he wouldn't get more than five miles before he was captured. Matt's teeth gleamed brightly in the morning sun as he considered that. He'd always been one to bet on long shots, and as often as not, they'd paid off. That brief smile flashed again as he sent the horse over a low stone wall and into the valley below it. The odds had been considerably higher this morning that he would be dead by now. Instead, he was alive, free as the air, the sun warm on his face and a horse beneath him. He just might manage to cheat the devil one more time. Thinking that, for the first time in a long while Matt laughed out loud.

chapter two

"Damn."

Lady Amanda Rose Culver took intense satisfaction from uttering a word that, had they heard it, would have sent the good nuns with whom she lived into a collective swoon. Savoring the feeling of wickedness it gave her, she said the word again, louder. But it didn't really make her feel any better. She doubted that anything could.

As if to punish her for her naughtiness, the pale ghost that was all that was left of the moon stared at her reprovingly from the still-midnight-black sky while the early-morning wind whipped her hair across her face. Muttering impatiently, Amanda dug the offending tresses out of her eyes with both hands. Her hair—a heavy, wayward mass that fell down past her hips when released from the neat braids in which the nuns insisted it be kept confined—was the bane of

23

her existence. Even the color annoyed her. It was a deep, true red, the shade of fine old port when the sun hits it. Coupled with the porcelain paleness of her skin, the inky blackness of her winged brows and thick lashes, and the strange, smoky violet of her eyes, it could be considered striking, she supposed. Certainly the nuns were much struck by it. They seemed to feel that it symbolized everything they found fault with in Amanda. Her quick temper, her impulsiveness, the many small rebellions with which she plagued them daily, they always attributed directly to the outrageous color of her hair. Which was why, she supposed, they required her to wear it in such a conventionally schoolgirlish style—braided and wound into a coronet on top of her head—a style she loathed. Which in turn was why she unbraided it every chance she got, and why it was free to fly in her face at that moment.

Tucking the offending tresses firmly behind her small ears, she walked farther along the beach, her arms automatically wrapped about her slender body for warmth. She should have worn a shawl; even in the springtime this isolated bit of Lands End was cold at night. But the only shawl she possessed—the good sisters practiced poverty, as well as chastity and obedience, and saw to it that their pupils did the same—was a spotless, gleaming white cashmere. Against the background of dark gray cliffs and black water it would have stood out like a beacon, whereas the unfashionably high-necked, long-sleeved gray merino dress she wore blended almost invisibly into the night. Even in the murky, predawn hours, when she loved to walk the small shale beach at the foot of the cliff on which the convent perched, it was possible that one of the sisters would be up and about. If they saw her, they would not hesitate to report her to Mother Superior, and that would mean punishment, as well as the certain end of her clandestine walks. Even pretty Sister Mary Joseph, the youngest and most sympathetic of the nuns, would betray her, feeling duty bound to do so. After all, it was neither safe nor respectable for a young lady to be out alone at night anywhere, much less on a deserted stretch of beach that had been notorious some years back as a smugglers' haunt; and just at present there was another, more acute danger: the whole of England was on the alert for Lord James Farringdon's murderer, who three weeks ago had made a stunning escape from the very gallows itself.

The man was said to be brutal and ruthless in the extreme—the exact details of his crime were too horrendous to have been told to Amanda or even to the nuns themselves—but it was known that he had callously slain a woman and several children, as well as the Tory lord, who had been his prime target. He was desperate, unlikely to stick at anything. Ladies across the land were being careful to stay in their homes at night unless escorted by a gentleman, and men were going about armed until the fellow was caught. As he would be; it was merely a question of when. He could be anywhere in England, although the authorities were most particularly scouring the coastal areas, certain that the man would try to flee the country. And Lands End was one of those areas under constant surveillance.

Not that Amanda was unduly worried about coming face to face with a murderer. Of all the places in England that he could choose to run to, it seemed unlikely that he would pick her own small stretch of beach. No, she had more pressing worries on her mind than a madman who was probably hundreds of miles away. Only last evening she had received word from her half brother, Edward, the sixth Duke of Brookshire, that he had made final the arrangements for her marriage—arrangements that had been undertaken with nary a word to her. In four months' time, he had written to her, just a week to the day before her eighteenth birthday, she would become the bride of Lord Robert Turnbull, a plumpish, balding forty-year-old, nephew to Edward's late mother, the first wife of Amanda's father, and cousin to Edward himself.

She would *not* do it. Oh, she knew she had to marry, and marry well. There was no other course open to a lady of her background and breeding, and she had long since come to accept its inevitability. But *not* to Lord Robert. Why, he was old and fat, and had already buried one wife—who had been a considerable heiress, if she remembered correctly. Amanda knew that she would, upon her marriage—if that marriage met with Edward's approval—come into a tidy fortune of her own. With that as her dowry and her own not-inconsiderable charms, she had thought to be able to look as high for a husband as she chose. She had always imagined she would be allowed to select a man from among the list of eligibles who would no doubt pay her court after her come-out. For years she had dreamed of a brilliant season—she would, of course, take the *ton* by storm and be the year's reigning belle—and of a handsome, wealthy young man of impeccable lineage who would fall madly in love with her and beg her to be his bride. There would be other gentlemen ready to die for the sake of her *beaux yeux*, of course, but she would have no one but him. At the end of the season there would be a dazzlingly lovely wedding, and she would waltz into the future with her adoring husband to protect and cherish her. But now Edward was going to spoil it all—as he had always tried to spoil everything for her—by insisting that she wed this cousin of his before any other gentleman had ever seen her, and make her bow to society as Lady Robert Turnbull.

Edward had always hated her, just as he had hated her mother. His sisters, Lilian and Charlotte, hated her too. No matter that she was their half sister. They bitterly resented the bond of blood that tied her to them, and never let her forget that her mother had been, of all things, *on the stage,* and a "scheming, immoral creature" who had caught the eye of their widowed father when he was in his dotage. No matter that the fifth duke had adored Isabelle, his beautiful young second wife, and their child, Amanda, who was Isabelle's mirror image. No matter that he had never fully recovered from his grief when Isabelle died when Amanda was only ten. No matter that he had loved Amanda dearly until his own death three years later.

The fifth duke had scarcely been cold in his grave when Edward, a ponderous frown on his face, had summoned Amanda to his study—her father's study— and told her that she was to be sent away to school. She had been pampered and indulged beyond belief all her life, he said, and there was to be no more of it. She was to learn humility and obedience and respect for her elders and betters. Amanda, still in shock from the loss of her beloved father, had born Edward's tirade in drooping silence until he had dared to call her mother a painted whore. Even at the tender age of thirteen she had recognized fighting words when she heard them. Flooded with the fiery temper that went with the color of her hair, she had flown at Edward, kicking him soundly in the shins. The next morning she had been packed off to Our Lady of the Sorrows Convent, where the sisters of the Order of the Magdalene operated a school for young ladies from some of England's best families who for one reason or another needed to be gotten out of the way. Amanda had heard only occasionally from Edward in the almost five years since, and every one of his communications had been unpleasant. But his letter of the night before was the worst yet.

Engrossed in her thoughts, Amanda had moved some distance along the beach without realizing it. Her feet had somehow managed to pick their way through the debris thrown up by the storm that had come upon them just before midnight. Now, in the hour before dawn, the rain had stopped, but the wind still blew strongly, sending angry-looking waves rushing across the small bay to knock themselves against the shore. Heavy black clouds rolled above the cliffs, partially obscuring the moon from time to time and giving the silhouetted convent the eerie look of a medieval castle. There was just enough silvery moonlight to see by; in the darkness every rock and piece of driftwood took on a menacing appearance that bothered Amanda a little, although she would have died sooner than admit it. She had always prided herself on her courage, and she had weathered too much in her short life to let a niggling little fear of the dark chase her away from the one place she had always sought solitude—and solace.

Then she heard the moan. Amanda stopped in her tracks, straining her ears, eyes wide as she assured herself that it was only the wind whistling through the caves with which the cliffs were honeycombed. But the sound came again, unmistakable this time. Throat suddenly dry, she stiffened, holding her hair out of her face while she looked warily around. She saw nothing out of the ordinary, but there were countless large rocks, scattered near the base of the cliffs, which could have hidden someone who cared to hide. If there were someone, which there probably was not. More than likely it was an animal, hurt or trapped. Of course it was.

She had been poised to run, but that idea stopped her in her tracks. She could not bear the thought of an animal out here, alone and possibly trapped, surely injured, from the sounds it was making. Perhaps it was a raccoon or even a dog. At the third moan, she knew she had to see if she could find it, help it.

She moved slowly in the direction of the sounds, looking carefully about her. The chances were high that it was an animal, but just in case . . . She picked up a sturdy chunk of driftwood from the shale, hefting it in her right hand while her left kept her hair out of her eyes. She would have no compunction about braining someone if it turned out to be necessary.

As she cautiously approached a large rock nestled near the foot of the cliffs, she heard another sound, this time more of a whimper than a moan. It clearly came from behind the rock. Edging forward, her makeshift club raised threateningly, she could just make out a large, dark shape lying against the shale. It was too large for a raccoon or a dog... Was it a man? It *was*. Shock made Amanda jump backward, a startled cry rising to her throat. The piece of driftwood dropped from her nerveless hand.

He made no move to come after her. Amanda relaxed a little, her hand pressing against her heart, which was pumping double time. Gradually it occurred to her that the man must be hurt: that would explain the sounds she had heard. Perhaps he was a local farmer, fallen from the cliffs while looking for a strayed animal, or even a sailor whose boat had sunk in last night's seas. She couldn't leave him there. She had to help him if she could.

Still, her movements were cautious as she took a step closer, and then another. When the man continued to sprawl, unmoving, in the shale, she concluded that he was probably only semiconscious at best, and breathed a little easier. Hesitantly she bent to touch him, first his shoulder, then his averted face. He was soaking wet, his clothing half frozen to his body, his hair dripping water, and yet his skin was fiery hot. Clearly he was ill. That realization made her feel much better, and she was almost at ease as she knelt down beside him, her hand firmer on his shoulder as she attempted to shake him to his senses. His only response was a groan as he tried to pull his shoulder away from her importunate hand.

"Can you hear me?" she asked insistently. "Sir?"

Whether in response to her hand or to her voice she didn't know, but he rolled over, lying now on his back, motionless, his eyes closed. His body looked long and large against the shale; it would be impossible for her to shift him without help. She started to get to her feet, knowing she had to summon assistance even if it meant that the sisters would find out about her nightly perambulations. Then the moon came out from behind a cloud to shine its light directly on his face. Amanda stayed where she was, crouched beside him, staring at his face, transfixed.

His hair was as black as coal and curling, and she guessed that his skin would be dark, too, without the twin influences of illness and moonlight. His brows were thick and as black as his hair, and his lashes curled with incongruous and oddly disarming innocence against his lean cheeks. The rest of his face was hard, aggressively masculine though he was unconscious, with chiseled cheekbones, an arrogant blade of a nose, and a jaw covered with thick black bristles that effectively obscured the lower third of his face. But it was not all this that arrested Amanda's attention, causing her eyes to widen with slowly dawning horror. It was the scar.

It was a long, thin scar, faintly raised and paler than the skin around it, which descended from the outer corner of his left eyebrow down across his cheek to disappear in the stubble at the side of his mouth. Amanda could not tear her eyes away from it. Not that the scar was horrible in itself; it wasn't, not at all. But Amanda had heard tell of a scar like that only once before, just recently, when one of the girls at the school had received a letter from her married Londonite sister. In the letter, the scar, as well as the man who bore it, was described thoroughly. And he was identified, too—as Matthew Grayson, the escaped murderer who had the whole country in a quake.

Thank the Lord he was unconscious. That was the first thought that went through Amanda's head as she made the connection. Her heart hammered against her breast as she imagined what would have happened to her if she had come upon him on this deserted stretch of beach when he was in possession of all his faculties. He would undoubtedly have killed her, to keep her from telling what she had seen... Dear God. At the thought of what could have happened, she quivered from head to toe. For once the nuns had been right. She should never have ventured out alone at night—and would never do so again. But now she had to get away, get to the authorities...

Amanda started to scramble to her feet. As she did so her unconfined hair fell forward to brush against his face. To her horror he lifted his hand a little, trying to push her hair away. Amanda jumped back— but it was too late. His hand closed painfully on the trailing ends of her hair, jerking her back to her knees beside him. Frozen with fear, Amanda could only stare dumbly into that dark face as his eyes slowly opened. They were light, she noted distractedly, almost silver in the faint moonlight, and as cold as death. They fixed on her face for a long moment before moving on to stare at the silken length of hair wound so tightly around his fist. The expression in his eyes made her tremble; she shrank back as he lifted his other hand to touch the imprisoned skein of hair.

"An angel," he muttered dazedly, turning his head so that his cheek nuzzled against her captured tresses. "An angel with red hair."

And then he began to shiver violently.

chapter three

He was delirious from fever, Amanda realized, and breathed a little easier. Plainly weakened by whatever it was that afflicted him, he surely couldn't do her any harm. All she had to do was to disengage her hair—gently—and run to fetch the authorities. She doubted that he would try to escape before she was able to lead them back here. He was clearly in no condition to run away; he probably couldn't even stand.

Those silvery eyes were still fixed on her. She could feel the hand that trapped her hair shaking convulsively. Her eyes never leaving his, she reached out tentatively to touch that hand. Her movements were as gentle and unalarming as she could make them as she sought to unclench the fist that held her prisoner. His flesh was burning hot to the touch; his long limbs were racked by tremors. Unfortunately he seemed to have no intention of letting her go—if he even knew he was holding her. From the glassy blankness of his eyes, she questioned whether he did.

Amanda was afraid to be too forceful in her attempts to free herself, afraid that any careless movement on her part might provoke him into violence: he had already killed half a dozen people that she knew of.

"I'm cold," he said suddenly, conversationally, sounding so normal that Amanda jumped. Inching a little farther away from him, as far as she could get without snapping her neck, she eyed him nervously. Was it her imagination, or did his eyes seem more aware than they had a moment ago?

"If you let me go, I'll... I'll fetch you a blanket," she promised with sudden cunning. He frowned, seeming to understand and consider her words.

"Will you?" He sounded doubtful.

"Y-yes." Amanda was willing to promise anything that might induce him to let her go. "I promise."

"They were going to hang me, you know."

Now, what on earth could she say to that? If he was even the least bit aware, and she let on that she recognized him, her fate was as good as sealed. He would kill her. He certainly couldn't let her go; even she could see that. She would immediately run to the authorities, as he must realize as soon as he regained his senses. She said nothing, her eyes wide in the pale oval of her face as she stared at him.

"But I escaped." He chuckled hollowly. "By God, I *escaped*. But they shot me, and then that damned horse went lame and I had to walk, and I fell, and then it rained. God, it rained. Does the sun never shine on this wretched country?" He lapsed momentarily into incoherent muttering. With his black hair straggling in wet curls all around his face, his thick beard bristling at her, and his eyes wild and staring, he looked out of his mind. And not just with fever. Amanda tugged despairingly at her hair, wishing vainly that she had a pair of scissors with her. She would gladly have cut the whole mane off if it would have freed her from this madman.

"Who are you?" His eyes were suddenly sharp on her face, and his voice was demanding. Amanda swallowed. He looked extremely fearsome, glaring at her as he was. And she was very much afraid that he had just regained his senses, if in fact he had ever lost them.

"My . . . my name's Amanda. Amanda Rose Culver." Then, desperately, she added in what she hoped was a confidence-inspiring voice, "And I'm going to help you."

"You know who I am." It was not a question. The words rang like a doomsday bell in her ears. She felt her muscles tense in horrible anticipation. Denial would be useless, she saw, staring wretchedly down into his set face, even if she could have found the right words and forced them from her lips.

"I—I can help you," she said again, weakly. His mouth twisted into a bitter grimace; his hand tightened painfully on her hair. Amanda cringed away from him.

"Don't lie to me," he said, his voice harsh. His fingers, embedded in her hair, dragged her closer, so that her face was just inches from his. "I'm not stupid."

"I'm sorry," she murmured frantically as he glared at her. His teeth were bared in what she could only think of as a snarl, and he looked like a dreadful beast bent on devouring her. Amanda shuddered. He must have seen the convulsive movement or correctly interpreted the fear in her eyes, because he relaxed his grip a little, a faintly satisfied expression flitting across his face.

For a moment neither said anything, the man seemingly bent on recouping his strength and his senses at the same time, and Amanda thinking furiously.

"Could you please let me go?" she ventured at last in a small voice. "You're hurting."

It wasn't much, but this appeal to any latent chivalry he might still possess was all she could come up with. As she had expected, it won her nothing but a grunt and a scornful look. But after a moment, to her surprise, his hand did readjust itself so that it was not pulling quite so hard on her hair.

"Thank you." Amanda couldn't quite keep the surprise out of her voice. He made no reply, only stared up at her in a considering way that chilled her more than the wind. He was probably wondering how, with his small store of strength, he could kill her, and where he could hide the body . . .

"What do you have on under that dress?" Whatever she had expected him to say, it certainly hadn't been that. She stared at him, her eyes going suddenly enormous.

"Well?" He sounded impatient. Amanda wet her lips before replying.

"A petticoat," she whispered. She was not going to describe her underclothing in any more detail than that.

"Is it clean?" he demanded.

"Of *course*," Amanda retorted, stung, before she remembered her situation and hastily subsided.

"Take it off."

Amanda blanched. Oh, dear God, surely he didn't mean to . . . to ravish her? Sheltered as she had been, she knew that low men sometimes forced women to perform indecent acts, and a murderer was about as low as one could go. She stared fearfully at him. He was eyeing her, his expression unreadable, his teeth clenched against the spasms that racked him, as they seemed to periodically.

"No. Please," she breathed, knowing it was useless to beg but not willing to resort to physical resistance unless she had no choice. Incapacitated as he was, she had little doubt that he was still considerably stronger than she, and she was afraid of putting her assumption to the test unless and until it became absolutely necessary.

At her whispered plea, his eyes raked her from head to toe as she crouched beside him, her head bent with the weight of his hand in her hair. Although she did not know it, her small, slender body looked very young—and very vulnerable. His mouth twisted sardonically.

"Despite anything you may have heard to the contrary, I'm not in the habit of raping children," he rasped. "You're perfectly safe from that particular fate, I assure you. Now, are you going to take off that damned petticoat—or do you need help?"

That threat, plus his assurance that he had no intention of raping her—which, oddly enough, she believed—sent her fumbling under her skirt for the tapes to her petticoat. But with his eyes watching her every move, and obviously noting with interest the slender, white-stockinged ankles that she could not help but reveal, she could not seem to untie the knot, and her awkward position made it doubly difficult.

"Hurry up," he said through his teeth. Amanda thought that he looked quite fierce as his eyes moved from her ankles to her face. She did her best to comply with his order, then swallowed nervously.

"If you would close your eyes—and let me stand up," she tacked on hopefully, "it would help."

"Oh, for God's sake," he muttered, but he did close his eyes. Amanda guessed that she would have to be content with that concession; she hadn't really thought that he would let go of her hair so that she could stand up. Moving as quickly as she could, wanting to get the business done before he could open his eyes and catch her with her skirts up around her knees, she at last managed to loosen the tapes of the petticoat. The white linen garment crumpled into a heap around her feet. His lashes flicked up just as she kicked free of it. Seeing his eyes on her fallen undergarment, she felt sudden color heat her cheeks.

"Tear a couple of strips off it," he directed. Amanda, thankful not to be told to remove anything else, obediently picked up the petticoat and proceeded to try to do as he bade her. It was, however, easier said than done. Finally she had to resort to chewing the edge of the linen between her teeth. When at last the material gave with a loud rip, she felt a small spurt of satisfaction as she tore several long strips out of the skirt. She looked up to find his eyes on her.

"I took a bullet in the hip," he said abruptly. "It's basically just a flesh wound, the bullet went on through, but it's been bleeding like be-damned. I want you to bandage it for me."

His fingers slid beneath the tails of his tattered, once-white shirt to unfasten the buttons of his rusty-looking breeches as he spoke. Amanda stared, horror-stricken, at the movement of that hand, then jerked her eyes back up to his face. He *surely* was not intending to remove his breeches in front of her?

He saw the frantic expression in her eyes and had no trouble interpreting it. One corner of his mouth turned down in an expression of pure disgust.

"I have neither the inclination nor the strength to pander to your girlish modesty," he said coldly. "I've been shot in the hip, and the wound is bleeding and needs to be bandaged. If I could do it myself, I would. But I can't. You, however, can—and you will. I've already told you that I have no intention of raping you. You'll be perfectly safe—as long as you do as I say."

His eyes were hard, his expression stony as he stared at her. Amanda swallowed, then nodded slightly. Of course, tending the sick was the Christian thing to do—the nuns did it all the time. The mere fact that he was male, and his body was therefore strange to her, should have no effect on her as his nurse. But still... She couldn't prevent the fiery scarlet color that spread from her neck all the way to her hairline.

The breeches were unbuttoned now, and he was lifting his hips from the shale, trying to pull the garment down with one hand. As Amanda watched, mesmerized, he winced and fell back against the ground. His eyes closed for an instant, his pain obvious. Then they opened again, faintly cloudy as they met hers.

"You'll have to help me," he muttered. "Pull these damn things down so that you can get to the wound. And don't worry—it's pretty high on my hip. You should be able to bandage it without swooning."

This last was said with such a sardonic inflection that Amanda bit her lip. But, she thought hotly, her confusion was very natural under the circumstances. No gently reared young lady could be expected not to feel some trepidation at the prospect of looking at an unclothed male body... He was glaring at her. Amanda closed her eyes, sent a brief SOS to God, and did as he'd told her. The material of his breeches was coarse and cold and wet under her hands; the furred, tautly muscled flesh beneath was fiery hot in contrast. He wore no underdrawers, Amanda noted with embarrassment as she eased the breeches down over his hips. The sight of a neat, round navel cozily nestled beneath a covering of curling black hair brought more color flooding to her cheeks. She averted her eyes abruptly, looking at the sky, the sea, anything except him. He groaned a little, bringing her eyes swinging back around, first to his face, which had paled, and then to his now-bared abdomen. She had uncovered the wound. It was, as he had said, fairly high up on his hip, a jagged gash plowed perhaps a half inch deep into his side. The edges of the wound did not mesh properly, which was probably why blood continued to ooze sluggishly through the opening, which was about six inches long. Dried crusts of blood here and there attested to the fact that the bleeding had stopped several times, only to start again. In order for the flesh to heal properly, she guessed, he would have to remain quiet for some time.

"What are you trying to do, memorize it?" he demanded testily. "Bandage the thing and have done with it."

Amanda flushed at the thought that he might imagine her to have been staring at his body, and reluctantly set to work. Folding a scrap of petticoat into a pad, she laid it over the wound. Then she picked up the strips that would bind the pad in place.

"Lift yourself up, please," she said faintly, trying and failing to achieve a fair imitation of Sister Agnes's no-nonsense voice. Sister Agnes was a weathered, salt-and-pepper–haired former fisherwoman who had taken the veil ten years before after losing her husband and two sons, fishermen all, in a sudden off-shore squall. Her keen eyes and brisk efficiency, to say nothing of her sharp tongue when provoked by slow or incompetent helpers, had won her the respect of every resident of the convent and, indeed, of the entire village. She had a knack for healing— Amanda often wondered if it didn't have a great deal to do with the fact that the sick were simply afraid not to get better when she ministered to them—and had taken on the role of lay doctor to half the population of the county. Amanda, whose unprecedented refusal to swoon or get sick when presented with a gruesome injury had won the old woman's curtly nodded approval, was often called upon to assist her. With females and children, of course. Sister Agnes tended to the needs of the men and boys herself.

"Yes, ma'am." There was a spark of humor in his voice that sent her eyes flying up to meet his. She must have been mistaken, she decided, meeting those stony eyes and seeing the hard, unrelenting set of his mouth, which was just barely visible through the bristly beard. Her eyes dropped back to her work; with commendable efficiency she wound the strips of petticoat around him, trying to make as little contact with his bare skin as she could. She couldn't help but notice that, from the feel of it at least, the lower part of his back was not covered with hair like his belly and chest. The pattern of hair on his front side was very interesting, she decided almost subconsciously as she knotted the ends of the bandage directly over the pad. His shirt was pulled up around his ribs, leaving bare the lower part of his chest and abdomen to where the breeches rested low on his hips. There seemed to be a thick growth of hair on his chest—at least, what she could see of it—that narrowed until it was hardly more than a silky trail once it got past his navel. From there the trail began to widen again down the center of his abdomen until the breeches abruptly cut off her view. She wondered how much hair he had lower down—and was horrified at the thought. This time her blush was almost painful. To hide her confusion, she quickly pulled the breeches back up over the bandage, apparently hurting him in her haste because he grunted. But he didn't say anything, and she sat back with a feeling of relief, leaving him to fasten the buttons himself, which he did one-handed. His other hand showed no signs of releasing its tether hold on her hair.

"Good job," he said approvingly as he fastened the last of the buttons. "Now see if you can dry my hair. It feels like it's turning into icicles around my ears."

It took Amanda an instant to realize that he meant for her to use what was left of her petticoat for that purpose. Hesitating only a moment, she picked up the ragged garment and, inching closer to his head, began rather gingerly to dry his hair. The icy wetness of the curling black strands soon penetrated the thin linen of her petticoat, chilling her fingers. He was soaked to the skin; she could feel the muscles of his neck and shoulders trembling with cold. If she hadn't been so afraid that he meant to murder her at any minute, she would almost have felt sorry for him. After all, she wouldn't have been able to stand seeing even a mad dog in his condition without wanting to do what she could to alleviate its suffering. But, then, a crazed murderer, sick or well, was a different proposition from even a mad dog...

Finally his hair was as dry as she could get it, and she sank back onto her heels, eyeing him, the petticoat in her lap.

"Wrap that thing around me as well as you can, will you?" he requested next, and it was a request, not an order, despite the gruffness of his tone. Amanda did as he told her, spreading the damp linen over his chest and tucking it in around his shoulders and neck. It covered perhaps a third of his body, leaving his hips and long legs protected from the wind only by the raggedy breeches. The petticoat could not have provided much comfort, but he snuggled into it as if it were the woolliest of blankets.

"What did you say your name was? Amanda? Amanda Rose?"

Amanda nodded, slowly backing away from him as she did so, eyeing him warily. Now that she had seen to his comfort to the best of her ability, would he decide her usefulness was at an end and wrap those long, strong fingers around her neck?

"What are you doing wandering around in the dark, Amanda Rose? Did you sneak out to meet someone? A man, perhaps?"

"Yes." Her voice must have been a shade too eager, because he looked at her silently for an instant before slowly shaking his head.

"Don't lie, Amanda." It was surprising how formidable he could sound, even lying flat on his back with his body racked by tremors and his shoulders huddling into her torn petticoat.

"I'm not," she began, then gave it up. She had always been a dreadful liar anyway; it was no wonder he could see through her clumsy attempts at subterfuge. "I often walk on the beach before the sun comes up. I . . . like to be alone."

"So you weren't looking for me?"

"No." She spoke so fervently that his lips moved in the semblance of a wry smile. Amanda stared at the crooked twist of those lips, thinking that it made him seem suddenly so much more human. Maybe he wasn't totally evil after all, she thought. Maybe, just maybe, he had done what he had out of sincere political convictions. If so, it meant that he was that much less likely to murder her out of hand... she hoped.

"No, I suppose not." He forced the words out through teeth that were clenched suddenly to stop them from chattering. The ghost of a smile vanished as suddenly as it had come, and for a moment he closed his eyes. Amanda watched him hopefully. If she was lucky, he might pass out...

"I presume your family has a house somewhere nearby?" His eyes were open again, but Amanda thought his voice sounded a bit weaker.

"N-no," she answered, then as he looked at her sharply her tone became defensive. "It's the *truth*. I live in the convent at the top of the cliff. I'm a pupil there."

"I see." He was silent for a moment, apparently digesting the information. When he spoke again, she knew she was not imagining the weakening of his voice. "Are there any outbuildings? A place where I could rest—out of the cold and this damned wind?"

Amanda thought quickly. The only outbuilding the convent possessed was a small tool shed well within the grounds. If she could get him up there, all she would have to do was scream and the entire population of the convent—eleven girls and twenty nuns—would be out upon them in a matter of seconds. And he couldn't possibly kill thirty-odd females. She didn't think he had a weapon.

"Yes," she said at last, but again she must have hesitated too long because he eyed her with some suspicion.

"If you're lying to me . . ." He let his voice trail off, but the threat was unmistakable. Amanda shivered. When he spoke like that, she had no difficulty believing that he was capable—more than capable—of cold-blooded murder.

"I'm not." Desperately she tried to infuse her voice with conviction. In an effort to persuade him further, she added eagerly, "Our gardener sleeps there sometimes. There's a cot, with blankets. And I could get you some food."

He groaned, and his eyes closed. "I haven't eaten in three days," he admitted under his breath. Then his eyes popped open to stare at her warily. "You know that I'll hang if I'm caught?"

Amanda returned his look just as warily. Then she nodded.

"Then you know that I don't have anything to lose if I kill you. And if you cross me . . ." His voice trailed off, but his eyes spoke for him. Amanda shivered. If she crossed him, he would kill her. Did she dare even to try? Looking into those silvery eyes that glittered so coldly back at her, she knew she had no choice. Even if she did everything he said, he would kill her eventually. She had to take the first chance of escape that presented itself, no matter what the risk.

"Is that understood?" He meant to have an answer. Amanda looked at him and nodded jerkily. She prayed that he wouldn't read her intentions in her eyes.

"Then I'll ask you again, and I want the truth: is there some place up there at that convent of yours where I can rest—without being found?"

For a barely perceptible instant Amanda hesitated,

thinking of the nuns and the other girls—people she had grown to care for—who were sleeping so peacefully in their beds. What guarantee did she have that he couldn't somehow manage to kill everyone who came to her aid? After all, he had had some experience in mass murder. But then she thought of the path up the cliffs. It would be almost impossible for him to make the climb in his present condition; surely it wouldn't be too difficult to get away from him on the steep, narrow path...

"Yes." She was proud of herself. This time her voice was just right: steady and confident.

"Good. Then you can help me to stand up. And remember what I told you: I don't have anything to lose." This last was growled so menacingly that Amanda shrank back.

"I-I'll remember." At the moment she didn't think it would be possible ever to think of anything else. Sheer fright was causing her hands to shake almost as much as his were. Why did she never do as she was bid? If she had listened to the sisters, she would be safely tucked up in her bed now, not trapped in a living nightmare with a man who could easily take it into his head to kill her at any minute.

"Are you asleep?" There was a note of exasperation in that gravelly voice. "I *told* you to help me up."

Thus adjured, Amanda made a hasty, abortive attempt to get to her feet, only to be brought up short with a whimper of pain as a sudden, sharp agony shot through the part of her scalp that was attached to the hank of hair wrapped around his hand. *Damn.* She had forgotten just for an instant that he still had a grip on her hair.

"What's the matter?" he asked, swiveling his head so that he could look at her as she rocked back on her heels. One of her hands rubbed at her tender scalp.

"I told you—you're hurting me." Her tone was resentful. Then, as a thought occurred to her, she continued carefully, "If you want me to help you, you'll have to let go of my hair. You must see that I can't do anything while you're holding me like this."

He looked at her consideringly. Amanda returned his look, her expression as innocent as she could make it.

"And as soon as I let go of your hair, you'll be off like a little doe," he said, sneering. "I told you before, I'm not stupid. You'll just have to manage to get up and get me on my feet the best way you can. And considering the consequences if you don't, I'm sure you'll contrive something."

Amanda swallowed. He was right; considering the consequences, she would contrive something. She positioned her feet beneath her and then straightened her knees so that she was upright from foot to waist, but still bent over him, anchored to him by her blasted hair.

"Very good," he said approvingly, and again she thought she detected a touch of humor in his voice. Crossly she wished the fever would come upon him once more, rendering him helpless. Why did nothing ever happen as it should?

After a moment's thought she reached down to grasp him under his armpits, pulling back with all her might. He barely budged, and she was soon panting as if she had run for miles.

"You're not very strong, are you?" he said critically

at last, his eyes disparaging as they moved over her slender body. Amanda started to stiffen indignantly, remembered just in time his hand in her hair, and contented herself with glaring at him instead.

"You'll have to help me," she answered coldly—or as coldly as she could with perspiration beading her forehead and her breathing ragged. "You're very heavy."

"Grab my hand and pull," he instructed, and when she had grasped his proffered hand, he unwound his other hand from her hair. Amanda felt a flood of mingled relief and surprise, and immediately jerked as hard as she could on her imprisoned hand, hoping to yank it free. But she only succeeded in hauling him into a sitting position. His grip was like a vise.

"I knew you could do it." His voice was faint but the tone sardonic. He was now leaning back against the rock that had sheltered him, and his eyes were closed. Her petticoat had slipped from his shoulders to lie like a crumpled flag of surrender against the dark shale. Amanda waited a second, watching him, then gave another surreptitious tug on her hand. Nothing happened—but his eyes opened.

"Don't try to run away, Amanda," he cautioned softly, his voice chilling her blood. "You won't succeed—except in making me very angry."

She stopped tugging. He leaned back against the rock again, his eyes closed, his breathing labored. Anchored to his hand as she was, Amanda could not help but be aware of the raging heat of his flesh and of the tremors that shook him. Despite her fear, she felt another of those odd little pangs of pity for him. He was clearly very ill . . . But there was nothing she could do for him, nothing she would want to do for him if she could. She was not foolish enough to aid, any more than she could help, a man who gave every indication that he planned to kill her sooner or later.

His eyes opened again, touching on her face like a silvery flash of fire before moving on to fix with grim concentration on his feet in their ill-made shoes. Moving slowly, as though it required tremendous effort to do so, he drew his knees up so that his feet were planted as close to his body as he could get them. Watching, Amanda saw his muscles tense as he braced his back against the rock.

"All right. Now see if you can help me stand up," he ordered. Amanda looked at him briefly, then did as he told her, pulling on the hand that imprisoned hers with all her might. To her mingled relief and dismay, he inched slowly upright until at last he was on his feet, leaning against the rock, his face as pale as a corpse's and his breath rattling in his throat in a way that made Amanda wince just to hear it. Throughout, he had never slackened his grip on her hand.

He stayed like that for several minutes, catching his breath, and then he looked at Amanda again.

"Come closer," he said, pulling on her hand to enforce his words. Amanda hung back, not liking to get too near him now that he was on his feet. His sheer size frightened her. He was huge, tall and broad-shouldered, easily dwarfing her own petite frame so that she felt like a little child beside him. Despite his leanness, the muscles that were clearly visible through his ragged clothes were corded and strong-looking. She was no longer left with even a shred of doubt about who would emerge the victor in any contest of physical strength between them.

"Amanda." His voice was a chill warning. Not knowing what else to do, Amanda reluctantly moved nearer, flinching as he drew her close to his side. He positioned her so that she was under his left armpit and he could lean on her. When his arm had clamped firmly around her shoulders—his fingers tangling in a strand of her hair again for extra insurance—he let go of her hand. Amanda could have sobbed with frustration. He was taking no chances on losing her.

When at last she was situated to his liking, he took a tentative step away from the rock, leaning heavily on Amanda, who staggered. He staggered with her, and for a moment she thought they were both going to fall on the rock-studded beach. But miraculously they managed to stay upright, although he was none too steady on his feet. They advanced a step, and then another—and then he stumbled over something, perhaps a jutting rock or even his own feet. Whatever the cause, he fell heavily, his arm slipping away from Amanda's shoulder and his hand wrenching the lock of hair he had held captive from her scalp. The pain made Amanda's eyes water. She clapped an instinctive hand to her head, rubbing vigorously in an effort to ease the ache as he crashed to the shale. His curses turned the air blue and would have put Amanda to the blush again—if she had stayed around to hear them.

But she did not. As soon as she realized that she was free—*free*—her feet seemed to sprout wings and she was off like a shot, scrambling away over the beach. She had not gone more than a yard when she heard a murderous growl behind her. Throwing a terrified look over her shoulder, she saw that he had somehow managed to get to his feet and was coming after her. Even as she tried frantically to speed up her escape, he was launching himself toward her in a flying tackle. She screamed as she felt his arms lock around her waist and his weight force her to the ground. The sound was silenced abruptly as the sudden jolt crushed the breath from her lungs. By the time she had recovered her senses enough to be aware of what was happening again, he had turned her onto her back and was leaning over her, his eyes flashing with an unholy light. His lower body crushed her legs into the shale.

"Damn it, you little bitch, I ought to . . ." What he ought to do she never knew, because his words trailed off in a groan. Throwing himself about like that must have hurt him badly. Trapped beneath him, her breasts heaving with fright and her thighs crushed by his much larger ones, Amanda stared up at him wide-eyed. He was as white as death, and his mouth was set in a furious grimace that struck fear into her soul. He would kill her now, she had no doubt, and terror set her to kicking and hitting at him mindlessly. He cursed and tried to capture her flailing hands. Instinctively they curved into claws, which she raked down his cheeks, feeling savage satisfaction at the bloody furrows her nails left in their wake. He cursed again, viciously, and caught her wrists in a grip that made her fear that he meant to snap the fragile bones. She squirmed and kicked frantically beneath him as he transferred both her hands to one of his; then her eyes widened with fright as he raised his free hand, fist balled to strike her. Her eyes were frantic as she stared at that fist, which was poised to descend upon her face with its delicate bones. He could, and undoubtedly would, beat her to a pulp before he killed her. She screamed with pure animal terror, her eyes locked with his all the while. To her surprise and confusion, she saw an emotion come into his eyes that she would have described as self-disgust in anyone else. Then his fist dropped; she felt his open hand cover her mouth, stifling any further outcry.

"It's all right. I'm not going to hurt you," he said, effectively quelling her struggles with his body while his hand continued to exert that strangely gentle pressure across her face. "Be still, and I'll let you go. Only you mustn't scream, Amanda. Amanda, do you hear me?"

She did hear him, and presently her terror eased, along with her struggles, as the calming note in his voice had its effect. Perhaps he really wasn't going to kill her. Perhaps he meant the words he was almost whispering to her. Her eyes were still huge and her breathing was fast, but she slowly allowed her tense muscles to relax until she was no longer fighting him.

"That's right, Amanda," he murmured soothingly. "Just be still, and everything will be all right. I'm going to take my hand away from your mouth now—only you mustn't scream again. Do you promise not to scream, Amanda?"

She stared up at him for a moment. His face was very close to hers, his beard tickling her cheek as he muttered in her ear. He raised his head to look at her, waiting for her response, and she saw that his eyes had lost their murderous gleam and looked merely very tired.

"Will you promise not to scream, Amanda?" he repeated, and this time she nodded once. As he had promised, he removed his hand. Instinctively she wet her dry lips with the tip of her tongue. He watched that tiny movement intently. Then he opened his mouth to speak.

Whatever he was going to say was lost forever as they both heard running footsteps crunching across the shale toward them. Amanda felt his muscles tense against her; as he turned his head to stare in the direction of the sound the look on his face reminded her of nothing so much as the heart-thumping fear of an animal before the hunters close in.

chapter four

The footsteps slowed, then stopped altogether. "Whoever is back there, *come out*," a stern voice called. Amanda felt her body sag with relief as she realized that rescue was at hand. All she had to do was to call out... She looked quickly up into the face of the man pressed so closely against her. He was not looking at her; every ounce of his attention was focused on the rock that shielded them from whoever was on the other side, as if by staring at it hard enough he could see through it, see who would finally bring him to justice. He was making no effort to silence her or even to hold her still. She wondered if he had forgotten her existence. The muscles of his arms and legs and chest were rigid against her as he prepared himself for the inevitable. He must know that he had no chance of escape, of fighting his way out of the trap. He was far too weak... She pushed urgently at his shoulders, trying to free herself. Only as a last resort would she scream again...Those silvery eyes were as hard as agates as they swung back to look down at her, but for one single, unguarded instant Amanda saw in their depths a flicker of something that might have been despair. Again she was reminded of an animal at bay...

"Oh, for goodness' sake, let me up," she hissed, annoyance and disgust combined in equal parts in her voice. "He'll be back here any minute if you don't."

His eyes flickered again with that same odd expression. His mouth compressed into a tight, controlled line. To her relief he rolled to his side without a word, freeing her. Amanda got quickly to her feet, making no effort to conceal herself as the upper half of her body became clearly visible above the low grouping of rocks.

"I'm so glad you've come," she called in a tremulous voice to the man standing perhaps three yards away. It was still dark enough to make it difficult for her to recognize him at that distance, but she had no trouble identifying the rifle that had been resting against his shoulder. He was slowly lowering the weapon as she moved out into the open. Apparently her sex had lessened his suspicions somewhat...

Matthew Grayson lay silently staring up at her as she passed around the side of the rock. His face was without expression as she threw him one last, quick glare. "Don't make a sound, and stay where you are until I come back," she whispered fiercely. Then she was limping toward the man with the rifle, saying, "I fear I've had a slight accident."

Though the gray light of the slow-breaking dawn partly obscured the stocky figure and square, ruddy face beneath the homespun cap, she recognized him as one of the local sheep farmers as she hobbled nearer.

"Oh, Mr. Llewellyn, thank goodness it's you." There was no mistaking the sincerity in her voice. She had helped Sister Agnes attend the man's youngest daughter through a bout with pleurisy the year before, and had come to know him rather well. Yves Llewellyn was as good-humored as he was stolid, and if he had a thought in his head not concerned with sheep or sheep farming, she had never heard tell of it. His buxom wife and four sturdy daughters had him firmly under their collective thumb. He was more than accustomed to feminine oddities, and Amanda doubted he would even bother to ask what she was doing on the beach, supposedly alone, at such an hour. At least, she hoped he would not. What could she possibly say?

"That be ye, Lady Amanda?" He peered at her doubtfully. Amanda didn't blame him. With her hair tumbling wildly down her back and her hands and dress smeared with dirt and bits of shale, she must look quite a sight.

"Yes, Mr. Llewellyn, it's me." She grimaced noticeably as she approached him, hoping the distortion of her features would pass for an expression of pain. She need not have worried. Mr. Llewellyn frowned and reached out a work-calloused hand to support her as she limped nearer. Amanda stifled a satisfied smile and used that helping hand to steer him as unobtrusively as possible back in the direction whence he had come.

"Hurt yerself, did ye, missy?" he asked gruffly as they progressed with maddening slowness down the beach. His rifle was slung negligently under the arm away from her, Amanda noticed with relief as she leaned heavily against him and limped for all she was worth. Clearly she had managed to allay his suspicions to the point where he no longer suspected that a source of danger might still lurk in the shadows. "Heard ye screechin'. Thought for a minute that it was one of my ewes—dogs been after 'em."

Amanda held back a giggle with some difficulty. Of course that was why Mr. Llewellyn had come running down to the beach, rifle at the ready: he had thought one of his precious sheep was being threatened. Although he had no doubt been informed of the manhunt—she would be surprised if anyone in the whole of England had not—the thought that he might encounter the bloodthirsty object of that search here on their own little bit of Land's End had plainly never entered his head. Just as it had never entered hers—until a little more than an hour ago.

"I came down to admire the sunrise—Sister Mary Joseph is always telling us that there is nothing so godly as a sunrise—and I got so caught up in watching what was happening in heaven that I forgot to watch where I put my feet." Was she laying it on a bit thick? Amanda wondered with a sidelong look at Mr. Llewellyn. But she could not detect the faintest hint of skepticism in his expression. "I tripped over a rock—I must have turned my ankle."

"Aye," was all he said. Amanda was afraid to risk

another look at him, afraid that her guilt would show in her eyes. She *hated* to lie. She had never been any good at it; the few times she had tried when she was younger, she had invariably been found out, and felt shame down to her toes. Not that she had been punished for it then. Her mother used to say that Amanda's own guilty conscience was punishment enough, and she was right.

"Think you can manage, missy?" They had reached the base of the path that sliced up the rocky face to the top of the cliffs. It was little more than a sheep trail, steep and treacherous with a sheer drop to the rock-strewn beach on one side and the unyielding gray stone of the cliff itself on the other. Even vegetation was scarce: only a few small scrub bushes dared to try cling to the rock.

"I can carry you, pig-a-back."

"Oh, no, thank you. I can make it." Amanda hastened to get the words out. Not for anything would she allow him to bear her on his back during that arduous climb, not when she was perfectly healthy.

It was awkward, trying to climb and limp at the same time, but Amanda did her best. Mr. Llewellyn stayed just behind her, the better to break her fall if she should slip, which aided her efforts considerably. To spare her modesty, he was forced to keep his eyes turned down to the path. There *was* no way to clamber up such a trail without revealing a great deal more of her legs than was proper. Despite his rough appearance, Mr. Llewellyn had the soul of a gentleman. Amanda was grateful, both because it allowed her to concentrate more on climbing and less on limping, and because it kept Mr. Llewellyn from looking out over the beach. Amanda had no such restrictions, and she had discovered to her horror that their lofty vantage point afforded an excellent view of every little nook and cranny of the curved shoreline. It was possible to make out Matthew Grayson's long body as he lay close against the rocks where she had left him. From such a height she didn't think that anyone who didn't know he was there would be able to discern that the dark form against the lighter gray shale was a man; he looked more like a large log. But, still, if Mr. Llewellyn should chance to glance that way, he might be moved to investigate.

By the time they reached the top of the cliff Amanda's heart was pounding furiously—and not from exertion. Helping a wanted felon to avoid the law was going to be a hair-raising business, she was just becoming aware. But for now, just for this moment, she had to put that thought out of her mind and turn her efforts to ridding herself of her self-appointed escort. And then she still had to get back down to the beach...

"Thank you so much, Mr. Llewellyn." Amanda turned to the man and smiled with a radiance that owed less to gratitude than to the fact that she had just discovered that the cliff overhang now hid Matthew Grayson from view. "I don't know what I would have done if you had not come along. Probably I'd have been down there on the beach all day."

"The sisters would've got up a search party, soon or late."

Amanda had intended her words as dismissal, but

Mr. Llewellyn refused to be dismissed. Plainly he was determined to see her safely back to the convent. There was nothing for it but to allow him to escort her to where the gray stone walls—made of rocks carved from the cliffs centuries ago—rose from the brown grass like silent sentinels. On the way, it occurred to Amanda that she was faced with another problem: if Mr. Llewellyn mentioned this morning's encounter to the nuns, as he undoubtedly would, if only to inquire about the progress on her nonexistent injury, the fat would be in the fire and she would be in for a grilling indeed. And the sisters were, for good or ill, considerably more suspicious than Mr. Llewellyn—and considerably more familiar with Amanda and her high jinks.

"Mr. Llewellyn," she began uncomfortably as they halted outside the small oak door that led into the convent's gardens and through which Amanda had presumably exited. He turned an inquiring eye to her. "I wonder if you would...That is, I would appreciate it very much if you would not..." Her voice trailed off, and hot color rose to her cheeks as she looked up at him appealingly.

"Ye'll be wantin' me to keep a still tongue in me head about this," he said, eyeing her with a twinkle. "I didn't have four girls for naught, missy. Many's the time I've helped them pull the wool over their mam's eyes. Don't fret. I won't tell the holy sisters on ye—this time. But ye must promise me to stay safe inside yon walls from now on, at least until the sun's good and woke up." This last was said with some severity, softened by the twinkle that still lurked in his eyes.

"I promise," Amanda said fervently. "Thank you, Mr. Llewellyn."

She smiled at him and stood waiting for him to go. But he didn't move, seemingly planted in the ground before her as solidly as a hundred-year-old oak. Amanda realized he was waiting for her to get safe inside the convent walls. Taking a deep breath, praying that the door was unlocked, she turned and tried the latch. To her relief it lifted, and she slipped through the door. Then she turned to smile at Mr. Llewellyn and watch thankfully as he took himself off in the direction of his farm. By the time he was out of sight, and she felt it was safe to retrace her steps, the crimson sun was just beginning to appear over the horizon. If she was to make it back to her room before her absence was discovered, she had to hurry.

When she was once again on the beach, it took her only a moment to rush back to where she had left Matthew Grayson. He was not there. She stared blankly at the spot where he had been, then started half walking, half running along the beach, keeping close to the cliffs, as she guessed he would try to stay out of the open as much as possible. Finally she saw him and heaved a small sigh of relief. She had been afraid that someone else had come along and discovered him in her absence.

He was leaning back against the face of the cliff, his long legs sprawled out before him, his eyes closed. He looked totally exhausted. Amanda approached him slowly, feeling suddenly wary, and stopped while she was still some feet away. After all, what assurance had she that he would not suddenly grab her again.

She looked at him critically, wondering for the first time if she was insane to have done what she had. A horrible, sneaking suspicion lurked in the back of her mind that she could get arrested for helping him—if he didn't kill her himself. Which he very well might: he was a convicted murderer...

She must have made some slight sound because at last he opened his eyes. Across the few feet of rocky beach that separated them, their eyes locked. For a long moment they stared at each other warily. He broke the silence first.

"Why did you do that?" He sounded genuinely curious.

Amanda glared at him. "I have trouble swatting wasps, too," she answered with more than a hint of bite. He grinned a little at that, seeming to relax as one corner of his mouth tilted up lopsidedly. Then he grimaced, his hand moving to press against his hip. Amanda saw that his breeches were wet with blood.

"I'm grateful," he muttered.

"You should be." Amanda's reply was tart. "I must be as crazy as you are." She hadn't meant to say that last aloud. Biting her hip, she eyed him.

"Yes." He didn't seem particularly offended. In fact, he was smiling faintly as those silvery eyes met hers. "I won't hurt you, you know. You're perfectly safe with me—I give you my word."

For what it's worth, Amanda couldn't help thinking, but still it was better than nothing. "You promise?" she asked, sounding uncertain all of a sudden.

A small part of her still wondered if she shouldn't go screaming for help.

"I promise," he answered gravely.

Watching him, feeling a ridiculous qualm of conscience as she saw the raw scratches her nails had raked in his cheeks, she gave it up. She was committed now, for better or worse. It was far too late to worry about the possibility of his wrapping those long fingers about her neck and choking the life out of her. To begin with, how could she explain why she had not denounced him at once? Amanda felt faintly sick; with her usual headlong lack of caution—another fault the nuns were always deploring—she had gotten herself into another scrape. And this one was no mere childish peccadillo. It was an out-and-out disaster.

"We're going to have to get you off the beach before it gets light." Amanda was thinking quickly. What couldn't be cured must be endured, as Sister Mary Joseph was fond of saying. If she was going to help Matthew Grayson—and it seemed as though she was—she had better do it right. She could worry about the moral aspects of the situation later. "There's a cave not far from here, behind that outcropping of rock." She pointed; his eyes followed the direction of her hand. "You should be safe enough there until I can think of something better."

"What about that gardener's shed you were telling me about?" He sounded only mildly curious, but his eyes were suddenly keen as they rested on her face. For the life of her, Amanda couldn't stop herself from feeling—and looking, she had no doubt—extremely guilty.

"I don't think that's such a good idea anymore," she mumbled.

"I see." She inferred from the tone of his voice that he did—all too accurately. Amanda looked at him warily. Would he fly into a murderous rage now that he guessed what she at first had planned for him? To her relief he continued to look calm. She took heart a little, but her next words were still faintly reluctant.

"You'd better let me bandage your wound again before you start moving around. You're bleeding quite badly."

He shook his head. "It's all right—I made a pad out of what was left of your petticoat and tied it up again. I think it's more urgent that I get off the beach before anyone else decides to come for a morning stroll.

"Yes," Amanda agreed slowly. What he said made sense, she knew, but... "Do you think you can stand up?"

He looked apologetic. "I'm sorry, but I feel as weak as a day-old infant. Do you suppose you could..."

"Of course." Amanda stifled an inward sigh. Well, she had known that she would have to put herself within his reach again. She couldn't help him from a safe distance, for goodness' sake. But...

"I really won't hurt you," he said, his voice oddly gentle. His eyes were knowing as they watched the emotions that flitted all too plainly across her face. "From a strictly practical standpoint, I would be a fool to, wouldn't I? Without you I'd be stuck on this damned beach until your friend or some of his cohorts came back and found me—and I'm counting on you to bring me food and a few other necessities, too. Hurting you would be the last thing I'd dream of doing."

Amanda thought about that for a moment. It made sense, she realized with a quiver of relief. Feeling a little better, she edged closer until he was once again grasping her hand in his. The feel of those strong fingers locking around hers brought a rush of panic with it. She tugged sharply at her hand, wanting instinctively to be free. He released it at once.

"See?" he said softly, meeting her eyes. Amanda returned his look for an instant, then nodded. And extended her hand to him again.

Helping him to his feet, feeling the warmth and strength and life of his body as he leaned heavily against her side, she began to feel a little better about what she was doing. Perhaps he deserved to be captured, deserved to forfeit his life for what he had done—and she knew that most people, the nuns included, would say that there was no perhaps about it—but she didn't see how his death could really benefit anyone. The people he had killed—as she thought of them she winced—were dead; nothing could bring them back. Matthew Grayson was alive. And whatever he had done, he was a human being and he needed her help. She couldn't just abandon him to his fate or, worse, turn him over to it herself. It just wasn't in her, and she knew it.

It took a little time and quite a lot of effort, but they managed to traverse the eighth mile of beach that separated them from the outcropping of rock that hid the entrance to the cave. The opening itself was just a narrow fissure running sideways through the hard stone of the cliff, barely wide enough for a grown man to slide through sideways. It was nearly impossible to see from the beach unless one knew it was there. In the old days—and still upon occasion, as Amanda knew full well—it was used by smugglers; as far as she was aware, she and the smugglers were the only ones who remembered its existence. And with the nightly patrol on the beach, she doubted that the smugglers would be using it anytime in the near future. She had to grin at that. How the smugglers must be cursing Matthew Grayson. He had undoubtedly put a severe crimp in their usual operations, not only here but along the entire English coast.

"Something funny?" He sounded faintly put out, and, glancing up at him, Amanda didn't blame him. Sweat was rolling freely down his face; he was pale and obviously in pain while she was grinning like a hyena. The thought made her grin again, wider than before, and he rewarded her with a sour look.

"Share the joke, why don't you? I could use a good laugh."

So Amanda did. He didn't appear to find it overwhelmingly amusing, but it did help to take his mind off the pain he must have suffered as he squeezed through the narrow opening. Once inside, it was so dark that Amanda couldn't even see his face as he stood right next to her. If it hadn't been for the weight of him leaning against her, and the feel of his hard arm wrapped around her shoulders, she might have thought she had imagined everything.

The cave was as cool and damp and dark as a grave. Before they could proceed any farther, they had to have a light. The candle Amanda always left inside was just to the left of the entrance, but before she could find it, she had to free herself of his crushing weight.

She stretched out her hand to feel for the stone wall behind them. It was cold and moist to the touch.

"Can you lean against the wall for a moment?" she asked, her voice sounding almost unnaturally loud in the tomblike quiet. "I have to light a candle."

"A candle?" He sounded surprised, but he obligingly allowed her to ease him against the wall; when he was reasonably secure, he released his grip on her shoulders. "You're full of surprises, aren't you, Amanda Rose? Do you always carry candles about in your pockets, or did you just have a feeling you might need one this morning?"

She thought she detected humor in his voice. When she struck a match from the box she always left beside the candle and touched it to the wick so that the flame caught and flared, she was sure of it. The flickering light made him look pale and drawn— and huge; his shadow crawled up the side of the cave like that of a dark giant—but a grin crooked his mouth and his eyes were whimsical.

"Are you a witch, Amanda? Or my guardian angel come to life? Although I must admit I never would have guessed that angels came with hair of such a devilish red. Or are you a hallucination? You're certainly too good to be true."

Amanda straightened, the movement slow and cautious, and eyed him uneasily. She was almost sure that he had been out of his head when she had first come upon him, and when he had first mistaken her for an angel. Was he going out of his head again? The thought alarmed her. A rational murderer was bad enough. An irrational one... She must have looked as nervous as she felt because his grin widened, and she could have sworn that his eyes teased her.

"Come on," she said, hoping that cold practicality would restore his possibly wandering senses. Candle in hand, she moved toward him, a little apprehensive about letting him touch her if he was going out of his mind. Perhaps he killed only during fits of insanity... But it was too late to worry about that now, she told herself, and fatalistically took his arm and draped it over her shoulder again. "It's not very far now, and then you can rest."

"Perhaps you're one of the devil's angels," he continued musingly as she urged him forward. "If the devil has angels, which I'm sure he must. He sounds like a smart old fellow. Perhaps he's sent you to tempt me down to hell. Ah, well, lead on. At this point even hell sounds good. At least it's warm. Or so I've heard."

Amanda threw another anxious look up at him as they staggered along the worn stone passage that led deep into the cave. His eyes were very bright—with fever?—and his skin was so white beneath the scraggly beard and smears of blood that it frightened her. He looked as if he might faint at any moment. Standing so close to him, with his arm around her shoulders and his big body pressed hard against her side, she could feel the unnatural warmth of him even through the wet chill of his clothes. He radiated heat like a stove. He needed a doctor, she thought, but she knew it would be impossible for him to be seen by one. He would have to live or die on her ministrations alone—and his own strength.

When at last they reached the round, high-ceilinged cavern that was Amanda's goal, she let out a sigh of relief. He was swaying, and Amanda knew she wouldn't have been able to support him much farther.

"We're here. You can rest now," she told him, and gasped as his knees buckled. It was all she could do to prevent him from pitching headfirst onto the stone floor.

"Sorry," he muttered as she eased him down and knelt beside him. He lay sprawled on his stomach on the stone with his head cushioned on his bent arm. "I'm just so damned tired."

Amanda touched his shoulder anxiously.

"Just lie still. I'm going to go get you a blanket," she said, feeling the heat of his skin through the damp shirt. "I'll be right back. I'll leave the candle."

She left him lying in the flickering pool of light while she groped along the wall to a small passage that led off to the right. Although the candle's cheerful yellow glow would have been nice, she had no real need of the light. In the almost five years she had been at the convent, she had walked along this passage hundreds of times—to the aged trapdoor that opened right into the convent's deepest cellar. In the days when the convent had been a castle—sometime in the sixteenth century, she thought—the lower cellar had probably been used as a dungeon. Now it served as an almost forgotten storage room, and Amanda was as certain as it was possible to be that the sisters had no notion of the trapdoor's existence. Presumably it had been designed as an escape hatch for the castle's original owner and was forgotten later when the land was confiscated and presented to the Church under James I.

Amanda had discovered the door and then the cave quite by accident just a few weeks after her arrival at the convent. She had been hiding from Sister Boniface, who was determined to quell the small, red-haired, rebellious Amanda by whatever means were necessary. A lady of good family who had chosen the life of a nun in preference to matrimony and motherhood, Sister Boniface had rigid notions of what constituted correct behavior for schoolroom misses. Being kicked in the shin by a child she had properly been chastising—for swimming in the open bay while clad in only the flimsiest of undergarments—outraged the sister. But the kick had allowed Amanda to escape, at least temporarily. She had fled and eventually found her way to the very darkest corner of the lower cellar, where she had lain hidden beneath a pile of old clothes while the search for her went on above. Lying against the cold stone, shivering as much with fright as with chill, Amanda had felt something hard and even colder than the floor pressing into her stomach. Upon examination, it had turned out to be a circular iron ring attached to a door cunningly fashioned out of flagstones to match the floor. Not without difficulty, she had managed to pry it open. A shallow flight of worn stone stairs led down into darkness. Step by cautious step, she had descended—and found the cave.

At first its dark, winding passages and echoing caverns had frightened her. But over the years she had grown quite fond of the place and had got in the habit of sneaking out of her bed before anyone else was up and following the passageway down to the beach. Except for the few occasions when the smugglers had used it—and when she had been careful to stay out of the way—no one else had entered the cave since she had first explored it. It should be a safe place for Matthew Grayson to hide and recover his strength in. And after that, she thought, pacifying her unhappy sense of self-preservation, he would be on his own.

There was an old blanket just inside the trapdoor, and an ancient feather tick. Amanda sometimes wrapped herself in the blanket and curled up on the mattress when it was too cold to go walking along the shore. Even on the iciest winter day the cave never got much colder than it was right now, and it was an ideal place to read or think...

The blanket and the mattress together were awkward to carry, but they weren't particularly heavy. Amanda lugged them back as quickly as she could. The sun would be up by now, she guessed, and she would be missed if she didn't get back to her room soon. And then there would be all sorts of questions...

Matthew Grayson was still lying where she had left him; he didn't appear to have moved so much as a muscle. Amanda felt a sudden spasm of alarm. Had he died? What on earth would she do if he did? But her fear was allayed as she saw his back move slightly. He was still breathing, at least.

She dragged the mattress until it lay beside him, then knelt to place a gentle hand on his shoulder.

"Mr. Grayson," she said urgently, shaking his shoulder just a little. "Mr. Grayson..."

One eye opened blearily. "You'd better call me Matt," he muttered, his words slurring.

"Matt," she repeated obediently. "I've brought you a mattress. Can you roll over onto it? You'll be much more comfortable once you're off this cold stone, and I have a blanket for you, too."

"See? I knew you were an angel," he said on a note of intense satisfaction, and painfully rolled so that he was lying on his back on the feather tick. He needed to be out of those wet clothes, Amanda knew, but she drew the line at undressing him.

"You'd better take your clothes off," she said, fighting hard to sound matter-of-fact. He made a dismissive gesture. "Too tired...later," he muttered, and closed his eyes. Amanda hesitated, then, not knowing what else to do, spread the blanket over him, carefully tucking it in about his shoulders and legs. He didn't move.

"I have to go now," she said. "If the sisters miss me, they'll ask all kinds of questions and I'm not a very good liar. I won't be able to come back until tonight, when everyone's in bed. I'll bring you some food then. I'm sorry I can't do more for you now, but..."

He nodded without opening his eyes. Amanda hovered for a moment, staring at him helplessly. There really wasn't anything more she could do.

"You'll stay right here, won't you?" she felt impelled to ask. "You won't try to go anywhere? You'll be perfectly safe here. No one comes here anymore but me."

"Where would I go?" he muttered, and Amanda

bit her lip at the desolation she thought she detected in his voice.

"I'll leave you the candle," she said softly, standing up. He nodded again, weakly. Amanda looked at him a moment longer, hating to leave him in such a condition, then shook her head. She *had* to get back to her room...

She almost made it. Without incident, she went through the trapdoor, across both cellars, and up five flights of stairs to the very top of the turret, where her bedroom perched in solitary splendor. The sun was full risen and the nuns must be risen, too. It was not until she actually had her hand on the latch of her chamber door that the voice spoke behind her.

"Where have you been?"

chapter five

Amanda jumped as if the voice had bitten her, then whirled about. The girl on the stairs below her jumped, too, and had to clutch the oak bannister to keep her balance.

"Oh, Susan, you almost scared me to death," Amanda gasped, her hand pressed to her frantically pounding heart as she stared at her closest friend. Lady Susan Hartwood was a pretty, dark-haired girl cursed with Amanda's own lack of inches, but compensated with a pleasingly plump body that made her appear several years older than her actual age of nineteen. She had been a resident of the convent for more than two years now, having been banished from the bosom of her family—and the eyes and, the family hoped, the memories of the denizens of the polite world—after she had had the misfortune to be raped by a gang of highwaymen while on her way to a weekend house party scant weeks after her come-out. From what she had told Amanda—and Amanda believed her, for Susan was not the type to tell a self-serving lie—the fact that she was blameless hadn't seemed to matter to her family. Her father, the Earl of Kidd, had blamed his daughter for the attack that had taken her virginity; he could no longer bear to have her in his house or to hear her name mentioned. Susan had told her that the Earl and Countess of Kidd felt that it would be best for everyone concerned—except, perhaps, Susan—if their disgraced daughter took holy vows and spent the rest of her life behind the convent's high walls.

Amanda knew that Susan was profoundly unhappy at that prospect—she had not the least vocation to be a nun—but what else was there for her to do? as Susan frequently asked. Without her family's support, Susan had no money and nowhere to go. Her eventual fate if she left the protection of the convent would be too hideous to contemplate. Amanda sympathized strongly with Susan's predicament because it was similar to her own, and the two had become fast friends. Over the years, Amanda had grown to love the other girl like a sister.

"Well?" Susan interrupted her musings impatiently. Then, looking behind her down the narrow stairs, added under her breath, "We'd better get inside. Quickly."

Amanda opened the door and Susan followed her. After closing it behind them, Amanda crossed to the utilitarian washstand that stood against one wall. She had to do something about her appearance before one of the sisters saw her...

"*Amanda*," Susan cried, exasperated, and when Amanda turned from sluicing her face with water to eye her blankly, she repeated in a long-suffering tone, "I *asked* you where you've been."

"Just . . . walking in the grounds." Amanda decided in that split second that she would tell no one—not even Susan, whom she knew could be trusted implicitly—about the fantastic events of the previous two hours. For one thing, she was fully aware that she held Matthew Grayson's life in her hands; she could not jeopardize his safety by letting her tongue wag too freely. For another, although Amanda was not sure of the penalty for concealing an escaped murderer, she was pretty certain it would be severe, to say nothing of the social disgrace that would inevitably accompany discovery. She didn't want to bring any more of *that* down on Susan's undeserving head. Susan had had enough trouble of that kind already. And there was Matthew Grayson himself; he had killed before and, except for his promise, what guarantee did she have that he wouldn't do so again? She would be no friend if she exposed Susan to a murderer, and one whose wits tended to wander . . .

"Oh, really?" Susan, who knew her pretty well, looked politely disbelieving. Amanda could feel her cheeks coloring—blushing was the curse of the fair-skinned—but she doggedly returned Susan's look. "Well, if you don't choose to tell me . . ."

"How did you know I was gone?" Amanda asked, hoping to distract her friend, who tended to be scatterbrained at times.

"Oh, Sister Boniface is looking for you." Susan threw a scared look over her shoulder at the closed door. "When you weren't in your room, she came to mine to see if you were with me. I told her you'd probably gone down to the library to get a book. I think that's where she is now. What are you going to tell her?"

Amanda felt her heart sink. Sister Boniface was still her nemesis. Charged with maintaining discipline among the convent's pupils, Sister took her duties seriously. The girls had dealings with her only when they were in trouble, which meant that Amanda knew her rather well. Before she could work out a plausible answer—obviously her tale of a predawn walk in the convent's nearly nonexistent grounds was not going to do, if even gentle Susan did not believe her—a sharp rap sounded at the door. Both girls jumped and swung alarmed looks toward the door; it was opened with regal disregard for the privacy of anyone within. The tall, thin figure of Sister Boniface stood looking down her rather long and bony nose at them. A simple crucifix was held in her hands, and a severe frown was on her face, lending even more remoteness to a countenance that was unapproachable at best.

"Amanda," she said sternly, her eyes passing over Susan to fix on the primary object of her displeasure. "I have been looking for you for the past half hour. Would you care to tell me where you have been?"

"Did you want me for anything special, Sister?" Amanda asked, desperately hoping that the question would sidetrack the nun while she thought of a believable tale. Sister Boniface, however, was made of sterner stuff than Susan—and Amanda's brain traitorously refused to function.

"Certainly I wanted you for a particular reason." Sister Boniface sniffed. Righteous indignation added a trace of pink to cheeks that were ordinarily as white as her whimple. "I would hardly seek you out otherwise. But we stray from the point: I want to know where you have been. At once, if you please."

Amanda knew there was no help for it. She would have to lie, and Sister Boniface, who was nobody's fool, would know it. But she had no choice.

"I went walking on the grounds, Sister," Amanda said miserably.

"Indeed?" It was amazing how much skepticism Sister Boniface could squeeze into one small word, Amanda thought, and wished she could cover her telltale cheeks with her hands. She could feel them burning with guilty color. But of course that would clearly give her away.

"You may make your explanation to Mother Superior," Sister Boniface continued coldly. "It is she, not I, who wants to speak with you. She said immediately you had risen, but I see that we will have to delay her further"—she examined Amanda with distaste, making her cringingly aware of the unconfined masses of her hair and her dirt-and-water-streaked dress—"while you put your person into proper order. You may meet me downstairs in Mother's office in a quarter of an hour. I trust that will give you time to do something about your appearance—and think well on the sin of lying. I wouldn't want it on my conscience."

She watched Amanda closely as she spoke, looking triumphant as the girl's color intensified until she was the shade of the cherries that graced the tree in the garden, then turned her austere gaze to Susan, who quaked.

"Come, Susan, you may assist me with my correspondence this morning before matins," she said, turning. Her black habit billowed out behind her as she began to descend the stairs. Susan, after one despairing look at Amanda, trailed the nun obediently, closing the door with a gentle click.

Amanda stared at the closed door miserably for a moment, then allowed her unhappy gaze to wander around the room. Ordinarily her bedchamber, with its funny round shape, whitewashed stone walls, and small, uncurtained windows like portholes overlooking the bay, never failed to please her despite its unconventionality. She knew she was lucky to have this room, which had been used mainly for storage before her arrival. But she had seen it and fallen in love with it at once, both for its quaintness and for its isolation from the rest of the convent. Sister Agnes, sorry for the deeply unhappy child hiding behind a facade of bravado, had interceded for Amanda with Mother Superior. Otherwise, Amanda knew, she would never have been allowed to have a bedroom so far away from the other girls. But this morning was too much of a disaster to allow her to be pleased by anything. Mother Superior wanted to see one of the girls only when she had done something so monstrous that Sister Boniface felt she couldn't handle it on her own authority.

For one horrible moment Amanda wondered if the sisters had somehow discovered that she had found and helped Matthew Grayson. But that was impossible, she was almost sure. She would have heard the outcry if he had been discovered. Another possibility was that someone in her family had died. Amanda brightened a little at the thought that Edward might have been called to his just reward. Mother Superior did call the girls into her office to give them such bad news from home. But, Amanda told herself glumly, she couldn't be that lucky. No, it must be something she had done.

But time was passing. If she wasn't downstairs in the allotted fifteen minutes, that would be one more black mark that Sister Boniface would no doubt convey to Mother Superior. Hastily she crossed the bare plank floor—rugs were luxuries the nuns didn't allow themselves, although winters in Lands End were long and cold—to the wardrobe and pulled it open. She wasted no time contemplating the scanty contents; all her dresses were either gray or black and cut in the same unfashionable, modest mode. Withdrawing a high-necked, long-sleeved gray wool dress that was practically indistinguishable from the one she had on, she laid it across the narrow bed and began to strip off her clothes. The absence of her petticoat brought Matthew Grayson—Matt, she must remember to call him that—forcibly to her mind. She hoped he was all right...Shedding her remaining underclothes, she pulled on a fresh chemise and pantalettes, then another petticoat, before pulling the gray dress over her head. She only hoped that Sister Catherine, who did the laundry, would not notice later that one of her few petticoats was mysteriously missing.

Crossing back to the small mirror that hung from the wall over the washstand, she picked up her brush and began to restore her hair to some sort of order. The nest of tangles where Matt had held her made her grit her teeth as she raked the brush through it. Her hair was being more impossible than usual this morning; she supposed it somehow sensed that she was in a hurry. But at last she had it secured in two long braids, which she wound around the top of her head and anchored with pins. The resulting hairstyle was too dowdy for words, she thought, peering into the somewhat wavery mirror and completely missing the way the severe crown emphasized the delicate perfection of her features. Without her masses of hair to veil them, the jutting angle of her cheekbones and the clean, rounded lines of her forehead and jaw were plainly visible. The silky blackness of her slanting brows and thick lashes added a touch of the exotic to her candid violet eyes; her small, straight nose and tenderly curved lips still retained the innocent sweetness of childhood. Only the barely perceptible firmness of her chin and the deep, glowing red of her hair—a vivid contrast to her milky-white skin—hinted that she might not be as biddable as her age and sex dictated. Dismissing her reflection with a shrug to hurry toward the door, Amanda smiled as she remembered that Matt had called her an angel. If only he were free to repeat that observation to Mother Superior before she was raked over the coals!

Amanda just made it in the allotted fifteen minutes. As she knocked rather hesitantly on Mother Superior's door she heard the clock in the front hall strike seven-thirty. The other girls would be saying grace before sitting down to breakfast. Amanda's stomach rumbled at the thought. She would undoubtedly miss breakfast, she thought glumly, and she was hungry. Then she felt ashamed of her own greed as she remembered Matt saying that he had not eaten for three days. Feeding him was going to be something of a problem. She couldn't very well make continued raids on the convent's carefully husbanded supplies without someone noticing.

Joanna, a young novice who served as Mother Superior's assistant while she waited to be allowed to take her vows, opened the door to Amanda's knock. She was about Amanda's own age, but there all similarity ended. There was a serenity about the round face beneath the simple white headdress that was utterly foreign to Amanda's nature. Amanda supposed it was there because Joanna had her life all planned, along calm and unswerving lines; since the age of ten Joanna, the middle of three daughters of a wealthy wool merchant, had known that she was destined to be a nun, and she embraced the prospect wholeheartedly. Amanda could barely look at her without shivering. She would rather be buried alive than consigned to such a fate. So much of life was missing here in the convent's gentle twilight, so many things to see and to do and to feel. Amanda practically quivered with impatience whenever she thought of the world beyond the walls that enclosed her. She wanted to be out there in it, living as life was meant to be lived. And one day she would, she vowed, no matter what it took...

"Mother Superior is waiting for you, Amanda," Joanna reproved gently as Amanda simply stood staring at her. With a quick smile at the other girl, Amanda shook off her thoughts and entered the small antechamber that led to Mother Superior's office. Joanna closed the door behind her and led the way to the other door; with her hand on the knob, she paused to say softly over her shoulder, "Sister Boniface is already with her," before opening the door and announcing Amanda.

Amanda thanked Joanna with another smile for the warning as she walked past her. She heard the gentle click of the door closing behind her as her attention focused on the two women watching her from the opposite side of the room.

"Come in, Amanda, and sit down." Mother Superior's voice was truly beautiful, as Amanda noticed every time she heard her speak. Amanda obeyed the instruction slowly, moving across to the chair indicated by a plump, veined hand. Seated behind her desk, Mother Superior was small and round in contrast to Sister Boniface's angular length as she stood with one hand braced on the polished wood surface. The expression on Mother Superior's time-worn face was as different from Sister Boniface's as her person. Whereas Sister Boniface frowned, Mother Superior smiled; whereas Sister Boniface's eyes were disapproving as they rested on the slender young figure seating herself with unconscious grace on the very edge of the hard chair, Mother Superior's were compassionate.

The older woman still bore discernible traces of the homely farm girl she had once been; Sister Boniface could never be mistaken for anything except a lady. Sister Boniface's habit and wimple were immaculate in every detail, a stark contrast in pristine white and gleaming black. Her rosary was of gold and ivory. Long, slender fingers bore evidence of scrupulous care as they tapped with the faintest impatience on Mother Superior's desk. Amanda knew that Sister Boniface was being groomed to fill Mother Superior's shoes one day, and only hoped that she herself would be long gone before that happened. Mother Superior was kind and tolerant of minor misdemeanors. To Sister Boniface's mind, there were no minor misdemeanors, only infractions of the rules. And, to make matters worse, Amanda didn't think Sister Boniface had ever forgiven her for that kick.

"You . . . you wanted to see me, Mother?" Amanda spoke hesitantly. Sister Boniface's lips pursed, and she frowned. Flushing, Amanda realized that she should have waited until she was addressed.

"Thank you for coming to me, Sister," Mother Superior said mildly to Sister Boniface. "I will certainly keep all you had to say in mind."

It was a dismissal, however gently given. Amanda looked on in surprise as Sister Boniface, lips compressed, hesitated only briefly before bowing her head in acquiescence to Mother Superior's directive and leaving the room.

There was a moment's silence. Amanda bit her lower lip as Mother Superior turned on her a faintly sorrowing, all-knowing look that made her all too conscious of her past and present misdeeds, the most notable of which was the presence of the murderer for whom all England searched not a hundred yards from where they were sitting. As the silence lengthened Amanda felt the palms of her hands grow moist with tension. Surely they couldn't already know . . .

"I have received a letter from your brother," Mother

Superior said slowly at last. Amanda heaved a silent sigh of relief. At least they didn't know about Matt. "He informs me that you are to be married soon. I trust that he has written to you himself to acquaint you with his plans?"

"Yes, Mother." Amanda was almost lighthearted with relief. Edward and her proposed marriage to Lord Robert were something she could deal with in the future. For now all her energies had to be focused on getting Matthew Grayson restored to health, and then ridding herself of him. She was beginning to perceive just how uncomfortable she was going to be while she kept her guilty secret. To say nothing of what would be in store for her if it were revealed . . .

"You no doubt received your brother's letter yesterday, as I did. That would account for your lack of appetite at dinner last night and this morning's unauthorized absence and general untidiness that Sister Boniface was just telling me about?"

"Yes, Mother. I was . . . a little upset."

Mother Superior nodded. "That is understandable. Very well, we will say no more about your misdeeds. I trust you have resigned yourself to obeying your brother about this marriage?"

Amanda hesitated. It was useless to appeal to Mother Superior for support against Edward in this matter. If Lord Robert had been a moral degenerate or impossibly ancient or deformed in some way, Mother Superior might have interceded for her. But under the circumstances she would not see the need for such intervention. After all, the only options open to a girl of Amanda's birth and background were marriage or the Church, and Amanda was clearly not cut out for the Church.

"Well, Amanda." Mother Superior prompted.

"Yes, Mother," Amanda replied with scarcely a guilty flush. "I have resigned myself."

"You're a good child, Amanda," Mother Superior said unexpectedly. "Impulsive, and a little too quick to anger at times, but a good child. It is a pity that your father died when he did—I have never felt that our convent was the right setting for one of your nature. However, your brother disagreed with me, and I did not push the matter for fear that you would find yourself in an environment even less suited to you than this. But think upon this: after your marriage you will be free both of this convent and of your brother's domination. Your husband's authority will be far kinder, I am sure, and you will soon have his children to fill up your life. It can be a good life, Amanda, if you let it."

"Yes, Mother." Amanda just managed to hide the rebellious flash of her eyes by meekly lowering her head. She had not the slightest intention of marrying Lord Robert, but until she had worked out just how she was going to contrive to avoid it, she would keep her own counsel.

"That is all I wished to say to you, Amanda. You may go along to breakfast now. Tell Sister Patrick that I said you may eat in the kitchen, since I caused you to miss the scheduled meal."

"Yes, Mother." Amanda rose, bobbed a little curtsy, and headed for the door. As her hand touched the knob Mother Superior spoke again.

"Amanda . . . you know that if you want to talk, to

discuss anything that may be troubling you, I am here. I will do whatever I can to make things easier for you, my dear."

Amanda felt swift tears rise to her eyes. She blinked rapidly, desperate not to let them fall. Kindness always brought her to the brink of tears, whereas harshness did not, possibly because she had known so little kindness since her father died.

"Thank you, Mother," she said huskily. "I will remember." Then, with a sudden, heartshaking smile at the old woman, she let herself out of the room.

The rest of the day seemed to crawl. Amanda ate on schedule, prayed on schedule, did her lessons and assigned tasks on schedule, and chatted desultorily with the other girls just as she did nearly every day. But inwardly she was a seething mass of worry and impatience. Every time the bell rang, announcing arrivals to the convent—and it seemed to jingle with a previously unknown frequency—her heart jumped into her mouth as she waited for someone to burst in with the news that the escaped murderer had been captured, and had named his accomplice. As the day wore on and that particular hideous fantasy remained just that, she began to worry more and more about Matt himself. He had seemed very ill. What if he were dying even as she sat here impatiently picking out the stitches she had set into a shirt for the poor. (The straggly things had not met Sister Mary Joseph's approval.) What on earth would she do if he died? Even alive and bearing much of his own weight, he was heavy. If he were dead—and she understood now the origin of the expression "deadweight"—it would be impossible for her to move him. But she couldn't just leave him in the cave, either. First, it would be barbaric to deny him a proper final resting place; second, he would inevitably begin to smell ... Amanda felt a gentle nudge in the small of her back from one of the girls who sat behind her, and looked up to find Sister Mary Joseph watching her with shrewd hazel eyes. Immediately Amanda dropped her eyes to her work and saw to her horror she had just sewn a neat seam—the neatest she had sewn all day—up the front of the shirt where she should have been setting in button holes. Gritting her teeth, she began to unpick the stitches and vowed to keep her mind on what she was doing if it killed her. It would never do if her behavior aroused suspicion among the nuns.

After dinner and evening prayers the girls were allowed an hour to spend as they pleased. Amanda usually joined her friends in the small sitting room, where they would talk and giggle until it was time to go to bed. But tonight she was too on edge to exchange mindless chatter. Pleading a headache, she managed to escape from Susan and Bess, another of her particular friends, to her bedchamber. She spent the next hour pacing her floor in a fever of impatience. Would they never go to bed? But at last the bell chimed for lights out. Amanda got into bed fully clothed, in case Sister Boniface decided to make one of her infrequent bed checks, and waited.

When the small clock near her bed told her that two hours had passed, she judged it safe to get up. Usually she never left the convent until the early-morning hours, but tonight she couldn't wait any longer. The conviction stayed obstinately with her that Matt had died and she would be left with the problem of his body, and she would never be able to rest until she was sure he was alive. Besides, he would be hungry—if he were still alive, that is.

She had decided that she would never be able to get him enough to eat if she merely saved the scraps of her own meals. Even if she didn't eat at all, the small portions Sister Patrick doled out to her, after long experience with her small appetite, would hardly make a light snack for a man of his size. No, she would have to take the chance of raiding the convent's supplies; not the pantry, which held food destined for the convent's own table—that would be missed immediately—but the larder for the needy poor. After all, Matt was quite as needy as any of the families in the parish; few of them could truthfully claim not to have eaten for days, as they all knew that the convent would provide food for anyone who asked.

During the day she had managed to accumulate a collection of supplies: a bottle of basilicum powder tucked in her pocket while she helped Sister Agnes nurse a child whose cut arm had got infected; a shirt and a pair of loose workman's trousers from the pile of clothes that she was supposed to be refurbishing for the poor; eating utensils, including a rather sharp knife, which she almost had second thoughts about; a battered washpan, a chipped mirror, and a sliver of soap for his toilette; and a couple of tallow candles she had spirited from the kitchen that morning as she ate her belated breakfast. To these articles she added her own towel, bundling everything in one of the two blankets that were always kept folded in the bottom of her wardrobe. Then, hoisting the burden to her back, she crept from the room.

The interior of the convent was pitch black. Amanda did not dare to light a candle, so she was left with no choice but to negotiate the stairs in the dark. With every cautious step, she prayed that someone had not been careless enough to leave one of their possessions on the stairs. The nuns were always preaching the virtues of neatness, and for the first time Amanda saw how right they were. A place for everything and everything in its place was the only way to live—especially if one was bent on nefarious activities. A single crash or thud, to say nothing of the terrible din that would result if she should tumble down the stairs, would bring the whole convent upon her.

She had to light a candle in the larder to see what she was doing, but she shut the door firmly behind her and was as quick as she could be. When the job was done and the candle extinguished, she let out a sigh of relief. From there it seemed almost easy negotiating the stairs to the lower level of the cellar, where she at last dared to relight the candle. It required a considerable amount of juggling to get herself, the bundle, and the candle through the trapdoor and down the shallow flight of rough stairs on the other side without setting herself on fire or dropping the bundle, but she managed. Then she made her way along the passage, the candle casting a flickering pool of yellow light to show her the way. When she reached the cavern where she had left Matt, she raised the candle high so that the light illuminated most of the room. There was the feather tick, and the blanket she had left him—but he was not in them. In fact, she thought with a tingle of panic, he did not seem to be anywhere at all...

"Matt?" she called softly, uncertainly, fear and worry combining to make the blood pound in her ears. Where on earth could he be? Perhaps he had gone berserk and was even now watching her from the shadows, awaiting his chance to silence her forever... Unnerved, she began to back quickly toward the passage and the haven of the trapdoor. Something closed over her shoulder. She screamed, whirling and dropping both bundle and candle. The candle immediately went out, and she was left in pitch blackness while arms locked roughly about her and a hand clamped over her mouth, cutting off her breath...

"Good God, you damn near scared the life out of me. What was the screech in aid of?" The gravelly voice coming from somewhere over the top of her head sounded sane, and faintly exasperated. Amanda sagged with relief and drew in a deep, shuddering breath as he removed his hand.

"You scared the life out of *me*," she retorted shakily, pushing away from the hard masculine chest that she had clung to in her relief. "What on earth were you thinking of, to grab me like that?"

"Did you think to find me lying meekly where you left me, waiting like a tethered goat for my fate? I wasn't sure you'd come alone—and I had to be," he said. Amanda thought for a moment, then nodded, forgetting that he couldn't see her in the enveloping darkness. After all, he had no more reason to trust her than she had to trust him. "Did you bring some food?" he added, the studied casualness of his voice doing little to disguise his eagerness for her answer.

"Yes, I did, but you made me drop it all. Serve you right if everything's ruined."

"Ruined or not, I'll eat it," he promised, and Amanda heard the faint scrape of a match head against stone. A flame flared as Matt lit the candle she had left him the night before, which he withdrew from a pocket of his breeches. By its light she saw that he looked pale and hollow-eyed, with the scratches she had inflicted on him standing out starkly against his skin and a bruise she hadn't noticed the night before purpling just above his temple...

"I don't want to rush you, but could you gather up whatever it was you dropped and bring me something to eat? I'm so hungry I could almost eat you."

A quirky smile accompanied this last as he eased himself away from the rock wall that had been supporting his weight and walked with slow, careful steps to the mattress, where he sank down with obvious relief. Amanda eyed him nervously. It was just possible that he might not be jesting.

"It was a joke," he said wearily, catching her eyes upon him and correctly interpreting the look in them. "A joke, Amanda. You can take it on faith that I wouldn't hurt you even if you never fed me. Just as I'm taking it on faith that you won't betray me."

Amanda looked at him thoughtfully. He was sitting on the feather tick, his long legs bent at the knees so that they were slightly raised, his head leaning tiredly back against a convenient rock formation as if he didn't have the strength to hold it upright any longer. His shirt and breeches were stiff with salt and filthy, but they were dry. His eyes, smoky-looking by candlelight, gleamed at her.

"All right," she said slowly. "I'll trust you if you'll trust me. Is it agreed?"

He smiled at her briefly. "Agreed."

Amanda smiled back at him, then knelt and began to gather up the food.

chapter six

"What did you bring me?" he asked, his voice, despite its growly overtones, so nearly that of a little boy on Christmas morning that Amanda smiled again.

"A blanket and some soap and—"

"I'm talking about *food*," he interrupted impatiently.

Amanda was on her knees searching for the slab of cheese she'd hacked from the large piece in the larder. Apparently the thing had taken refuge behind one of the irregularities in the stone floor. She found it and added it to a plate that already contained cold gammon and two thick slices of bread. He was watching her every move avidly; instead of answering, she carried the plate to him. He took it and was already sinking white teeth into the meat when she turned away to get the water bottle, which fortunately had survived the fall intact. No doubt he would have preferred wine, she thought as she returned to sink down onto a rock near him, the rest of the edible provisions she had brought in her lap, but if she started raiding the convent's meager store of sacramental wine, the fat would soon be in the fire, indeed.

"That was good. Did you bring anything else?" Matt asked after he had sucked the marrow from the round bone of the gammon. The bread and cheese had vanished long since.

"Some slices of roast lamb. And an apple. And more bread and a piece of cake."

"Well, don't just sit there staring at me, pass them over. Haven't you ever seen anyone eat before?"

"Not like you," she answered truthfully, handing over the rest of the food, which he wolfed down almost as soon as he got his hands on it. Fascinated, Amanda watched as those white teeth made quick work of her offerings. He was clearly ravenous. Much of his weakness, which she had attributed to his wound and the resulting fever, might have sprung instead from starvation, she thought. He was a big man, tall, with large bones, still well-muscled despite his leanness; undoubtedly he required a lot of food. She wondered how long it had been since he'd had a decent meal. As he finished the cake and started on the apple she asked him.

"About four months, give or take a week or two," he answered absently, his teeth crunching pleasurably into the apple.

Amanda was horrified. "*Four months!* But you escaped only a couple of *weeks* ago. Surely they fed you while you were in . . . while you were waiting?"

Matt chuckled. It was the first time Amanda had

heard him laugh, and she liked the wry, husky sound.

"Of course they fed me. Two slices of bread and a mug of scummy water a day. Once a week they added a slice of what they called meat, and occasionally they would provide a few moldy vegetables so we wouldn't die. It got so bad that I was actually fantasizing about food. Have you ever dreamed about a haunch of venison and gravy? No? Well, it was quite a switch from my usual fantasy companions, too, I can say. Since I escaped, I've eaten anything I could get my hands on. It's been difficult because I don't dare walk into an inn and ask to be served a meal. Then, a few days ago, I got this damned fever, and I became too weak to trap anything or fish. So I haven't eaten."

Amanda's brow crinkled. "If you were so weak, how on earth did you get down onto the beach? You could never have made it down the path."

"No," he agreed, finishing the apple and eagerly licking the juice from his fingers. "I fell."

"You *fell*?"

He nodded. "I'd been hiding out on a ledge about halfway down one of those cliffs since I felt the fever coming on. Last night I thought I saw something I'd been waiting for. I stood up, moved closer to the edge so that I could see better, and my damned knees buckled. I half slid and half fell down to where you found me. I must have hit my head, because I've got a bump the size of an elephant." He touched the bruise above his temple. "And I don't remember a damned thing until I woke up to find an angel leaning over me, tickling my face with her red hair."

He grinned teasingly. When Amanda didn't smile back, he added softly, "I'm sorry if I scared you."

"'Scared' doesn't suffice. You *terrified* me. I thought you were going to murder me at any minute."

"Yes, well," he said apologetically. "How was I to know that you were the one female in a million with a kind heart? I was sure you were going to run screeching for help as soon as you got away from me. The only thing I could think of to do was to scare you into keeping your mouth shut."

Amanda looked guilty as she met those silvery eyes.

"I almost did—run screeching for help, I mean," she confessed.

"Why didn't you?"

Amanda looked at him, considering her answer. He still looked extremely fearsome—that bristly black beard and thin white scar had a lot to do with it, she thought—but she was somewhat surprised to discover that she no longer felt afraid of him. Why, she wasn't quite sure. Maybe it was the way he had devoured the food she had brought him. Nobody who ate with such greedy enthusiasm could be the inhuman monster she'd pictured.

"I suppose I felt sorry for you," she replied truthfully. His eyes darkened.

"As I said, a kind heart," he said after a brief pause. "I hope somebody treasures you, Amanda. What you have is more precious than rubies."

Amanda half smiled as she recognized the amended passage. She was right in her new assessment of him, she thought. No one who knew the Bible well enough to misquote it could be all bad.

"Thank you," she said softly. As her smile warmed on his face she noticed that he was starting to shiver. He gritted his teeth in an effort to control the spasm as it gained strength.

"I brought some medicine with me, too," she said, getting up from the rock and fetching the rest of the supplies she had brought. Sister Agnes swears by this for fever"—she held up a small glass vial containing a brownish fluid—"and I brought some basilicum powder and some real bandages for your wound."

He eyed her somewhat dubiously. "Are you sure you know what you're doing?" he said through clenched teeth. "I'd hate for your cure to succeed where the hangman didn't."

Amanda looked affronted. "I help Sister Agnes nurse people all the time," she replied with dignity. "However, if you'd rather not trust me..."

The spasms seemed to be growing stronger. She could see his limbs trembling despite his obvious efforts to control them.

"Oh, for goodness' sake, stop being so silly," she said, losing patience. "Drink this and lie down. I promise it won't poison you."

She held out the opened vial as she spoke. He took it, looked at it with loathing, then, with the air of a man throwing his cap over the windmill, bolted it down. Removing the now-empty bottle from his lips, he grimaced horribly.

"Now lie down," she ordered, taking the vial and standing over him with a vaguely threatening air.

"Bossy little thing, aren't you?" he murmured, grinning as he stretched out on the mattress. Amanda chose to ignore that, setting the vial aside and reaching for the blanket, which she spread over him. He was still grinning when she finished.

"Now, if you don't object, I think I should clean those scratches on your face," she said, pouring a little water into the bowl she had brought. "They could get infected."

"I'll probably be scarred for life," he said, his voice mocking. "You've put your mark on me forever, Amanda."

She looked at him, frowning. "I'm teasing you," he assured her in a resigned voice, seeing her troubled expression. "You shouldn't take everything so seriously, Amanda. Learn to laugh a little. It makes life a lot easier."

Amanda gave him a wry look. "Hold still, please," she said crisply, kneeling beside him, and half smiled when he jerked away as she dabbed at his scratches with water and strong lye soap.

"That stings," he said accusingly, huddling closer in his blanket.

"Laugh at it," she advised, and proceeded to clean each scratch thoroughly despite his occasional wince. When she had finished with the scratches, she carefully wiped the rest of his face clean and then sat back on her heels.

"Did I call you an angel? I mean fiend," he said feelingly. Then he smiled at her. Sitting so close to him, she noticed how the corners of his eyes crinkled when he smiled. He was really quite an attractive man, she thought. Of course, he was far too old for her—from the silver hairs that glinted among the coal-black ones she guessed that he was in his forties, although that ubiquitous beard made it difficult to be certain—and not at all the type that she found appealing. However, she didn't doubt that many women would differ with her there...

His shivers were easing, she noticed with relief. She let him rest quietly for a few minutes, until they seemed to be completely gone. Then she spoke again.

"Matt, you'd better let me dress the wound for you. Properly this time."

His eyes flicked open to meet hers. "Are you sure your maidenly modesty can stand it? I thought you were going to burst into flames, you became so red the last time."

To her chagrin Amanda felt herself blushing at the mere reminder. He grinned, his eyes gleaming wickedly.

"I have my answer," he said dryly. "Don't worry, Amanda, I'll do it. I've recovered quite a bit since this morning. If you'll pass me the powder and bandages and turn your back..."

"I'll do it," she replied, determined despite the warm rosiness that obstinately refused to fade from her cheeks. "It needs to be done properly if you don't want that wound to get infected. And if it gets infected you could die—and I'd be left with a body to dispose of." A glimmer of a smile curved her lips. He looked at her strangely for an instant, then grinned back, his eyes warming.

"You're learning," he said approvingly. "All right, Amanda, do your worst. I can stand it if you can."

It didn't take her long to fetch the powder and bandages, and pour fresh water in the bowl, but by the time she was finished he was ready for her. As though to spare her as much embarrassment as possible, he had unbuttoned his breeches and rolled them down just far enough so that she could get at his wound. He had pulled up his shirttails no farther than his waist. Amanda appreciated the care he had taken to spare her blushes, but she couldn't control the wave of color that crept up her face as she surveyed even that small expanse of hair-roughened, muscle-ridged, and unmistakably masculine flesh. She was thankful that he made no comment, although he eyed her pinkening cheeks sardonically. Amanda forced herself to concentrate on removing the makeshift bandage without hurting him. But it was stuck to his skin with dried blood, and despite her best efforts, his forehead was beaded with sweat when at last she succeeded in prying the bloodied pad from his skin. Seen by candlelight instead of moonlight, the wound looked worse than she remembered, raw and jagged and caked with crusts of dried blood. Fresh blood welled where she had torn away the bandage, and the flesh around the wound was reddened and obviously very tender.

"This may hurt a little," she warned as she moistened a folded section of bandage and began to gingerly wash away the crusts of blood that clogged the wound. He said nothing, but shut his eyes as she worked. By the time the wound was clean he was sweating profusely; Amanda felt the moist heat of the skin beneath her fingertips and bit her lower lip hard. Clearly he was in pain, and she hated to watch anyone suffer. But if the wound was to heal properly, it had to be done, so she set her teeth firmly and did it.

When finally the ugly gash lay open, she sniffed at it cautiously. So close to his skin she smelled sweat, and man, but no sickly, putrid odor that Sister Agnes had taught her meant gangrene. Satisfied, she sat back and sprinkled the basilicum powder liberally on the oozing wound. As she had expected, he yelped, and his eyes popped open to glare accusingly at her.

"That burns like the devil."

"I told you it might hurt," she said apologetically, folding a clean section of bandage into a pad and pressing it against the wound as she spoke.

"You were right—it did," he answered through set teeth, but as she began to wrap more bandages around him to hold the pad in place his tense muscles gradually relaxed. By the time she had finished and was securing the whole with a knot, he was breathing normally and watching her through speculative and slightly teasing eyes.

"Very nice," he said approvingly as she sat back, having completed the task. She smiled at him, and a devilish glint appeared in his eyes as he continued smoothly. "If you've finished, I could use a bath."

Amanda's eyes widened on his face, her horror at the implication evident. He chuckled, clearly pleased to have elicited a response from her.

"You mean you still have a few maidenly scruples left?"

"I'm certainly not going to bathe you, if that's what you're suggesting. You're not *that* helpless."

"I suppose I'll have to do it myself, then," he said placidly, and from the satisfied curl to his mouth she deduced that that was what he had intended all along. "If you'll just turn your back..." He was sitting up, his movements slow and careful, as if his wound pained him.

"You really shouldn't be moving around," she said, her eyes worried as she watched him. "If nothing happens to break the wound open again, it should heal without any problems. I won't change the bandage for a week or so—if you behave. But if it starts to bleed again..." Her voice trailed off, but the implication was obvious.

"After this I'll be still as a corpse," he promised. "But I've been sweating like a pig, and I stink so much I offend myself." He finished with the buttons. The shirt hung open, revealing such an expanse of black-furred muscles that Amanda's eyes widened. "Pass me the soap, will you?" he added casually. "And then turn your back, Amanda."

Amanda passed him the soap, then obediently turned her back. She heard the splash of water and out of the corner of her eye saw him lift an arm to scrub beneath it. She shut her eyes, and immediately the tantalizing image of the hair-roughened masculine flesh his opened shirt had revealed was imprinted against her closed lids. How would he look with his shirt off entirely? she wondered. And, cheeks pinkening, immediately banished the thought. It was positively unseemly to be so curious about a man...

"Oh, I brought you some clean clothes," she said, recollecting. Her eyes opened as she spoke, but she carefully kept her back to him. If he should somehow divine the incomprehensible curiosity the thought of his unclothed body inspired in her, she would die of shame.

"Pass them here, would you?" he asked. Amanda did so, careful not to look at him as she complied. Out of the corner of her eye she got a hazy impression of wide shoulders and flexing, sinewy arms...

"You can turn around now—I'm decent." Amanda heard the amusement in his voice, and as she turned rather hesitantly to look at him she saw it in his eyes as well, although they were not unkind. But they left her in no doubt that he was aware of her embarrassment and found it funny. To her chagrin she blushed furiously. He was watching her with keen eyes. In the clean and whole white shirt with loose black trousers she had brought he looked slightly less disreputable, despite the bristly beard, scratched face, and tumbled hair.

"How old are you, Amanda?"

Matt lay back on the feather tick as he spoke, folding his arms under his head and surveying her from beneath raised brows. Amanda was all too conscious of his gaze as she knelt on the stone floor some few feet away. She had to force herself to meet those too-knowing eyes.

"Almost eighteen." Her voice sounded strangled.

"And shy with it, hmm?" He laughed, but the sound was comforting rather than mocking. "Don't worry about it, Amanda. You'll outgrow it soon enough. All you need is a little more experience of men. Don't you have a father, brothers?"

"My father died almost five years ago. I have a half brother, who inherited his title."

"Title?"

Amanda nodded. Her embarrassment was fading somewhat as the subject changed. "My father was the fifth Duke of Brookshire. My half brother is the sixth."

His eyes widened, and his lips pursed in a soundless whistle.

"So you're 'milady,' are you? You should have told me at the outset—I would have been more polite."

"You weren't polite at *all*," she retorted, meeting his eyes without discomfort now.

"I wasn't, was I? You'll have to excuse me on the grounds that I've never met a titled lady before. In America, where I'm from, we don't have such things."

"What part of America?"

"New Orleans. That's in Louisiana, in case you don't know, milady."

She gave him a look designed to tell him what she thought of his mocking use of her title. "And Louisiana's in the South, I know. I'm not ignorant. And even if I were, I'd be able to tell where you're from by the way you talk. That slow drawl is very... distinctive."

"So are your clipped English vowels, milady, believe me. Tell me something: if your brother is a duke, why are you buried in this godforsaken place? It's not exactly the hub of English high society."

"My brother hates me." Amanda tried to make a joke out of it, but she could not quite prevent the forlorn thread of truth that laced her words. Matt's eyebrows lifted questioningly.

"Does he indeed? The man must be insane—you're the most eminently lovable person I've ever met."

Amanda smiled at him. It was a nice thing to say,

even if he didn't mean it. With a shock she realized how very few people had thought her lovable since her father died...

"Tell me about it, Amanda," Matt commanded softly. Amanda looked at him for a moment, hesitating. Keeping her troubles to herself was second nature to her, partly because there was only Susan who was really interested in hearing about them, partly because of her innate pride. But Matt's eyes were kind as they met hers, and she suddenly found herself craving that kindness. So she crept closer to the fearsome murderer who had practically terrified the life out of her scant hours before, and soon she had poured out to him everything that had happened from the time of her father's death to Edward's recent plan to marry her to Lord Robert Turnbull. By the time she had finished she was sitting on a corner of the mattress near his head, and he had taken her hand in his. She was vaguely conscious of the warmth and strength of that big hand cradling hers, and comforted by it.

"Poor little angel," he said softly. His hand tightened around hers and then he lifted it to his mouth, pressing his lips against the back of it briefly before releasing it. "And what do you plan to do if you do manage to avoid being married off to this Lord Robert?"

Amanda made a face. Her hand tingled slightly where he had kissed it and she pressed it absently against her skirt. "That's the thing: I don't know. My father left me some money, but Edward controls it until I marry—with his consent. And then it will pass directly to my husband. I could stay here, I suppose.

I know Mother Superior would let me, but I'd almost rather be married to Lord Robert than become a nun."

"The lesser of two evils, hmm? I wonder. You don't know very much about men or marriage, do you, Amanda?"

"No."

He shook his head. "I must tell you about it sometime. You should at least know what you're getting into before you make up your mind. Amanda..."

She looked at him inquiringly.

"Could you pass me that blanket? I'm getting cold."

She saw that he was beginning to shiver again. All the time she had been talking, he had been lying in the cool, damp air with no cover. Contrite, she fetched the blanket she had brought, then shook it out and smoothed that and the other one over him. He was shivering in earnest by the time she had finished. She sat beside him until the spasm passed, not speaking. Although talking about her situation had not changed it one iota, she felt much better, lighter almost, as though some of the burden had passed from her shoulders to his broad ones.

"Thank you, Matt," she said softly when he was still again. His eyes opened, the expression curiously brooding.

"There's something you haven't asked me, you know," he said abruptly. Those silvery eyes beneath the thick black brows were almost accusing. "Something that I would have thought you would have wanted to know before anything else."

Amanda looked down at him blankly. "What?"

"Don't you want to know if I did it?"

"Did what?" Amanda, befuddled by the unexpected change of topic, wondered momentarily if his mind was wandering again. She stared down at him, concern plain in her face. He made an angry sound that was almost a hiss.

"The murders, Amanda. Don't you want to know if I committed the murders?"

Amanda flinched. For the last hour or so she had forgotten what he was, and she hated being reminded of it. He had been so kind, so gentle with her. It was hard to reconcile this facet of him with the ruthless, cold-blooded killer who she knew must lurk somewhere within.

"Please . . . don't tell me about it, Matt. I don't want to know. I don't even want to think about it. You've been very kind to me, and that's all that matters."

He stared at her in silence for a moment. Amanda was surprised to see his eyes start to snap.

"Good God, you think I did it, don't you?" he demanded furiously, sitting up so that he was scant inches away from her. "You actually think I murdered six people—slit the throats of a woman and four children—and you're sitting here alone with me? You're not safe to be let out."

He sounded so angry that Amanda flinched away from him. The movement was involuntary, but his expression turned ugly as he observed it.

"A little late to be frightened of me, isn't it,

Amanda? What could you do if I decided to kill you, too? We're all alone—I could throttle you in an instant." He reached out to lay ungentle hands against the base of her throat. Amanda, eyes staring, looked at him with disbelief that rapidly turned to fear. He was so close, and so big... But his hands weren't hurting her, and as she realized that, everything he'd said took on a clear meaning.

"Do you mean—are you telling me—you *didn't* kill those people?"

"No, I didn't," he growled, removing his hands from her neck but looking angrier than ever. "It so happens that I'm as innocent of that particular crime as you are. But you had no way of knowing that. I thought you were helping me because you had decided that I was innocent. But you hadn't, had you, Amanda? You thought I was guilty as hell—and yet here you are, totally at my mercy. Do you think you could stop me from doing anything I chose to you? Which might include murder but certainly not at first. Have you ever heard of rape, Amanda?" Her eyes widened at that, and her cheeks flushed a deep pink as he continued relentlessly. "Believe me, my girl, it's not an experience you'd enjoy, and unless you want to experience it firsthand, I'd advise you to take more care in choosing your lame ducks. A soft heart is one thing, but a *soft head* is something else entirely."

He flung himself back against the mattress as he finished, but his eyes continued to glare at her. Amanda returned his gaze with the first stirrings of indignation.

"You got over being grateful for my help pretty

quickly, didn't you?" she demanded. "Would you rather that I'd left you on the beach—or screamed when Mr. Llewellyn told us to come out? I imagine they'd have hanged you by now—which might have been a damned good thing but I was too *softheaded* to realize it at the time."

Matt stared at her, his angry expression turning to one of surprise, then dawning amusement, as though a silky kitten had turned and bitten him.

"Don't swear, Amanda," he rebuked, his eyes beginning to dance as he took in the full extent of her loss of temper. "It's not ladylike."

"I'll swear if I *want* to," she shot back, jumping to her feet before he could put out a hand to stay her. "And since you're not a murderer, there's not a damned thing you can do to stop me."

And with that Parthian shot and a final, killing glare, she flounced toward the passage.

"Tut, tut, milady, where are your manners? Aren't you going to say good night?" he called after her retreating figure, and it was obvious from his tone that her anger had restored his own good humor. Stalking toward the trapdoor, Amanda quivered with fury at the laughter in his voice. After his insults and rank ingratitude, being the butt of his amusement was simply too much to be borne.

chapter seven

The next day, like the one before it, was excruciatingly long for Matt. Alone in the echoing quiet of the cave, both too weak and too wary to venture out on the beach, he occupied himself with getting his strength back—and with thoughts of the girl who had literally saved his life. The first was fairly straightforward, though painful and arduous. He forced himself to walk the length of the cave, over and over, until he was exhausted, but his muscles were becoming more reliable. Finally he collapsed on the feather tick, taking a hearty swig from the bottle of water that Amanda had left him. He was hungry—he always seemed to be hungry lately—but that didn't bother him particularly. Hunger had been an almost constant companion for months; he was getting used to it. The thoughts of Amanda that he could no longer seem to keep at bay were far more trouble-some than the gnawing in his empty belly.

She was beautiful. He had known—in every sense of the word—many women over the years, but Amanda had somehow managed to catch his fancy to a degree he previously would have said was impossible. His imagination dwelled pleasurably on the madonnalike loveliness of her features: the great, black-fringed eyes set aslant like a pair of sparkling amethysts against the magnolia-blossom texture of her skin, the still-childish line of her cheeks, her small, straight nose and rosy lips—sweet Jesus, yes, her lips. Lips clearly made for kissing... Their tender fullness fascinated him almost more than the glorious color of her hair. Before he had set eyes on Amanda's ruby-hued mane, he would have said that he preferred females whose locks were as pale as his own were dark. But Amanda's tumbling masses of fire-shot-with-gold silk lured him like a moth to the flame it resembled. Even the prim coronet of braids she had worn when she had come to him the night before had not lessened the almost irresistible compulsion he felt to bury his face in it, to see if it could possibly be as soft as his fingers remembered...

His thoughts wandered to the enticingly curved shape of her. She was slender as a young girl is slender, but there was a hint of fullness about her breasts that held out tantalizing promise of the wom-an she would one day become. Her breasts would be soft to the touch, like her hair... He felt his loins begin to heat. Thoroughly annoyed at himself, he wrenched his mind away from the further delights of her body. She was very young and very vulnerable, although she didn't seem to realize it, and he would not repay her for her care of him by rutting after her like a stag after a doe. He felt a curious urge to protect her, had done since he had opened his eyes on the beach to look into hers, huge with fright. Protectiveness was not something he usually felt toward women; desire, yes, liking, sometimes, but not this overwhelming urge to stand between her and anything that might threaten her, including the base stirrings of his own passion. He supposed he could ascribe it to a very natural gratitude—not many others would have put themselves at risk for a dangerous stranger, as she had done—or even to his instinctive recognition of an innate goodness in her that transcended mere physical beauty and transformed her into something quite outside his ken.

He wanted her, of course. He would have to be a eunuch not to. Her budding womanhood enticed him while the lusher charms of more experienced members of her sex had begun to pall. It would be enjoyable to teach her what it meant to be a woman... But the shining innocence that was so plain in her eyes stopped him cold. No matter what else he might have become, he was not that big a cad.

The trouble was, he told himself, that he hadn't had a woman in almost half a year. Not since two nights before they had arrested him... For him, who hadn't been celibate since a friend of his mother's had initiated him at the tender age of fourteen, that was almost unbelievable. Certainly it must be that which intensified his very natural interest in an indisputably lovely girl into this hot, raging desire that gnawed at his vitals like a starving rat.

To take his mind off the increasing tumescence between his legs, Matt stood up and began to pace restlessly back and forth. He winced as every movement of his right leg sent a knifelike pain plunging through his body, but he persevered. By the time exhaustion once again compelled him to sink down on the feather tick, his thoughts weren't on the girl but on the pain...

After he had rested for a while, the pain receded and Amanda's face and form returned to torment him despite his best intentions. In pure self-defense, Matt finally decided to shave. Scraping nearly four months' worth of whiskers from his face with nothing more than a knife and cold water should be a sobering enough experience to keep his thoughts where they belonged, he told himself. Picking up the knife, he grimaced at its dullness and proceeded to sharpen it as best he could on a stone. When the blade was honed to as near razor sharpness as he could get it, he found the small, chipped mirror Amanda had brought and propped it on a rocky protrusion that jutted shelflike from the wall. Then he positioned the candle strategically, poured a little water into the bowl, stripped to the waist, and set to work. As he turned the blade this way and that, he grimaced at the marks Amanda's nails had left on his skin. They were fading, but he still looked as though he'd been tangling with a wildcat, which he supposed was as good an analogy as any... Just as he scraped the last trace of stubble from his throat, wincing at the abrasiveness of the dulling blade, he heard the soft swish of skirts coming down the passage. Amanda. He would recognize that sound in a dark hole in China.

Clad in another of the severe gray dresses that were, oddly enough, a perfect foil for her bright coloring, Amanda was juggling several items, including a tureen of hot soup. All her attention was concentrated on not dropping anything as she entered the cavern. In consequence, she did not look up immediately, not until after she had safely deposited the tureen on the floor. The other items followed, and she heaved a sigh of relief as she looked around for Matt.

"I've brought you something hot," she began, smiling at him. He had been kneeling when she came in; now he stood up, coming toward her, and Amanda felt her cursed cheeks grow hot as she saw that he was naked to the waist. Hastily she averted her gaze, retaining only a fleeting impression of black-furred planes and broad shoulders. Her eyes moved up to his face—and her mouth dropped open.

He was handsome, she discovered with a shock, more than handsome, in fact. Without the bristly black beard that had obscured the firmness of his lean jaw and the cut of his beautifully shaped mouth, he was marvelous-looking. His black hair was still overlong and untidy, but its waving thickness framed a rampantly male face that God must have designed expressly to appeal to the female of the species. The silver-gray eyes beneath the thick black brows, the straight, almost aquiline nose, the high, flat cheekbones, were brought into exquisite symmetry by the newly revealed lines of cheek and jaw and chin. A chin that was square, and looked as though it could be obstinate. A chin that was not softened in the slightest by the faint cleft in its center. As her dazed eyes moved back over his face, seeking to reconcile the man who stood looking down at her rather quizzically with the fearsome murderer she thought she had come to know, another fact became crystal clear to her: he was young; much younger than she had supposed.

"You'll catch flies," he said, gently teasing as his thumb came up under her chin to close her mouth. Amanda continued to stare at him, not even blushing, so intense was her surprise.

"How old are you?" She gasped out the first coherent words that popped into her brain. He grinned, and one of his eyebrows lifted at her inquiringly. She had seen that expression on his face before—his mockery was something she was rapidly becoming thoroughly familiar with—but now the crooked grin had a charm that almost made her mouth drop open again. Just in time she got a grip on the remnants of her self-possession and managed to keep her mouth closed.

"Thirty-three," he answered equably, watching her with a glint of unholy amusement in his eyes. "Why, how old did you think I was?"

"I-I didn't know." Amanda stumbled over her tongue. Try as she might, she could not seem to tear her eyes away from the mind-boggling splendor of his face. The proximity of his naked chest paled into insignificance in comparison. "I thought about forty, or a little more," she added feebly.

"Not quite, although thirty-three must seem nearly as old to you," he answered, and to her relief took his eyes from her face to look with interest at the steaming tureen near her feet. "That looks good. What is it?"

"Potato soup," she replied automatically, still unable to look anywhere but at his face. Even half averted from her, as it was at the moment, it was devastating. "I volunteered to take what was left from dinner to the Morells. Mrs. Morell just gave birth to her eighth child, and Sister Patrick thought she would appreciate the soup. Which she did, even though there wasn't a lot left after I kept back half for you..." Amanda's voice trailed off as she realized that she was rambling. Sudden annoyance with herself set in. So he was handsome, and not horribly old, she told herself fiercely, so what? He was still the same man she had rescued and begun to regard almost as a friend. To her relief he didn't seem at all interested in her continued reactions to his changed appearance. Instead, all his attention was focused on the soup. Thank goodness his primary concern was his stomach! With luck, he hadn't even noticed what a fool she was making of herself.

"You'd better eat it while it's hot," she said, grasping for composure. To her relief her voice sounded almost normal. "There's fresh-baked bread, too, and butter."

"It sounds wonderful." He bent, picking up the tureen by its handle and gathering up the bread and butter in his other hand, then straightened, carrying his booty over to the flat-topped rock that served as his table. Retrieving a spoon and knife from the utensils she had brought him the night before, he sat cross-legged on the floor and began to eat with gusto. It was some few minutes before he stopped, looking a little self-conscious, and gestured to the food. "Will you have some?"

"What?" Amanda was still assimilating the shock to her system. "Oh . . . no, thank you. I've had dinner."

"All the more for me, then." He grinned with unabashed greed. Amanda was still coming to grips with the dazzling attraction of that grin, unobscured now by bristling whiskers, when he returned his attention to his meal. It was some little time before he spoke again.

"Still angry at me?" he asked casually, barely glancing up at her as he spread butter on a chunk of bread with absorbed pleasure.

Amanda blinked. It took her a moment to remember that she had been furious with him when she had stormed out the night before.

"No." She shook her head, smiling faintly. "I get over being angry almost as fast as I get angry."

He looked reflective, or as reflective as it was possible to look while crunching on a piece of bread. He must have finished the soup, because he was looking into the tureen with a faintly regretful expression and laying aside his spoon.

"You're not still afraid of me, are you?" He looked up at her again, swallowing the last of the bread, his eyes suddenly keen.

"Of course not," Amanda answered, then wondered if it was true. Oh, she was no longer afraid of him physically—that he would harm her, that is—but without his beard he was suddenly a stranger. An impossibly handsome stranger.

"Then why are you standing way over there? I don't bite—at least, not if you feed me." He grinned a little. Amanda realized with a burn of embarrassment that she had been rooted to the same spot since she had come in. She moved jerkily, turning her back to him and crossing to the place she had left the basilicum powder and bandages. At the memory of her fingers brushing against the hard wall of his abdomen—the abdomen of a young and unquestionably virile man—her blush deepened.

"Do I embarrass you?" he pursued softly. "Would you like me to put my shirt back on?"

Amanda turned to look at him. He was still sitting cross-legged on the floor, his eyes narrow as he regarded her thoughtfully. To tell the truth, she had almost forgotten about the bareness of his chest. So much male flesh was overwhelming, it was true, but in her shock she had hardly registered it. Now she did, her eyes automatically absorbing the wide shoulders and deep chest, the sinewy arms and flat, hard-looking muscles blurred by a soft covering of black hair. Foreign to her, certainly, but not the reason for her odd behavior...

"Yes, please," she said, hoping that he would think it was his state of undress that had caused her confusion. Her embarrassment would increase a hundredfold if he should realize that it was the sheer masculine beauty of his face.

He shook his head, standing up with a single fluid movement and reaching for his shirt, which lay across the rocky shelf that also held the mirror.

"You're going to have to learn to control yourself, Amanda." He was teasing her; she could tell from his

123

tone. "You can't go on blushing like a brushfire every time something makes you feel a little shy." He was holding his shirt in his hand, smiling wickedly at her as he spoke.

Amanda bristled. "I don't..." she began, only to break off as he half turned to shrug into his shirt. It was the first time she had seen his bare back. She froze, staring, her hand flying to her mouth. The smooth, rippling flesh of his shoulders merged with a mass of half-healed scars.

"Matt—your *back*," she gasped. Matt swiveled to look at her, his brows meeting in a thick black line above his eyes. His shirt hung loosely from his shoulders, still baring a considerable expanse of chest. "What on earth happened to your back?"

"I forgot about that," he said after a moment, his voice gruff. "I'm sorry, Amanda. I would never have let you see it if I'd remembered."

"What difference does my seeing it make?" she demanded impatiently, moving toward him as she spoke. "It looks so *painful*. What happened to you?"

He smiled, a crooked, rueful twist of his lips. Her hands went out to him automatically, and just as automatically he caught them in his, drawing her toward him so that only a foot of space separated them. "It's customary to beat a prisoner—especially a condemned one," he explained, looking down into her upturned face. "Unfortunately they did not make an exception of me."

"Oh, Matt." Amanda's throat closed with the sheer horror of it. He had been beaten, beaten in a way that would have sickened and infuriated her if it had been done to an animal. How it must have hurt! Tears welled in her eyes. *"Matt."*

"Good God, you're not going to cry about it, are you? It's not that bad, I promise—and it's certainly not the first time I've been beaten. My mother's gentlemen friends used to lay into me regularly when I was growing up. Said it was good for my character—and no doubt it was." He smiled, obviously hoping to relieve Amanda's distress with humor. She dutifully tried to smile back, but the effort was wobbly at best. And then it was spoiled entirely by a large tear, faintly golden in the candlelight, which spilled from the corner of one thick-lashed violet eye to traverse a shining path over the creamy pale curve of her cheek.

"Oh, for God's sake, Amanda, you're too damned softhearted for your own good." Matt's voice was almost a growl as he reached out to flick the tear away with a gentle forefinger. It was immediately followed by another. Seeing it, Matt groaned and pulled her against him, one arm going around her waist while the other hand cradled the back of her head. Amanda burrowed her face into the soft, faintly moist fur of his chest, her arms going instinctively around his waist so that she could get closer. He felt so warm against her, warm and strong and solid. In his arms she felt safe... She thought again of the horror of abuse that his back was mute testament to, and despite everything she could do to stop them, tears fell thick and fast from her eyes.

"Don't cry, Amanda." His voice was faintly rough. "I'm not worth one of your tears. Please don't cry."

Perversely this only made her cry harder. Matt

swore under his breath, cradling her closer, bending his head so that his face rested on her soft crown of braids. Amanda sobbed against his chest, eyes closed, arms locked tightly around his waist. Almost unconsciously she registered the salty taste of his flesh wet with her tears, the warm, faintly musky smell of him . . .

"Hush, now, Amanda," he was murmuring into her hair. "I can't stand to see a woman cry—it makes me want to cry myself. You wouldn't want that to happen, would you?"

The image his words conjured up—that totally masculine face awash with tears—was so ridiculous that Amanda giggled despite herself. The sound emerged half strangled, but Matt apparently had no trouble interpreting it correctly.

"That's my girl." The words were partially muffled as he spoke into her hair. "Come on, Amanda, dry your eyes. If you don't, you're liable to cause a flood that could wash us right out of here."

He was putting a little distance between them as he spoke. One hand still rested loosely on her waist while his other hand came up to dry her cheeks gently with the corner of his shirttail. Amanda's own arms had released their death grip on his middle; her hands now lay almost unconsciously on his bare chest. When her face had been dried to his satisfaction, he let his shirttail fall back into place and gripped her chin instead. Tilting her face so that he could see it properly, he regarded her with a quizzical, faintly worried expression.

"Better now?" he asked. Amanda nodded, then sniffed, the small sound prosaic. Matt's eyes warmed on her face, and one corner of his mouth crooked upward. Amanda's eyes were still misty with tears as they met his, but she smiled at him. An achingly sweet smile that touched Matt to the heart.

"I'm sorry," she whispered.

"Don't be." His voice was husky, and his eyes were disarmingly gentle as they moved over her face. "I don't think anyone's ever cried over me before. I like it. I like it very much."

Amanda stared wordlessly at him as his finger tilted her chin even more, and he bent his black head to brush a soft, sweet kiss across her mouth.

The touch of his mouth had a strange effect on her. She felt almost dizzy, and her hands slid automatically from his chest to his shoulders to steady herself. The feel of his lips, firm and warm against hers, the rasp of his chest hair beneath her fingers and then the satin-over-steel strength of his shoulders under her palms sent a quiver of sensation through her. She drew a breath, more of a little gasp; Matt had already begun to draw back when he felt the faint flutter of her lips under his. Amanda felt him begin to pull away, felt the moment when he stopped, standing like a statue for an instant, his eyes darkening as they locked with hers. Then his breath drew in sharply, much as hers had done but louder, fiercer; his eyes closed, and he bent over her again, his mouth on hers, but harder this time, and hotter.

She had never thought a man would kiss like this. That was Amanda's last thought as his arms tightened around her, drawing her up against him until they were pressed so tightly together that it seemed as though the heat of his body must fuse them into one.

His mouth was moving against hers, his tongue moist and urgent as it slid between her still-parted lips. It stopped at the barrier of her small white teeth, tasting the inner flesh of her lower lip before drawing it into his mouth and nibbling on it in a way that was part pleasure, part pain. Amanda opened her mouth to say something, anything, but before she could force words out, his tongue slid past her teeth to explore the warm, moist sweetness within. Amanda felt her knees weaken as the world seemed to revolve around her, and her hands instinctively crept around his neck for support as she closed her eyes.

He was bending her backward, one arm locking her to him while his other hand stroked restlessly over the curve of her back, kissing her as greedily as he had devoured his food earlier. Amanda clung tightly to his neck, her body bent over his arm, knowing that if he released his grip, she would fall in an ignominious heap to the floor because her knees had turned to butter, as incapable of supporting her as she was of stopping his kiss.

His tongue touched hers, stroked it, coaxed it. Without knowing exactly what he wanted of her, Amanda returned the caress. Against her breasts she could feel the sudden thud of his heart. He drew her tongue into his mouth, letting her taste him. His mouth was hot and moist and musky sweet... Shyly at first, then with increasing boldness, Amanda explored his mouth, brushing her tongue against his, letting it slide around the inside of his teeth. She felt his heart speed up until it was pounding as though he had run for miles. He was shaking against her, and to her surprise Amanda discovered that she was shaking, too, trembling from head to foot as he had when in the grip of the fever. She was barely conscious of his arms tightening around her, so caught up was she in the unbelievable sensations his mouth was awakening in her. But when his hand slid all the way around her to close over her breast, she felt it like a shaft of fire clear down to her toes. She stiffened, and her eyes flew open. He continued to kiss her, shaking, his face so close that she could see every pore in his skin. His eyes were tightly closed; his lashes lay like black fans against cheeks that were darkly flushed . . . His hand tightened on her breast, his thumb brushing against a peak that was sensitive in a way Amanda had never guessed it could be. She felt an unfamiliar tightness deep in her belly, a quick heating of her blood that made her feel as if she were burning up. Then his thumb repeated the caressing motion. Amanda's hands tightened around his neck, her nails digging deep into the flesh of his nape. Her lashes, strangely heavy, fluttered shut.

chapter eight

Matt ended it. No sooner had Amanda relaxed fully against him, surrendering herself without words to anything he might demand of her, than he jerked his mouth from hers with a muttered oath. His hand tightened momentarily on her breast, and then it too was removed, leaving Amanda feeling oddly bereft as she opened her eyes to find him looking down at her, a restless glitter deep in the silvery eyes.

"Matt?" she breathed, unconsciously clinging. His eyes blazed as they moved from her eyes to her mouth, and then he was pushing her away from him, his hands hard on her waist as he held her at arm's length.

"For God's sake, Amanda, *don't*," he said harshly. A little muscle jumped convulsively in his jaw. Amanda stared up at him, her eyes dazed with a passion she could barely put a name to. She felt totally unlike the girl she had been scant minutes ago. Impossible that he didn't feel the same. But he was looking down at her with eyes that were now as hard as agates, and his voice was hard, too, as he said her name again.

Amanda flushed. Suddenly she realized that she was clinging to him like a limpet, her eyes dreamy on his face, her mouth soft and trembling with his kisses. Her nails were embedded in the skin of his nape; as she became aware of that her flush deepened until she was the color of a wild rose, and her arms dropped to her sides. Her eyes dropped, too, and she would have pulled away from him but his fingers dug hurtfully into her waist as he refused to let her go.

"You're supposed to slap my face, not burst into flames in my arms." The humorous overtone to the voice that was still slightly husky with passion was the last straw. Laugh at her, would he? The temper that matched the bright heat of her hair burst into flaming life. Eyes flashing, she drew back her hand and slapped him across the cheek with all her might. His head rocked back with the force of the blow. He clapped one hand to his abused cheek, releasing his hold on her waist, and regained his equilibrium to regard her with astonishment.

"Satisfied?" She practically snarled the word, her mouth taut and her eyes blazing with temper. To add to her fury, as he took in the full extent of her outrage he began to look amused.

"Don't you *dare* to laugh at me." Boiling over with anger fueled by rising humiliation, she drew back her hand for another assault.

"Whoa, there." He grabbed for her, ducking to

miss the blow she aimed at him, catching her around the waist and pinning her to his side with one hard arm. Her arms were clamped to her sides so that she could only wriggle furiously, glaring at him.

"For such a little girl you have a remarkable wallop." He grinned as he rubbed his cheek with a rueful hand. "Stop squirming, Amanda. I was only teasing you."

"Let me *go.*" The words were spoken with such deadly menace that Matt's grin widened. "Let me go, you..." Amanda couldn't bring to mind words bad enough.

"Temper, temper." Matt was openly laughing now. Amanda twisted so furiously in his hold that he used his other arm to lift her clear off her feet. Infuriated by the physical superiority that allowed him so easily to subdue her, Amanda was spluttering with rage as he sat down on a rock, setting her on her feet again. Her back was to him as he pulled her between his spread legs, his arms locking hers to her sides.

"Let me *go,*" she spat again, rigid with fury. The way he was holding her, there was no hope of escape.

"Not until you calm down and listen to me," he said into her ear. She flinched from the feel of his warm breath against her skin. "Are you listening?"

As she said nothing his arms tightened fractionally around her waist. The feel of his big body pressed so intimately against her back was evoking sensations that even her anger couldn't blind her to.

"Amanda?"

Defeated, she nodded jerkily. The first hot blaze of her temper was beginning to drain away, letting the shame that had been the cause of its start to surface.

"I wasn't laughing at you, Amanda." The soft drawl was more pronounced than she had ever heard it. "I was laughing at myself. I never meant to kiss you— I've been fighting the inclination ever since I woke up and found you leaning over me on the beach. But you looked so sad just now, and so sweet, you confounded all my good intentions."

"I'm sorry if I embarrassed you," Amanda said stiffly, feeling her face flame. She was supremely conscious of the feel of his big body all around her as he held her enfolded against him. His arms were like iron bands constricting her own arms and waist, and she could feel the moist heat of his bare chest burning through her dress to the skin of her back. His thighs were hard as they held her legs still, and her head was tucked neatly under his chin. She couldn't have moved if she tried.

He gave her a slight shake. "Honey, you're not listening. You didn't embarrass me. You excited me— quite madly. I wanted you, Amanda, in the way a man wants a woman and you're probably too young to understand. I had to force myself to let you go. If I hadn't... I'm many things, Amanda, and most of them not particularly nice, but I try to draw the line at seducing sweet young virgins I've grown rather fond of."

Amanda stood very still.

"Are you saying... you're fond of *me*, Matt?" she asked at last in a small voice. His arms tightened around her waist in a quick hug.

"Very fond," he said huskily against her ear. "You're the sweetest thing I've ever seen—and I want to keep you that way. If I'd gone on kissing you, Amanda, pretty soon kissing wouldn't have been enough. I'm a man, not a boy, and while kissing may thrill you right down to your little pink toes, it merely whets my appetite for the main dish. And you don't want to be a meal for me, Amanda. I'd gobble you up just as I've gobbled up dozens of females before you, and then I'd go on about my business. But you'd be shattered. I don't think you could give your body without giving your heart, Amanda, and you don't want to give your heart to me. I'd break it, honey, and that's the truth."

Amanda felt her cheeks burning as his words sank in. No matter how he phrased it, he was warning her against falling in love with him. The *conceit* of him. With that face, no doubt he'd had females swooning over him in his pram. And he thought she was in danger of joining the queue. When pigs fly, she told herself stiffening.

"Please let me go. I have to get back before Sister Patrick sends someone to look for me. I've been gone far too long already." Her voice was carefully even. She knew her cheeks had to be hectic with color, but she hoped he couldn't see them from where he sat behind her. Not that she was embarrassed any longer, mind. She was angry.

"Damn it, Amanda, I'm telling you this for your own good. Don't you think I want to kiss you, make love to you? You're a beautiful girl, and I have all the normal instincts. But I like you too much to take advantage of your innocence. Believe me, I could make you want me so much you wouldn't care what was happening until it was all over. Then you'd be sorry, but it would be too late. You're only a virgin once, honey. Don't be in such a hurry to lose it."

"You think an awful lot of yourself, don't you?" Her voice was rigid with fury. Impatient with being held captive in his arms, she twisted violently. To her surprise he let her go. And she was under no illusion that "let" was not the operative word. He could have kept her captive until doomsday if he'd wanted. The knowledge didn't mitigate her anger one scrap; if anything, it increased it. She whirled to glare at him, skirts flying, hands on hips. He remained where he was, watching her, his long legs in the loose black trousers casually apart, his hands braced against the surface of the rock on which he sat. His unbuttoned shirt hung loosely from his shoulders, baring a considerable expanse of black-furred chest. A dawning exasperation mingled with the amusement that still twisted his mouth and gleamed in his eyes. The candlelight gilded the hard planes of his face, adding a touch of gold to the silver-gray eyes. Just looking at him fueled Amanda's outrage. He was, in a word, beautiful. The knowledge that his warning might be just the tiniest bit justified maddened her.

"Are you so conceited that you mistake simple kindness for... for something else entirely?" Her eyes shot violet fire at him. He looked mildly intrigued as he observed the effect. His refusal to be angered maddened her as much as his dazzling good looks. Her voice quivered with temper as she continued to hurl words at him. "You kissed me, you oaf, not the other way around, remember. And contrary to what you may think, it wasn't so marvelous that I'm in danger of losing my heart as well as my... well, anything else to you. In fact, I'm surprised that you had the nerve to touch me. I know in America things may be a little more democratic, but here in England a *lady* is usually safe from that type of vulgar advance."

He lifted his eyebrows at that, then slid off the rock and onto one knee, lifting his clasped hands toward her in a gesture of entreaty. Laughter danced like twin demons in his eyes.

"Forgive, oh, forgive, my lady," he intoned wickedly.

At his teasing, Amanda felt her temper shoot through the roof.

"Go to hell, you . . . you . . ." she spat, and just managed to stop herself from stamping her foot before she whirled and stalked away. Behind her, he gave a shout of laughter, and she sensed rather than saw him get to his feet. But he made no move to come after her.

By the time she reached the kitchen again, she was still flushed with anger, so much so that Sister Patrick looked at her in concern and asked if she felt feverish. It was all Amanda could do to return a civil answer, and she received a sharp look from the kindly sister for her pains.

"And did Mrs. Morell like the soup?" Sister Patrick prompted. Amanda, already halfway through the kitchen door, looked around guiltily.

"Oh, yes, she . . . appreciated it very much. They hadn't anything else for supper." The memory of Laura Morell's pale face as she had thanked her so fervently for the half tureen of soup flashed before Amanda's eyes. Barely thirty, with one babe still at her breast and another under her apron while seven more under the age of twelve crammed the tiny cottage, Mrs. Morell was one of the most pitiful—and deserving—of the poor the convent had taken under its wing. Mr. Morell was a sailor, and he came home perhaps once a year to drop a few dollars on the table and plant a new babe in his wife's belly. To support herself and the children, Mrs. Morell took in washing and did whatever other odd jobs she could get. But this last pregnancy had made her ill, and now she was unable to work. Amanda had felt a severe twinge of conscience as she had delivered the half portion of soup and bread, barely enough to make a good supper for two and yet fallen upon so thankfully by the seven hungry children. Amanda doubted that Laura Morell, who needed it more than her youngsters, would get more than a spoonful. If she hadn't already separated Matt's portion from the rest, hiding it in a separate tureen under the Morells' stoop until she could smuggle it down to the cave, she would probably have given in to pity and left the whole. But Matt was hungry, too, and there would have been nothing left for him...

I'll take them some of the vegetables from the cellar tomorrow, she told herself, somewhat quieting her conscience, and a cheese, too. How she would explain distributing such largesse to Sister Patrick she had no idea. Oh, well, maybe she wouldn't tell her. She already had the sin of theft on her conscience, to say nothing of all the lies she had told lately. What were a few vegetables and a cheese?

"And my dish?" Sister Patrick sounded faintly put out. Wisps of iron-gray hair peeked out from under the wilted and somewhat askew wimple that framed the nun's perspiring face. She eyed Amanda with a trace of exasperation, her hands emerging from the large pan within which she had been washing the last of the supper dishes. "Really, Amanda, where is your mind tonight? That's the third time I've asked you."

"I'm sorry, Sister, I wasn't attending," Amanda murmured desperately. "I left the dish. I'll collect it in the morning." Interpreting Sister Patrick's scarcely mollified sniff as dismissal, Amanda turned and practically fled, all the while praying that Sister wouldn't discover that yet another tureen was missing before she could restore them both, one discreetly washed and put away, in the morning. Sister Patrick was extremely careful of the convent's supplies . . .

As was their custom, the girls were gathered in the back parlor to gossip and giggle. Amanda almost pleaded another headache so that she could escape to her room—it wouldn't have been far from the truth—but she was afraid that a headache for the second time in a week, when she was never ill, might give rise to the curiosity she was at such pains to avoid. Besides, to tell the truth, she really didn't want to be alone with her thoughts. As much as she tried to prevent it, they seemed to be concerned with that black-haired devil's mockery—and his kisses . . . Later that night, when she was alone in her narrow bed and the convent was quiet, she gave it up. Her breast still burned where he had held it, and her mouth seemed to be permanently branded from the touch of his. When her eyes were closed he seemed to be beside her; she could almost taste him, touch him, smell him . . . Furious at herself, her eyes popping open, she got up, abandoning all attempts to sleep. Now her head did ache, so she carefully unbound the single plait, running her fingers through the long strands in an effort to ease the niggling pain. Which was a waste of time, she knew. The source of her discomfort was not a too-tight plait, but a living, breathing annoyance who was too handsome for his own good and too aware of it for hers. Picking up her hairbrush, she went to stand in front of the window. More for something to do than in any real hope it would soothe her headache, she began to stroke the brush rhythmically through her hair.

The sea and sky were dark, barely lit by a sliver of moon. From her vantage point high in the convent, Amanda could see the white tips of the waves as they rolled toward the beach. The thick black clouds blowing in from the ocean reminded her, against her will, of the near-dawn when she had found Matt . . .

She had liked him almost from the first. Even when he was scaring her half to death—and now that she had come to know him better she guessed that his role of vicious murderer must have amused him mightily—she had felt a kind of sympathy for him. When she could have turned him in, she hadn't, but steered in the opposite direction the man who would have solved all her problems. Although she was generally softhearted, she was not, despite anything Matt might say to the contrary, generally softheaded. There had been something about him that had touched her heart . . .

Much as she hated to admit it, there was some basis for his warning her not to lose her heart to him. It would be all too easy to do. He was the handsomest man she had ever seen, but even when he had been bearded and dirty, when she had felt not the slightest bit attracted to him, she had liked him. He had made her feel safe, as if she had at last come across a calm port in the midst of a stormy sea. She had confided in him things she had never told anyone before, not even Susan, and that worried her.

He was right: she mustn't fall in love with him. Because he would soon be gone, and she would be left behind with nothing but hurtful memories. And he was much better now. He seemed to be over the fever that had racked him with alternate periods of raging heat and chills, and his wound seemed to be troubling him less, too. At least, he appeared to have little trouble moving about, and he had lifted her clear off her feet with no sign of strain. It was inevitable that he should leave. She couldn't even wish otherwise. The longer he stayed in one place, the greater the likelihood that he would be caught. Sooner or later he would venture outside the cave and someone would see him, or Sister Patrick would notice the inexplicable depletion of her carefully husbanded larder, or... There were a dozen possibilities, but they all had the same ending: he would be caught and hanged. Her always too-vivid imagination conjured up a picture of that long body dangling at the end of a rope, that handsome face blackened and twisted, and she winced as a pain stabbed her heart.

Something glimmered far out in the bay. Amanda saw it out of the corner of her eye, but it took some seconds to penetrate to her absorbed brain. Then she snapped to sudden attention, staring anxiously out at the dark sea. After a moment it came again—a quick flash of light against the blackness. This time it was answered by another. She blinked, disbelieving the conclusion her mind had jumped to even as she could find no other explanation. Despite the increased surveillance along the coast, the smugglers were out in the bay.

She had to get to Matt, she thought, dropping the brush and speeding silently to the door. If the smugglers were in the bay, it was a definite possibility that they were making for the cave, where they sometimes stored their cargo... They *mustn't* find Matt. She had no idea what their reaction would be, but she didn't want to find out. Big Matt might be, and strong, but he was no match for half a dozen armed men.

She was panting as she wrenched open the trapdoor and leaped down the stairs. There was no time to be lost if Matt was to be got safely away and the cave cleared of all traces of his presence.

He was sitting on the feather tick with his back against the wall, frowning as he carved a piece of driftwood. He must have heard her coming because he didn't even glance up as she stopped just inside the cavern, her hand pressed to her heart as she tried to catch her breath.

"Over your tantrum already?" he asked, looking up at last, his voice mocking. As he saw her standing there clad only in her thin white night rail, her hair unbound and tumbling around her face and shoulders to her hips in thick, glinting red waves, his teasing expression altered dramatically.

"What has happened?" he demanded in a totally different tone, surging to his feet and coming to stand in front of her, his hands reaching out to grasp her shoulders.

She looked up at him, her eyes wide with urgency. "Smugglers," she gasped. "The smugglers are in the bay, and they'll probably come here. You *must* get out of the cave."

He frowned. "What exactly did you see?" he asked sharply.

Amanda shook her head, impatient that he was not immediately getting ready to leave.

"Smugglers," she repeated, her tone anxious. "I saw their lights—I'm almost certain they're on their way to the cave."

"You saw lights in the bay?"

He was not normally obtuse. Amanda reached up to grip his forearms, her nails digging into his flesh beneath the sleeves of his shirt.

"*Yes.*"

His hands tightened briefly on her shoulders.

"*Stay here,*" he ordered, then he was releasing her to stride toward the entrance to the cave—the entrance that opened onto the beach.

"Where are you going?" she gasped, flying after him to catch urgently at his arm. "Didn't you hear what I said?"

"I heard you—and I told you to stay here. I want to see those lights for myself, and you'll only be in the way."

"But why?" Amanda practically wailed the question.

He frowned down at her, disengaging her hands from his arm and turning away.

"I'm expecting someone." He threw the words over his shoulder. "Now do as I say and stay where you are. Whoever it is will be able to spot you a mile away if you come outside in that white thing."

It was so true that Amanda stopped in her tracks. If he was insane enough to go out to meet the smugglers, she wasn't going to go after him and give his presence away. Biting her lower lip, she watched despairingly as he disappeared toward the entrance. For a long moment she didn't move, and then her common sense reasserted itself. At least she could clear the cave of all traces of his presence in hopes that he himself would have the good sense to stay out of the smugglers' way.

He came back just as she returned from dragging the mattress and blanket to their old place in front of the steps leading to the trapdoor. To her knowledge, the smugglers had never penetrated that far into the cave.

"You're right, they're smugglers," he said, throwing a quick glance around the now-cleared chamber as he came across to her with long strides, snatching up the candle on his way.

"I told you . . ."

"Hush," he said, grasping her arm and blowing out the candle in the same breath. "They're close behind me—luckily they're carrying some barrels that seem pretty heavy. We'll have to hide."

"We can go through the trapdoor into the convent," Amanda whispered, already moving toward the passage. Matt's arm was around her waist as he followed her lead.

"There's no time—they'll hear it open. That damned thing squeaks."

It was pitch black inside the cave. Amanda couldn't

see Matt, though he was scant inches away from her. Lucky she knew the way so well... She had no sooner had the thought than she heard muffled voices behind them, and a spreading beam of light reached from the cave's entrance toward the cavern they had just left.

"Hurry—and be quiet. They mustn't find us," Matt breathed in her ear. Amanda nodded silently, forgetting he couldn't see her. She didn't like to contemplate the smugglers' reaction if they should be discovered... The voices were louder behind them as her feet touched the hard edge of the steps that led up to the trapdoor.

"We can't go any farther. But this should be all right. I don't think they ever come back this far."

"Let's hope not." His voice was a scant breath of sound. She felt him move, heard a faint clink, and guessed that he had set the candle in its brass holder on the floor.

Again she felt him move, then his hand was tightening on her waist.

"Come here," he murmured. Obediently she let him pull her forward until she was resting against his body. One arm stayed around her waist while his other hand came up to press her face into the soft cloth that covered his chest. He was leaning back against the wall, letting it bear his weight. Amanda rested against him without protest. His arms seemed the safest place to be.

"Don't worry. I won't let anything happen to you." His voice was the merest whisper in her ear. Amanda nodded in silent reply, believing him. Whatever happened, she knew he would protect her if he could. Odd how much she trusted him, she thought, and her lips shaped a wry smile as she remembered that this man who cradled her so protectively against him was a convicted murderer—of a woman and children. Even if he hadn't told her he was innocent, she thought that in this moment she would have known.

"Come on, put the bloody thing down and go fetch another one. We ain't got all night." The rough voice came from the cavern they had so recently vacated. At the end of the twisted passageway Amanda could see the warm glow of a lantern. The smugglers were obviously stowing their cargo. She prayed that they would not feel a sudden urge to explore the rest of the cave. Instinctively she burrowed closer against Matt's chest, and felt his arms tighten around her.

"I wish they'd catch that blasted convict," said a different man, who seemed to be moving away from them. His last words were faint and indistinct. Amanda felt Matt stiffen against her.

"Bloody nuisance," the first voice agreed. It seemed closer than the other, and she guessed that its possessor was staying in the cavern to oversee the bestowal of whatever they had carried in. "Turn him over to the law myself if I could catch him. Interferin' with business."

The reply was unintelligible. Amanda huddled against Matt's hard form, listening to the tramp of booted feet and to the sometimes comprehensible mutter of gruff voices. No further mention was made of Matt, and as the minutes ticked past with no suggestion that the smugglers meant to do anything more than store their cargo in the cavern and leave, she felt him gradually relax. She relaxed, too, letting him bear the full weight of her body, growing more and more conscious of the feel of him against her. Despite her best intentions, she could not help but be affected by his nearness, by the solid strength of his body against hers, by the faintly musky smell of him that rose to tantalize her nostrils. She should step away from him, she knew. His arms had loosened their hold on her waist, and all she had to do was take a single step backward to be free of his touch. but she didn't. She told herself that she didn't want to make it obvious to him how much his closeness disturbed her, but deep inside she knew the simple truth of the matter was that she didn't want to move. The very warmth of his body held her in thrall.

She could feel his muscles gradually stiffening against her, and her brow wrinkled as she puzzled at it. The smugglers seemed to be going about their business, with no hint of anything disturbing, and she could think of nothing else that would account for the growing tension she could sense in his body. Perhaps she was hurting his wound? She shifted slightly, though she didn't think she had touched it. He tensed even more. Concerned now, Amanda pressed lightly against his chest with both hands, tilting her head to peer up at him. The darkness made it impossible for her to see his face.

"Matt?" she whispered, his name a question.

His hands clenched on her waist.

"Oh, hell," he growled softly, and began to shake.

chapter nine

"What's the matter?"

"Nothing." The word seemed to force itself out from between clenched teeth.

"Something must be the matter. You're trembling."

"Your perceptiveness is amazing." His hoarse whisper did nothing to disguise the intentional sarcasm.

"Don't be rude, Matt," she reproached him in the same barely audible voice. "Are you ill again?"

"No, I'm damned well not ill again." This time there was no doubt about the clenched teeth.

"Then what's wrong with you?"

"You've felt me shake before. Figure it out."

The terse comment made her eyes widen. Yes, she had felt him shake before—just a few hours before, to be exact.

"You want to kiss me." It was more statement than question. Amanda didn't know whether to feel frightened or elated. She knew she ought to step away from him now, do what she could to guard her vulnerable heart, but she couldn't seem to move. And he wasn't pushing her away.

"As I said, your perceptiveness is amazing." His arms still cradled her waist despite his forbidding growl. She could feel the tremor that coursed through the encircling muscles—and the rest of him. Her fingers curled against his chest in involuntary response, the nails rasping against his chest hair through the linen shirt. He drew in his breath, the sound like a groan. His fingers clenched on her waist so hard they hurt her.

"Then, why don't you?" Amanda couldn't believe that sultry whisper was really her own voice. She hadn't meant actually to say the words, although they had immediately jumped to the forefront of her mind. But now that they were out, she couldn't take them back. She *wanted* him to kiss her . . .

"Are you hell-bent on suicide?" He sounded almost angry. But he still wasn't pushing her away. Amanda could feel the heat of him burning through her night rail to her skin. Her breasts seemed to swell against his chest, separated from his hard flesh by only two thin layers of cloth. No matter the consequences, she wanted him to make her feel that strange, hot urgency again. She needed him to.

"Kiss me, Matt. I want you to." The total darkness was making her bold. That was the only way she could account for her temerity.

"Amanda . . ." The harsh tone was a warning and nearly a plea. "Amanda, I told you . . ."

"Please." It was little more than a breath. She

could feel his heart slamming against his breastbone. Compelled by some instinct she'd never even guessed she possessed, she pressed her lips to that wild throbbing. A long shudder rippled through him, and Amanda was suddenly conscious of a little prickle of triumph. No matter how hard he protested, he was going to give in...

"Amanda, damn it, didn't anything I said to you before penetrate that beautiful skull? A kiss is one thing, and I'd kiss you if I thought I could stop there, but I wouldn't be able to. I'm on fire for you, Amanda, and you're the one who's going to get burned, not me."

She silenced his protest by the simple expedient of raising herself on tiptoe and placing her lips on his. He didn't move for a long moment, standing as though frozen in place, his hands instinctively gripping her waist to give her balance while she clung to his shoulders. Then, with a muttered oath, he surrendered, his arms circling her so fiercely that for a moment he stopped her breath, his mouth taking starved possession of hers as he bent her backward over his arm.

"Matt..." She breathed his name into his mouth as the blood in her veins turned to liquid fire. Her eyes closed, and her arms slid up around his neck, her fingers closing on the thick, silky hair at his nape. It felt cool and a little rough under her hands. He was trembling against her, his arms shaking as they held her to him, his mouth shaking, too, as it probed and stroked and plundered...

"Sweet Jesus." He tore his mouth from hers, swearing softly but fluently under his breath. If his arms around her hadn't held her upright, she would have fallen. Her hands refused to release their grip on his neck. Disappointment and disbelief combined to make her forget their circumstances, the smugglers in the cave, everything except the fact that he wasn't going to kiss her after all.

"*Matt.*"

"*Hush.*" One big hand came up to cover her mouth, reminding her irresistibly of another occasion when he had silenced her. Then she had been terrified of him; now she was furious. She bit down hard, catching the fleshy part of his palm between her teeth with the clear intention of biting right through it. He snatched his hand out of harm's way, then immediately put it back, the palm carefully cupped so that she could not bite him. His fingers sank warningly into her cheek, and the arm holding her waist gave her a little shake.

"Behave yourself," he said sharply into her ear. He was tense but not because of anything she was doing to him. Amanda was beginning to recognize the difference. He seemed to be listening... "They're leaving."

Amanda's eyes widened as she realized she had completely forgotten about the smugglers. If he hadn't silenced her... She had no doubt that, in the first fierce burst of rage and disappointment his abandonment of their kiss had engendered, she would have given them both away. With consequences too horrible to think about. Matt would surely have died, either murdered by the smugglers or turned over to the authorities for hanging, and she might have been killed, too. And all because she couldn't control her temper... Shuddering, she went limp against him, letting him hold her as he would as they both listened to the sounds of booted feet dying away.

At last he took his hand from her mouth. Amanda ran her tongue over lips dried by the contact with his skin. She was no longer angry; the thought of what her quick temper might have brought about had cooled her rage quicker than a douche of cold water.

"All right?" He was being careful; his whisper was no louder than before. Amanda nodded. He must have felt the movement of her head, because his arms slid away from her, releasing her, leaving her to stand on her feet without support from him. Amanda felt almost bereft as the warmth and strength of his body moved away.

"Stay here." That was all he said. She didn't hear the sound of his shoes on the stone, but she knew he had left her alone in the dark. Wrapping her arms around her suddenly cold body, she leaned back against the cool, moist wall as she waited for him to return. Clearly he was taking no chances that the smugglers might have left a man to guard their cargo. He was less careful coming back; she heard him stumble over something and curse, making no effort to lower his voice, from which she surmised that he had ascertained that they were indeed alone.

Only moments ago she would have been delighted at the prospect, but now she felt a tingling embarrassment. She was uncomfortably aware that her behavior tonight had been something less than circumspect. Gently bred young ladies did not kiss men or beg men to kiss them; they certainly did not feel the aching longing that she did whenever Matt held her in his arms. At least, she didn't think they did. Having had no experience of the more intimate types of contact between a gentleman and a lady, she couldn't be sure. But Susan had confided the horror and shame she had experienced at having her virginity taken, and some of the other girls who had been sent to the convent precisely because they knew about such encounters had described men's kisses as unappealing things at best. Their giggling recital of their own cold response had included no mention of a sudden surge of fire in their blood, or a compulsion to lock their arms around the gentleman's neck and press their bodies to his...

Suddenly Amanda remembered the things Edward had said about her mother. Isabelle had been low born, an actress with beauty but no background when Amanda's father had married her. Was it possible she had inherited from her mother this shameful inability to control herself? Edward had called Isabelle a whore. For the first time the description frightened rather than infuriated Amanda. If it were true—and Amanda felt a stab of contrition as she remembered her beautiful, laughing, loving mother—then was it something that was passed on from mother to daughter, like a disease? She shivered at the prospect.

Amanda was so caught up in her uneasy speculations that she didn't hear Matt return. The scrape of a match head against stone and the sudden flare of light made her start. She watched him as he bent to light the candle, her hands clenching as she felt a tingle of pleasure just looking at him. Surely a real lady wouldn't be so affected by a man's face and form?

"What's wrong now?" The tone was resigned, but the silver-gray eyes were sharp as he surveyed her pale face and clenched hands from beneath frowning brows. Amanda said nothing, but her cheeks grew hot as she looked at him. Just the sight of that beautifully shaped mouth awoke feelings that she could only think of as wicked . . .

"Out with it, Amanda." It was an order, and when she didn't comply he sighed, set the candle on the floor, and reached for her. Amanda flinched at the feel of his warm hand on her upper arm through the thin stuff of her night rail, but he drew her inexorably forward despite her obvious reluctance. When she was close enough, he lifted his other hand so that his thumb was beneath her chin, and tilted her face up so that he could study it.

"Can't you tell me, honey?" The gentleness of the question made her shut her eyes. More than anything she wanted to rest her head against that broad chest, to pour out her confusion to the one person who had so ridiculously come to represent security to her. But if she told him what was in her mind, he might think worse of her than he must already.

"You're not angry at me." It was a statement, made in a thoughtful tone, as if he were considering and dismissing the possibilities one by one. Amanda refused to answer, refused even to open her eyes and look at him for fear he might read what he wanted to know there.

"You're not scared of the smugglers." She could feel him watching her, sense the scrutiny of his eyes even through her closed lids.

"You're embarrassed." There was sudden convic-

155

tion in his voice. Despite everything she could do to prevent it, telltale color heated her cheeks.

"You *are* embarrassed." There was a wealth of triumph in his tone. "You should never try to hide things, Amanda. Your face gives you away every time. All right, now that we've got that out in the open, would you care to tell me why?"

Still she said nothing, keeping her eyes resolutely closed. His hand tightened on her arm, and his voice was laced with exasperation when he spoke again.

"I'm getting tired of asking questions, Amanda. And I can make a pretty good guess at what's bothering you, so you may as well tell me. Come on, Amanda. Open your eyes and tell me."

He would only keep badgering her until she did as he said, she knew, so she slowly opened her eyes. His face was serious as he studied her expression. Amanda looked up at him helplessly, part of her wanting to rid herself of the whole sorry tangle of her feelings, part of her dreading his reaction if she did. She remained miserably silent.

"You're embarrassed because you kissed me, aren't you, Amanda?" That shot was close enough so that her cheeks grew hot again. Her thick lashes fluttered down in a futile effort to shield her eyes from the hard probe of his. Not that it would do any good, she thought. Her blasted skin would tell him everything he wanted to know.

"You're worried about the way I make you feel, right, Amanda?" The hot surge of color was his answer. His fingers left her chin to close over her other arm and he shook her, hard this time. Her eyes flew back to meet his, and she was taken aback to find an almost grim look on his face.

"If you don't start talking to me, I'm liable to commit a real murder," he warned tightly. To her surprise as much as his, she smiled. The taut line of his mouth relaxed, and he smiled back at her, his eyes gentling. That crooked smile made mincemeat out of the last shreds of her resistance.

"Do you think I'm...bold, Matt?" The question made her cheeks flush scarlet, and she quickly dropped her eyes. If he despised her, she didn't want to see it on his face.

"No bolder than you should be. Why?" To her relief his reply was almost negligent. She dared another glance at him. He didn't look shocked or horrified.

"Nobody else has ever kissed me," she confessed in an almost-whisper. The answering quirk of his eyebrows told her that he knew this. "I...don't know how I'm supposed to feel. I know you've kissed lots of other girls. Do most of them...Well, do they react as I do?"

"No." The cold certainty of the word shattered her. Her eyes were enormous and defenseless as they flew to meet his. Stricken, she felt her lower lip tremble. His eyes fastened on that betraying quiver, and his hands on her arms tightened almost cruelly. "What you have is a precious gift, Amanda," he went on, his voice rough. "The gift of a warm and loving nature. You're a passionate little thing, honey, or at least you will be when you've had a little more experience, and that's something you should thank God on bended knees for. A passion like yours is the

157

best gift a woman can give the man she loves. Believe me, whoever he is will treasure it."

Amanda regarded him with an expression that was somewhere between relief and suspicion. "Are you telling me the truth, Matt? You're not just trying to make me feel better?"

His mouth twisted in unmistakable annoyance. "Of course I'm telling you the truth. Whatever else I may do, you can trust me not to lie to you."

"Then why—"

He interrupted with a fierce gesture. "Why don't I take what you're doing your best to give me?" Watching her blush, he looked grimly satisfied. "I told you, Amanda: I like you too much. That passion of yours is a gift for the man you'll love—the man who will marry you and give you children. And that's another reason: children. Whether you know it or not, and I know you probably don't—it's criminal the way we keep young girls so ignorant—the way you feel results in children. If I made love to you the way I'd have to if I had very much more of your kind of kissing, you'd soon have a baby growing in your belly. And that's not what you want, is it?"

Amanda stared at him. Matt's baby growing in her belly—the thought made her toes curl involuntarily. Mortified, praying that this time he wouldn't be able to guess what she was thinking, she dropped her eyes and pulled away from his hands.

"No, of course not." Her voice betrayed embarrassment, but if she was lucky he would think that it stemmed from discussing such an indelicate subject. She stole a look at him. He was watching her with keen eyes. Quickly she searched her mind for a topic to distract him. Thank goodness there was an obvious one at hand. "Matt . . . you can't stay here tonight."

"I can't? Why not?" He drawled the words, plainly aware that she was trying to change the subject but willing to follow her lead.

"The smugglers will be back to pick up their cargo, probably in a day or two. They don't usually leave it any longer than that."

"I'll stay out of their way."

Amanda shook her head. "No . . . that would be too dangerous. They could come again at any time, even later tonight. And if they found you . . ." She didn't have to go on. Matt knew as well as she did what would happen if they found him.

"What do you suggest?"

Amanda thought for a moment. "The cellar's out. Sister Patrick goes down there fairly often—she stores vegetables there. And you certainly can't just wander about the convent. Someone's bound to see you." She frowned. "I think you should stay in my room," she said slowly. "It's way up in one of the turrets, by itself. No one ever goes in there except with me. And if by some mischance someone should, you can always hide in the wardrobe." Her eyes moved over him, and she grinned. "No, not the wardrobe—you're too big. Under the bed." He gave her a speculative look.

"So long as you're not planning any more assaults on my virtue," Matt said dryly. "I don't think I could stand it."

Cheeks flushing with indignation, Amanda glared at him and opened her mouth with the fixed intention of leaving him in no doubt as to what she thought of such an ungentlemanly suggestion. He grinned suddenly and silenced her by holding up a restraining hand.

"I'm truly sorry. I apologize for that. Now suppose you quit spitting fire at me, and we make sure that you cleared everything away properly in there. Next time, the smugglers might not be in such a hurry."

He picked up the candle and moved past Amanda as he spoke. Amanda was left with no option but to follow. This she did, after favoring Matt's disappearing back with a last glare. Handsome or not, it was the outside of enough for him to suspect she meant to attack him.

Matt stopped just inside the cavern, holding the candle high so that the room was illuminated, and Amanda stopped, too, some few paces behind him. Besides the usual stalagmites, stalactites, and other rock formations, the circular chamber was now embellished by the addition of perhaps forty brass-bound barrels, stacked haphazardly. Matt passed Amanda the candle without speaking, then crossed to the barrels, rolling one free to pry at the lid. It didn't take him long to get it open; when he did, he looked faintly surprised at its contents.

"They're smuggling grain."

Amanda, having lived in the area for some years, was well aware of that. The smugglers' activities were rather an open secret, one that she, like the rest of the peninsula's inhabitants, was not particularly concerned about. Live and let live was the way most of the local residents felt about the smugglers, who were almost thought of as family. Black sheep, maybe, but family. Nearly everyone took a proprietary interest in their goings-on, and no one would have dreamed of turning them over to the local authorities.

"It's because of the Corn Laws," Amanda explained. She moved a little farther into the chamber and peered into the nooks and crannies to see if there was anything that might betray Matt's presence. There was an unraveling bandage peeking out from behind a rock. Amanda picked it up and looked around for anything else. As Matt had said, next time, the smugglers might not be in such a hurry. "They probably brought the grain over from France. Tomorrow night or the one after that, a boat will come across St. George's Channel to take it to Ireland. That's what they always do."

"And how do you know so much about it?" Matt was looking at her rather strangely. Amanda grinned.

"Oh, I've been watching them for years," she admitted. "I can see the bay from my bedroom window, and whenever I see their lights I go out on the cliff and watch them work. When the moon's out, I can see quite a lot."

"You seem to have any number of nighttime adventures," Matt said dryly. "Did it never occur to you that it might be rather dangerous for a young girl to go wandering around alone at night?"

Amanda threw him a saucy look. "Not until I stumbled across a murderer on the beach. Since then, I've been more careful."

Matt's mouth quirked upward in a somewhat reluctant answering smile. "And so you should be. Next time, there actually might be a murderer."

"Yes." Matt was still looking at her strangely, and Amanda frowned. She did not realize that in candlelight, her thin night rail was almost diaphanous, that only the glittering skeins of hair flowing past her hips in any way preserved her modesty. She only saw Matt's eyes move over her once before they were abruptly averted. Her frown deepened, and she would have questioned him, but he had already replaced the lid on the barrel and was crossing to her, taking the candle from her hand.

"Let's go," he said brusquely. "Dressed—or should I say undressed—as you are, you're likely to catch your death of cold. Next time you go flying out into the night, take a moment to slip into your dressing gown and slippers. They might preserve your health in more ways than one."

Only then did Amanda remember the scantiness of her attire. Looking down at herself, she blushed scarlet. Matt's lip curled at her embarrassment.

"Just so," he said curtly, then left her to follow him to the trapdoor. Amanda stopped only long enough to tuck the tureen under one arm before scrambling after him. Once they were inside the cellar, the going became more difficult. The candle was of necessity blown out, leaving them in total darkness. Amanda knew the way and alone would have had little trouble returning to her room, but guiding Matt added hair-raising dimension to the exercise. He bumped his shins more than once and cracked his head on a low beam so hard that it sent him staggering. The words he uttered under his breath should have had the convent walls tumbling about his ears, but though Amanda momentarily held her breath, nothing happened.

She made a quick stop in the kitchen, daring to

light a candle as she hurriedly washed the tureen and put it away, all the while praying that no chink of light would show beyond the closed kitchen door. When she was at last able to blow out the candle, she let out a sigh of relief. Thank goodness no one had awakened. Matt had been sitting at the scrubbed pine table, watching her. He stood as darkness descended upon them once more. Amanda groped her way to him, grasping his arm and secretly marveling at the hardness of the muscle beneath her hand, and steered him toward the stairs. By the time they had negotiated the remaining three flights of stairs to her room, he was limping and leaning reluctantly on her shoulder.

Amanda was panting now, as out of breath as if she had run every step of the way. When at last she eased them both through the door of her bedroom, which, she was thankful, was illuminated by moonlight, she heaved a sigh of relief.

"Are you all right?" she whispered, anxiously looking up at Matt, who was resting wearily against the closed door.

"Yes." The word was clipped. Amanda bit her lip, but she knew Matt well enough by now to say nothing.

"You take the bed. I'll curl up with a blanket and pillow on the floor." He looked so exhausted she had to make the offer, although she guessed that it was not likely to be well received. She was right.

"Don't be ridiculous. I'll sleep on the floor—I'm used to it. Believe me, it won't be any more uncomfortable than many of the places I've slept recently,

163

and it's certainly a damned sight cleaner. Get into bed, Amanda."

This last was tacked on so abruptly that Amanda looked up at him in some surprise. She saw how his eyes, their silvery glitter restless, were once again moving down her body, and she realized that the streaming moonlight affected the material of her night rail in much the same way that the candlelight had earlier. She started to say something, thought better of it, then obediently crossed to the bed and climbed between the sheets. He followed her, more slowly, coming to stand between her bed and the window, looking down at her with his face in shadow so that she could not read his expression.

chapter ten

For a long moment he remained motionless, saying nothing. Amanda returned his look gravely, wishing she could see his face, thinking how tall and broad he seemed with the moonlight pouring in around the dark shape that was his body, silvering the outline of him. He looked like something from her worst nightmare—or darkest fantasy. If she had awakened to find him looming over her bed as he was now, not knowing him, she knew that her scream would have roused the dead—if, indeed, she had screamed at all.

Finally he spoke.

"Sleep well, Amanda," he said, turning away. His voice was husky; the words were almost inaudible.

"Good night, Matt." Her voice was husky, too. Strangely, she felt almost on the verge of tears. With every fiber of her being she suddenly realized that she wanted this man; not just his kisses or his lovemaking, but his arms around her to hold her, his voice to soothe her, his very presence to cherish and protect her as she had longed to be cherished and protected for years. She felt so safe in his arms, so warm and secure... She wanted him; it was as simple as that. And there wasn't any hope that she could have him. He would be in her life for only a few brief days, and then he would be gone, like the dream figure he resembled. And no one except herself would ever know how he had affected her.

At the thought of his going, she was horribly afraid that she would start to cry in earnest. Hearing her, he would probably, with his despicable conceit, imagine that she was trying to lure him into her bed. Indignation stiffened her spine and effectively banished her tears. He was settling himself on the floor near the bed, sitting with his back against the wall and his knees bent so that his arms could clasp them loosely. His black head rested against the whitewashed wall just a foot from where the simple, carved-wood headboard of her bed ended. His face, still veiled by shadow, turned toward hers. Silently she offered him a blanket and pillow. He rejected both with a gesture. Then he chuckled.

"Your eyes shine like a cat's in the dark. Very unnerving. Go to sleep, Amanda."

"Why don't you?"

"Unlike you, I'm used to getting by on very little sleep. And at the moment I'm not feeling particularly sleepy."

"Neither am I. Talk to me, Matt."

"About what?" His voice was indulgent, as if he

were humoring a child. Amanda knew she should feel indignant, but she didn't. She liked having him near.

"In the cave, when I told you about the smugglers, you said that you were expecting someone," she said, suddenly remembering. Her eyes widened as she stared at him, wishing she could read his expression in the darkness. "Who, Matt?"

He was silent for so long that she began to think he wasn't going to answer. When at last he did, his voice was low, and he turned his head toward the window. Amanda didn't mind because with the moon illuminating his profile, she had a better view of his face. She thought he looked wary.

"Some friends of mine."

The clipped answer made her stiffen. "I see. I shouldn't have asked."

He sighed, turning his head so that he was looking at her again. The moon silhouetted a quarter view of his face, painting a silvery wash over his chiseled cheekbone and down the flat plane of his cheek to his jaw.

"I'm sorry, Amanda. I'm so used to not trusting anyone that I occasionally forget you're not a treacherous mortal like the rest of us. As my personal guardian angel, you have the right to know anything you like." His voice was whimsical, but his continued allusions to her as an angel disturbed her for some reason. She was as much flesh and blood as he.

"I'm not an angel, Matt."

"Allow me to be the judge of that, if you please. And don't argue—it could get you in trouble with the rest of the angels. I'm sure arguing is against the rules . . . Have you decided that ignorance is bliss, or do you want to know whom I'm expecting?"

For a moment Amanda thought about insisting that he acknowledge that she was as much a human being as anyone else, as capable of petty and not-so-petty sins as he, but the tantalizing lure of his last question sidetracked her.

"I want to know."

He smiled faintly. Amanda could see the twisted curve of his mouth in the pool of moonlight.

"I thought you would. Very well, Miss Cat-Eyes, I'll tell you: I'm expecting my ship and my men and my brother, anytime now."

It took her a moment to assimilate that. She stared at him, astonished.

"But how on earth can they know where you are?"

"Zeke—my brother—and I have been here before. We once took shelter in the bay from a storm. He was sailing with me then. Now he generally captains his own ship. The day after I escaped, I sent word to him to meet me here. I imagine my letter must have been quite a shock—he can't have had the one I bribed a guard to send him while I was in prison or he would have been in London before the ink dried. It's probably waiting for him in New Orleans. In any case, if he's on schedule, he should have arrived at Le Havre ten days ago to deliver a load of cotton to a buyer there. He should get my message as soon as he lands or, to be precise, as soon as he visits a certain lady who keeps a house near the docks, which if I know Zeke will be his first port of call. I've been expecting him anytime for the last few days."

"You've been watching for a ship. That's how you

fell onto the beach and why you rushed outside tonight when I told you I'd seen lights in the bay." Amanda spoke slowly. She was having trouble coming to terms with all he had told her. It was strange to think of him with a brother who cared what became of him. She was used to considering him as hers and no one else's . . .

"Tell me about your brother. Is he older than you or younger?"

"Younger, by seven years, to be precise. Ezekiel Peter Grayson. Quite a mouthful but no worse than Matthew Zacharias, which is my full name, by the way. Our mother was fascinated by the Bible." His mouth twisted wryly. Amanda was too absorbed to do more than vaguely register his expression.

"Is your mother still alive? Do you have any other family?"

"There are just my brother and me." The words were faintly clipped.

Amanda's brows drew together. She was suddenly inordinately curious about him. Strange she had never given any thought to the life he must have led before he was arrested for murder. "And you're both sea captains?"

"Zeke is. He works for me. I'm more businessman than anything else these days, though I started out being hired to captain someone else's ship. But I managed to persuade the owner—a New Orleans merchant with no stomach for the sea but a hard head for money—to pay me a percentage of the profit on each successful voyage. I saved everything I made, and it wasn't too long before I was able to buy part interest in a ship of my own. Now I own half a dozen and spend more time securing business than I do sailing, although I occasionally take a cargo across just to keep my hand in."

"Matt, how did it happen? Your being arrested, I mean."

Even through the obscuring shadows she caught the teasing glimmer in his eyes.

"I thought you didn't want to know," he reminded her softly.

"That was when I thought you were guilty," Amanda retorted. "Now that I know you're not going to recount the gory details of your crime, I'm curious."

His teeth gleamed in the darkness.

"Are you, now? All right, then, my curious cat, I'll satisfy your curiosity: I was in London to see a gentleman about a contract for shipping molasses. I was alone. When it became obvious that it was going to take more time than I had expected to come to terms, I sent my ship on to Lisbon to deliver its cargo under the captainship of my first mate, who's a very capable seaman himself. His instructions were to head for Morocco after he had delivered the cargo to Lisbon and pick up a load of silks at Rabat, which he was to take back to New Orleans. I planned to sail on one of my ships or to book commercial passage home. In either case, I should have arrived about a month ago. I imagine that Zeke was intending to make a detour by London to see what was detaining me when he finished his business in Le Havre." He paused, frowning. "Considering the isolation in which I was held and the brevity of my trial, I could easily have been hanged before any of my people found out what had become of me."

Amanda's brow wrinkled. "But why did they think *you* were the murderer?"

Matt smiled mirthlessly. "Ah, there's the rub. I was drinking with my prospective customer in a London inn near the docks when I pulled from my pocket a timepiece I had recently purchased. His eyes bulged as he watched me open it, and he excused himself and left the bar rather hastily. I assumed he had had too much to drink and thought no more about it. I was sitting there, finishing my drink, the only thoughts in my head concerning whether or not I would get the shipping contract, which was a rather large one, when a dragoon of soldiers burst in. They asked me if I was myself. I said yes. They searched me, removing my watch for 'evidence,' they said, and hustled me away with them.

"The next day, I was charged with murdering Lord Farringdon and his family. I had heard of the crime, of course. Who hadn't? But I had never, to my knowledge, set eyes on the fellow. Certainly I had no motive for murdering him. But that watch was one he was known to have possessed, and it was believed that he had had it in his pocket the night he was murdered. Not that mere possession of the watch was enough to convict me. Oh, no, after they found that, they searched the rooms where I had been staying and found another item I had purchased at the same time and in the same place: a jeweled dagger, a pretty toy, I thought. What I had no way of knowing at the time I bought it was that it had been used, most recently, to slit the throats of Lord Farringdon and his wife and children."

Amanda made an inarticulate sound of horror.

"My reaction exactly. Well, to continue, I told them I had purchased the items from a young girl who had offered to sell them to me so she could buy milk for her child. She had the babe with her, and it cried the whole time and looked extremely undernourished. Like a fool, I had felt sorry for her and so paid her a good price for the watch and knife. The soldiers were unable to find a trace of her, although I was assured they had tried. Then came the decisive factor: aside from being in possession of a personal item belonging to the victim, as well as the murder weapon itself, I didn't have a shred of an alibi for the night in question. I was in bed asleep. Alone. The officers in charge of the investigation seemed to find that almost impossible to believe. I pointed out to them that if I had really committed the murder, I would have taken good care to arrange an alibi. They were not impressed. Within three months of being arrested, I was tried, found guilty, and brought to the very brink of the gallows before fate intervened. And I may hang yet. I have no doubt that they'll string me up without ceremony if ever they get their hands on me again."

Amanda was silent for some time after he had finished.

"What will you do? Now, I mean." Her voice was troubled.

"Go home, first of all. They'll manage to trace me there eventually, but I think they'll find that arresting me in New Orleans, where I'm well known, is a very different kettle of fish from arresting me in London. And in the meantime I plan to send someone over here to try to find that blasted girl. Without her my story falls apart."

"What if whomever you send doesn't find her?"

"Then I'll take good care never to come to England again. Which would be no great hardship. I haven't found your country to be particularly hospitable. Quite the opposite, in fact."

He was staring at the opposite wall, his expression brooding. Amanda impulsively reached out to lay a gentle hand on his shoulder. He turned to look at her, his face once again shadowed so that she could not see his expression. Then he lifted a hand to cover hers, pressing it to his shoulder for a moment before lifting it carefully and carrying it with infinite tenderness to his mouth. Amanda felt her breath catch in her throat as he placed a deliberate kiss on the very tip of each of her slender fingers. When at last he turned her hand over to press his mouth to her palm, heat seemed to radiate from the spot. Amanda was conscious of a sudden wild desire to leave the shelter of the bed and join him, to wrap her arms around him and soothe his hurts with soft words and softer kisses. But she knew he would only push her away...

"Is your curiosity satisfied now, my cat-eyed angel?" He pressed a last brief kiss on her knuckles before returning her hand to her, tucking it gently beneath the blanket as though to put it safely out of harm's way. Amanda caught her breath in a deep, shuddering sigh and cradled the hand against her breasts.

"Yes. Thank you." The words were indistinct. She hardly knew what she was saying.

"Then I suggest you try to get some sleep. I'm

relying on you to keep the wolves at bay tomorrow. I really don't relish having to spend the day under the bed." A brief smile glimmered.

"I don't think you'll have to." Her voice was soft, dreamy.

"Good. Go to sleep, Amanda."

"Yes, all right. Good night, Matt."

His reply was little more than a grunt. Amanda obediently shut her eyes, hugging the feel of his mouth on her hand to her. Just thinking of his mouth inevitably brought to mind the occasions when he had kissed her. Twice now . . . She shivered at the memory.

"Matt." Her eyes opened to find him. He hadn't moved.

"Hmm?"

"I'm sorry I slapped you."

He turned to look at her. His teeth shone white in a slow smile.

"Think nothing of it. Go to sleep, Amanda."

"You keep saying that." The words were plaintive.

"Because I mean it. Go to sleep."

"Oh, all right." Crossly she turned so that she was facing away from him and closed her eyes. She thought she heard him chuckle, but she was not going to give him the satisfaction of looking at him so that she could be sure. But she would *never* go to sleep . . .

His hand gently shaking her shoulder woke her. When she felt that unmistakably masculine touch, her eyes flew open and she rolled onto her back with a startled gasp. Just for a moment she could not imagine who on earth . . . Then she looked up into silver-gray eyes and a lean, handsome face roughened by a day's growth of beard, and she smiled. The silvery eyes darkened to the color of gun metal as they observed her flushed with sleep, her unbound hair tousled and vivid against the virginal night rail and equally virginal sheets. She had kicked the covers off during the night; the hem of her night rail had ridden up around her thighs, baring legs that were slender and shapely and the color of warm cream amid that cocoon of white . . . Amanda followed the direction of his glance and flushed as she realized how much of herself was unveiled for him. But her movements were almost languid as she pushed the offending garment down. It startled her to realize that she liked having him look at her. It was Matt who moodily turned away.

"You'd better get up." His voice was harsh, and Amanda could see him clenching and unclenching his fists. "A bell rang a few minutes ago."

Reminded now of their situation, Amanda sat up, swinging her legs over the side of the bed. After one hard glance at her Matt turned his back and moved to the window, where he stood looking out at the sky and the sea.

"I have to get dressed." As the last remnants of sleep fled, her sense of propriety returned—and with it came consternation. She could not simply remove her night rail and get dressed as he stood not five feet away. But what else *could* she do? He couldn't leave—and she couldn't remain in her night clothes all day.

He must have sensed her dilemma. "Don't worry,

I won't look," he said wryly. Looking uncertainly at him as he stood with his back to her, his broad shoulders nearly blocking the window, she realized that regardless of his pedigree or lack of one, he was a gentleman to his fingertips. At least where she was concerned. In fact, she thought, sometimes she wished he had just a shade less chivalry. But this definitely wasn't one of those times.

He was as good as his word. While she hastily removed her nightdress and washed, a wary eye fixed on his tall form, he continued to look pensively out the window. If she hadn't known better, she would have said that he had forgotten her presence in the room. She dressed as quickly as she could, putting on a fresh chemise and stepping into panta-lettes, knotting the tapes of her petticoat with fingers that were made slightly clumsy by Matt's silent presence, then slipping into one of her plain gray dresses. Fashion decreed the addition of at least two more petticoats as well as stays, she knew, to say nothing of a very different style of dress, but the sisters had nothing but contempt for fashion and their pupils willy-nilly followed their lead. But Amanda was suddenly assailed by a vision of herself in a dazzling white ball gown with skirts so wide that she had to pass through a door sideways, and short, puffed sleeves and a neck cut down to *there* . . .

It would be satisfying to watch Matt's reaction if he could see her dressed so beguilingly. She had an image of him on his knees at her feet, his arrogant black head bowed as he begged humbly for the favor of a dance. She chuckled at the absurdity of the notion. The convent was far more likely to fall into the sea. *And* she didn't know how to dance.

"You can turn around now. I'm almost finished," Amanda said, standing on one shod foot as she slid the other into a flat black slipper. Matt turned obediently, one eyebrow rising as he surveyed her.

"Don't you have anything besides gray dresses?" he asked impatiently. Amanda looked at him in some surprise. He sounded testy, and she wondered what she had done to cause his ill-humor. She was ready to swear that he had been perfectly even tempered when he awakened her.

"A black one, for Sunday best," she answered flippantly. He frowned at her, studying the unfashionable gray dress with such a sour expression that Amanda raised her eyebrows at him. His mouth tightened as he observed her expression. "Your brother treats you shamefully. He isn't short of cash, I take it?" Amanda shook her head. "He should be shot." Matt thrust his hands into his pockets as he spoke. Through the rough material of his trousers Amanda saw his hands ball into fists. Puzzled, she considered questioning his odd behavior, but then thought better of it. There was no time for a discussion if she was to make it downstairs before matins; besides, she was often cross herself for no apparent reason. Wasn't he allowed the same privilege? Perhaps he was simply one of those people who never spoke a civil word before noon. That was possible. After all, she had never seen him in the morning before.

"I suggest that you quit staring at me as if you're afraid I might explode at any moment, and do something about your hair. You can't go downstairs like that."

The tone was still disgruntled, but the advice was so eminently practical that Amanda did as he suggested. As she stood in front of the small mirror struggling with the heavy, wayward mass, she was conscious of his eyes watching her intently. Putting her hair up was more difficult than usual this morning; because she had slept with it unconfined the night before, it was a mass of tangles and rat tails. Finally, dragging the weight of it over one shoulder, she began to rake her brush through it so hard that tears came to her eyes.

"Here, let me help you." She had been concentrating so on her blasted hair that she wasn't aware that he had moved until he stood directly behind her. Even as he spoke, he removed the brush from her hand and swept the mass of hair over her shoulder so that it waved and spiraled down her back. With infinite gentleness, he began to work his fingers through the thick strands, separating knots and tangles before at last smoothing the whole with her brush. Amanda stood very still as he ministered to her, loving the feel of his hands in her hair but afraid to give him the slightest inkling of how she felt. If he guessed what the mere touch of his fingers against her hair did to her, she knew that he would immediately abandon his task and put the width of the room between them. Still, there was nothing to stop her from watching him in the mirror ...

He looked so tall and dark standing behind her, his expression intent as he worked on her hair. Positioned in front of him, her bright head barely reaching his shoulder, she admired the breadth of his shoulders, the rippling muscles of his arms, the strong brown neck and hint of silky chest hair revealed by the open collar of his shirt. He was so big that he would easily make two of her, she thought, big enough to break her like kindling between his two hands if he wished. But for all his size and enormous strength, he had been nothing but gentle with her . . . A stray beam of sunlight sneaked through the window to touch the glossy blackness of his hair. The few silver strands shimmered in the sunlight, almost matching the color of his eyes, which she knew by heart now, although his lashes were at present veiling them from her gaze. The lean strength of his jaw and slightly cleft chin were faintly blurred by black stubble that was not yet long enough to obscure the chiseled masculine beauty of his mouth . . . She was staring at that mouth when he glanced up to catch her eyes on him in the mirror.

His jaw clenched. Amanda watched, fascinated, as a tiny muscle began to twitch at the corner of his mouth. His eyes darkened as they met hers. He stared at her silently for an instant before those smoldering eyes shifted to rest almost unwillingly on her mouth. Amanda felt the touch of his eyes like a physical caress. Her lips parted involuntarily, and her breathing quickened. More than anything in the world she longed to turn and slide her arms around his neck . . .

"You'd better finish it yourself," Matt said harshly, tossing the brush on the bed, and while she watched in the mirror he turned on his heel and crossed to stare out the window again. Amanda gritted her teeth against disappointment so acute that it was almost an ache. Then, with clumsy hands, she retrieved the brush from the bed and finished putting up her hair.

She was just stabbing the last pin through the coronet of braids when a light rap sounded on the door. Amanda whirled to stare at the portal, and Matt dropped to the floor behind the bed so quickly and silently that it was almost as if he had never been there. And just in time, too. The door opened before Amanda could respond. Susan stood framed in the doorway, a worried frown marring her pretty face.

"I'm just coming," Amanda began, moving quickly toward the door, hoping that her drumming heart was not audible to anyone else. "I didn't realize it was so late."

'You have visitors." Susan gnawed her lower lip. "I was sent to fetch you. It's your brother, and another gentleman."

The two girls stared at each other in dismay. Susan knew better than anyone except Matt how Amanda felt about Edward. Amanda didn't have to say a word; the sudden consternation in her eyes said it all for her. Her first, cowardly impulse was to remain in her room, to send Susan down to tell Mother Superior that she was ill. Then she thought of Matt, who could undoubtedly hear every word from his hiding place. Whatever happened, she could not do anything that would cause the sisters or, God forbid, Edward himself to come to her room. Anyway, she thought, squaring her shoulders defiantly, she was *not* afraid of Edward.

"I'll be right down." Amanda's chin lifted as she

braced herself for the inevitable. Then she turned back to the mirror, ostensibly to check her appearance but really to give herself a precious few seconds to regain her composure. Moving with conscious deliberation, she tucked in a wayward strand of hair. Then she was ready. Susan followed her silently down the stairs. Amanda could feel her friend's unspoken sympathy enveloping her.

"They're in Mother Superior's office," Susan said softly as they reached the ground floor. Amanda nodded but, despite her best intentions, hesitated. What could Edward want? Nothing pleasant, she was sure. Never in all the years she had been a pupil here had he deigned to visit her. Impossible to hope that this was a mere social call. No, if she knew anything of Edward, he was here on business—business that boded no good for her. Then another possibility struck her forcibly, causing her face to whiten. Could it be that the nuns had somehow found out about Matt and had sent for Edward before confronting her with their knowledge? He was, after all, her legal guardian, and presumably would be interested to know that his half sister and ward was concealing England's most notorious murderer.

"Oh, Amanda, you don't think they're going to take you away?" Susan's worried question was so in line with what she had been thinking that Amanda started. A dragoon of soldiers to drag her off to prison might even now be waiting behind Mother Superior's closed door. Then she realized what her friend had meant. Susan was afraid that Edward might have come to remove Amanda from the convent for some purpose of his own. And that was possible, too.

"I hope not," she said slowly. Susan's pansy-brown eyes, meeting hers, misted with sudden tears.

"I-I do, too." Her voice was husky. "If you left, I would be so . . . lonely."

"I would miss you, too." It was all Amanda could find to say. Susan knew as well as she did that if Edward wanted to remove her from the convent, Amanda would have no say in the matter. Just as Susan would, in the end, have no choice but to obey her parents. Except for the few who were lucky enough to have financial independence, females were mere chattel, expected and, indeed, legally required to do as they were told. It was terribly unfair, but it was the way of the world.

The door to Mother Superior's office opened, interrupting Amanda's thoughts. Joanna looked out into the hallway, saw Amanda and Susan standing at the front of the stairs, frowned, and beckoned.

"Mother Superior is waiting for you, Amanda," she said reprovingly.

Amanda squared her shoulders, then on impulse reached over to give Susan's hand a quick squeeze. Susan returned the gesture for an instant. Then, gritting her teeth, Amanda moved past Joanna into Mother Superior's office.

Despite her small size, Mother Superior radiated authority as she sat like a queen behind her desk. Amanda thought that she had never seen her look so totally in command. Clearly she disapproved of her visitors. Not Edward, whom she had met before and who now stood in front of one of the many-paned

windows with the morning sun streaming in to high-
light his fair hair. (Amanda suspected that he had
taken up that stance for just that reason.) No, Edward,
who managed to greet her with a civil word, was,
outwardly at least, a gentleman. It could not be he
who had irked Mother Superior.

Which left the other gentleman. He rose to his
feet from the small chair before Mother Superior's
desk as Amanda entered.

"You remember Lord Robert, Amanda," Edward
murmured by way of introduction, not moving from
the window as the other man stepped forward to take
the hand that Amanda automatically held out to him.
She could only stare in liveliest dismay as her prospective betrothed raised her hand to his lips, planting a
damp kiss on its unresponsive back. Yes, indeed, she
remembered him. But in his case memory had been
kind. Surely he had not always been so short or
plump, and surely his scalp had not always gleamed so
brightly through the thinning ginger strands that were
unsuccessfully arranged to conceal his baldness. And
surely he had not always dressed his rotund form in
such a ridiculous fashion. Why, his collar points were
starched so high that he could scarce turn his head,
and his lavender coat ill suited his florid complexion.
She had no doubt that, combined with his biscuit-
colored breeches and intricately tied cravat, the coat
was the height of fashion, but, quite apart from its
color, the wasp-waisted, shoulder-padded style made
him appear more than a little ridiculous. And *this*
was the man Edward had chosen for her husband.

"It is a great pleasure to see you again, Amanda,"
Lord Robert was saying. "I may call you Amanda?

After all, in one way or another, we are very nearly related. And may I say you have improved far beyond my wildest hopes—er, expectations—since I last saw you."

He released her hand at last and sent a significant smile to Edward, who smiled in return. Both men eyed Amanda, one with satisfaction, the other with avidity. Amanda surreptitiously wiped her hand on her skirt and barely repressed a shudder. Lord Robert looked as if he would like to have her for breakfast, and Edward, she knew, was perfectly capable of feeding her to him.

"Have you nothing to say, Amanda?" Edward demanded with an edge to his carefully smooth voice. Amanda realized with some surprise that she had not uttered a word since entering the room. First nervousness and then shock had rendered her tongue-tied.

"Of course. It's merely that I'm surprised to see you," Amanda said with some composure to her half brother. Not for anything would she let Edward see she feared him; he would enjoy that and take full advantage of it. Then she turned to Lord Robert, who was beaming at her fatuously. "It's good to see you again, Lord Robert. And of course you may address me by my given name. After all, we *are* cousins."

Edward glared at her, clearly disliking her implicit disclaimer of any closer relationship with Lord Robert. Amanda returned his look unflinchingly, though she had to swallow once to combat the sudden dryness in her throat. Mother Superior, seeing this deadly exchange of glances, chose that moment to intervene.

She rose unhurriedly and came around the desk to stand beside Amanda. The slender girl with her vivid coloring and the old nun in the somewhat limp habit were nearly of a height.

"Your brother and Lord Robert have asked permission to take you out for the day, Amanda. I have consented. I suggest you return to your room and fetch your shawl. They will await you here."

Amanda looked into Mother Superior's kindly old eyes and nodded slowly. For the moment, at least, she would not openly defy Edward. Later was the time, when she was safely rid of Matt.

"Yes, Mother," she said meekly and, with a small curtsy dropped in the general direction of the two gentlemen, quitted the room.

Susan was hovering just outside the door, as Amanda had known she would be. She reassured her friend quickly. Then, gathering her wits and realizing that she might be gone for most of the day, she managed to sneak away to the larder and take some food for Matt. Bread and cheese merely, but that would have to do until she could get more . . .

Matt was clearly not pleased when she told him her visitors' identities, and what they wanted. He frowned, staring at her thoughtfully with his hands thrust into his pantaloon pockets. But there was nothing she could do but comply, and they both knew it. Besides, what harm could possibly come to her on an outing in broad daylight with her half brother and stepcousin, be they ever so unpleasant? She put the question to Matt with a smile, but his frown did not lessen in return. He of all people knew how much she hated and feared Edward.

"I must go," she told him, snatching up her shawl and moving quickly toward the door. Matt put out an involuntary hand, as though to stop her. She hesitated, looking into that lean, handsome face that was dark with concern for her. Then she smiled her heartshakingly sweet smile. "I really must, Matt," she said softly. He stared at her for a moment, unspeaking. Then his mouth twisted in wry acceptance, and his hand dropped to his side.

"Take care," she thought she heard him murmur as she went out the door...

The day was like a bad dream. That was the only way Amanda could think to describe it. She felt as though she had been split into two persons: one rode in Edward's carriage on a tour of the local sights, making innocuous conversation with an eager Lord Robert while Edward watched and listened with grim pleasure; the other was worrying about Matt. Suppose he was discovered? Amanda found that she had no idea what Lord Robert was saying to her or what she was replying. The strain of knowing that England's most wanted murderer was secreted in her bedroom, coupled with the strain of trying to appear totally unconcerned about anything but her two companions, was addling her wits. She had no doubt that, if Lord Robert had proposed in the last few minutes, she had absently accepted. She could only hope that he had not.

Edward had not changed one iota, Amanda discovered as the day wore on. She also discovered that absence had not made her heart grow fonder. What she found most painful was that he was so like their father physically. Seeing the distaste in his eyes when he looked at her, hearing the cold voice that made no effort to conceal its dislike, was like watching a cruel caricature. Every time Amanda looked at that sneering, supercilious face she felt as though a knife were twisting in her heart.

As nearly as Amanda could figure it, they had come because Lord Robert wanted to get a look at his prospective bride before irretrievably committing himself to the betrothal. Neither he nor Edward actually said so, but from chance remarks they let fall, and from the smiles and nods that Lord Robert bestowed on Edward through the day, Amanda guessed this must be the case. After all, the last time her stepcousin had seen her, on the day of her father's funeral, she had been a scrawny, carrot-topped thirteen-year-old with eyes red and swollen from weeping. No doubt he objected to buying a pig in a poke and wanted to see for himself what changes the intervening years had wrought. For her part, she could not discover that he had changed at all, except to become a little more puffed up in his own conceit. If she had found him unappealing at thirteen, now, at almost eighteen, she found him repulsive. Probably because she knew now that he intended to make her his wife, with all that that entailed. And also because she now had Matt's kindness and hard male beauty with which to compare him.

It was long after dark when, after providing her with an excellent dinner at the inn where the two men would pass the night, Edward returned her to the convent. Amanda wondered why Lord Robert, who had stuck to her side like a cocklebur to a dog's back all day, did not accompany them. No sooner had

Edward said his good-evenings to Mother Superior than Amanda had her answer. Edward wanted to speak with her alone.

Mother Superior graciously allowed them the use of the little parlor that was usually reserved for visiting priests. As she followed Edward through the door and watched him shut it behind him, Amanda felt her stomach lurch. Now Edward would tell her what she both wanted and dreaded to know.

He wasted no time on the preliminaries. His eyes followed her closely for a moment as she took a chair near the unlit fire, determined to present as cool a facade as she could, despite her drumming heart. He did not sit down but strolled closer until he towered menacingly over the chair in which she had seated herself. Edward was tall, though not so tall as Matt, with slender bones and their father's fair hair. His clothes were the height of fashion, and so were his gleaming boots, or at least Amanda assumed they were. She had lived retired from the world for so long that she was not conversant with male sartorial standards. At any rate, the pale yellow coat and biscuit-brown breeches became him admirably. He would have been a handsome man—except for his eyes, which were of so cold and pale a blue that they resembled chips of ice.

"You've turned out just as I expected: the image of your mother."

"Thank you," Amanda returned composedly, although from the sneer in Edward's voice she was well aware that the words were not meant as a compliment. But, if she were to have a chance of emerging victorious from this encounter, she knew she could not afford to give her temper free rein. "Why are you here, Edward?"

He looked faintly startled. It was clear that he had not expected her to take the initiative. Amanda hoped that his slight surprise would give her an advantage.

"Robert wants to make sure that you give your assent to this marriage before he signs the papers. For some reason which escapes my comprehension, he does not want you if you are unwilling. But you are willing, aren't you, Amanda?" His voice held a veiled threat. Amanda swallowed, then looked up to meet his eyes steadily. The expression in their pale blue depths chilled her.

"No, I am not," she answered, taking her courage in both hands. Edward's eyes narrowed until they were little more than cruel slits in an equally cruel face.

"You will be. By tomorrow, when the fool has it in mind to ask you. Because if you're not, Amanda, if you refuse him or make him think you don't want to be his wife, I'll make you sorry your bitch of a mother ever gave you life. And I can do it. I can take you back to Brook House and lock you in the attic and tell everyone that you are mad. Who will gainsay me? Or I can beat you. And make no mistake about it, Amanda, I will. You are not going to ruin this for me."

Amanda's first impulse was to jump to her feet and tell him with what contempt she viewed his threats. But for almost the first time in her life, caution stayed her. Edward could, indeed, do as he said.

And if she didn't obey him, she knew his vengeance would be terrifying.

"Why is this marriage so important to you, Edward?" Her tone was carefully even. His mouth relaxed slightly as the defiance he had expected was not forthcoming.

"Robert has promised to deed your inheritance back to me on your wedding day. Without that money, Brook House and all the land with it must be sold."

Amanda's eyes widened. She had assumed that Lord Robert wanted to marry her for her money. To discover now that he was prepared to deed it back to Edward greatly surprised her. But *why* should Edward need her money?

"Why is the money so important? There was always plenty—"

"Are you questioning me, girl?" His mouth hardened, and his eyes glittered ominously. Then his gaze shifted as a thought occurred to him. "You want to know, do you? Very well. Perhaps it will make it clear to you how far I am prepared to go to see to it that you marry Robert. Over the last few months I have had rotten luck at cards. Now there is only Brook House left. And I won't lose that, Amanda. Not while I have you to sell instead."

The calculated cruelty of the words should have hurt, but it didn't. She was too used to Edward's animosity.

"But why should Lord Robert want to marry me?" she asked slowly. "I had thought it was for the money."

Edward laughed briefly, the sound harsh. "No, my

dear half sister, he's not after your money. It seems that he was one of the legion of men fascinated by your mother—and apparently one of the few who didn't have her. He thought he might be able to realize his long-standing desire with you, Isabelle's daughter. And when he saw you, he was sure of it. You're so like your mother, Amanda—in every way, I'm sure."

Amanda had had enough. "Don't you *dare* talk about my mother that way." She jumped to her feet and glared up at her half brother. He was only scant inches from her. One hand came up to grip her hard by the arm.

"I'll talk about that whore any way I please. And you *will* marry Robert. Won't you, Amanda?" His fingers tightened on her arm, squeezing until Amanda winced at the pain.

"No, I *won't*."

"Yes, you will. Think about it, Amanda. If you refuse, I'll take you away with me tomorrow. Won't that be nice, Amanda, coming home at last? And if you're still unsure about what that means, I'll give you a little sample of what you can expect if you force me to take you home."

With that, he lifted his hand and slapped her very deliberately across the face. The blow was so hard that it made her eyes water. Amanda raised a disbelieving hand to her sore cheek as Edward released her.

"That was just a sample, little sister. Refuse Robert tomorrow and there will be more." He turned away as he spoke.

Amanda, knees shaking, moved to the door and

walked out into the hallway. It was deserted; the lack of light meant that everyone except herself and Edward had retired. Edward would soon be leaving to join Lord Robert at the village inn. Tomorrow they would be back, and Lord Robert would want her answer. Amanda pressed her cool hand to her throbbing cheek again as she made her way along the corridor and up the stairs toward her room. He would want her answer—and she knew already that there was only one answer she could give. She was trembling all over with dread as she let herself into the bedroom and stood leaning against the door. Moonlight streamed in through the window, bathing the narrow bed in a pool of light. Matt lay on the bed, his long legs crossed, his arms folded under his head, which turned toward the door as she entered.

"Have a nice day?" he asked mockingly as he got to his feet with lithe grace. Amanda didn't answer, didn't move. She couldn't. She was afraid her knees would buckle if she took a step, and her mouth was shaking so that she couldn't form words. Matt came closer, peering at her curiously in the darkness. Then his hand was beneath her chin, and he was tilting her face so the moonlight caught it. There was an instant's silence. She felt his hand beneath her chin grow tense.

"What in the name of hell happened to your face?"

chapter eleven

"Edward..." Her voice shook.

"*I'll kill him.*" The deadly menace in his tone brought Amanda back to reality. Matt's hand fell from her chin to join its fellow in closing about her waist. Clearly he intended to lift her out of his way. "Where is he? Downstairs?"

"Matt, *no.*" Shocked into horrified awareness, Amanda lifted her arms to lock her hands behind his neck. Her head tilted back on the slender stem of her neck as she stared up beseechingly into his face. It looked grim and determined. Amanda was once again reminded of the ruthless murderer she thought she had discovered on the beach.

"If you think I'm going to let him get away with abusing you, you can think again." His voice was a deadly rasp. "I'll beat him to a pulp with the greatest pleasure imaginable."

"Please, Matt, *no*." She was frantic now as she tried to hold him. It was useless, of course. His strength was many times greater than hers. He lifted her with no more trouble than if she had been a small child and set her down on the floor behind him, turning so that he faced her while she still clung to his neck. His hands came up to pry her arms from around his neck; Amanda knew that if she did not stop him now, at once, he would go downstairs and find Edward and very likely kill him. Not that she was worried about Edward, but in the ensuing uproar Matt would undoubtedly be caught—and then hanged.

"Don't leave me, Matt," she moaned, cunningly letting her body go limp so that he was forced to abandon his attempt to remove her arms from about his neck and support her sagging weight.

"Amanda." The sound of her name on his lips was harsh. She sagged more completely against him, feeling relieved as he cursed and shifted his grip so that one arm was sliding beneath her knees while his other arm cradled her shoulders. She felt herself being lifted as if she were weightless, and clung to his hard chest while he strode toward the bed. When he lowered her to the mattress, she panicked, thinking that he meant to leave her and see to Edward. Her hands tightened on his shoulders as he leaned over her, and her lashes fluttered up so that she could look at him as she felt the softness of the mattress accepting her weight.

"Please don't leave me, Matt," she begged again, something suspiciously resembling a sob making her voice break. His lips compressed, and she saw his eyes flicker as if he, too, were hurting; then he sat down on the bed beside her, his hands gentle as they eased her back against the pillow.

"I won't leave you, honey," he promised tightly. Amanda relaxed then. He had promised, and she would hold him to it. Which meant that he was safe for now, at least—but so, too, was Edward, Amanda thought with a twinge of regret.

"Let me look at your face, Amanda." Matt's hand came up to tilt her face gently into the streaming moonlight, which did little to disguise the bruise that was already beginning to darken beneath her cheekbone. As Matt looked at that mark of abuse on the tender white skin, his mouth compressed into a hard, straight line and his eyes glinted dangerously. Amanda lifted a hand to catch his wrist as it rested below her chin, suddenly afraid again as she saw the rage in Matt's eyes.

"That bastard," Matt said through his teeth, the words flat although the glittering eyes belied his tone. Then, his voice softening as he saw the worry clouding her face, he added, "It's all right, honey, I'm not going anywhere. Lie back and relax, and let me bathe that bruise for you. It must be sore as hell."

Amanda looked up at him for a long moment, relieved to see that, although the ominous glitter still lurked in his eyes, some of the coiled tension had left his muscles. He would not do anything rash, she was almost sure. She allowed herself to do as he'd said and relax against the pillow, her fingers moving up to touch the throbbing bruise almost ruefully.

"The whole side of my face feels numb," she

confessed. She heard a faint, gritty sound that she identified at last as Matt's teeth grinding together, and her gaze flew to his face once more. Those silvery eyes were blazing with an icy fire, but as he caught her eyes upon him he managed to twist up one corner of his mouth in the semblance of a reassuring smile.

"It's all right," he said again. "Just lie still a minute. I'm not going anywhere."

He got up off the bed and stepped over to the washstand, where he doused the linen towel and wrung it out. Then, cloth in hand, he came back to sit beside her on the bed.

"Look up, Amanda." She did, and he gently wiped her face, his hands very careful as they worked over the sensitive area of the bruise. When her face was washed to his satisfaction, he reached down and caught her hands, and very gravely wiped them, too, as if he had been tending a little child. Amanda smiled mistily at him as he took such tender care of her. Only Matt had ever made her feel so cherished and protected. Finally he got up again to rinse the cloth and wring out the excess water, then brought it back folded to lay it gently against the sore cheek. The compress felt wonderfully cool and soothing. Amanda nuzzled her face into the cold cloth and the hand holding it, and smiled at Matt again.

"You're very good to me," she said softly. His eyes darkened.

"You deserve to have people be good to you," he said, his free hand coming up to smooth back the disordered tendrils of her hair. "Your brother must be mad to treat you so. And I'd like to make him suffer."

This last was muttered under his breath, but Amanda heard. She gnawed on her lower lip, looking up at him with anxious eyes. "Matt, you mustn't do anything to Edward—he'll make sure that everyone knows you're here. One little slap in the face isn't worth hanging for."

"Isn't it?" His mouth twisted wryly. "I'd do far more than hang for you, Amanda, if I thought it would benefit you. But short of killing your brother— which I may yet do if he dares to lay a hand on you again—I don't see how anything I could do at the moment would be of much help to you. So you can take that worried look off your face. I told you I'd stay here with you and I will."

"Thank you, Matt."

He took the compress from her cheek and stood up to wet it again. When he came back, Amanda tried to hold the cloth in place herself, to save him from having to do so. To her surprise, her hand shook so badly that she had to let it fall back to the bed. Matt frowned as he watched.

"Tell me what happened, Amanda. Why did he slap you? Did you quarrel?" His voice was incredibly gentle.

Amanda looked at him for a long moment. She wanted to tell him—longed to tell him. But she feared to raise his ire against Edward any further. If Matt knew how Edward had threatened her, she had little doubt as to what his reaction would be.

"It was nothing, really. Edward told me that he had arranged my betrothal to Lord Robert. When I said that I didn't want to marry him, Edward slapped me. He's never struck me before—and it shocked me."

"Is that the truth?" Matt sounded faintly disbelieving, and Amanda prayed that the darkness would keep him from seeing the betraying color that she could feel rising in her face.

"Yes." She comforted herself with the reminder that it was, indeed, the truth—if not all of it.

"And did you agree to marry this Lord Robert?"

"No. At least, he hasn't asked me yet. Edward says that he is planning to propose tomorrow. When he does, I-I haven't decided yet what I'll do."

Matt took the compress away from her cheek and studied the bruise contemplatively for a moment. Then he met her eyes, his own narrowing.

"You told me before that there was no question of your marrying the man." There was a barely discernible edge to his voice. "What has changed your mind?"

Amanda looked at him mutely. He seemed very big and dark sitting on the edge of her bed, his hands resting lightly on his thighs in their loose black trousers. His eyes were fixed on her face, searching her expression, waiting for an answer. Amanda wavered. She didn't want to lie, but she couldn't tell him the truth about Edward's threats, either. She had no doubt that Matt would kill Edward if he knew how her brother had threatened her...

"Edward pointed out... He told me of the life I would lead as Lady Turnbull. It wasn't as... as disagreeable as I had imagined. Now I'm reconsidering, but I haven't decided one way or the other yet."

"I see." The two words were drawn out. He looked

down at his hands for a moment, then up again at her face so swiftly that if it hadn't been for the darkness, Amanda had no doubt that he would have seen her lie written clearly in her eyes. Hastily she lowered them. "Care to talk about it?"

Amanda shook her head. There was nothing that she would rather do then tell her troubles to Matt, but under the circumstances it was impossible. To distract him, she raised her still-trembling hand to touch her brow.

"My head aches, Matt." The words sounded so forlorn that Amanda nearly congratulated herself on her acting ability. Then it occurred to her that she wasn't acting. She felt just as forlorn as she sounded—and she craved his comfort.

"No wonder, after that brutal slap." He reached up to touch the braided coronet of her hair. "But these probably don't help, either. Let me take them down for you." His hands were busy removing the pins that held her braids in place as he spoke.

"I can do it." Absurdly, the feel of his hands in her hair was making her feel shy. She reached up to remove the rest of the pins herself, only to find that her arms were too weak to allow her to do so. That scene with Edward had drained her more than she had realized.

"Can you?" The question was dry. "Just lie there and let me take care of you for once, Amanda. After all, you've done as much for me."

At the memories his words conjured up, she smiled. When he had first ordered her to bandage his hip, she had been terrified—but that seemed very long ago now. "I have, haven't I?" she murmured.

"Mmm." He continued to take the pins from her hair, dropping them onto the bedside table one by one. When at last they were all out, he drew her braids down over her shoulders and began to loosen them, running his fingers through the strands until at last her hair lay smooth and gleaming in thick waves.

"You have beautiful hair," he murmured, picking up a lock and studying it as if it were a rare and curious specimen. The moonlight streaming in through the window fell in love with the vibrant ruby color and shimmered it with hundreds of hidden lights that glittered like diamonds. Matt turned the lock of hair this way and that, absorbed as he watched the bright silk reflecting and refracting the light. Amanda watched him, her eyes taking on a warm, almost secret glow as she traced the planes and angles of his face. Even two days' growth of beard could not disguise the masculine splendor of his features. A man had no right to be so outrageously handsome, she thought, and wondered how she had failed to recognize his beauty from the moment she had laid eyes on him. Even a full beard would no longer be able to hide from her the lean strength of his jaw and square, determined chin, or the classic cut of hard masculine lips that were tender now as he examined her hair with grave attention. His nose was classic, too, straight as a blade and arrogant, while the harsh curves of his proud cheekbones and wide brow could have been carved by a master sculptor. His lashes lay like thick, stubby black fans against cheeks that had regained much of their natural bronze, veiling eyes that she knew were as silver as coins within a darker ring of smoke. Even his eyebrows were beautiful, thick and black with a faint sardonic arch, and very expressive in conveying his moods without words. Just now one was lifted fractionally, as if he were curious about something. His hair was as black as his brows, so black that it shone with faint blue highlights under the wooing influence of the moon, curling as it fell down over his forehead and skirted around his ears to nestle at the nape of that strong brown neck.

"So is yours—your hair, I mean. It's beautiful." The words sneaked out of her mouth before Amanda was aware that they were there. The first three were spoken dreamily, but the rest were rushed as she realized what she had said. If Matt even guessed at the warm, tingly feeling she got from just looking at him, she had no doubt that he would move away from her—and she didn't want that.

"Thank you." Incredibly, he smiled. The amused curve of his lips and the gleam of white teeth lent a rakish charm to his face that threatened to render Amanda speechless. "It's nice to receive a compliment for once. Usually we poor gentlemen have to bestow them all day long, with nary a one in return."

"You're welcome." Suddenly shy, more from her thoughts than from anything he had said or done, she let her lashes droop down over her eyes. He replaced the lock of hair on her breast and lifted his hand to touch the length of her lashes with an experimental finger.

"Soft as silk, black as sin, and long as the devil's tongue," he murmured caressingly. Startled at some indefinable note in his voice, the lashes that he had described fluttered up again. Her eyes looked almost purple as she stared up at him. His hand slid away from her lashes to rest warmly against her uninjured cheek. Abruptly his expression changed to a forbidding scowl. Amanda blinked at him, bewildered.

"Your skin is like ice," he said, his tone completely different from the gentle murmur of just seconds before. His hand dropped from her cheek to pick up one of hers. It lay small and defenseless in his large palm, her slender fingers dwarfed by the length and strength of his. Amanda stared down at their joined hands, hers white and slender with delicate fingers and buffed oval nails, his brown and strong, a blatantly masculine hand with a calloused palm that was clearly no stranger to physical labor. She could sense the warm vitality of him flowing to her through his palm.

"Your hand is cold, too," he continued. "You've had a shock—you need to be in bed. If you'll tell me where it is, I'll get your nightdress for you and we'll get you tucked up."

He stood up as he spoke, letting her hand drop back onto the bed. Amanda felt bereft as she stared up at him, suddenly becoming aware of how very cold she was. Without his presence beside her to warm and comfort her, she was beginning to shiver.

"In the wardrobe, the second drawer." It was all she could do to keep her teeth from chattering. Matt turned away as she spoke and crossed to the wardrobe to rummage among its contents with masculine disregard for the neatness of the items within. In a moment he was back, towering over her as he stood beside the bed, one of her prim white night rails dangling incongruously from his hand. He dropped it onto the bed beside her, and before she quite knew what he was about, he caught her by the ankles and deftly slid the black slippers from her feet.

"Beautiful feet, too—small and slender and most definitely female." He held one foot in his hand as he spoke. Amanda felt a tingle surge through her body as he caressed the white-stockinged instep with teasing fingers. Her toes curled involuntarily. Before he could see her reaction, she pulled her foot from his grasp and burrowed it down against the blanket.

"Turn over and I'll undo your dress buttons," he instructed, apparently unaware that he had caused every cell of her body to be aware of him. At the thought of those large hands on the legions of tiny buttons on the back of her dress, Amanda shivered. She hoped that he mistook the chill of the room as the cause of the convulsive little movement.

Apparently he did. Without waiting for her response, he gently rolled her over so that she was lying on her stomach and, after brushing the waving mass of her hair out of the way, proceeded to unbutton her dress. Amanda felt the warmth of his hand against the cool skin at the nape of her neck, and couldn't suppress another shiver as it traced down between her shoulder blades before the thin muslin of her chemise afforded her vulnerable senses some protection. By the time he had unlooped the last button somewhere in the vicinity of her hips, she was lying rigid, her teeth clenched as she fought the sensations his touch aroused in her.

"Finished," he said, straightening. His hands slid up her sides to grasp her under the armpits, and then he was lifting her from the bed and setting her on her feet on the floor. Amanda caught at his arms to steady herself as he bent to catch the hem of her dress and lift it around her waist. She had no time to register anything before he coolly instructed her to raise her arms, then eased the dress over her head. She was left standing in her chemise and single petticoat, a figure all in white except for the dark fire of her hair and the amethyst glow of her eyes. As much from embarrassment as from cold, she wrapped her arms around herself, hoping desperately that he had not noticed her body's humiliating reaction to standing before him clad only in her underclothes. Her breasts seemed to swell, and her nipples hardened until they stood out like tiny pebbles against the thin muslin of her chemise. This unprecedented response shamed her so much that she could feel hot color creeping up her neck to wash over her face like a tidal wave. Mutely she thanked the Lord for the darkness that masked her shame. No matter what Matt had said about the virtues of possessing a warm and loving nature, she was convinced that such an intense longing for him to look at her with those silvery eyes, touch her with those long fingers, and kiss her with that hard mouth was incontrovertible proof of the wantonness she had suspected in herself since he had first kissed her.

"I can manage the rest myself," Amanda said hurriedly as Matt turned back to her after dropping her dress negligently over the single straight chair.

"All right." His answer was agreeable, but Amanda thought he gave her a rather comprehensive look before he obligingly crossed the room to stare out the window. Amanda clenched her teeth at the thought that he might have seen and correctly interpreted her response to him. He would be very kind about it, she knew, but she also knew that kindness and forbearance were the last things she wanted from him at the moment.

Her fingers were clumsy as she struggled with buttons and ribbons and ties, but at last she managed to get her underclothes off and her night rail on. She left her stockings for last, slipping off her garters and then rolling down the flimsy cotton stockings. When she straightened after removing the second stocking, she was taken aback to find that Matt had turned his back on the window and was watching her. His face was deep in shadow; only the glint of his eyes was visible to her.

"Get into bed. You're cold." The words were abrupt, the tone almost harsh. Amanda looked down at herself, at her breasts neatly covered by the prim, pin-tucked white muslin night rail with its demure high collar and long sleeves, and saw to her dismay that her nipples were as visible through the thin garment as they had been through her chemise moments before. Quickly she crossed her arms across her chest, then blushed again as she realized that this would only call Matt's attention to her difficulties—if he hadn't noticed already.

"Matt, I . . ." Too late, she realized that one should never attempt to explain the unexplainable, but mercifully he interrupted, saving her from floundering in a morass of deepening embarrassment.

"Get into bed, Amanda."

Thankful, she did as he said, so grateful to be safely hidden from his eyes as she crawled beneath the covers that she barely noticed that his tone was even harsher than before. When she was lying back against the pillow with the covers pulled up to her chin, she dared to look at him. His gaze was on the slim outline of her body beneath the blanket. Then, as if aware of her attention, he abruptly turned and stared across the room at the dark hearth.

"We need a fire. It's cold as be-Jesus in here."

"We're not allowed to have a fire in our bedrooms in the spring. Only in winter."

Amanda realized they were both talking at random; Matt didn't seem to have his mind on what he was saying, and she certainly did not. She was far too busy considering the almost hungry look in his eyes as he had stared at her body beneath the bedclothes.

"Damned barn of a place," he muttered, and his eyes shifted so that he was looking at her again. His hands slid into his pockets and his feet moved restlessly. "How do you feel now?"

"Much better," Amanda answered, returning his gaze reluctantly and then finding that she was quite unable to tear her eyes away. His eyes smoldered at her in the darkness, making her burn with a heat that made a mockery of the chilled room.

"You will have quite a bruise. How are you going to explain that to Lord Robert tomorrow?" Amanda thought she detected a trace of a sneer in his voice when he said the name.

"I . . . don't know. I suppose I shall say that I bumped into something in the dark."

His lips compressed. "You won't tell him the truth? That your bastard of a brother hit you to persuade you to marry him?"

"No." Her voice was low.

"Of course not." He moved toward the door. Amanda sat up in bed, her eyes widening.

"Where are you going?"

His hand was on the latch as he turned to look at her.

"I think it would be better if I found somewhere else to sleep tonight."

"But why?" There was shock in her voice.

"Because if I stay here another minute, I'm going to have to choose between strangling you and kissing you, and I'll be damned if I'll do either."

He sounded almost angry, and his stance was rigid as his eyes raked over her. Amanda felt her heart speed up at the suppressed violence in his voice. She wanted his hands on her, she realized with an odd, sinking sensation in the pit of her stomach, whether in anger or in passion. But he was clearly determined not to touch her.

"Would you do me a favor before you go?" The meekness of her tone contrasted sharply with her pounding heart. "There's another blanket at the bottom of the wardrobe. Would you fetch it for me? I'm cold."

She met his eyes with beguiling innocence. As she had thought, he could not resist such an appeal to the protectiveness he seemed to feel for her. The twitching of a muscle in his jaw was the only sign of protest he made as he did as she asked. Amanda subsided against the pillow as he shook the blanket over her bed. Her lashes veiled her eyes as she admired the rippling muscles in his arms and shoulders through the thin white shirt as he performed the simple task; then, as he bent over her to smooth the blanket about her shoulders, she lifted her lashes to look frankly at the starkly beautiful face so close to her own. Her eyes met his. Dark embers glowing in those silver-gray eyes seemed to sear her. The sudden blast of heat made her mouth go dry. Unconsciously she wet her lower lip with her tongue. Matt's eyes were riveted on the tiny movement.

"Dear God, Amanda . . ."

The hoarseness of his tone and the tormented blaze in his eyes provided the impetus she needed. Swallowing, she eased one hand from beneath the piled covers to catch his. His skin was burning hot—and not with fever.

"You promised you wouldn't leave me," she reminded him in a voice grown suddenly husky. Impulsively she lifted his hand and pressed it against her uninjured cheek. His skin felt hard and hot and abrasive against the softness of her face.

"I've changed my mind." But he made no effort to pull his hand away from her cheek. Instead, she was almost certain that the long fingers made an abortive caressing movement before being abruptly stilled. "You don't know what you're asking for, Amanda." These last words were almost desperate.

"No, I don't, do I?" Her eyes met his again, their expression soft and seductive beneath the long lashes that half veiled them. "But you could teach me, Matt."

And she turned her mouth into his palm.

chapter twelve

The touch of her soft little mouth against his palm seemed to scorch his flesh. Matt could feel the heat of it shoot along his veins like an explosion of molten fire. The desire he had been battling for days threatened to consume him in its flames. Gritting his teeth, he fought the impulse to pull his hand away from her lips and replace it with his mouth, to drop down on the bed beside her and take her in his arms and never let her go. She wanted him, he knew. He could clearly read the passionate invitation in her huge purple eyes. But she had no more idea than a baby what it was she was inviting; it would be criminal of him to take advantage of her innocence and her affection for him. She was just a child, despite her heart-stirring beauty and the enticing, womanly shape of her.

"Teach me, Matt," she repeated huskily. Her mouth

slid from his palm to the inside of his wrist just above the loose cuff of his shirt. Matt felt the moist heat of her mouth against his drumming pulse, and was so tempted he could have screamed. He wanted to, oh, he wanted to...

"Amanda," he said unsteadily, knowing he should leave her now, this instant, but unable to force himself to take what his mind told him was the only rational action. She silenced him by the simple expedient of placing her fingers against his mouth. To make the gesture she had loosed his hand; without his volition it lay feather light on the blanket just over her breast. With every fiber of his being, Matt was conscious of those slender fingers against his mouth and the soft female shape of her beneath his hand. Desire rose in him like a raging demon, screaming to be fulfilled. But still he fought it, grimly.

"Hold me, Matt," she whispered. "Please—won't you just hold me?" She met his eyes beseechingly. Matt thought that her eyes looked both pleading and bewildered, like those of a child who has been punished for something she cannot understand and is being denied comfort for an equally incomprehensible reason. A rush of tenderness for her accompanied the thought; Matt welcomed it, thinking it would provide a shield against the passion that threatened to overwhelm him at any instant. He looked down into her face, so small and defenseless on the white pillow, his eyes unconsciously absorbing the perfection of each feature and the loveliness of the whole. Her hair was the color of fine old wine in the moonlight, providing an exquisite frame for the pale serenity of her brow, the smooth curve of her cheeks, the elegant little chin. Her eyes beneath the silky black brows gleamed up at him with soft fire in their depths, like amethysts caught in the sun. Her nose was small and delicate, like the rest of her, and beneath it her mouth swelled, lushly red like a rose...

Matt stared at that mouth, unable to help himself as he remembered how it had felt to kiss those sweetly curved lips—and remembered, too, her response. She had gone up in flames in his arms... To his dismay Matt felt the tenderness he had counted on for salvation turn tail and join forces with the desire he found so difficult to control. Together, they tortured him with a hot, throbbing need that was almost impossible to resist.

Amanda's fingers slid from his mouth to caress his cheek, her hand cool and soft against the whisker-roughened hardness of his skin. Matt stood rigid beneath her touch, fighting a passion that was almost crippling in its intensity. And he might have won—if she had not chosen that moment to run her fingers lightly, oh, so lightly, along the narrow, raised outline of the scar that twisted across his cheek, memento of a childhood beating with a riding crop administered by one of his mother's gentleman friends. The gentleness of Amanda's touch soothed a pain that had seared its way from his cheek to his heart years ago, and which he had thought long since forgotten. Suddenly Matt realized that he needed Amanda's gentleness desperately, craved it, had to have more of it or perish...

With a muffled groan he gave up the fight, lowering himself to the bed beside her and enfolding her in his arms in a single violent movement. He sought her lips with his, finding them readily as she lifted her mouth to him without fear or restraint.

"Darling," he murmured hoarsely before he began to kiss her with a savagery born of desperation. She should have shrunk from the barely controlled violence of his embrace, but, to his wonder, he felt her arms slide around his neck—and she was kissing him back.

After that his kisses gentled. Amanda gloried in the feel of his lips against hers, hard, hot, masculine lips that promised and demanded, stroked and caressed, took and gave. She gave herself up to their expert tuition, returning kiss for kiss. No longer shy when she felt his tongue invade her mouth, she met it with her own, and discovered to her delight that exploring his mouth was as deliciously dizzying as having him explore hers. When at last his mouth left hers to trace a hot pattern along her cheek to her ear, she trembled at the exquisite sensation his teeth aroused as they nibbled lightly on her lobe. Then his lips left her ear to slide hotly down the slim column below it. Amanda arched her throat against the moist heat of his mouth, feeling her toes curl as his lips rested finally on the throbbing pulse at its base. Her hands were in his hair, pressing against his scalp through the thick black strands as she held him to her. He rested against her for a moment, his breath hot against the skin of her throat, and then he lifted his head to look at her.

"Amanda, you're going to have to stop me," he said, the words so indistinct she could barely understand him. "Because, before God, I can't stop myself."

She smiled at him, a small curving of her lips barely visible through the silvered darkness, and allowed her hands to caress his silken black head.

"I don't want to stop you," she told him softly. His eyes smoldered and then blazed in response; then his mouth was on hers again, hard and hot and devastating in its impact on her senses, while his hands moved to the ribbon that secured her night rail at the throat.

Amanda trembled as she felt the brush of his fingers against the soft skin of her throat. This was what she wanted, she told herself, this man, this moment. She so desperately wanted him to kiss her and hold her and love her that she thought she would die if he were to draw back now. But she didn't think he would—not this time. The fine tremor that shook his hands, the dark flush straining his cheeks, the hoarse, uneven sounds of his breathing, told her that he was as much under her spell as she was under his.

She watched the intense concentration on that hard face as he slowly and methodically worked his way down the dozen tiny buttons on the front of her night rail. With each button that he freed, he pressed a tiny, stinging kiss to the sensitive flesh thus exposed. Amanda felt the hardness and heat of his mouth, the rasp of his unshaven chin, the touch of his hands against her, and thought that her bones would melt from the sheer ecstasy. Her hands never left the black head as he worked his way down between her breasts to just above her navel, barely parting the material of her night rail so that a long, triangular section of her skin was exposed. When the last button slid out of its hole, unfastening the night-dress to the waist, his hands slid up her rib cage and then flattened just below her breasts.

Amanda felt the heat and strength of those hands burning through the thin linen to her skin, and instinctively pressed closer against him. She could feel the muscular length of his body burning her as he lay stretched on the bed beside her; the bed-coverings twisted around her hips prevented her from fully feeling the urgent pressure of his thighs as he moved them closer against her. But only the thin linen of her night rail shielded her breasts from his touch—and then, moving very slowly as if he feared to frighten her, his hands folded back the unfastened edges of her night rail to expose her breasts.

As she felt the cool night air against her bare skin, Amanda quivered and shut her eyes. Nothing happened, not a movement, not a sound except the stentorian rasp of his breathing. When eventually she dared to peep up at Matt from beneath the thick veil of her lashes, she saw that he was propped up on his elbow beside her, one hand supporting his head while his other rested with disturbing weight and heat against the bare skin just below her breast. His eyes were fixed on her breasts, his silver gaze darkened to smoke by a hunger that she, even in her innocence, had no trouble recognizing. A dark flush stained the flesh high on his cheekbones, and a leaping nerve in one corner called attention to the long, straight line of that beautiful mouth. As if he felt her gaze upon him, Matt looked up then; Amanda felt her own mouth quiver as she met his eyes.

"You have beautiful breasts, Amanda," he said, his

voice hoarse. He lifted the hand beneath her breast to run a gentle finger over the flesh he praised. Amanda drew in her breath sharply at his touch. Her eyes dropped from his face to the hand that caressed her; the contrast between the milky skin of her small, pointed breasts and the swarthiness of his large hand made her heart pound. Then he lifted his hand again to touch her nipple with that same seducing finger. Amanda could not stop the small moan that escaped her as her nipple quivered to life beneath his touch. She watched, half shamed, half fascinated, as her breasts swelled beneath his caress, seeming to beg for more. As if in answer, his hand moved to her other breast, and his palm rasped lightly against her second nipple. The sensation of mingled pain and pleasure thus aroused quivered down to her belly, where it curled in a tight, pulsating ball. She gasped at its intensity.

"So beautiful," he murmured, his eyes on her breasts again as he traced concentric circles from her nipple to the outer edge of her breast and then back before cupping the whole in his palm. "Your skin is so soft, like gleaming white satin. I could touch it forever." He drew in his breath on a ragged sigh; his hand tightened possessively over the breast it entrapped. His eyes came up to meet hers. Amanda thought she would be consumed by the smoldering heat she saw in their depths.

"If you have any sense at all, you'll tell me to remove my hands and get out of your bed and leave you the hell alone," he muttered roughly, the growling timbre of his voice telling her how difficult he was finding it to give her that advice. "But if you're going to do so, for God's sake, do it now. In another minute it will be too late. I won't be able to stop if you begged me on your knees."

Amanda looked up at him, her eyes moving over the hard, handsome face so near her own, thinking again how incredibly beautiful he was, beautiful in a purely masculine sense that left her devastated. The silver-smoke eyes, the hard planes of his face, the chiseled mouth, and even the profusion of thick black curls stirred her profoundly. Her hands came up to cradle his face. The gesture was shy at first, but as she felt the sandpaper roughness of his cheeks under her palms she lost every last scrap of her shyness in a blinding rush of emotion.

"I love you," she said, wondering, knowing it was true even as she said it. He tensed, and then his eyes began to blaze with a fire so intense it all but liquefied her bones.

"Dear God, Amanda, you just sealed your fate," he groaned, his voice strangled, and then he was bending down to her, his arms going tight around her as his mouth found hers again.

He kissed her desperately, his mouth devouring hers, as if he could never have enough of her, could never let her go. His arms around her locked her so closely to him that she could feel every hard muscle of his body through his clothes and even the entangling bedclothes. He was lying on top of her, his big body completely enveloping hers, his weight crushing her into the mattress while his hips moved in odd little thrusts against hers that seemed to increase in force and urgency as she caressed his broad shoulders with her hands. Even through his shirt, the feel of those sinewy shoulders intoxicated her. She wondered how it would feel to touch him without the barrier of his shirt to impede her hands. She wanted to touch his bare skin, as he had touched, was touching, hers . . . Her hands moved of their own volition until they found the V opening of his shirt and slid within. The feel of his chest hair against her fingers intoxicated her. She ran her nails over the soft mat of hair, loving the crispness of it against her fingers, loving, too, the moist heat of the flesh beneath. He stiffened at her touch, his mouth leaving hers to rest hotly against her neck, and then he was pulling away from her, his hands on her wrists restraining her as she tried frantically to hold him.

"*Matt* . . ." There was a world of anguish in the sound. He bent down to kiss her quickly, his hard lips reassuring her without words, and then he was impatiently freeing her from the covers that shrouded her from the hips down like a mummy. He threw the offending covers on the floor, leaving her lying defenseless on the white-sheeted mattress.

"Let's get your nightdress off," he said, his voice hoarse, and bent to catch the hem of her night rail and draw it up over her head. The night rail joined the covers on the floor. Amanda was left lying on the bed with only her hair to hide her body from his eyes. She had not guessed that he would want her naked; her hands came up in an instinctive movement to cover herself.

"Don't be shy with me." He was kneeling beside her, his eyes both tender and passionate as he brushed aside first her hands and then the clinging strands of hair so that her body was totally exposed to him.

Amanda flushed but made no other move to shield herself as his eyes traveled from her slender shoulders to the high, firm breasts whose rosy nipples seemed to ache as his eyes caressed them, to her narrow waist and flat stomach, on down to her long legs and the dark triangle of hair between them. She could see the rapid rise and fall of his chest as he stared down at her, and then he was standing beside the bed, his movements clumsy with haste as he shed his own clothes. Amanda watched, quivering with fear and anticipation as he pulled his shirt over his head and dropped it on the floor, then sat down on the bed beside her to remove his shoes and hose. His broad, bare back was turned to her, and the fear she had briefly felt died and was replaced with an aching tenderness as she saw the mass of scars. She sat up, her arms sliding around his waist as she pressed her lips softly against the ridged flesh. Matt's breath caught on a ragged groan; Amanda felt the strong body tremble against her. Then he was turning, lying on top of her as he pinned her to the bed, his mouth shaking as it slanted across hers. Amanda's arms slid around his neck. She clung to him shamelessly, trembling as violently as he.

She could feel him everywhere, with every inch of her flesh. His chest hair rasped harshly against the softness of her breasts, arousing them until they burned with longing. The hardness of his stomach and abdomen pressed into hers while the thrusting strength of his thighs crushed her hips and legs. He was still wearing his trousers, but Amanda could feel grinding against her the hot, bulging outline of the part of him that made him a man. She had seen that part only on a baby boy whom she had diapered at Sister Agnes's instruction, and then she had hastily averted her eyes. But her memory of that small, innocent maleness bore no resemblance to the feel of this huge thing that importuned her so insistently. She trembled as it pressed boldly against her; her hands clutched at his shoulders and then ran with increasing need over his back. She was intensely curious about him, about the look of him, the feel of him; her fingers were unsteady as they explored first the muscular breadth of his shoulders, marveling at the smooth hardness of his skin, and then traced gently over the outline of the scars on his back.

This was Matt, her Matt, who was disfigured so, and the small flaw in his physical perfection touched her to the heart. The words she had said a few moments ago, words she had not known were in her mind, came back to her: she loved him. Never in her life had she felt anything like the intensity of the emotion that shook her as she stroked his broad, scarred back.

He was kissing her throat, his mouth hot against her skin while his hands cupped her breasts. Amanda stiffened, first with shock and then with something perilously close to ecstasy, as she felt his mouth leave her throat to nuzzle at her breast. The feel of his unshaven jaw abrading her softness as he brushed his face back and forth against her nipples caused a moan to rise unbidden from her throat. Amanda heard the wanton little sound as if from a distance, wondering vaguely where it had come from until she realized to her horror that it had come from her own throat. And continued to come. She couldn't seem to stop the animalistic little cries no matter how hard she tried. Then his lips closed gently over her left nipple and she stopped trying as her body went wild under his hands.

If she had been aware of anything except the intensity of her own pleasure, Amanda would have wanted to die of shame at the way her body writhed and twisted beneath Matt's hands and mouth. He stroked her, first her silken belly and then her thighs, as his mouth continued to tease and torment her nipples. He moved from one breast to the other, first suckling and then catching the nipple between hard white teeth and biting down gently until her nails dug deep into his shoulders and she cried out his name. He shuddered as he felt her pleasure, and his mouth slid down from her breasts to trail burning kisses over her flat stomach, stopping momentarily to explore her navel with his tongue, before moving on down her abdomen to the place where her thighs joined. Amanda quivered with shock as she felt his mouth nuzzling her there, and her eyes flew open as she tried to squirm away from him. She was not yet so completely depraved as not to realize that the way he was kissing her now was wrong; he had to stop . . . But his hands were holding her in place, not letting her move away from him, and the pressure of his mouth against that place where no one had ever touched her before was doing funny things to her insides.

"Relax, Amanda," he murmured in a low, thick voice, "and let me kiss you."

Still she lay stiffly beneath him, resisting the nibbling little kisses he was pressing up the inside of her thighs. Her hands were in his hair, but gradually they stopped trying to pull him away. Instead they rested quietly, the fingers tensely entwined in the thick strands. She wasn't resisting anymore, but she was no longer responding as she had, either. Matt's hands slid down her sides to cup her hips, holding her loosely but making no effort to force her to do anything.

"Amanda." His voice was hoarse with passion. Amanda looked down and met his eyes as he lifted his head so that he could look up at her. He was half lying, half kneeling astride her legs, and the contrast between his black hair and swarthy skin and the pearly glimmer of her stomach and thighs made her catch her breath. "You trust me, don't you?"

Amanda thought about that for an instant, then nodded hesitantly. She did trust him: more, she loved him.

"Then open your legs for me, and let me love you properly." Despite the husky overtones, his voice was cajoling. Amanda shivered at the image his words conjured up, but when his hands slid down between her thighs she let him part them and settle himself between them. Her nails dug deep into his scalp as she felt him press first gentle kisses and then hot lingering ones against the quivering softness of her. As he found each sensitive spot with his tongue, her heart began to pound so hard that she thought she must die from it. Instinctively she tried to squeeze her thighs shut, but he was fixed firmly between them now and she only succeeded in imprinting the feel of his rough cheeks against the silky skin of her inner thighs. Tugging at his hair, writhing in frantic protest against the sensations he was arousing in her, she tried her best to make him stop, but he would not. And then she didn't want him to. Her body responded with a will of its own, arching itself against him, shivering and pulsating and clutching him to her with hands and legs.

"Sweet Jesus." He was lifting himself away from her, his hands shaking as they moved to the buckle of his belt. "I know this is probably going too fast for you, but I can't wait any longer. I'll try not to hurt you."

Amanda was in such a daze that his words barely penetrated. She lay as he had left her on the bed, her legs parted, her breasts quivering, and watched him fumble with the fastening of his trousers and then kick them aside as they fell down his legs. She had just a brief glimpse of his nakedness, of the white bandage adorning his hips; just enough of a look at him to register vaguely that he was as hairy lower down as he was on top and that that thing was really as huge as it had felt. Then he was on the bed beside her, his arms sliding around her, his mouth crushing hers as his knees slid between her thighs. She no longer had any thought of denying him. She was drunk with passion, scarcely aware of where she was or who she was or anything else except the feel of his big body against her much smaller one. She felt the rasp of his body hair against her breasts and belly and thighs, and trembled; she felt the hardness of his shoulders under her hands, the sinewy strength of his thighs between hers, the shaking passion of his mouth on her own, and wanted to die from sheer bliss. Never had she experienced anything like it, or even dreamed it existed. Never had anything felt so wonderful.

Something hard and hot probed insistently at the softness between her thighs. It managed to wedge itself a little way inside, and Amanda squirmed, trying to escape it. It was annoying to be distracted in such a way when she was trying to concentrate on an elusive, pleasurable something that she sensed was almost within her reach. The thing poked at her again, harder this time, and Amanda had to arch her back to escape it. She knew Matt wasn't hurting her deliberately, but he was ruining the dazzling glow that his lovemaking had engendered in her. In fact, with that thing prodding her, she was barely able to enjoy the pleasure he was giving her with his hands and mouth . . . She had to tell him, or their lovemaking would be quite spoiled.

"Matt," she began breathlessly as his mouth fastened on the pulse at the base of her throat while his hands closed over her breasts. Not knowing quite how to put her problem into words, she moved her hips so that he would be able to feel what he was doing to her. To her amazement, the simple sideways movement made him gasp, and his hands tightened painfully on her breasts. Amanda's own hands flew to his wrists, seeking to ease the crushing pressure; she had opened her mouth to protest again when he surged against her with a groan. The thing that had been prodding and poking at her impaled her now, tearing through her flesh to embed itself deep inside her. The pain was so unexpected that Amanda screamed. Matt's mouth on hers swallowed the agonized cry, but he could not have mistaken the frantic squirming of her body beneath his as she fought to get away from him.

"You're *hurting* me," she cried into his mouth as she tore at his hair. But if he in fact heard, he ignored her, pinning her beneath him with the sheer weight of his body and pulling her head back with his hand in her hair as he took her mouth in deep kisses that should have drugged her pain but didn't. Then, when the first terrible pain began to recede and she was able to relax a little, he moved, thrusting into her again with a force that brought tears to her eyes.

"Let me *go*, Matt." She was beating against his shoulders with her fists as he thrust into her again and again. He did not slacken his movements, but he did reach up and capture her hands and force them down beside her head on the pillow. When she turned her head away from his kisses, he buried his face in her throat without altering by so much as a heartbeat the hard, driving rhythm of his movements.

Amanda stopped fighting, knowing that it was useless and that he would not release her until he had reached whatever goal he seemed to be striving for. Feeling his sweat drip down from his shoulders and chest onto her skin, hearing the impeded rasp of his breathing, seeing the dark flush that mottled his face as he surged over and in her, Amanda shuddered. When Susan had told of how her virginity had been taken from her, she had been too embarrassed to go into much detail. Amanda had imagined that the horror and pain her friend had described had been due to the fact that she had been forced into the act by strangers bent on degrading and defiling her. But now she herself had been hurt, although the pain was subsiding, and as Matt heaved and panted over her shrinking body Amanda felt degraded and defiled as well. If this repulsive act was what men and women did together, she wanted no part of it, she thought, biting her lip to keep an ignominious sob from bursting forth.

"Oh, *God*, Amanda." He thrust into her so hard then that she feared he must split her in two, then held himself inside her while a long shudder racked him. Amanda moaned in shame; he seemed to like that because his hands released hers to close about her, hugging her tightly to him. Amanda lay unmoving beneath him, stiff with anger and revulsion. It was some little time before at last Matt eased himself away from her.

chapter thirteen

"Christ, I'm sorry." Matt was lying beside her, leaning over her, his head propped on one hand while his other hand made a tentative gesture as though to wipe the tears from her cheeks. Amanda turned her face away from him, stonily regarding the wall, wishing with all the strength left in her that she could reach her night rail, a blanket, anything to shield her body from his eyes. Whereas before the thought of being naked with him had been oddly exciting, now it made her cringe.

"Amanda." His voice was insistent; his hand was insistent, too, as it captured her chin and forced her to look at him. His eyes flickered as they took in her mouth swollen from his kisses and the tear stains on her cheeks.

"You hurt me." The words were bitter, accusing.

Matt winced. "I know—I'm sorry." He let go of her

227

chin gently to brush away the tears that still dangled from her lashes. Amanda jerked her face away from him, and he dropped his hand. "I wouldn't have hurt you for the world, Amanda. But—I lost control."

"It was *horrible*."

He flinched. "It's always painful for a girl her first time, Amanda. But the next time, there won't be any pain, I promise."

"The *next* time." An almost hysterical laugh burst from her throat. "There never will be a next time—I *hated* it."

"And me?" The question was very quiet.

"What?"

"Before, you said you loved me. Have you changed your mind?"

Amanda stared up at him. He looked so big and dark, looming over her with the moon just touching his shoulder, making her shudderingly aware of his nakedness and strength, of the sinewy muscles of his shoulders and arms, of the thick black pelt that covered his chest and more—and of the thing that had done its best to rend her in two. It wasn't quite as hard and angry-looking now, she noticed before she jerked her eyes away.

"I don't want to talk about it." To tell the truth, she didn't know what she felt. At the time, she had been more certain of her love for him than she had ever been of anything in her life. But now—now she didn't know. And she didn't feel able to analyze her emotions at the moment.

"I see." He levered himself off the bed, uncaring of his nakedness, and reached for his trousers.

"Where are you going?"

"To sleep somewhere else, as I would have done earlier. Only, if I remember correctly, you wouldn't let me." There was bitter mockery in his voice. Amanda sat up, folding her arms over her breasts and raising her knees to her chin in an instinctive gesture of modesty, and glared at him. Her reward was a scornful glance as he turned his attention to fastening his trousers.

"That's an ungentlemanly thing to suggest."

"I'm not suggesting anything. I'm stating the plain truth, and you know it. You've been wanting me to make love to you for days. Haven't you heard the old saying about being careful what you wish for because you just might get it? Well, you wished for it—and you got it. I am not a monster who forced you to do something you didn't want to do."

"I didn't want to—you *know* I didn't. I *tried* to stop you."

He was shrugging into his shirt, closing the buttons with one hand as his mouth curled derisively at her.

"Only when it was too late, Amanda. Don't delude yourself. You were deliriously happy until the very end—until you decided that making love wasn't pleasurable anymore and you wanted to stop. Next time I suggest you pick a partner as callow as yourself. He just might manage to oblige you."

"Get *out* of here." Hurt and disillusionment combined with outrage at his remarks to make her furious. Her voice shook as she hurled the words at him. If she'd had anything to throw, she would have thrown it. As it was, hampered by the need to keep her arms over her breasts, she could only kill him with her eyes.

"I'll leave—immediately." He bent to pick up his shoes and hose, then padded barefoot toward the door. When he reached it, he turned to look at her. Even at that distance she could see the cold glint in his eyes and the hard set of his mouth. "Aren't you curious about where I'm going? There are quite a few people looking for me, remember. Or don't you care, now that you've found that your new toy isn't quite as much fun as you thought?"

"How *dare* you say that to me. You..." Indignation strangled her, and he cut her off smoothly.

"I'll tell you so you won't worry." The taunting voice made her long to scratch out his eyes. "I'm going back to the cave. Oh, yes, it's safe: I saw the smugglers' lights from the window earlier. By now they should have retrieved their cargo and gone. There's no need to distress yourself about what might happen to me."

"I don't give a *damn* what happens to you." The words fell far short of expressing the full extent of her rage. He had no right to say such things to her—and, anyway, why was he so angry? *She* was the one who had been hurt and shamed; *she* was the one who should be angry—and she was. "It would serve you right if they *did* catch you. Perhaps you've been lying to me and you really *did* kill those people. Hanging's probably too good for you, you...you...

"Don't you know a word that's vulgar enough?" His voice was harsh with mockery. "What a pity. I shall have to teach you some."

"*Oh.*" This time she did throw something: her

pillow. She snatched it and hurled it straight at his head. He caught it deftly in one hand, laughed shortly, and threw it back at her. Amanda clutched it with both hands as he left the room.

She glared at the closed door for some little time, curiously aware of feeling almost as hurt as she was angry. In the short time she had known him, Matt had become her dearest friend in the world, her father, brother, and confidant. Now he was her lover as well—and that had changed everything. She had trusted him implicitly, and he had hurt her. She had loved him, and he had responded by taking her body with an animalistic passion that still made her shudder to remember. He had said he'd lost control, but she had no idea what that meant. He had also said that it would be better the next time. Not that she intended a next time, but might he be right? Surely men couldn't force such a disgusting, degrading act on their wives for years if each time the hapless female suffered as she had tonight. Or maybe they could. In her experience most men were selfish at best, and would have little compunction about hurting a woman if in the process they themselves were pleasured.

One of her problems was resolved, however: now that she knew for certain exactly what the marriage act entailed, she would never consent to marry Lord Robert. If she had found Matt, who was certainly handsome and usually kind, bestial in his passion, how much worse it would be with someone like Lord Robert, whose plump body and slack mouth nauseated her. If she were honest, she would have to admit she had enjoyed the touch of Matt's hands, and the touch of his mouth as well. In fact, she had enjoyed everything he did to her—more than enjoyed it—until that final, unexpected possession had changed everything. She had never in her wildest dreams imagined that he would do that . . . Was that the way it was always done? If so, how did women stand it?

Amanda looked down at her nakedness, at the pale gleam of her breasts and belly and thighs, and wondered what there was about them that could make a normally very controlled man go wild as Matt had tonight. At the end, when he had plunged endlessly into her softness, she knew that he had had no thought of her. His one desire was to take what he wanted from her defenseless body . . .

There were brown smears on her thighs. Looking more closely, Amanda touched the drying spots and discovered to her horror that they were blood. For a bewildered moment she thought that Matt's wound must have broken open during the act and bled on her without her being aware of it, and then she realized that the blood was hers. She was *bleeding*. From the pain she had experienced she had guessed that he had injured her in some way, and now she had proof of it.

Panicked and furious, she got up off the bed to dab at the blood with a damp cloth. She wished that he were present so she could show him what he had done to her. Then it came to her that he already knew. Of course, this was her virgin's blood, her proof of purity meant to be proudly displayed before her husband on the morning after their wedding. Susan and the other girls had told her of this secret symbol of innocence, but she had never understood just how one produced blood on demand, or how that blood could prove anything at all. Now she realized that the man made his bride bleed by roughly tearing through her delicate tissues. How horrible, she thought, shuddering. Then the thought came to her that she was no longer a virgin and thus no longer eligible to become the bride of a respectable man. If anyone found out, she would be a social outcast, like Susan. Amanda felt a hard knot form in her stomach as she realized just what it was that she had done.

At least she no longer had to worry about being a wanton, she thought with a humorless smile. If nothing else, tonight's debacle had settled her doubts on that score. She hated the thing that men and women did together and had no desire to repeat it. Her father's blue blood must have prevailed.

By the time she had cleaned herself and was respectably clad in a fresh night rail, and had sponged the bloodstains from the sheet, she was as exhausted as she was heartsick. At least she didn't seem to be bleeding any longer, and she thanked God for small mercies. She hoped that He would not condemn her utterly for what she had done. However much she might wish to do so, she knew that she could not put all the blame on Matt for what had happened between them tonight. Susan had been forced to yield her virginity and thus, in the eyes of God, at least, was guiltless. She herself had been a willing, nay, an eager participant, at least until the very end. She had allowed Matt to take off her clothes, to touch and kiss her—had wanted him to, in fact. Would she burn in hell forever for that?

Her eyes were so heavy she could barely keep them open. Murmuring a brief plea for forgiveness, she threw the discarded covers on the bed and crawled beneath them. Perhaps things would look better in the morning; they could hardly look worse . . . Almost before her head touched the pillow she was asleep. Matt's dark face was the last image to float across her mind.

The next morning she overslept. No sooner had she become groggily aware of sunbeams slanting across her face than someone began shaking her shoulder. For one brief, happy moment she thought it was Matt. Then she remembered what had happened between them the night before, and realized that it wasn't likely to be him: he was angry at her for some reason she still didn't properly fathom. Besides, the small, soft hand shaking her so insistently could in no way be mistaken for Matt's hard grip . . .

"Amanda, *wake up*." It was Susan who was shaking her, Amanda discovered as she opened her eyes. "Mother Superior wants us all to come downstairs at once. The constable is here, and he's brought some of the local militia with him. They believe that there has been a man living here secretly, and now they're going to search the convent. Amanda, they think the man is that *murderer*, Matthew Grayson."

"*Oh, no*." Amanda sat bolt upright in bed, her eyes wide with alarm as she stared at Susan's excited face. Just in time she kept herself from blurting out anything more revealing. At all costs, she had to keep her wits about her to protect Matt. At the thought of their finding him and dragging him off to be hanged, Amanda felt her skin pale. Despite everything—the pain and shame he had caused her last night and the angry words later—she had to save him if she could...

"Yes, can you believe it?" Susan sounded almost awed. "They actually think that he's been hiding out here, at our convent. Of course, it's probably all a hum, but wouldn't it be exciting if it turned out to be true? Just think of it, a mass murderer skulking through the halls at night, hiding in the shadows... Why, he could have killed any of us." She shivered theatrically.

Amanda surveyed her friend with a jaundiced eye as she swung ler legs from beneath the covers and got out of bed. "You've been reading too many novels, Susan," she said tartly.

"I have *not*. You know we're not allowed to read novels." Susan sounded affronted. Amanda crossed to the washstand and splashed her face with water. Looking at her reflection, she was relieved to see that the bruise just below her cheekbone was not as noticeable as she had feared. It was nothing more than a faint, dark smudge. Susan hadn't even noticed it.

"Just because Becky's sister sent her *Glenarvon*," Susan continued a shade sulkily. Amanda wasn't listening. How could the authorities have found out about Matt? she wondered feverishly as she began to dress quickly. If the sisters or the girls had somehow discovered that she had been hiding him, she felt sure they would have let her know at once. But perhaps not. This was such a serious matter that Mother Superior may have felt that it could be properly handled only by the constable and his men.

Perhaps they knew everything, even had Matt already in custody, and were waiting downstairs until she appeared so that they could arrest her, too.

At the thought of being arrested and imprisoned, perhaps even beaten and tortured, as Matt had been, Amanda felt sick to her stomach. But Matt's fate would be even more horrible: he would be killed. At the thought of that long, strong body dangling at the end of a rope, his handsome face swollen and blackened, she was afraid for one hideous moment that she might throw up. And how would she explain that?

"You're doing up the buttons of your dress wrong: you've missed one," Susan said, breaking into her thoughts. Amanda silently said "damn," then struggled to undo what she had done. But it was difficult to match the tiny buttons behind her back properly when her hands were none too steady, and her heart felt as if it would pound through her chest at any moment. Susan saw her difficulty and clucked with disgust, then came over to help her with the recalcitrant buttons.

"Are you all right? You're sweating and your hands are shaking," Susan observed with concern. Amanda rolled her eyes heavenward—a gesture that Susan, who was standing behind her, couldn't see—and did her best to get a stern grip on herself. It would never do to arouse suspicion where none existed—*if* she was lucky.

"I-I think I'm coming down with something," Amanda improvised, thinking wryly that her association with Matt had certainly improved her ability to lie convincingly. "That's why I overslept. My head aches, and my stomach feels rather queasy." Which was true, for the exigencies of this dangerous situation had, in fact, caused her symptoms.

"Oh, that's too bad. Perhaps you should go back to bed. I'll tell Mother that you're ill. I'm sure she won't object if you don't come down in that case."

"*No.*" At her vehemence, Susan looked puzzled. Her buttons securely fastened, Amanda stepped away from her friend and began to brush her hair with hasty strokes. "I don't feel that bad. And I wouldn't want to miss the excitement," she tacked on, hoping the excuse sounded more reasonable to Susan than it did to herself.

Apparently it did. Susan didn't say anything else as Amanda began to braid her hair, thinking once again what a nuisance the thick mass was. But today it was especially annoying. She had to get downstairs as quickly as possible, so that she could determine more accurately what was going on. If the constable and his men didn't really know anything but were just here on a suspicion, she could slip away and warn Matt. Yes, she must warn him; if they were searching the convent, the cave would no longer be safe. Under the influence of all the excitement, someone was bound to remember its existence. She had to let Matt know, give him a chance to escape...

"Hurry up, Amanda. We're going to miss everything," Susan said impatiently. Amanda thrust pins into her hastily coiled hair, wincing briefly as one impaled her scalp. She *had* to go to Matt...

"I'm ready."

Susan needed no urging. Amanda took a deep,

steadying breath and followed her friend out the door.

The large front hall was so full of people that it resembled the square of the nearby town of Penzance on market day. Scarlet-coated militiamen milled about under the apparent direction of the heavy-set constable, whose plain buff coat and brown breeches set him apart from the men who were nominally under his command. The nuns in their black habits stood like a flock of crows near the entrance to the dining hall, watching the giggling, gray-clad girls as if they were so many kernels of corn. Apparently the girls weren't to be allowed to associate with the men.

"Come down, girls," Mother Superior called up to Amanda and Susan, who had stopped halfway down the stairs to stare at the unusual spectacle with wide eyes. When they had obediently joined the group of ladies, Mother Superior said to the constable, "You may proceed, Mr. Ives. But allow me to say that I think this affair is *ridiculous*." Her voice was stiff with disapproval.

"Sorry, Mother. We received word from an unnamed source that that fellow Grayson has been hiding here, and we must make a search. It's our duty, ma'am." Sweating with discomfort, his round face turning beet red, the constable turned to his men with palpable relief.

"Let's get on with it, then," he bellowed; then, with a sideways glance at Mother Superior, whose usually serene face expressed unmistakable outrage, he muttered, "Don't upset things any more than you have to, men."

As she watched the soldiers disperse in a somewhat haphazard manner—they seemed to go just where they liked, with no direction that she could perceive—Amanda's tense muscles relaxed slightly. It was clear they hadn't an inkling that she had helped Matt, and they weren't even sure that he was or had been in the convent. "An unnamed source" had told them to search the convent, and so they were. But if they found nothing, which they would with just a bit of divine intervention, they would go away again, and Matt would be safe—and, not so incidentally, so would she. But she had to manage to sneak away to warn Matt...

When Edward walked through the door, the first thing Amanda felt was harassed. She could not possibly cope with Edward and his threats—to say nothing of Lord Robert—at the moment. Then she realized that here was a possible diversion if she could just determine how to make use of him. Perhaps she could provoke him into an argument—admittedly not too easy a task in front of an audience, for Edward was careful to maintain the illusion of being a kind brother and gentleman. But then the solution occurred to her, and it did not involve Edward in the least. In fact, it was simple.

Casting a cold glance at Edward, who gave her a malevolent smile in return, Amanda moved to Sister Mary Joseph and whispered in her ear. As she had expected, the kindly nun nodded. Amanda started to quit the hall, only to be brought up short by Edward's hand on her arm.

"Going somewhere, little sister?" A slight smile was on his face for the benefit of the watching females, but Amanda looked up into his eyes and saw

239

the hatred there. She tilted her chin at him defiantly, determined that, if he frightened her, he would never know it.

"Like all of us, I must sometimes answer nature's call," she said haughtily, and tugged her arm free of his grip. He made no further attempt to hold her, which surprised Amanda. She supposed she could thank the presence of the nuns for his restraint.

"Go, then, but don't be long. We have a discussion to continue, you and I." Amanda did not reply but hurried from the room. From the corner of her eye she saw Edward turn away to say something to Jamison, his valet, who accompanied him everywhere. Her lip curled as she remembered that Edward liked the constant attentions of a personal servant. She thought of the discussion they would shortly have, and shivered. He was more than capable of striking her again . . . But for the moment she had to push all thoughts of Edward from her mind. Her first concern was to warn Matt.

The privy was in the back garden, situated a discreet distance from the convent and afforded even more privacy by the concealing shelter of a large pine. Amanda headed toward it only until she was sure she was out of sight, then, with a hasty look around to make certain she wasn't being observed, she picked up her skirts and sprinted for the stairs. She would have to be quick to get down to the cave and back without someone wondering what had taken her so long. Her feet practically sprouted wings as she flew down both sets of cellar stairs, thankful that her soft-soled slippers made no noise.

The trapdoor creaked. Oddly, she had never noticed

that until Matt had pointed it out, but now the sound seemed as loud as a gunshot. Wincing, Amanda let herself through, leaving it open behind her so she could return quickly. Warning Matt should take no more than a minute...

He was not in the cave. Amanda became convinced of that as she walked through the darkened rooms, calling his name in a voice that was as urgent as it was soft. Either he had already left—perhaps he had somehow learned of the intended search of the convent—or he was on the beach. But she had to make sure.

He was on the beach. Amanda saw him walking moodily along the shoreline some distance away, his dark head bowed and his hands thrust into his pockets. The morning sun striking blue sparks off the gleaming blackness of his hair would have fascinated her at any other time, but not today. She was furious at him for taking such a chance as to walk along the beach in broad daylight. Although it was usually deserted, there was always the possibility that someone else would have a like impulse. And *why* had he chosen this morning to be so reckless? She didn't dare call his name but ran toward him on silent feet as he continued to stroll with his back to her. He didn't hear her coming until she was almost upon him. Then he whirled, his stance wary, as if he were poised for battle. When he saw who it was he visibly relaxed, and his hands came out to grip her arms.

"*Matt ...*" She was panting so hard she had to draw a deep breath before she could continue. His eyes grew warm and faintly amused as they surveyed her flushed cheeks and the fiery tendrils of hair that had escaped the prim coronet to curl wildly about her face.

"In a hurry to make amends for the brutal way you treated me last night?" He was teasing, and she wanted to scream. How could he laugh when she was in such deadly earnest? Couldn't he read the agitation in her eyes? "Don't worry, Amanda. I'm quite ready to forgive you—if *you* can forgive *me*."

His tone became serious as he asked her to forgive him, and Amanda saw that, though he might have been joking about the rest, he meant that last. He sounded truly repentant . . . But there was no time now to savor the thought or to forgive him sweetly even if she had been so inclined, which to her surprise she found she was. She had to warn him . . . She drew a deep, shuddering breath.

"Matt, there's something I must tell you . . ." But he was no longer listening. He was staring over her shoulder in the direction she had come, and as she looked up at him his face hardened until it could have been carved from stone.

"Matt?"

He looked back at her. Amanda was startled to find that his eyes were ablaze with bitterness.

"You little bitch," he gritted, and his hands tightened around her arms until she gasped from the pain. Then he was thrusting her away from him and sprinting toward the water, running out into the waves.

"In the Queen's name, *stop*." A shot rang out at the same time as the cry, and Amanda whirled to see the constable thundering down the beach with four militiamen at his heels. One of the soldiers was clutching a smoking rifle while another stopped to jerk his weapon to his shoulder. Another shot rang out. Amanda heard a cry behind her and turned back just in time to see Matt topple headlong into the waves.

chapter fourteen

Amanda passed the next three days in a daze. She felt as if she were trapped in a waking nightmare. Matt was almost certainly dead, although with all their efforts at dragging the bay, the constable's men had not yet recovered the body. But she, and they, had heard the shot and Matt's agonized cry, and had seen him fall. The vicious undertow, known to lurk in the depths of the bay, could account for the absence of a body. The constable was well satisfied that it had been swept out to sea. As much as it pained Amanda to do so, she was slowly being forced to admit that it must be true. For, if not, where was Matt? Surely he would have come to her...

But perhaps not. After turning over and over in her mind his last furious words to her, Amanda had reluctantly come to the conclusion that he held her responsible for the presence of the soldiers on the beach. That he believed she had betrayed him, in fact. The thought that he might have died believing that made her sick at heart.

No matter whether Matt was dead or alive, she loved him. Amanda knew that love was the only thing that could account for the awful desolation she felt. The world, which had once seemed a bright and shining place full of endless possibilities, had faded to a uniform shade of gray. She could not eat or sleep or smile or cry. It was all she could do to get up from her bed in the morning, get dressed, and go through the motions each day. She was certain she wouldn't have been able to manage even that if she had not been terrifyingly conscious of eyes watching her every move, weighing her actions and demeanor. The question in the minds of everyone, from the constable to the girls and nuns, was, had she known that Matt Grayson was on the beach before she had gone there that day?

Edward alone knew the answer. In the first horrifying moments after Matt had been shot, when she had joined the soldiers in running out into the waves, Edward had appeared from the mouth of the cave and dragged her back. It was Edward who had insisted upon her innocence, Edward who had used his authority to save her from immediate arrest. If Amanda hadn't been so grief-stricken, she would have been astonished and disbelieving. As it was, she had been conscious of a mild softening in her feelings for him. He must care for her in some fashion after all, she thought dully, since he had gone to so much trouble to save her from jail.

In less than two hours he had disabused her of that

notion. When the constable had at last left her alone to return to direct the dragging of the bay, Edward had steered her into the same private parlor they had used for their previous talk. Once the door was closed behind them, he dropped all pretense of brotherly concern. Pushing her into a chair, he sneered as he informed her that he knew all about her disgraceful, immoral behavior and—what was worse, at least in the eyes of the law—how she had sheltered and protected an escaped felon. She could spend the rest of her life in prison if he told what he knew—if they didn't hang her in lieu of her lover.

Amanda had been too horrified to question how Edward had come by his knowledge. That he had, she accepted. And that he would have no compunction in betraying her to the authorities, she also accepted. Edward's hatred of her was too ingrained to allow for a sudden surfacing of affection or even of familial responsibility, as she would have known at once if her mind hadn't been fogged by grief.

In return for his silence, he demanded her immediate marriage to Lord Robert. If she showed the slightest hint of unwillingness and it put him off, or if she told her prospective bridegroom that she had made a whore of herself with a criminal, Edward would immediately turn her over to the authorities. He told her he would, relishing her helplessness. And she believed him.

The wedding was to take place Sunday week, in the little chapel at the convent. Since she was willing, Lord Robert saw no reason to wait, and Edward's urging was all that was needed to make him decide in favor of an immediate marriage. The banns were already being read; Amanda knew there was no escape, even if she had had the will, which she no longer did. If she protested in any way, she would be arrested, and her fate would be even more dreadful than marriage. If she tried to run away, it was almost inevitable she would be found and brought back. She could consider herself lucky that she was being allowed to remain here, among her friends, until the wedding. Amanda knew that was only because Edward thought that the presence nearby of the constable, who was already suspicious of her, would help to keep her in line.

She spent much time in her room as the wedding day drew inexorably closer. Mother Superior had relieved her of all her schoolwork and other duties, as she was soon to be married and leaving them. The other girls tended to regard her as if she had suddenly grown horns and a tail. Either they gigglingly demanded to be told what the murderer had been like, or they fell silent and looked guilty when she entered a room. Only Susan still treated her much the same, her obvious affection overlaid by a silent sympathy. Amanda was grateful for her friend's support, but she preferred her own company to Susan's. Confiding in Susan was a luxury she could not afford to indulge in, for Susan's sake as much as her own.

If she had not been so heartsore over Matt, Amanda's one consolation during that time would have been the acquisition of the skeleton of a wardrobe. So as not to be shamed by her obvious lack, Edward had been forced to pay for a simple wedding dress and a few other garments that would serve as a modest trousseau. Anything else she needed could be purchased after the wedding. Lord Robert assured her that it would be his pleasure to dress her properly once she was his wife and they had returned to London. At the reminder that she would soon be Lady Robert Turnbull, Amanda shuddered. The thought was enough to spoil even the slight pleasure she felt in the new clothes.

The first of the gowns for her trousseau had been delivered that day. After supper Amanda retired to her room and, for lack of anything else to occupy her thoughts, decided to try it on. She was still young enough, and feminine enough, to appreciate the softness and shimmer of primrose-yellow silk. It felt cool and slithery against her skin. Settling the gleaming folds of the full skirt about her feet, Amanda was suddenly conscious of how impossibly shabby her underclothes were. Although her pantalettes and petticoat and chemise were spotlessly clean, the unadorned white linen, with the discreet repairs to the fabric, looked almost pitiful against the elegance of the gown. Not that it mattered. There was no one to see her underclothes—at least, not yet. When they married, Amanda supposed that Lord Robert would want to see her in various stages of undress. Unlike Matt, he might be repelled by her poor clothes. Fiercely she hoped he would. Maybe her lack of finery would disgust him enough to keep him out of her bed.

Matt... Amanda could not swallow the lump that rose in her throat as she thought of him. His dark face rose before her in such sharp detail that she had to blink to make sure he wasn't there. But he wasn't— and was never likely to be again. She had to accept the near certainty that he was dead, and get on with her life. And Edward had killed him; she knew without being told that Edward was the "source" who had alerted the constable, perhaps had sent the soldiers after her onto the beach. How he had found out about Matt she had no idea; she knew only that she would hate Edward for the rest of her life.

Amanda gave up trying to get out of the dress. Her fingers were shaking so badly she found it impossible to free the few hooks she had managed to fasten. Instead, in an effort to soothe her painful thoughts, she picked up her brush and crossed to the window. She would watch the sea while she brushed her hair, and perhaps tonight, for the first time since Matt had disappeared, she would be able to sleep.

Tonight there was no moon. Only the rolling white-caps as the waves crashed to shore allowed her to separate sky from sea. Amanda slowly unpinned her hair and loosened the braids, then began to pull her brush through the waving thickness. The night was lonely, like herself, she thought, staring out into the inky darkness without really seeing much of anything. Cold and alone and lonely. She shivered.

A faint silvery flash caught her eye briefly, then vanished. A school of fish, probably, or one of the dolphins that occasionally came to frolic in the bay. But it was early yet for dolphins... The flash came again. Amanda strained to see through the darkness. When it was repeated a third time, she was sure. That flickering glimmer was not a school of fish or a dolphin but a light, perhaps from a lantern in the bow of a small boat. Most likely it was the smugglers, returned to the scene of their recent expedition earlier than usual. But perhaps it was Zeke Grayson, come for his brother, as Matt had seemed so sure he would. She had to find out. If it was Zeke, she owed it to Matt to try to contact him and tell him what had happened. And there was always the tiniest possibility that Matt might be alive, and Zeke might know it and tell her. Of course, if that was the case, Amanda realized with a resettling of the knot in her stomach, Zeke would hardly come here. Either he had no knowledge of Matt's fate or he had come to find and claim the body.

Amanda shook off the horrible thought as the light glimmered once more, then vanished. The boat, whatever it was, whoever was in it, must now be fairly close to shore, for the overhanging cliff hid it now from her sight. She had to hurry if she was to catch it . . .

Amanda sped around the end of her bed, barely pausing to slip on her flat black slippers before hurrying from the room. Moments before, the ringing of the bell had signaled the girls to extinguish their candles, and now the convent was dark. The easiest, most convenient way to the beach was through the cave, but Amanda shivered with distaste as she thought of making even one more journey into its cold darkness. For her, it would always be haunted with memories of Matt; to go that way would be to increase her pain tenfold. Besides, the practical part of her cautioned, it was just possible that the constable had stationed one of his men down there, on the off chance that Matt had survived and might return . . .

She would go along the cliffs and down the path. This route would be longer but less harrowing in her present state of mind. Until she determined who was in the boat, she would stay well out of sight. How she was to recognize Zeke or his men Amanda had no idea; but, she reasoned, if it wasn't the smugglers, it almost had to be someone coming for Matt. Nocturnal visitors were a rarity in Lands End.

It was a cold night. The wind was the first thing Amanda noticed as she let herself out through the back garden. She shivered, clutching her arms around herself for warmth, reminded irresistibly of the night she had first discovered Matt on the beach. The wind had been blowing then as now . . . But she had been dressed in a long-sleeved wool dress, and now she was wearing a frivolous concoction of pale yellow silk, with little puffed sleeves that left most of her arms bare and a lace-edged neckline that revealed her shoulders and the tops of her creamy white breasts. Only her long, thick hair provided even a modicum of warmth, but suddenly the wind caught it and whipped it out behind her back like a crimson banner.

She had to bend her head against the wind as she hurried along the top of the cliffs. It was blowing in bursting gusts that Amanda suspected presaged a storm before morning. Whoever was out on the bay in the small boat would be well advised to take shelter before the wind increased.

She could no longer see a flashing light on the bay. Either the boat had reached shore or it was running without a light—dangerous in a sea like tonight's. But perhaps she was imagining things, and the silvery flash she had seen had been only a leaping school of fish.

It was so dark she could barely see a foot ahead of her. Instead of staring down at the bay to watch for the reappearance of the light, as her every instinct urged her to do, she was forced to watch where she put her feet. At this height, so close to the edge, one misstep could be fatal. The short brown grass beneath her feet provided fairly even walking, but she knew that in a few places treacherous rocks protruded nearly invisibly from the ground. And if she should trip...

The path could not have been more than a few yards ahead of her when she first heard it: a creaking sound not in keeping with the wind-born noises of the night. Her head jerked up and her eyes peered suspiciously at the darkness around her, but she could see nothing. Still, she could not shake an uneasy feeling that something was out there with her, watching her.

She was being fanciful, and she knew it. What she had heard could have several explanations: a creaking branch, say, or a cricket. No matter what she told herself, however, the sense of not being alone stayed with her, refusing to be shaken off.

As she drew closer to the path her speed increased until she was practically running. If there was something abroad in the night, it would not be able to follow her down that steep, winding trail unless it was a mountain goat—or a ghost. The latter thought raised prickles on the back of Amanda's neck. Could it be a ghost, Matt's ghost, feeling betrayed and seeking vengeance?

Pure, unreasoning terror rose like bile in her throat. She was not alone—she knew it. Someone, or something, was right behind her. She whirled, tripping over the hem of her skirt in her panic, and felt herself falling backward only to be brought up short as a man's hard arm grabbed her around the waist.

She screamed. Or, at least, she tried to, but a thick, broad hand smelling faintly of turpentine clapped painfully over her mouth, stopping the sound. She tried to kick, to hit out, but to her horror her feet were caught and roughly bound, then her hands were bound, too, behind her back. The ropes were tied tight, as if whoever it was didn't care if he hurt her. She could feel the bonds cutting off the circulation to her hands and feet... The hand was removed from her mouth. She opened her mouth again to scream, only to have a smelly, oily-tasting rag thrust between her teeth, choking her. She gagged and tried to spit out the loathsome piece of cloth, but it was already being tied securely in place.

A light flared in front of her as someone struck a match. It came to her then that there was more than one of them, whoever they were. As the man holding the match used it to light a lantern and then lifted it high over his head, Amanda saw that there were three of them: three big, burly men dressed in rough clothes with faces in varying degrees of unshavenness. In one respect, however, they were identical. They were all staring down at her with an expression that, she recognized with a shock, bordered on hatred.

Amanda was still trying to come to terms with that when the lantern was abruptly doused. The man who had been holding her against his chest swung her up in his arms, and from there to his shoulder, where she was left to hang facedown, like a sack of meal.

With one of his partners in skulduggery in front and the other behind, they moved off, their pace becoming slower and more cautious as they headed down the path to the beach.

Amanda's head throbbed painfully as blood rushed to it; her stomach felt as if a knife were lodged in it from the pressure of the man's hard shoulder on which it rested; her feet and hands had lost all feeling; and she was shivering with cold. But she was scarcely aware of these physical discomforts. One thought occupied her mind to the exclusion of all else: who were these men, and what did they mean to do with her?

She could do nothing while they were on the path, no matter how intense her terror, for she would only precipitate her own end. If she kicked or otherwise struggled, she might succeed in knocking her abductor off the path—but she would go with him to certain death. Bound hand and foot as she was, she had no chance of escape. The rational part of her mind recognized that. But still she strained her eyes and ears to gather all the information she could. If she could learn who these men were, it might help her to prepare for what lay ahead.

At last they were safely on the beach. Amanda closed her eyes in relief.

"You sure she's the right one?" Amanda despaired as her abductors were joined by a group of three men. It was one of the newcomers who spoke.

"Yeah." A rough hand caught at her hair, holding it out from her head. A match flared. "Look at that hair. There can't be two up there with hair like this."

A grunt signified the other man's agreement. The

match went out. Amanda lay deathly still, hoping they would think she had fainted and perhaps leave her alone. Apparently they had been looking specifically for her. But *why*? Her heart throbbed sickeningly as she pondered that question.

"Did you signal the boat?"

"Yes. Up there on the cliff. It should be here soon."

They were standing at the water's edge. Amanda could feel the nervous movements of the man holding her as he occasionally turned to look over his shoulder. From the faint crunch of booted feet against the shale, Amanda deduced that the other men were similarly uneasy.

"Here she comes."

The faint slap of oars on water told Amanda that a boat was approaching. Obviously they were expecting it—and equally obviously it was the same boat whose light she had seen from her window when it had come ashore to drop the men off. Why had she not stayed safely put instead of haring outside like an irresponsible child? And why did she always ask herself these questions too late?

The boat must have been near shore, because the men were wading into the water. Amanda jumped as a surging wave sprayed her head with cold water.

"Easy, now," the man holding her growled, and placed his hand on her rump to steady her. At the familiarity of his touch, Amanda's instincts took over. She jerked frantically, trying to free that most personal part of her anatomy from his hand. When that didn't work, she lifted both her bound feet and kicked him squarely in the stomach. The man cursed and flinched. To her horror Amanda felt herself slide off his shoulder and land in the water with a tremendous splash.

Amanda struggled frantically, but the cold water closed over her head and, bound as she was, she could not seem to find the surface. She was sinking, sinking—she would surely drown . . . But then something caught at her hair, jerking her head free of the water. The pain was intense, but Amanda was so glad to be able to breathe again that she was almost grateful for it. She sucked in a deep, shuddering gulp of air—and was simultaneously scooped from the water by a pair of strong arms.

"Christ, man, you weren't supposed to *drown* her. Can't you hold on to a little-bitty thing like this?" The voice was younger than the others', and the face was younger, too, from what Amanda could see of it in the darkness and with the water streaming across her face. She could taste salt from the sea on her lips, feel the bite of the wind as it traveled over her soaked body . . .

"The little she-devil kicked me." The man who had been carrying her earlier spoke with a strong sense of ill-usage. Another man guffawed; the sound was quickly muffled. The men's movements increased in tempo, as if they were anxious to be gone.

Then Amanda was dumped unceremoniously into the gunwale of a small boat. The six men heaved themselves in after her while the two manning the oars began to pull away from shore. Sitting upright, her arms clutched around herself in a futile effort to control her shivering, Amanda got her first good look at the men who had abducted her—and what she saw struck fear into her heart.

They looked like pirates. They were all cut from the same cloth, hard-bitten men ready to cut a man's throat as easily as lend a hand at the oars. And she was at their mercy. Her shivers intensified as she wondered once again what they had in store for her.

"Peake, pass me your nor'wester. Much as I'd like to give her pneumonia, I don't reckon we'd better."

"Aye, sir."

So the younger man, the one who had scooped her out of the water, was addressed as "sir." Amanda pondered the significance of that as he dropped a burly wool coat over her shoulders and carelessly fastened a couple of buttons up the front to hold it in place. He said nothing to her, didn't even look at her, in fact. Amanda felt that he disliked her intensely, but for what reason she couldn't fathom.

No one spoke to her as the men took turns at the oars, pulling strongly for the open sea. Rowing against the incoming tide was hard work under the best of conditions, Amanda knew. Tonight, with the waves whipped into frothy peaks and an icy wind blowing in from the sea, it was doubly difficult. The men labored silently for the most part, with only an occasional muttered remark filtering to her ears over the lapping of the waves and the whistling of the wind.

She was left alone and unguarded in the gunwale. Amanda wondered at that briefly, then realized they were confident she couldn't escape. And they were right. Although she could swim, it would be suicide to throw herself into the sea bound hand and foot. And no matter what fate they had planned for her, she knew she was not prepared to end her life rather than risk it. Death was the ultimate horror; she couldn't think of anything they could do to her that wasn't preferable to that.

The boat was passing the point, nearing the open sea. As the last bit of land receded, Amanda's fears increased. The seas were rough, and growing rougher with every passing moment. The small boat bucked up and down like a child being bounced on its father's knee. If she had eaten anything at all in the last few hours, Amanda knew she would have been ignominiously sick. As it was, her stomach churned in protest, but the emptiness prevented outright nausea. None of the men seemed affected. She supposed they were all used to this never-ending pitch and roll. But far worse than being seasick, even with a gag in her mouth, which might cause her to choke to death, was the fear that they would capsize at any moment. Boats of this size weren't meant to take on the full fury of an angry sea. If they did not reach their destination soon, be it land or a ship anchored well outside the bay, she did not like to think of what the probable outcome would be. The men might just manage to make it back to shore, although, unless they were exceptionally strong swimmers, she doubted it. She herself, bound hand and foot, would certainly drown.

When the dark outline of a three-masted ship appeared on the horizon, Amanda nearly sagged with relief. She would rather face anything than be pitched headlong into the sea.

The men brought the small boat alongside the much larger ship with practiced ease. Amanda was forced to admire their skill: it was no easy task in tonight's seas. A flurry of activity on the deck high above them announced that they had been spotted. Ropes were tossed down to them. Peake, the man who had given her his coat, and another man secured the ropes at bow and stern, elbowing Amanda aside in the process. When that was done, the ship hands dropped a rope ladder. Before Amanda had time to do more than blink, she was scooped off the gunwale and into the strong arms of "sir."

"Kick me, missy, and you can play patty-cake with Pluto for all I care," he warned grimly, then tossed her up over his shoulder and proceeded to climb the ladder. After one horrified look into the swirling black water below, Amanda shut her eyes. And was very careful not to give him the least excuse to drop her.

In what was actually a very short time, though it seemed long to Amanda, they were on the deck. Instead of putting her down, as Amanda had expected, and helping his men raise and secure the small boat, which she thought from overheard remarks might be called a gig, he strode along the deck with her in the same ignominious position over his shoulder. Amanda was too miserable to wonder where he was taking her or for what purpose. Her hands and feet were numb, the ropes around her wrists and ankles cut into her soft flesh painfully, she was soaking wet and icy cold, and her stomach, besides churning wildly, felt as if it were badly bruised. She only hoped that wherever he was taking her was warm and dry. Everything else she would worry about later.

Dangling upside down as she was, she did not

have the best view of the ship, although she did register that it seemed large and that an inordinate number of men were bustling about the deck. Amanda caught fleeting glimpses of coils of rope, partially opened hatches, and booted feet. Then her abductor paused to shoulder through a door; they were inside a small cabin, Amanda deduced, though she could see only part of the floor and the lower half of the door.

"Well, I have your red-haired she-devil," the man carrying her announced cheerfully. "Where do you want her?"

And without waiting for a reply flung her on the floor.

chapter fifteen

A man rose from a straight-backed chair that had been pulled up to a small table. From her vantage point on the floor, Amanda's eyes touched first on gleaming Hessian boots, then slid slowly up long, muscular legs clad in superbly fitting buff-colored pantaloons, to a hard waist and broad chest covered by a spotless white shirt made of fine linen and lace. Her gaze traveled upward to wide shoulders—then her eyes widened with shock as they registered the dark, masculine splendor of that face. *Matt*. She would have cried his name out loud, but the gag prevented her from making any sound more intelligible than a moan.

"What happened?" Incredibly, Matt didn't seem concerned at finding her, soaking wet, bound, and gagged, at his feet. He made no move to approach her or to remove the bonds that cut into her soft flesh. Amanda's eyes were huge purple pools as she stared up at him disbelievingly. It *was* Matt, wasn't it? The face and body were the same, but she had never seen him so richly clad before—and she had never dreamed that those silver-smoke eyes could regard her so icily.

"She kicked Grumman in the gut," the man who had carried her replied negligently. Amanda didn't look at him; her eyes were riveted on Matt's face. It was Matt, without a doubt. Why, then, was he making no move to come to her aid? "He—uh—was taken by surprise and dropped her."

"In the sea, by the look of her." There was no doubt that that was Matt's voice discussing her plight in that cold, dispassionate tone. Amanda wanted to scream. What ailed him? He looked like a stranger— a cold, frightening stranger.

"Yes." The other man's agreement was laconic. Amanda's eyes left Matt for just an instant to touch on the stranger's face. It was narrower than Matt's, with a longer nose and chin, and the eyes were hazel instead of silver and the hair was rusty brown. But there was something that was similar, more in facial expression and voice inflection than any physical resemblance. This man was tall, too, nearly as tall as Matt, and though he bordered on being thin, she knew from her own experience with him that he possessed a whipcord strength...

"Thanks, Zeke." Matt confirmed what she had begun to surmise. This, then, was his brother—the younger brother he had been so sure would come for him... "You can get on about your business. I want to catch the tide."

Zeke looked from Amanda to Matt. His lips compressed. "Are you sure you want to take her with us? If you ask me, she's going to be a peck more trouble than she's worth."

Matt smiled tigerishly. "Oh, yes, I'm sure. Amanda would be heartbroken if I left her behind, wouldn't you?" It was the first remark Matt had addressed directly to her; Amanda felt sick at the harsh derision. This cold, hard, angry man was not her Matt... Her eyes must have conveyed her bewilderment to him because his smile widened and became tinged with hateful mockery.

"You're the boss." Zeke was clearly none too happy with his brother's decision, but just as clearly he was not going to argue about it. He turned toward the door. Matt's voice stopped him.

"Have a couple of the men bring in that old hip bath and some hot water. Milady here looks a tad bedraggled. And that will never do at all—not for what I have planned for her."

Zeke nodded once in reply, then left the cabin, closing the door behind him. Amanda was left to stare apprehensively at Matt—a Matt altered almost beyond recognition.

"Well, well, Amanda—how lovely to see you again." His voice was laced with an awful affability as he came to stand behind her, then knelt to work the knot on the gag. "A most unexpected surprise—for you. As for myself, I must admit that I've been anticipating this meeting for some days—ever since I had to swim for miles to escape the little party you had arranged for me."

265

The gag was loosed at last. Amanda spat out the crumpled rag, then ran her tongue around dry lips.

"You can't believe I planned that," she croaked, swinging her head around so she could look at him. He was kneeling, his head bent as he labored to undo the knot that bound her wrists. At her words his eyes came up to meet hers. They were as cold as the sea in winter.

"Can't I?" The tone was silky. "Oh, I believe I can. You told me yourself that no one else knew of the way to the cave through the convent. And following hard upon your latest temper tantrum... Yes, I can believe it—and I do."

"It was *Edward.*" Her words were despairing, for he clearly was convinced of her guilt. But why should he so readily believe the worst of her? "Matt, it *was* Edward. Somehow he learned where you were and told the authorities. They were searching the convent that morning. That's what I came down to the beach to tell you—only I never got the chance. I didn't think anyone saw me go there, but I *must* have been followed."

"Like hell." For just an instant something ugly blazed in his eyes. Then the fire was once again swallowed by ice. He smiled unpleasantly. "Allow me to congratulate you on the improvement in your ability to tell lies. Except for a bit of overacting—barely noticeable, I assure you—that was really quite good."

"Matt, I'm telling you the truth—I *swear* it."

"I don't believe you." Her hands were freed, and she brought them forward to rub them together, absently trying to restore the circulation. His voice

266

had been brutal, final. She was very much afraid she would be unable to change his mind.

"Matt..." She was determined not to give up. He *had* to believe her. She loved him, had thought she would die when she believed he was dead. At least, she loved the Matt she thought she knew. This icy stranger with the blazing eyes terrified her.

A brief knock on the door interrupted her before she could say anything else. Matt called out a brief assent, and the door opened to allow two burly seamen to enter the room. One was carrying a battered tin hip bath; the other held two buckets of steaming water. Wet and cold as she was, Amanda would have welcomed the sight of the bath at any other time, but now she was too preoccupied with convincing Matt.

"Matt..." she began. He was in front of her now, pushing her sodden skirt out of the way as he worked to free her ankles. Her hand came out to touch his shoulder beseechingly. He shrugged away from her touch, and Amanda winced as her unwanted hand fell to the floor.

"If you insist on continuing with that imbroglio of lies, I suggest you wait until we're alone. My men aren't too kindly disposed toward you, and it wouldn't take much to persuade one of them to tip you quietly over the side. Unlike you, they're intensely loyal."

The words were said so quietly that Amanda didn't think the seamen, one of whom was busy filling the tub with water, heard. But the very softness of his voice made it seem all the more menacing. He talked as if he hated her—and, looking into those glittering eyes, Amanda began to be very much afraid he did.

She was obediently, despairingly silent as the sailors finished their task. Matt meanwhile freed her feet, and she occupied herself with rubbing life back into her numbed limbs while he rose to stand towering above her, his hands jammed in his pockets.

"Anything else, Captain?" The tub was full now, and the men were gathering up the empty buckets and moving toward the door. They paused to look respectfully back at Matt.

"That's all, thank you." His tone was abrupt, but the sailors didn't seem to be offended. Taking his words as dismissal, they left the cabin. Amanda was once more alone with Matt—and the thought made her shiver.

"Matt..." she began again, swiveling so she could look up at him. He loomed above her like a mountain while she huddled, shivering and dripping, at his feet, not sure whether her limbs retained sufficient strength to support her if she should try to stand. She never had a chance to try, for, ignoring her attempt at speech, he stooped and caught her under the armpits, lifting her to her feet. Amanda hung swaying between his steadying hands, gripping his forearms for support. His mouth twisted with an emotion Amanda couldn't quite recognize. Perhaps it was nothing more than distaste at her sodden state. She was making quite a puddle on the highly polished floor.

"Can you stand?"

Amanda nodded. "I think so."

The supporting hands were withdrawn. Amanda found that she could, indeed, stand, but that she was shivering so hard from the cold her teeth chattered.

"Strip off." The words were harsh, the tone almost brutal. Amanda, clenching her teeth as she felt another spasm of shivers, could only stare at him in disbelief. Surely he couldn't mean that terse command? Even angry as he was, he surely couldn't expect her to submit meekly to the humiliation of undressing in front of him?

"Did you hear what I said?" The bite in his voice made her jump.

"You can't be serious," she managed at last in what she hoped was a reasonable manner. His lip curled, and he shoved his hands in his pockets as if he were having trouble keeping them from shaking her.

"Why can't I? If you're planning to claim maidenly modesty, don't. I've seen every inch of your delectable white skin—and you're no maiden."

"That's a *horrible* thing to say." She was staring at him, her eyes wide with hurt.

"But true." He smiled. Amanda feared the look in his eyes. It seemed predatory, like a wolf's glare. "Will you take off your clothes, or must I do it for you? My plans for you don't include having you die of pneumonia—at least, not yet."

Amanda gave up. From the look on his face, he meant what he said. Either she took off her clothes or he would. And she didn't want his hands on her, not while he was in his present mood. He might take it into his head to exact vengeance—in the most primitive way—for her supposed betrayal of him.

"I will." His eyes glinted at her, as though her capitulation both pleased and annoyed him. As Amanda reached behind her back to feel for the fastenings of her dress, the thought came to her that he would have enjoyed forcing her to his will.

The silk was cold, wet, and slippery. Amanda struggled with the few hooks she could reach, separating no more than two from their eyes. After watching her lack of progress for some little time in brooding silence, Matt made a harsh sound under his breath and caught her by the arms, turning her so that her back was to him. She flinched at the touch of his hands on her back as he began to manipulate the hooks. Her hair was dripping icy water down her back, and with an impatient sound he threw it over her shoulder.

"A lovely dress," he said, sneering, as he apparently noticed her changed apparel for the first time. "How did you acquire it—with your thirty pieces of silver?"

"*No.*" Amanda started to turn toward him, only to be stopped as his hands tightened savagely over the material at her back. There was a loud tearing sound as the material separated under his fingers. "Matt, *no. Stop it.*" He was ripping the gown from her body, his face dark with blood as the ugly fire that had blazed at her earlier returned to his eyes. Ignoring her protests and frantic attempts to get away, he tore the dress until it was little more than a rag lying in tatters around her feet. She stepped quickly away from him, clad only in her chemise and pantalettes, both of which were sopping wet and did little to conceal her body from his gaze. Wrapping her arms defensively over her breasts, she stared at him from a distance of five feet. Dark blood still suffused his face; his hands were clenched into fists at his sides as he fought to regain control.

"Undress and get into that tub—now." The words were growled from between clenched teeth. Amanda hesitated, sorely tempted to do as he said and warm her frozen body in the water that steamed enticingly, but she was both afraid and embarrassed to take off the rest of her clothes in front of him. In his present mood, rape was not beyond him, and even if he didn't descend to that level of violence, she didn't want him to look at her—not like this. Before, when he had made her naked, it had been an act of passion if not of love. Now it would be just one more method of punishing her. She could read in his eyes his desire to humiliate her.

"Amanda, if you're not out of those clothes in the next minute, I'll tear them off you."

There was no doubt that he meant it. Amanda looked into that dark, implacable face, saw the harsh set of the beautifully cut mouth and the steely color of his eyes, and felt more afraid of him. Always before, he had been quick to laugh, to smile at her. She realized she had never seen him truly angry— until now. Now he was furious; the knowledge made her heart pound.

Before he could carry out his threat, she began to remove her soaked underclothes. Better not to risk a repetition of his violence. But her hands were shaking, from cold or fright, and the tapes to her petticoat were wet. What had once been a bow had now become a knot, and she couldn't untie it for the life of her. She struggled with it, despairing, while violent shivers racked her. When she heard him rap out

271

an impatient oath, she jumped. He was walking toward her, his stride quick and menacing, and he held a long-bladed knife in one hand.

Amanda uttered a choked cry and would have cringed away from him, but he caught her by one arm and held her still as his knife sliced through the sodden knot. Her petticoat immediately dropped to lay in a soggy heap around her feet. Pulling her free of it, he folded the knife and put it back in his pocket. Then his hands were at her waist, stripping off her dripping pantalettes, leaving her standing in nothing but her chemise.

"Matt, I can do it." Amanda tried to speak calmly, not wanting to provoke him further. He ignored her, catching the hem of her chemise and lifting the icy-wet garment over her head. Her words of protest were muffled by the folds of cloth. Then he was flinging the chemise aside, and she was left standing before him with nothing but her dripping hair to preserve her modesty. She wrapped her arms over her naked breasts, blushing furiously as she tried to look everywhere but at his face. He was looking at her, she knew. She was all too aware of the heat of those metallic eyes as they moved over her body.

"Matt . . ." Whatever she had intended to say died in her throat as he took a step toward her and scooped her up in his arms. Her head fell back against his wide shoulder as he held her against his chest. He seemed not to care that her hair was soaking his shirt. Amanda quivered as his eyes roamed insolently over her body, lingering on her breasts, which had grown rigid with cold, and her bare, slender thighs. Then he was lowering her without ceremony into the tub. A muscle jumped convulsively in his jaw as he moved away.

Amanda watched that broad back as he walked away from her to rummage in a sea chest pushed against one wall. The hot water was wonderfully warming, and one part of her mind acknowledged its comfort, but the rest of it concentrated on Matt, and what he meant to do next.

"Can you bathe yourself, or do you want me to do that, too?"

He had turned back to look at her, with a cake of soap in one hand and a towel in the other.

"I can do it." Her voice was low, her eyes wide with appeal as she looked at him. If anything, her expression made his own harden. Clearly he was determined to believe the worst of her—and while she was sitting naked in a bath, vulnerable and defenseless, was not the ideal time to try to persuade him otherwise. She would get warm first, and clean and dry, and then she would try again to convince him of her innocence. It couldn't be that difficult. The Matt she had come to know was kind and fair, and at the very least fond of her. He had to listen, and believe...

"Don't be all night about it. You and I have some business to attend to, milady." There was that sneering mode of address again. Amanda's lips tightened, but it was not difficult to restrain her own quick temper. She had never been a fool, and it would be foolish to lose it now; in a confrontation with Matt, she was bound to lose. She cast a quick, apprehensive look at him. He was walking toward her, the soap and towel in either hand. When he was perhaps a foot from where she sat in the tub, he tossed the soap to her. Taken by surprise, she missed, and had to scrabble around the bottom of the tub for the slippery cake.

"Are you certain you don't want me to scrub your back?" His jeering question made Amanda flush, and she looked at him quickly. He had walked back to reseat himself in the straight-backed chair. Only this time he tilted the chair against the wall so that it balanced on its two back legs. One hand was in his pocket and the other idly drummed the tabletop as he watched her. Amanda flushed under that mocking perusal, supremely aware that the shallow water left her body from the waist up clearly visible to him. And from the expression on his face, he was intent on enjoying the sight.

"You make me feel like a . . . a wanton," she said, voice quivering, then could have bitten her tongue out. She had not meant to say the words aloud. As she had suspected he would, he looked pleased at her discomfiture. That long mouth twisted into a nasty, mocking smile.

"If the shoe fits . . ." he said softly. Amanda stared at him in angry disbelief, her soft lips trembling with hurt, her eyes huge with reproach. With her long, water-darkened hair trailing around her in the water, its sodden state making it of very little use in hiding her charms from him, she looked like a mermaid. Or a siren. One of those deadly sea sirens who sang so prettily until they lured besotted sailors to their graves . . .

"Take your bath. And hurry. I'm not feeling very . . . patient now." He watched her from beneath half-lowered lids as he added this last. Amanda flushed, for his meaning was unmistakable. He meant to force her to endure another of those degrading, painful performances with him.

"Matt, why are you acting like this? You *must* know that I didn't betray you. We were friends, Matt—at least I thought we were."

"Is that how you would describe what we were to each other, milady? Now, I would have said we were lovers—and that you didn't like having a lover. Oh, you liked the kisses and the caresses, but when we arrived at the consummation, it wasn't quite genteel. So you decided to put the memory—and me—behind you in the most effective way you could think of. Do you have any Borgia blood in your veins? I wonder. If I remember correctly, that family boasted a lady who rid herself of unwanted men by killing them off."

"Matt, that's *not true*." She was glaring at him and beseeching him at the same time. His mouth twisted into a snarl, and his eyes glittered as the front legs of the chair hit the floor with a bang. He was on his feet, glaring at her as if he hated her. Amanda cringed.

"Finish your bath," he gritted. "And be silent. If you say another word, I won't be responsible."

Amanda watched, biting her lower lip, as he took a quick, angry turn about the small cabin. Temper emanated from him in waves. It came to her then that Matt Grayson was a dangerous man when he was angry—and she had made him very angry indeed. Prudently deciding to say nothing more for the moment, she began to soap herself.

She worked the soap over her arms and shoulders

and breasts and belly, then extended first one long, slender leg and then the other to be lathered. Throughout, she felt Matt's eyes on her, his gaze growing hotter and angrier with every new movement. But she refused to look at him. Bathing in front of him this way was humiliating in the extreme, and it would be made even more so if she acknowledged that he was watching. But she could not prevent the blush that spread from her face to her neck and even to her breasts. The usually pale peaks were rosy and glowing... Amanda saw a trickle of soapy water run down the slope of one breast to dangle from the nipple, and she absently wiped it away. Then, compelled by instinct, she looked up to find Matt's eyes fixed on her, their expression unnerving. His jaw was clenched so tightly that a nerve jumped at the corner of his mouth. His hands were balled into fists at his sides, the knuckles whitened by the force of his grip.

"You've had long enough. Get out," he ordered tersely, his eyes, with that same frightening expression, never leaving her body.

"Matt..." Now was the time to try to reach him, if there was ever to be a time. Now, before he got his hands on her body, as she could read in his eyes that he meant to do. But he didn't give her a chance. At the wide-eyed fear in her expression, the soft appeal in her voice, his mouth twisted savagely. He crossed the floor in two quick strides, catching her under the armpits to haul her dripping and still partially covered with soap to stand before him. His eyes raked her contemptuously, the sneer not quite able to hide the desire. Amanda shrank from him, twisting to try to preserve as much of her modesty as she could, but he wouldn't let her go. One hand bit into the soft flesh of her upper arm while the other caught up the towel and ran it roughly down her body. To her shame, the abrasion of the rough material made her nipples harden. He laughed as he saw her body's involuntary response, and tweaked one nipple insolently. Amanda cried out at the sudden touch that was almost painful, and her eyes flew to meet his. What she read in them made her knees tremble.

"Matt, please, don't," she breathed, shivering at the thought of being taken by him in anger. Before, when he had been kind and gentle with her, it had been a horrible, disgusting experience. What would it be like now, when he hated her, and seemed bent on proving it?

"Oh, yes, you're the little virgin who decided she didn't like making love," he said, smiling unpleasantly at her as he stopped drying her body to wind the towel around her hair. "Isn't that unfortunate?"

"Matt, *please.*" She was begging, shamelessly, terrified by what she read in his eyes. He meant to deliberately hurt and humiliate her.

"Not this time," he snarled softly. "*This* time I mean to please *me.*"

And he picked her up in his arms.

Amanda lay as still as death as he carried her to the bunk, which was built into the far wall. He wanted her to struggle, she realized, so he could have the pleasure of taming her. If she fought him, it would only inflame him further. She knew that instinctively.

"What, no maidenly protest?" He was mocking her, his silver-smoke eyes gleaming at her nastily, his arms like iron bands around her as he held her close against his muscular chest. She could feel the heat and strength of him through the fine linen of his shirt, feel the flexing muscles of his arms as he lowered her to the bunk and sat beside her, his hands on either side of her, imprisoning her. Her eyes were huge purple pools of fright as she stared up at him. He smiled tauntingly.

"Matt, won't you please listen?" Her teeth were chattering, from fear this time instead of cold. The fate he intended for her was too horrible to contemplate. She remembered the stabbing pain that had felt as if it would rip her in two, and shuddered. If she didn't convince him of her innocence now, at once, it would be too late... "I didn't betray you, Matt." She spoke slowly, as if to a child. "I swear it. It was Edward."

"Say any more, and I just might strangle you." His voice was almost pleasant, but it was belied by both the ominous glitter of his eyes and the savage snarl that revealed most of his white teeth. Terrifying in their slowness, his hands moved to unwind the towel from about her head and drop it to the floor. Then he began to spread out her still-damp hair across the pillow...

He wasn't listening, wasn't going to listen, Amanda realized with a sick feeling at the pit of her stomach. His face wore that absorbed, almost blind look of passion that she had seen on it only once before, when he had forgotten everything except his own desire and the slaking of it... Despairing, she tried one last time.

"Matt, *please* listen to me. I would never betray you: I *love* you."

He looked at her then, his eyes hardening and darkening until they appeared almost black.

"You lying little bitch," he gritted. "You'll try any trick, won't you?"

And then he reached for her.

chapter sixteen

Amanda jerked helplessly as she felt his hands close over the soft flesh of her upper arms, but it was useless. His mouth came down over hers, his lips hard and hot, taking what they wanted from her shaking mouth, his tongue thrusting insolently between her teeth, daring her to fight him. When she tried to wrench her mouth away, his hand came up under her chin, his long fingers biting into her jaw as he held her still. He kissed her, over and over again, long, hungry kisses that gave no quarter to the remnants of her innocence. His hands were everywhere, not hurting her but shaming in their familiarity, roaming her body as if it were his to touch and explore. Despite her fear, the feel of those long, strong fingers with their faintly calloused tips running possessively over the crests of her breasts caused a tingle in her belly. Her nipples swelled to quivering life against the stroking hands. She felt him smile against her mouth at this evidence of her reluctant arousal, and then one hand was trapping the tender prey while his mouth moved to torment it. Amanda gasped as his teeth closed over the rosy nipple with a force that stopped just short of pain. Her eyes flew open, and her hands came up instinctively to clutch at his head. A pair of lanterns lit the cabin; by their soft glow, she could see every detail: the blackness of his hair against the pearly gleam of her breast, the whiteness of his teeth as they mouthed her quivering nipple, the bronze of the large hand that cupped her softness, holding it helpless victim to his mouth. The rough texture of his jaw and chin against her silken flesh reminded her vividly of the first time he had taken her. He had seduced her then as now, exciting her unsuspecting body to blind enchantment before destroying her girlish illusions forever with hard, thrusting pain. Remembering that pain, Amanda went rigid. Her hands, which had been curling around the back of his head, now tried to push him away.

"*No,*" she gasped. At her protest, he moved away from the nipple he had been alternately tormenting and enticing. His eyes as they met hers seemed to sizzle, their silvery color darkened to the shade of molten iron.

"Yes," he said softly, baring his teeth at her in what was more a snarl than a smile. Then, to her surprise, his hands fell away from her and he stood up. Amanda lay blinking up at him, bemused, too amazed that he was letting her off so easily to do more than stare at him. She completely forgot about her nakedness until his eyes raking her body reminded her. Then she blushed and turned onto her side, groping for the rough-textured cover beneath her to pull over her quaking body.

"Be still," he said, reaching down to remove the fold of blanket from her clutching fingers. Then his hand on her shoulder turned her onto her back again. Amanda tried to resist, but his strength was far greater than hers and reluctantly she surrendered to it. She lay on her back, one leg slightly bent as she instinctively sought to hide the silky triangle of black hair. Her arms came up to cross over her breasts in that age-old gesture of self-protection, but he wouldn't allow that. He bent, catching both her wrists, pulling them away from her breasts and pushing them down until her palms lay flat against the bunk. When he released his grip, she would have returned her arms to their original position if a predatory gleam in those smoldering eyes had not stayed her. He watched her expectantly for some few seconds; when she made no move to defy him, his muscles relaxed slightly and one hand went to the buttons on his shirt. His eyes never left her.

"You have a beautiful body, Amanda." His words were more a taunt at her helplessness than a compliment. "I like looking at it. It heightens the . . . anticipation."

Even without the drawling emphasis on the last word, the movements of his fingers as they leisurely unfastened his shirt would have told Amanda that he had no intention of letting her go. He wanted her, and he would take her, whether she was willing or not. At the thought, Amanda shuddered. Matt's eyes narrowed slightly at the convulsive tremor, and his mouth hardened and tightened.

"Please don't do this, Matt." At any other time Amanda's pride would not have allowed her to beg, but the memory of the stabbing pain and subsequent degradation drove out every other consideration.

"You beg so prettily, Amanda." Even the silky-smooth mockery of his voice frightened her. She stared up into the dark, handsome face, so familiar and yet so terrifyingly unfamiliar, with the wide-eyed fascination of a rabbit mesmerized by a snake. "I shall teach you to beg me to make love to you. I'd like that."

"*Stop* it, Matt." As he unfastened the last button and pulled his shirttails from the waistband of his pantaloons, she shuddered. Then, despite any possible consequences, she scrambled to the far corner of the bunk and huddled so that her knees came up to her chin and her arms wrapped around her legs. Her every instinct screamed for her to run, but there was no place for her to go. Matt loomed between her and the door, and even with fright sharpening her speed and strength, she knew she would never get by him. He had her trapped; she was totally at his mercy— and from the harsh gleam of his eyes, she guessed that he was not feeling merciful at the moment.

"You'll make me hate you," she warned, her eyes enormous as he shrugged out of his shirt and then crossed the few steps to the bootjack, where he inserted in the grooved slot first one heel and then the other, which allowed him to draw off his boots easily.

"I'd rather live with your hatred than with your

love," he said, his voice gritty with anger. "At least that's an honest emotion. Your so-called love almost got me killed."

"I *didn't* betray you, Matt," she cried despairingly, and then the words died in her throat as he unbuttoned his pantaloons and pushed them down his legs, then stepped out of them. As he straightened to throw them over the chair, Amanda stared at his body. Before when he had been naked, the room had been dark and she had been too dazed with passion to observe much. But now lamplight bathed the room in a soft, golden glow, illuminating every hair and sinew. And passion was the furthest thing from her mind. Her eyes grew enormous as they moved over him.

He was magnificent—and frightening. There was such strength in the broad, bronzed shoulders and muscled arms, such masculinity in the thick black hair covering the wide chest and hard, flat abdomen. His hips were narrow compared to the breadth of his shoulders, and he had dispensed with her bandage so that his wound was now exposed to the air. It had healed over, no longer raw but still a red, angry-looking gash against skin that was paler than the teak of his arms and chest. His legs were pale, too, silent testimony to the fact that they were usually decently covered when he labored in the sun. Their long, straight muscularity was not softened by the faint blurring of dark hair. Her eyes slid back up his legs to rest with a horrified inevitability on the thing between them. It was enormous, she saw as a sick feeling rose in the pit of her stomach. It jutted out from the wiry nest surrounding it with blatant male aggression. It looked swollen and hungry—and she was the meal it wanted.

"Look as long as you please," he said softly. "We have all night."

Her eyes jerked up to his. Mortified to have been caught looking at him, she blushed scarlet. He smiled nastily. At the unrelenting intention she could read so clearly in his eyes, she felt her throat grow dry. She swallowed, then her tongue came out to wet her parched lips.

His eyes narrowed as he observed the tiny movement.

"Then again, perhaps we have less time than I thought." And with that husky warning, he moved, coming toward her with savage grace while she cowered away from him, gasping, huddling back into the corner, shaking her head as if to ward him off. It was useless, as she had known from the beginning it would be. Nothing was going to stop him from taking what he wanted from her. One steely hand closed over her ankle, dragging her across the bunk. She kicked at that imprisoning hand with the other foot, squirming, frantically trying to free herself from the fate that was now so close. He controlled her by capturing her other ankle as well, using them both to drag her sprawling toward him. Then he pinioned her with his body, lowering himself on top of her, his hard thighs crushing her softer ones into the thin mattress. Made reckless by fear, she tried to claw him, only to have her hands captured by his.

"Oh, no, my sharp-clawed little cat, none of that. I forgave that trick once. If you had succeeded in doing it again, you wouldn't have liked the consequences."

There was increasing passion as well as warning in that drawling voice. Suddenly Amanda realized that her squirming attempts to free herself were merely exciting him further. She stopped moving, her wine-red hair like spilled skeins of bright silk against the white pillow and her eyes bottomless wells of smoky purple as she stared up at him.

"Please let me go, Matt." Her voice was breathless, husky with fright and threatened tears. He stared down at her, his eyes hard as diamonds as they moved over the pleading softness of her face, the fear plain in her wide eyes and quivering pink mouth. His face darkened, closed.

"Never in this life," he muttered thickly, and then he was transferring her wrists to one hand, which imprisoned them over her head while his other hand came up to capture her chin. She shut her eyes helplessly as his mouth came down on hers.

Even as he kissed her he was nudging her thighs apart with his knees. Amanda tried to keep her legs together, tensing her muscles and straining against him, but his strength defeated her. At last, with a sob muffled by his devouring mouth, she gave up. He spread her legs wide and settled himself between them. She tensed as she felt the fiery hardness of him probing at her softness.

Oh, God, please help me, she thought, every muscle stiffening as she remembered the pain that had come before. Now he was pushing at her, thrusting against her, demanding entrance.

Then, as if he felt her resistance, the thrusting

movements suddenly stopped. The hand that had been curled around her chin deserted its post to slide down over her body, pausing briefly to fondle first one breast and then the other before moving over her flat belly to the soft mound of hair below. Amanda gasped and began to struggle again as she felt his hand between her legs, knowing that he was bent on doing something indecent to her. His hand stoked and caressed, gentling the soft tissues he had frightened earlier. Amanda felt her muscles gradually begin to relax. No sooner had she done so than he took advantage of this lowering of her guard to slip one long, strong finger inside her.

Immediately Amanda stiffened, horrified, crying out her protest against his mouth. He drank in her cry, kissing her deeply while refusing to remove that shameful invading finger. Amanda tried to squirm free, but he held her too securely. She arched her back, fighting—and then he began to move his hand.

His finger slid softly in and out in gentler approximation of the movements his body had made before. Sometimes he withdrew it altogether, stroking the outer flesh, which had begun to grow warm and moist, then returning to the dark cave he was claiming as his own. Amanda stopped fighting him. What he was doing to her was not painful at all, unlike the other thing. It was almost pleasurable. Gradually, as he showed no sign of relenting, her muscles went limp altogether. She was actually anticipating the movements of that finger. Her hips moved once, twice, in involuntary response. The finger was abruptly removed. Amanda's eyes opened, and she squirmed in silent protest at the cessation of that gentle teasing. Matt's mouth, which had slid down to her breasts, came back up to cover hers. And it was while he was kissing her with hot, expert urgency that that thing began to probe once more between her thighs.

Amanda felt it and stiffened—but it was too late. It was already sliding inside her. To her surprise there was no pain, only a hot, throbbing fullness that seemed to expand as it moved deeper and deeper within her. She gasped, astonished. It was not at all like the time before... And then he was moving, sliding that thing in and out of her as he had his finger. Only it was infinitely more exciting.

Despite herself, Amanda began to get caught up in the urgency of his movements. Her nails dug into his shoulder, and when his mouth left hers to bury itself in the hollow between her shoulder and neck, her head tilted submissively back against the pillow, her eyes closed, making no protest. She didn't want him to stop...

"Wrap your legs around me," he whispered hoarsely in her ear. Amanda quivered, obediently moving her legs. No sooner had she done so than he stiffened, his arms tightening around her. Then he groaned, thrusting once, twice, three times into her body, the movements hard and urgent. Amanda cried out at this sudden change from gentleness to savagery. At her cry he thrust again, harder and deeper, as if he would embed himself forever in her body. Then he shuddered and became limp.

Amanda's eyes slowly opened as she lay beneath him, feeling the heat and weight of him crushing her into the mattress, smelling the musky man-smell of him and feeling his sweat dripping onto her body. Her body felt tense, as if it were waiting for something—something that only he could give her. But he was not moving. She stared down at the top of the black head buried against her throat, at the wide, bronzed shoulders that blocked her view of the rest of their entwined forms. He was still inside her, but the hard urgency was gone. He felt softer, smaller... Amanda wanted to cry with frustration. She had been on the verge of something—something momentous. She knew it, though she didn't know quite how she knew. But he had stopped...

He moved then, his eyes opening so that they looked into hers. They stared at each other for a long moment, unspeaking. Then he levered himself off the bunk, reaching for his pantaloons. Amanda watched him dress, unable to think of anything to say. She felt tired, drained, depleted, and also curiously on edge.

"I'm going out on deck for a while," he said, his voice curt, his eyes remote as they slid over her. "Go to sleep."

Amanda closed her eyes, turning on her side, pulling the bed coverings over herself. She refused to so much as look at him as he left.

It was a cold, clear night, and the driving wind was fast whipping itself into a storm. The *Clorimunda* was a good ship, a New England-built clipper like four of the six others he owned, but even she was having a little difficulty making headway against that wind and the surging waves. Matt watched as a sail was expertly repositioned to take maximum advantage of the wind without allowing it to overpower them, and he smiled, albeit a trifle sourly, at Zeke's seamanship. He had taught the boy well; it was hard to remember that the "boy" was a twenty-six-year-old man and as capable a captain as Matt himself. Which was a mighty good thing for him, Matt reflected as he climbed the stairs to the quarterdeck from the captain's cabin below it. If Zeke and the *Clorimunda* had not appeared when they had, he would more than likely have drowned.

After diving to escape the fusillade of bullets, he had been caught in a vicious undertow, which had pulled him willy-nilly out to sea. To fight it would have been suicide. He had had to swim with it, praying that its strength would give out before his did. It had been a close run. He had been swimming for hours, and the sun had begun to sink below the horizon, when he spotted a sail in the distance. The chances that it was even marginally friendly were not good; more than likely, he'd considered, it had been sent out to search for him. But no matter; if he had to die, hanging wasn't so much worse than drowning, and at least if he signaled the ship—and if it saw him and picked him up—he had a chance. If it didn't, he might not last the night. Certainly no longer, not with his muscles aching and weighing him down like lead, and the sea rising. A bitter anger was all that had kept him alive so long. He wasn't going to die yet if he could help it. Not until he'd settled the score with Amanda.

Zeke—and if there ever was a miracle, it was that the ship had been the *Clorimunda* with Zeke at her helm—had thought, and freely said, that he was mad to risk so much for a girl, no matter what she had done to him. What else could one expect from a woman? Zeke had asked. They were no more than a hank of long hair and silky skin, and if they had a brain at all, it was concerned solely with their own comfort. Back-stabbing was as natural to them as fleas to a dog, and as little to be remembered or punished. That this was a fair assessment of his own usual attitude, Matt recognized. And he stubbornly refused to explain why this incident, this girl, was different. He hadn't felt angry at a woman in years, not truly angry, not the gut-wrenching, fire-breathing kind. But now he did; he wanted to hurt Amanda as she had hurt him, to teach her what it felt like to be alone and frightened and at the mercy of something over which one had no control. He wanted her to beg for mercy... He had insisted that they turn about and fetch her, and Zeke, reluctantly, had bowed to the habit of obedience ingrained in him and had given in. With the proviso that he and a few of the men, not Matt himself, would go ashore...

"Come up for air so soon?" His brother's jovial voice broke into his thoughts. Matt had crossed the quarterdeck and now stood beside Zeke at the wheel.

"Mmm." He would not discuss Amanda, or his feelings for her, with anyone, not even with his brother, who had shared most of his waking thoughts for years. At the noncommittal reply, Zeke cast him a sideways glance, then rubbed the bridge of his nose in a thoughtful gesture that was characteristic of him.

"She's a pretty little thing, but I wouldn't have said she was quite your style. Too young, for one thing." Zeke made this observation in a dispassionate voice, staring out at the dark waves that were growing ever taller. Matt leaned against the wheel casing, crossing his arms over his chest and regarding his brother with brooding eyes.

"She's almost eighteen," he said. No need to tell Zeke that Amanda was something different, special—or had been until she had betrayed him.

Zeke raised his brows and risked an inquiring look at his brother. "Want to talk about it?" he asked softly. Matt shook his head.

"No."

"All right." Zeke knew when to let a subject drop. For a while both brothers were silent, intent on the sea and sky and their own thoughts. Then Zeke spoke again.

"I sent Van Horn on to London to see if he can resolve your difficulties. I thought he would be best."

"Yes." At the moment Matt was not interested in whether Van Horn would be able to find the vital witness who would enable him to have his murder conviction reversed. The image that kept returning to his mind was Amanda, naked and lovely beneath him, Amanda frightened at first and then responding until he had once again lost control and let himself be carried away too fast for her, Amanda smiling at him, crying, trembling in his arms . . .

"Are you asleep?" Zeke's half-humorous, half-exasperated voice finally penetrated Matt's absorbed consciousness. "I asked you if you wanted to take the wheel."

For a moment Matt hesitated. He was tempted, sorely tempted, to return to his cabin and Amanda, to join her in his bunk and make love to her until she discovered the ecstasy whose memory was even now heating his loins. But, he told himself, if he went below now, it would be an admission, an admission that, no matter what she had done to him, he could not resist her ...

"I'll take it." He made up his mind in that instant.

"I'll get some sleep," Zeke said, a note of humor in his voice. "I'll bunk with Kidd."

Matt grunted in reply as Zeke left. Matt stood at the wheel, his hands absently enjoying the feel of the smooth wood, his feet braced against the rise and fall of the deck and his face lifted to the wind. It was good to be free again, to have a deck beneath his feet and know that tomorrow was a better than fair possibility. It was good to look up at the velvety black sky and at the endless expanse of sea ...

Amanda. He could not get her out of his mind. She haunted him like an earthbound ghost. He didn't have to close his eyes to see her as if she stood before him, her glorious hair blowing in the wind, her lovely face, with its exquisite bones pink and glowing. He thought of her eyes, which changed from amethyst to smoky violet to purple according to her mood, and remembered that her eyes had been as purple as pansies when he had made love to her. From fear at first, then from passion ... As he had thought, she was marvelous in bed. She excited him as no other woman had ever succeeded in doing. It seemed that he was always losing control when she was around, both of his temper and of his passion, and his control and ability to pleasure a woman were two things on which he had prided himself. It galled him to admit that a schoolgirl could reduce him to the endurance level of a white-hot boy with his first woman, but it was true. Just the thought of that slender, perfect shape, of those pale breasts like small melons with their strawberry tips, of the narrow waist and curving hips, the long, luscious legs and the dark triangle of hair between them was enough to make him tug uncomfortably at his crotch. She excited him, even now, when she was as untutored as a baby. What would she do to him when he had taught her a little more of what it was all about?

The knowledge of her betrayal sat like a stone in his stomach. He thought he knew why she had done it; it had happened in a fit of temper, because of the way he had taken her and his anger afterward. At least, he hoped that was how it was. He could understand, if not forgive, a sudden burst of anger. He had, he supposed, behaved badly that night. But his emotions had been as raw and confused as hers. He had wanted her more than he had ever wanted a woman in his life; not just her body but Amanda herself. And she'd said that she loved him. He hadn't acknowledged the admission in any way, but it had wormed its way into his heart and lodged there, warming him. At the time she had said it, he had been too caught up in the needs of his body to give the words the attention they deserved; later, afterward, when he had pulled them out to examine them, she had been cold and angry with him, refusing to repeat them or give him any hint that she had meant them. It had hurt damnably, if he was honest, and the hurt had made him angry, too. So he had stalked out and she had gotten even. By turning him over to the authorities, to be hanged, as she must have thought.

Throughout that long swim, he had promised himself he would make her pay for what she had done to him. Tonight, when Zeke had dumped her on the floor at his feet, he had felt a cold, hard anger and a colder satisfaction. He had meant to rape her, to punish her for what she had done to him in the oldest, most primitive way known to man. But when it came to the point, when he had felt her soft, silky body stiff with fear beneath his, heard her voice breathing his name, husky with pleading, seen the fright in the huge purple eyes, he had not been able to. He had realized, with a sick sensation in the pit of his stomach, that he would sooner cut off his arm than harm a hair of her head.

He had realized something else, too: he loved her. And the thought terrified him.

chapter seventeen

The promised storm broke before morning. Amanda was jolted rudely awake by the violent pitching of the ship, which tossed her from the bunk to land with a hard thump on the floor. She lay blinking for a moment, trying to catch her breath, then scrambled to her feet. Were they sinking? From the steep tilt of the floor beneath her and the rolling motion of the ship, it seemed quite possible. Amanda shivered as the ship dipped again, then rose up on end like a rearing horse. She had to find out what was happening. Scrambling to her feet, she started for the door, only to remember her nakedness. That was easily remedied, she thought, turning back. Then, seeing the tattered remnants of her lovely yellow gown on the floor where Matt had thrown it, her eyes widened in dismay. She had literally nothing to wear. And not for any consideration would she appear on deck, in front of all those men, clad only in her underclothes.

As the ship pitched again, Amanda staggered, grabbing the table, which had been bolted to the floor for just such an eventuality. Clinging to it for dear life while her feet slid wildly on the slippery wood, she noticed the sea chest from which Matt had extracted the towel and soap last night. More than likely he kept clothing in there, too.

Taking a deep breath, timing her action so that it coincided with a downward plunge of the ship, Amanda let go of the table to dart across the floor. No sooner had she reached the sea chest than the ship was tilting the other way. Amanda grabbed the sea chest for support, finding, to her dismay, that it was not bolted down or secured. Clutching it, she began to slither helplessly across the floor. The sea chest slithered with her and they landed with a thump against a table leg. Amanda hooked one arm around that blessedly stable post and managed to wedge herself against the table so that she was relatively secure. She took several deep breaths to steady herself again, then turned her attention to opening the trunk. If the ship were sinking—and it seemed as if it might well be—the sooner she was decently covered, the sooner she could leave the cabin. Though what she would do once she was on deck she didn't know.

As she had guessed, the trunk contained several articles of clothing. Matt's shirt was huge on her, she realized with a grimace as she pulled on one of fine white linen. Its tails hung way past her knees, and the cuffs dangled ludicrously past her wrists, but at the moment all she cared about was that she be adequately covered. She rolled up the sleeves and rooted through the chest for something to cover her lower half. She found a pair of charcoal-gray knee breeches; but, though the length was reasonable, the waist could wrap around hers twice, she realized as she slid into them. There was neither belt nor any type of rope in the chest, so she gathered up the excess material at her waist and tied it into a clumsy knot.

"I hope that holds," she thought, looking down at the bunched cloth rather doubtfully. Then, with a shrug, she dismissed the problem. Now all she had to concentrate on was reaching the door. That was no small feat, but eventually she managed.

Once she was on deck, she braced herself against the wall of the captain's cabin, clinging to a hook just above her head. Her eyes were huge as she stared around her. The deck was awash with water. Towering gray waves rose on all sides like mountains; some the ship rode, which accounted for all that bucking and pitching, and some broke over her bow, sending icy water cascading over the deck. Men were everywhere, running across the slanting deck, wrestling with ropes and sails, climbing in the rigging. They paid her no mind, in fact did not appear to see her. Amanda looked up at the lowering sky, listened to the ominous howling of the wind and the sharp crack and pop of the rigging, and understood perfectly. They were battling for the ship's life; they had no thought to spare for her.

Where was Matt? Try as she would, she could not make out his form among the bustling figures. He had not returned to the cabin last night, and it occurred to her that he might be avoiding her. But surely, when they were faced with such danger, he would put aside such petty considerations as pride and anger?

He would be on the quarterdeck, of course. After all, it was his ship. He would surely be at the helm. She had to get to him. Despite everything, he represented security to her. He would take care of her, she knew, if anyone could.

Negotiating the steep, narrow stairs from the main deck to the quarterdeck was a nightmare. Twice she thought she would be thrown back down on the hard boards below as the ship rolled wildly. Once, she nearly lost her grip on the handrail as a deluge of icy water washed over her. When at last she arrived, clinging to the railing that ran all around the quarterdeck as if it were a lifeline, she was soaking wet and shaking from fear and the cold. And still she couldn't see Matt.

Zeke was at the helm, barely recognizable in an oilcloth coat. Three other sailors were working feverishly, trying to free a large sail that had broken away from its lines and was now hopelessly tangled in the rigging. Another sailor stood near Zeke, holding tightly to a spar with one hand while he fought to take a compass reading.

Zeke would know where Matt was. He might not think very highly of her, but from what Matt had told her of him, she felt she could trust him. If Matt hadn't prejudiced him against her, as it had been obvious he had from the very beginning, they might have become friends.

Taking a deep breath, she waited until the ship was on a downward roll, then let go of the railing. The motion of the ship propelled her toward where Zeke stood at the wheel. She crashed into the shoulder-tall wooden shelter built around the wheel and hung on for dear life as the ship rolled the other way.

"What do you want?" If Zeke was surprised to see her, he didn't show it. He scowled at her, shouting to be heard above the wind. His brown hair was darkened with water, plastered to his skull. The hazel eyes were cold with dislike as he looked at her.

"Where is Matt?" She had to scream the question. Zeke heard her—she could tell by the way his mouth tightened—but for a long moment she thought he wasn't going to answer. Then he shrugged and made a curt upward gesture with his thumb.

For a moment Amanda thought that this was some piece of sailor's crudity. Her cheeks colored angrily, though her eyes instinctively followed the direction his thumb had indicated. And froze, widening with horror.

Matt was high in the rigging, clinging to a spar with both legs and one hand as his knife worked to cut loose the crippled sail. He was dressed only in a shirt and pantaloons. His black head was bare and wet, gleaming like a seal's, and his feet were bare, too. The distance between them precluded Amanda from seeing his expression, but as she watched him she could have sworn she saw a flash of white teeth in that dark face. She stared, swallowing. She hadn't been mistaken: the lunatic was actually grinning.

"Dear God," she breathed. Zeke looked at her

curiously, but her eyes were riveted on Matt and she was barely conscious of him.

"You'd better go below," Zeke instructed curtly, the shout all but lost in the wind. Amanda ignored him. She wouldn't leave until Matt was safely back on deck. If he fell from that height... She couldn't bear to think about that.

Just then Matt whooped, and as Amanda watched, the tangled sail fluttered toward the deck like a dying swan. He had succeeded in cutting it free. The three sailors below were catching it, gathering it up, while Matt put the knife between his teeth and started to lower himself to the deck. And then it happened.

A wave, larger than the others, caught them unaware, bathing them in a violent deluge of icy seawater. At the same time the ship stood almost on her bow, then plunged into the trough left by the huge waves. Amanda clutched at the wheel casing to keep her balance, felt Zeke's hand close over her arm like a vise as he tried to hold her in place, and thought for a moment that she might be swept over the side. Then Zeke, looking up, let out a hoarse shout. Amanda looked up, too, to see Matt falling, hurtling through the rigging toward the deck far below.

For the first time in her life, she fainted.

When she regained consciousness, she felt as if a horrible, crushing weight had settled on her chest. Matt had fallen. If by some miracle he was not dead, he must be grievously injured. Zeke was kneeling beside her, leaning over her as she slowly opened her eyes. With the small part of her mind that was still functioning rationally, Amanda noted that the man who had been using the compass had taken the helm.

"Matt..." she groaned, struggling to sit up, looking for and yet not wanting to see his broken body. Why was Zeke not with him?

"It's all right—he managed to catch a line. He's not hurt," Zeke yelled over the storm. For the first time he was looking at her without dislike.

"What the hell's going on here? Amanda?" It was Matt, his voice sharp with anger and concern. Amanda shut her eyes. He was not dead or injured, after all. She thought she might faint again from sheer relief.

"She fainted. She saw you fall," Zeke said briefly. He stood up, looking at his brother with a frown while Matt, ignoring him, knelt beside Amanda.

"Amanda?"

She opened her eyes, dwelling on every plane and angle of that handsome, beloved face. "Are you all right?"

He snorted. "Yes, but *you* don't seem to be. What were you thinking of, to come up on deck?"

"I was frightened—I wanted to see you."

"Don't ever do that again. You could be washed overboard. Come, I'll take you back to the cabin—and this time stay there. I'll come for you if there's need."

His arms were around her, gathering her up. He lifted her high against his chest, staggering a little as the ship pitched again. Amanda rested limply against him for a moment, relishing the hard arms that held her, the beat of his heart against her side, the flush of blood that rose in his face as she looked up at him. Then she shook her head, regaining the use of her muscles and pushing at his chest determinedly.

"You can't carry me in this storm," she shouted. "Put me down, Matt, I can walk."

He looked at her for a moment, his arms tightening around her as if he would never let her go, then, as he had to brace himself to withstand another roll of the ship, he seemed to see the sense of what she had said. It would be difficult to carry her down the narrow stairs to the main deck under the present conditions. Slowly his grip eased, and he let her slip to her feet. His arm stayed around her waist as she caught her balance.

"All right?" he asked. She nodded, not wanting to waste any more breath shouting into the storm. His arm stayed around her to the stairs, and then he insisted on going before her, making her back down while holding to the rail with both hands, poised to catch her if she should slip. They achieved the bottom with no mishap. Amanda would have clung to Matt's hand when they reached the cabin, fearing to let him out of her sight, but he pushed her inside the cabin without ceremony, to stand staring at her for a moment from the open doorway. With his arm braced over his head for support, he completely filled the opening.

"Stay here," was all he said, but he looked as if he had wanted to say more and then thought better of it. He closed the door behind him. Amanda's knees began to tremble as she crossed to the bunk and sat down. At least he no longer seemed angry . . .

The storm lasted for three days. In that time

Amanda, as well as everyone else on board, lost an appreciable amount of weight. With the violent pitching of the ship making a cooking fire dangerous, all they had to eat was dried fruit and pieces of hardtack washed down with water—all of which had been somewhat affected by salt from the seawater that was continually washing over them. Not that Amanda was hungry. If her stomach hadn't been so empty, she feared that she would have disgraced herself completely by being horribly ill. As it was, she was more frightened than anything. From the ominous creaks and groans of the timbers, and the ripping sound of canvas being torn to shreds over her head, she feared the worst. And came to accept it. Whether they sank or not was in God's hands.

She did not wholly obey Matt's edict about staying in the cabin. On the second day, when it occurred to her that every man must be needed to battle the storm, she made her way to the ship's galley and told the exhausted cook that she would be pleased to assist in the distribution of food. Unaware of Matt's instructions to the contrary, he was equally pleased to let her.

The sailors accepted the bits of food and water she brought them with gruff thanks, some of them even unbending sufficiently to warn her to look tight when the ship heeled. They were not unduly friendly, but after the third time she brought them food, they were not unfriendly, either. Perhaps they were beginning to question their earlier judgment of her. At least she hoped they were.

It was inevitable that Matt should see her. She had carefully avoided the quarterdeck, knowing he would immediately order her back to the cabin as soon as he set eyes on her. But toward the middle of the third day, he observed her as she made her way across the deck, clinging for dear life to the safety lines that had been run from one end of the ship to the other. And he swooped down upon her like a hungry hawk.

"Damn it, I *told* you to stay in the cabin," he roared. Amanda had not heard him come up behind her, and his angry bellow made her jump. It also made her lose her grip on the safety line. She staggered, then fell heavily to her knees. The supplies of dried fruit she had been carrying scattered around her on the deck, only to be washed away by an enveloping wave.

"*Good Christ.*" Amanda would quite likely have been washed away with the fruit if Matt had not reached down and grabbed her by the single thick braid in which she had confined her hair. Wincing with pain, she was nonetheless grateful to be caught. Being washed overboard was not the fate she fancied for herself. Then it occurred to her that she wouldn't have been in the least danger if Matt had not startled her, making her lose her grip on the safety line. She was scowling as blackly as he when he hauled her to her feet.

"Damn it, don't you have any sense?" Even over the howling of the wind, his angry bellow was audible. And not only to Amanda. Looking around, she saw that to nearly every man on board they were the objects of fascinated attention.

"Don't shout at me," she cried, incensed and embarrassed at being publicly upbraided. "I was perfectly all right until you came along and frightened me."

"If I frightened you this time, wait till you see what I do to you if I catch you out on deck again." Dark blood rising high in his cheekbones said more than words about how angry he was. His silvery eyes took on the menacing gleam of twin knives as he glared at her. With his black hair wet and curling wildly around his head, his clothes soaked with seawater and plastered to his body, showing every sinewy muscle, and his mouth set in a grim line, he looked formidable. Amanda lifted her chin and returned glare for glare, her eyes shooting purple sparks and the color of her hair no redder than the haze before her eyes. She was not about to allow him to intimidate her.

"Don't threaten me, you *bully*." She was furious now. Matt looked down at her slender shape, ridiculously clad in his too-large clothes, and noted her arms-akimbo stance that threatened to send her sprawling with the next pitch of the ship. Then his lips twitched. Until he noticed how the drenched clothes clung to her skin, revealing every luscious hill and valley. Her nipples, rigid with cold, were straining against the material of the shirt she wore. The laughter vanished from his eyes, to be replaced by another hot flare of anger.

"I'll do more than threaten you next time. And that's a promise," he said grimly, snatching her off her feet and throwing her over his shoulder as he spoke. Amanda kicked and squirmed furiously, scarlet with humiliation, as he strode back toward the cabin with her, one arm locking her in place over his shoulder and the other hand holding tightly to the safety line. When at last he shouldered his way through the door, he tossed her on the bunk and turned to leave. Amanda was spluttering, too angry to be coherent about the insults she would like to have flung at him. He stopped at the door, turning back to fix her with a stony glare.

"If you leave this cabin again before the storm clears, I'll hog-tie you to the bunk." Before she could reply, he left, closing the door behind him.

By the next morning the storm had vanished as though it had never been. The sea was as smooth as blue-green silk, and the sky was equally halcyon. The sun shone brightly down, reminding the world that it was indeed spring, and a gentle breeze chased a few fluffy white clouds across the sky. Amanda, waking to find that the rolling and pitching had miraculously ceased, poked her head cautiously out the cabin door and smiled with pure delight. It was a beautiful day and, best of all, she no longer had to worry about the possible consequences of defying Matt. Because, of course, she had no intention of staying in the cabin.

Quickly she stepped back inside the cabin and tidied herself as well as she could. Besides splashing her face and hands with water and pulling her chemise on under the shirt and breeches, there wasn't much else she could do. The bit of string with which she had bound the end of her braid the day before had fallen off when Matt had grabbed her hair; finding a comb in Matt's sea chest, she merely ran it through her hair, then tucked some carelessly behind her ears.

She left the cabin, padding barefoot toward the quarterdeck—and Matt. Now that the storm was past, it was time for him to answer a few questions, such as where he was taking her, although she had a fair idea. Hadn't he said once that the first thing he would do after escaping from England would be to head for New Orleans, his home?

Men were sprawled all over the main deck, most lying facedown in attitudes of exhaustion. Amanda would have thought that some dreadful plague had visited the ship overnight, killing off her crew, if it had not been for the stentorian snores that rose all about her. From the look of things, only a very groggy skeleton crew remained to see to the operation of the ship.

Zeke was at the wheel again, Amanda saw as soon as she set foot on the quarterdeck. There was no one else about. With some trepidation, she looked up into the rigging, but Matt was not there either. Hesitating only a moment, she walked toward Zeke, who was whistling as he stared out to sea. He might not like her, but surely he wouldn't harm her.

"Good morning," she said, hoping that civility would win a like response. To her surprise it did. He didn't smile at her as he returned her greeting, but his eyes no longer shouted his dislike.

"Matt is below, having something to eat," he added dryly, anticipating her question before she could ask it. "That's what you were going to ask me, isn't it?"

"Yes." Amanda smiled at him, wanting to be friends. She had no idea how that sweet and faintly mischievous smile affected him. It was the first time he had ever seen her smile, and it made her look very young, and very lovely. Not at all the monster in maiden's clothing who had betrayed his brother.

"Why did you do it?" he blurted out, then was immediately angry with himself. Matt would wring his neck for butting into Matt's private business; besides, it didn't matter why. The only important thing was that this dazzlingly beautiful and deceptively innocent-looking chit before him had nearly gotten his brother killed.

"Do what?" For a moment Amanda was at a loss. Her smile faded as she stared up at Zeke. He was not anywhere near as handsome as Matt, she noted abstractedly, but he had a certain charm of his own. A friendly, open charm that did not extend to her. He shrugged curtly in answer to her question, his mouth tightening as he returned his eyes to the sea.

"Betray Matt?" Amanda queried softly, and the look he sent her was answer enough. "I didn't, Zeke. I swear it. I went to the beach that morning to warn him. My half brother, Edward, had told our local constable that Matt was hiding at the convent. Edward hates me, you see. I don't know how he found out about Matt, though. Anyway, I wanted to give Matt a chance to escape. The soldiers must have followed me. I suppose I was responsible in that way, but I didn't deliberately betray Matt."

Zeke was silent for some time after Amanda's earnest little speech, and she suspected that he, too, thought she was lying. Then he turned to look at her, a sharp, judgmental expression in his hazel eyes.

"Did you tell that to Matt?"

Amanda nodded miserably. "He doesn't believe me."

"Why not?"

She shook her head, her eyes clouding over as she pondered the question that had tormented her so many times. "I don't know. I don't know."

Zeke pursed his lips, looking thoughtful. He frowned at Amanda, his hands idly tracing patterns on the wheel's wooden surface.

"I believe you," Zeke said suddenly. His eyes were intent as they fixed on her face. "And I think I can explain to you why Matt doesn't—although he'd probably slit my throat if he knew what I was about to tell you." He hesitated. "Before I do, I need to ask you a personal question. Amanda"—this was the first time he had used her name—"are you in love with my brother?"

Amanda felt the heat rise in her cheeks. It was embarrassing to admit such a thing to a stranger, but . . .

"Yes," she said softly.

Zeke stared at her hard for a moment, then nodded.

"All right, then, I'll tell you. But for God's sake, don't tell Matt that I did."

chapter eighteen

"Has Matt told you anything about our mother?"

Amanda shook her head. "No. Only that she's dead."

He gave her a sharp look. "Did Matt actually say that?"

Amanda nodded, then frowned. "No, he didn't. What he said was that you are the only family he has. I assumed, then, that your mother was dead."

"She isn't," Zeke said flatly. "Cristabel, our mother, is very much alive. At least as of six months ago, when Matt last heard from her."

"Matt never mentioned her." Amanda frowned again. "I take it that there is an estrangement?"

"In a way. I suppose I'd better tell you the whole story. That's the only way you'll understand why Matt sometimes behaves as he does."

"I'm listening."

Zeke chewed his lower lip for a moment, still plainly hesitant about revealing so much that his brother preferred to keep secret. Amanda gazed up at him encouragingly. She very much wanted to hear the story of Matt's past, and she had a strong suspicion that Matt himself would never tell her.

"Cristabel—we always called her Cristabel, never Mother, on her instructions—was, according to her own version of events, the daughter of an aristocratic Southern family, the Graysons," Zeke began slowly, shifting his gaze from Amanda's wide eyes to the sea. "Though there are some Graysons living in Charleston, where she says she was born, I have my doubts that she is related to them. Sometimes I even doubt that her name is Grayson. But that's what she says, and that's the name Matt and I grew up with." He glanced at Amanda again, noting her puzzled frown as she absorbed the information that Matt and his brother used their mother's maiden name.

"Oh, yes," Zeke continued, the lightness of his tone not disguising an underlying bitterness. "Cristabel never married. Matt and I are both—begging your pardon, Amanda—bastards."

"Matt never told me," Amanda breathed, her eyes fixed on Zeke's face.

"It isn't something one brags about," Zeke returned dryly. "Does it make a difference to the way you feel about Matt?"

"Of *course* not." Amanda was clearly indignant. Zeke nodded, the movement brusque.

"Good. Because that's merely the beginning of the story. According to Cristabel, after a debut that would have put Queen Victoria's to shame, she eloped with a handsome young man from New Orleans. She thought he came from a wealthy aristocratic Creole family. Later, when they arrived in New Orleans, she discovered that he was nothing more than a professional gambler. Again according to Cristabel, when he learned that she didn't have any money of her own, he abandoned her. Left her at a seedy hotel one night and never came back. The next night, when he still hadn't appeared, she went to the hotel where he had set up his games and asked about him. A lady— and I use the term advisedly—came out to talk to her upon hearing whom Cristabel had been asking for. The lady was also Paul Mareschel's wife—that was his name, Paul Mareschel. And since their marriage was solemnized some years before Cristabel's, obviously it took precedence. And just as obviously Cristabel was not Mrs. Mareschel at all, but still Miss Grayson. And Miss Grayson was alone, frightened, and with child."

"Matt."

"That's right." Zeke nodded. "Well, Mareschel's wife—if she was his wife, any more than Cristabel was, is open to speculation. Apparently he was quite a lady's man." Zeke grinned suddenly and added in an aside, "Matt must take after him. Cristabel always said that Matt's daddy was as handsome as the devil himself and as popular with the ladies." Then, recollecting himself, he went on hastily. "Mrs. Mareschel felt sorry for Cristabel and took her in. Oh, not to the hotel, but to a little business she owned in partnership with an aristocratic New Orleans gentleman. They gave her a place to stay until Matt was born, and then she had to start earning her room

315

and board. Which she did, without any qualms that I ever noticed."

Amanda's eyes were huge as they met Zeke's. The implications were clear.

"You mean . . ." She faltered.

He nodded. "I mean she became a practitioner of the world's oldest profession: a prostitute, if you'll forgive my bold speech. And she plied her trade with talent and enthusiasm, from all accounts. I was born seven years after Matt, when Cristabel, according to her calculations, was twenty-six; I think she must have been closer to thirty. I have no idea who my father was. Some nameless fellow who bought my mother for the night. Since I don't look like Cristabel— who is blonde and small, although she now makes up in girth what she lacks in height—I assume I resemble my father. Good looking son-of-a-gun, wasn't he?" This last was accompanied by a flashing grin that reminded Amanda again that this man was Matt's brother.

"Then Matt is ashamed because his mother is a . . . prostitute?" Amanda colored a little on the last word, but got it out nonetheless. This conversation was too important to leave vital points unclarified for lack of a little plain language. "I don't really see what that has to do with why he won't believe me when I tell him I didn't betray him."

Zeke shook his head. "I don't think Matt is ashamed, not anymore. You get used to it, over the years. What he is, is hurt and angry—and bitter toward women. You see, despite what she was, Matt thought the sun rose and set in our mother. When I was a child, he would come into the room we shared in the attic of Cristabel's place of employment, his face all bruised and bloody from fights with boys who'd called his mother a whore. For a long time Matt wouldn't admit to himself what Cristabel was. He would even be angry at me when I tried to tell him." Zeke paused to take a deep breath. "When I was seven and Matt fourteen, Cristabel was offered better circumstances. There was a man who wanted to take her away from the sordid life she'd led until then, and give her everything she didn't deserve. She left us then. Merely kissed both of us on the forehead, said good-bye, and left us. That was the first and only time I've seen my brother cry: the day our mother left us. He was a big boy, tall but rather thin and gangly, and he sat there on the end of our bed and tears ran down his cheeks. It frightened me more than Cristabel's leaving did. I'd never depended on Cristabel, but I did depend on Matt. And Matt was crying."

Zeke's eyes clouded as he remembered. Amanda's heart ached at the image he was creating for her, the image of a tall, thin boy with Matt's face, weeping for the mother who had abandoned him.

"But Matt stopped crying and went to work," Zeke continued softly. "He supported me from the time he was fourteen until I could do it myself. He's a remarkable man, my brother."

"Yes," Amanda agreed softly, her eyes misting. She thought about what Zeke had said. Matt's mother, whom he had adored, had betrayed him, and that had led him to expect betrayal from all women. He was harboring a deep-rooted fear. She would have to be kind and patient and, most of all, loving...

317

"But you've had contact with Cristabel since?" she asked, suddenly remembering that Zeke had said they'd heard from her just six months ago. Zeke's mouth twisted.

"Oh, yes—whenever she needs money. When Matt was about twenty-two, she came back to New Orleans and learned that he was part owner of the *Lucie Belle*, his first ship. And she thought it was charming that the son she had abandoned had done so well. She tried for a reconciliation, but her money-grubbing little claws were showing. Matt gave her some money— he has a soft heart beneath that tough exterior. At the end of their last interview, when she saw she wasn't making headway, she gave up acting the prodigal mother and screamed about being destitute—and Matt wouldn't leave her in want no matter what she'd done to him. Now we hear from her once or twice a year, whenever she's penniless. And Matt always sends her money. But she's never tried to see him again and he never speaks of her. And I think she's forgotten that I ever existed."

"I'm so sorry, Zeke," Amanda murmured impulsively, sensing the pain that was as real in him as he'd said it was in Matt. She laid a gentle hand on his arm in an instinctive gesture of comfort. He looked down at her, smiled Matt's smile, and patted her hand. And then both of them became aware of a tall figure looming behind them.

"Making advances to *my* girl, little brother?" Matt asked. His tone was light, but as Amanda and Zeke both started and turned a guilty look on him, his eyebrows knitted in the faintest of frowns. Those silvery eyes were keen as he surveyed them in turn.

"I acquit you of trying to steal my girl," Matt said slowly, his eyes fixed on Zeke. "But the two of you are clearly up to something. Come on, brother, out with it. If you don't, Amanda will. She's the worst liar I've ever seen. She's even worse than you."

There was a taunt in his voice as he said that last. Zeke looked uncomfortable, and Amanda, feeling sympathy for a fellow habitual truth teller, stepped into the breach.

"We were deciding to be friends," she said, tilting her chin defiantly as she looked Matt straight in the eye. "Just because *you're* stubborn and mule-headed doesn't mean Zeke has to be."

Matt's eyes widened fractionally. "Is that right?" he drawled as Zeke chuckled.

"She has you there, brother." Zeke grinned, obviously not a whit disturbed by the frown Matt directed at him. "You *are* stubborn. And mule-headed. Only, I never thought to hear a little chit of a girl tell you so."

Matt looked back at Amanda. She looked very small and slight as she stood there staring impudently up at him, her bright head barely reaching the top of his shoulder. For what must have been the thousandth time, he thought what a lovely thing she was, with her violet eyes and delicately carved face, pinkened now by the breeze, and the sun finding golden threads in the cascade of ruby curls. His stomach twisted as he looked at her, and his mouth was grimly set.

"You can go below," he said shortly to Zeke, moving to take command of the wheel. "You need some sleep."

"I'm fit," Zeke protested. Matt silenced him with a look. Zeke pursed his lips, shrugged, and obediently went below.

"What were you and Zeke talking about?" Matt asked abruptly when he and Amanda were alone.

"Oh, nothing. Just...just this and that," Amanda stammered, caught by surprise. A faint flush rose in her cheeks. She knew she must look guilty, and she also knew she could not betray what Zeke had told her in confidence. She decided to take the offensive, hoping it would throw him off the track.

"What do you suppose we were talking about, how to cause a mutiny?" she added tartly. Matt looked at her, one corner of his mouth quirking up.

"I wouldn't put it past you," he retorted. "But I do trust Zeke."

She bridled at the implication. But there was nothing surprising in that. After all, he thought she had betrayed him, made no bones about thinking so. He was a low-down, suspicious...She opened her mouth to tell him so, then remembered why he was the way he was. The image of that gangly fourteen-year-old crying for his mother superceded the reality of the tall, tough man who looked as though he'd never needed anyone in his life. Her harsh words were swallowed before she could speak them. She would win him with kindness, get him to trust her with love...

"Where are we headed?" she asked, changing the subject, although she had a fair idea of their destination.

"Home," he said, confirming what she had thought. "New Orleans."

She didn't say anything for a moment, wondering

how best to penetrate his defenses to the man within the hard, distrustful shell. Finally she decided to ask the question that had been plaguing her for days.

"Why did you come back for me, Matt? Why are you taking me with you?" Her voice was soft, her eyes searching as they moved over his face. His mouth tightened, but the silvery eyes were mocking as they glanced down at her.

"Why do you imagine?" he asked musingly. "Because of your irresistible beauty, perhaps? Because I feared I wouldn't be able to live without you?" He was mocking her. Amanda's chin tilted at him, but she didn't say anything. She was going to be kind and loving to him if it killed her. "It wasn't either of those things, Amanda," he continued softly. "I went back for you because we had—still have—some unfinished business. Business that I plan to finish before much longer."

"You mean that you came for me because you wanted revenge."

His eyes narrowed slightly. "That, and other things. You have a lovely body, Amanda. I had just started to teach it what pleasure's all about. I wanted to feel it squirming beneath me, begging me to make it mine."

He was trying to embarrass her, Amanda knew, but that did not stop the hot color from flooding her cheeks. Her eyes sparkled indignantly as she glared at him. Weeping fourteen-year-old or not, he was pushing her tolerance too far.

"Well, in that case, I'm afraid you're going to be disappointed. I'll never beg you to . . . *you* know. I don't even like it particularly."

His eyes narrowed, then he smiled. "Don't you?

321

Well, I'll just have to see what I can do about that, won't I?"

Amanda fairly quivered with temper. "Chance is a fine thing," she retorted, and turned her back on him, stalking away before he could reply. Because of course he knew as well as she did that he would have the chance, and there was nothing she could do to stop him from taking it. But at least she would make no secret about her lack of enjoyment. And as she stomped away down the stairs to the accompaniment of his low chuckles, all her good intentions of winning him to her with loving kindness were forgotten.

For the rest of the day Amanda was careful to keep well away from the quarterdeck and Matt. The weather was gorgeous, sunny and bright with just the hint of a breeze. Even to avoid Matt she refused to stay in his cabin. Besides, she reasoned, he would surely return for some much-needed sleep before too long, and she didn't want to be there when he settled down for a rest. She had an uncomfortable suspicion that he wouldn't think twice about taking her to bed with him.

She spent the afternoon on the poop deck, above the main afterdeck. Most of the men were sleeping, and the few who moved about ignored her. She was able to enjoy the day, at least, as long as she firmly banished any thoughts of Matt. Just imagining that tall, strong body and handsome face, not to mention the sneering smile that was its usual adornment lately, made her angry. And sad at the same time.

Without Matt's handsome, if maddening, self to occupy her mind, her thoughts turned eventually to those she had left behind at the convent. What an uproar there must have been when she disappeared. What did they imagine had become of her? she wondered. Did they think that she had run away or perhaps even drowned herself in the bay rather than face marriage to Lord Robert? Amanda shook her head. Mother Superior and the other nuns, with the possible exception of Sister Boniface, who was always ready to think the worst of her, would never believe that she could be guilty of such a mortal sin. But Edward and Lord Robert did not know her quite so well. Amanda grinned as she pictured Lord Robert's embarrassment if word should get about that she had drowned herself rather than become his bride. He would be furious at being made to appear so foolish. Then there was Edward. Amanda shivered as she thought of facing his anger. Fervently she hoped that he believed her dead. If he did not, he might try to find her. And the thought of what he might do to her if she came into his power again made her shiver despite the warmth of the day. How he would enjoy making her pay for ruining all his plans. But, then, she told herself bracingly, even if he did not believe her dead, he was hardly likely to look for her in New Orleans. He could have no notion that she had gone there, and with Matt...

Susan would be grief-stricken. Her friend knew her too well to believe that she would take her own life, but for a young woman of Amanda's background and breeding, being on her own with no money and no one to come to her aid could be a fate almost worse than death. But she had no way to allay Susan's fears—not now. Later, when they reached New Orleans, she would write and let Susan, and through her the nuns, know that she was alive and well. Although she wouldn't be more specific than that. Not for anything in the world would she bring the authorities down on Matt's head.

The sun had sunk below the horizon in a blaze of crimson glory, and a few stars had begun to twinkle in the darkening sky before at last, reluctantly, she decided to go below. She was cold and hungry now. With a start, she remembered that she had eaten nothing all day. At the realization, her stomach growled loudly in pained reproach.

The first thing she saw as she walked through the cabin door was Matt. He was stripped to the waist, turned away from her so that his scarred back was plainly visible. Amanda stared at those marks and felt a pain in her belly that had nothing to do with hunger. It reminded her that, despite everything, she loved him. How had she, even for a few hours, forgotten that?

"I was about to come fetch you," he said, turning to look at her as she leaned against the closed door. From the soap that obscured half his face, and the gleaming razor in his hand, Amanda realized that he was shaving. And if the energy he exuded was anything to go by, not to mention the rumpled bedclothes and the half-filled hip bath.

"I was on the poop deck," Amanda answered, glad she had learned the name from one of the sailors. The sight of that broad, hair-covered chest awoke sensations in her that she refused to analyze. Best not to dwell on them at all.

He smiled at her. Amanda stared at that smile. It was utterly charming, the sort he hadn't bestowed on her since her supposed betrayal. Clearly he was up to something—but what?

"I know. I saw you. You don't suppose you could disappear for the better part of a day without my coming to check on you? When I climbed up on the poop deck, you were happily engaged in conversation with Foster. I went back to work, but never think I didn't know where you were."

"I'm surprised you bothered." Amanda couldn't control the caustic edge to her voice. He turned away from her, apparently no longer minding if she had an unimpeded view of his scars, and continued to shave.

"In that case you must have forgotten what I said about our unfinished business," he replied softly. Amanda stiffened. She hadn't forgotten, but she had hoped that he had—or at least that he'd just been tormenting her. But as she looked at the gleaming silver eyes in the small mirror he had hung from the wall, she realized that he was serious. He reminded her of a large dog eyeing a particularly juicy bone, one he had selected for his dinner.

"If that's what you have in mind, I'll leave," she said coldly, and turned to suit the action to the words. But she had forgotten how quick he was. Before she could open the door, he was beside her, his hand on her arm spinning her away from it. Then, smiling at her evilly, he produced a large brass key from his pocket and inserted it in the lock. Amanda heard the faint click of the lock and felt both excitement and anger as he withdrew the key and dropped it into his pocket with a mocking smile.

"No, you won't." Now that he had her securely trapped, he strolled back to the washstand and resumed shaving. "You'll have a bath and then we'll eat dinner. Then..." His eyes met hers in the mirror. She glared at him furiously; his eyes taunted and smoldered at the same time. He didn't have to finish his sentence. His meaning couldn't have been more obvious.

"I'm not going to...sleep with you," she announced, the militant sparkle in eyes that had begun to darken to purple daring him.

"Not until much later, anyway," he agreed smoothly, wiping the remnants of the lather from his face with a towel and turning to look at her. His lips twisted as he added, "What I have in mind has very little to do with sleeping."

"You know what I mean."

"I do—but I don't remember asking your permission. You'll do as I say."

"I *won't.* You can't make me."

He eyed her lazily. "We both know I can—but I won't. By the time I make love to you, you'll be begging for it. And that's a promise."

"The hell I will."

"Oh, you will—and don't swear, Amanda. I've told you before, I don't like it."

"Isn't that too damned bad?" He infuriated her. His mocking smile and air of confidence made her want to hit him over the head with the closest hard object. Unfortunately, if she gave in to that most worthy impulse, she had little doubt that he would retaliate, and that she would not enjoy whatever form his retaliation might take. So instead she chose to hurl words at him—words she knew perfectly well he disliked her to use. She hoped that her language would make him as angry as his arrogance made her.

"Has anyone ever washed your mouth out with soap, Amanda?" He was drawling, always a sure sign that she was ruffling his temper. Her eyes widened as she looked from him to the cake of soap he picked up from the washstand and tossed idly in one hand. He wouldn't dare—would he? "I suggest you quit talking and get into the bath, Amanda. Otherwise I might be tempted to teach you who's in charge—in more ways than one."

There were several points in that speech that Amanda took exception to, but she decided to focus on the most tangible.

"I'm not about to provide a peep show for you. If you want me to bathe, then leave the room."

His eyes narrowed. "We both know I could strip you in about two minutes flat and put you in that tub whether you liked it or not." Amanda tilted her chin at him in silent defiance. "But, as it happens, I need to take a compass reading. If you're quick, you can have your bath in privacy."

Her muscles relaxed slightly. She had fully expected him to force her obedience. His unexpected concession disarmed her belligerence slightly, although she was still wary. He *had* stated that he meant to make love to her.

"Thank you." Her words were stiff, and the eyes she ran over him were mistrustful. He was shrugging into a shirt. Perhaps he did mean to leave her alone to bathe.

He did. With a curt nod as his only reply to her

muttered courtesy, he left the cabin. Amanda plainly heard the click of the lock as he secured the door after him.

Left alone, Amanda looked longingly at the bath. She felt filthy and, grimacing, realized she had not had a complete bath since the first night she had been brought aboard. And that had been nearly a week ago. More than anything in the world, she wanted to shed her clothes and slide into that warm water.

Matt might be waiting outside the door, waiting until a sound told him she had done just that before reentering, but that was a chance she would have to take. Besides, whatever else Matt might do, she didn't think he would stoop to such a shabby maneuver. If he had wanted to watch her bathe, he would have stripped her himself and put her in the tub. That was much more his style.

It didn't matter, anyway, Amanda told herself as she removed her clothes. Matt had seen—and more than seen—every centimeter of her skin. It was pride more than modesty that forbade her to undress in front of him. If he had loved her, it would have been different. But he obviously did not, and she refused to serve as an object for his passing amusement.

She was still wearing Matt's shirt and breeches, and she had to struggle with the knot in the breeches before she could get them off. But at last she succeeded in working it loose; the breeches, with their too-big waistline, dropped around her feet. Amanda stepped free of them and slipped her chemise over her head. Then she stepped into the tub.

The water was faintly soapy from Matt's earlier

bath, and it had cooled until now it was no more than tepid. But still it felt marvelous. Amanda would have loved to have luxuriated in it, but there wasn't time. Quickly she scrubbed her face, body, and hair, then rinsed off the soap. She was just stepping from the tub when the lock clicked faintly, and Matt entered the room.

He stopped for a moment on the threshold, his eyes darkening in a way that made her heart speed up. Then he stepped inside the cabin, closing the door behind him. Her hair hung around her like a deep crimson curtain, its water-darkness emphasizing the creamy pallor of her skin. Her eyes were a vivid purple as she stared at him, and her cheeks flooded with rosy color as his eyes traveled the length of her. Naked, she was more than beautiful: she was slender, alluring, graceful as a flower in the breeze. Her shoulders were narrow and fragile-looking above breasts whose girlish tautness caused them to tilt at him with natural provocation. A study in strawberry and cream... Her waist was tiny, and below it her hips curved in a way that was still more girl than woman but that he found utterly irresistible. He caught just a glimpse of the silky dark triangle of hair that hid the very essence of her femaleness before she snatched up a towel and covered herself. But that flimsy cloth did not prevent him from admiring the lines of shapely, slender thighs and calves, and perfectly modeled knees.

Amanda saw the blaze that kindled in his eyes as he stared at her, and swallowed, sure that he meant to catch her up in his arms and carry out his threat to make love to her. To her surprise he did not. Instead, after one final searing look at her legs, he turned away, crossing to the sea chest, where, on one knee, he rummaged through the contents. Eyeing his back warily, she dried herself as well as she could while still holding the towel in front of her, and was just reaching for the protection of her discarded shirt when he closed the lid on the chest, straightened, and turned back to her, moving toward her with quick strides.

"You won't need that," he said brusquely, indicating the shirt with one hand. Amanda looked at him doubtfully, clutching the shirt in one hand and holding the towel in front of her like a shield with the other. She mistrusted the look in his eyes. They were a dark gun-metal color, and they seemed to smolder...

"If you think..." she began, backing away. He shook his head, the gesture impatient, then held up his hand so that she could see what he was holding. It was a dressing gown of dark blue silk. From the size of it, it was clearly his. But somehow she had trouble picturing Matt wearing such a luxurious but unfunctional garment.

"I don't think anything," he said. "At least, none of the very vivid thoughts that I can see are running through your head at the moment. Put this on. I'm sure you'll find it more comfortable—and certainly cleaner—than those ridiculous clothes you've been wearing for the past three days."

Looking at him doubtfully, knowing he could read her every thought, she wondered if he had an ulterior motive in offering his dressing gown to her. But for the life of her she could not imagine what—unless it was simply that he found it hard to make love to a woman dressed in his own too-large and not overly clean clothes. She looked from the gleaming blue silk of the dressing gown, which he was holding out invitingly, to the crumpled and spotted linen shirt she still clutched in one hand—and cleanliness won out. She dropped the shirt and reached for the dressing gown.

Turning her back, she shrugged into it, not dropping the towel until she was safely covered. The silk felt cool and slithery against her bare skin. She didn't notice how the dampness of her skin caused the thin material to cling to her in places, but Matt did. His eyes darkened even more as she turned back to him.

"Blue becomes you," he said gruffly, eyeing her. She looked back at him, her expression uncertain as he bent suddenly to retrieve the towel from the floor. He was very close, not more than two feet away, and as usual when he was so near his sheer size took her by surprise. The top of her head barely reached his shoulder. The breadth of his muscular shoulders and width of his chest dwarfed her. He straightened, towel in hand, and she took an instinctive step back. His other hand came out to grip her upper arm, not roughly but to keep her from moving farther away.

"It's customary to say thank you for a compliment, Amanda." His voice was grave. His eyes were grave, too, as he studied her. She was puzzled by his mood. He was no longer angry, no longer hostile, but he wasn't the charming friend she had come to know and love, either. This man looked suddenly older, remote—except for the tiny flicker in his eyes.

"Thank you," Amanda whispered. She looked up at him, her eyes searching every plane and angle of that handsome face. He met her eyes, and for a long moment they simply stared at each other silently. He opened his mouth as if to speak—and was interrupted by a quick knock at the door.

"Our dinner," he said briefly, tossing the towel to her as he turned away to open the door. Amanda caught the towel, her eyes never leaving that broad back. She felt a terrible sense of disappointment, as if he had been on the verge of saying something important. His hand on the latch, he turned to look at her over his shoulder. Although she didn't know it, her eyes gleamed with hope and entreaty as she returned his look.

"Dry your hair," was what he said, and Amanda could have cried with disappointment. She *knew* that was not what he had been about to say before the interruption. But it was too late; He was opening the door, allowing Timmy, the slight youth who served as cabin boy, into the room with his tray. Amanda stared at Matt helplessly as he exchanged meaningless pleasantries with the boy. Then she bent her head and began obediently to dry her hair.

There seemed nothing else to do.

chapter nineteen

She had had too much to drink. Amanda wasn't sure where that thought had come from, but it filtered through the golden haze induced by the seemingly innocuous concoction she had been drinking. The realization should have brought shame with it: a lady never allowed herself to become intoxicated. But, she comforted herself, she wasn't truly drunk. Only a bit—what were the words her father had used?—"on the go."

It was Matt's fault, of course. He was sitting across the table from her, idly sipping at a glass of port, his eyes gleaming faintly as he watched her. He had mixed the fruity-tasting beverage she had been consuming, and had said not a word to stop her as she had drunk several glassfuls. Punch, he had called it. She tried to eye Matt sternly, but her eyes now saw two of him. Two Matts. The thought was appalling and, at the same time, so appealing that she giggled.

"You're drunk," he said indulgently, his lips crooking into an amused smile as he observed her.

"I am *not*." Amanda meant to sound dignified and might have succeeded—if not for the wayward hiccup. Matt's grin broadened while Amanda scowled at him. He was laughing at her. He always seemed to be laughing at her. For a moment her befuddled brain tried to tell her something, to remind her that lately he had not laughed at all, but she could not quite grasp the memory. But it didn't matter anyway. This was Matt, her Matt. If she had to get drunk—loathsome word—she could have picked no better companion. He would watch out for her.

"Do you want any more of that pudding?"

Amanda looked down at the remains of the blanc mange and barely repressed a shudder. The sight of it made her stomach queasy. She shook her head and stood up... The room seemed to swim around her, and she had to clutch the edge of the table for support. Matt caught her arm, steadying her. Amanda shook her head to try to clear it, and only succeeded in making the room spin harder.

"I feel dizzy," she said, surprised. Matt now slid his arm around her waist. Amanda leaned thankfully against that supporting arm as he drew her toward him. He was still seated, leaning negligently back in the hard chair he had pushed away from the table. Amanda felt his hard thigh against hers, and then he was pulling her down onto his lap. She curled up against him docilely, enjoying the warm comfort of his body. He felt so hard and strong and male...

Luxuriously she let her head slip sideways to rest against his shoulder. Sighing, she looked up into his face.

He was looking at her with an expression that was not quite a smile. Amanda studied him, a faint frown knitting her brows. His eyes were more gray than silver as he returned her look, and one thick black eyebrow was tilted up as though in question. He had shaved, leaving his cheeks and jaw smooth and clean-smelling, with just the faintest dark shadow under his skin to remind her of the bristly whiskers that would roughen his face before morning. After his bath he had clearly not bothered to comb his hair. It lay in a blue-black tangle of curls about his forehead and ears. The scar gleamed faintly pale against his bronzed skin. Amanda followed it from his temple to where it ended beside his mouth. That strong, decisive mouth with its slightly fuller lower lip that was parted now, revealing even white teeth as he smiled at her.

"You're beautiful," she said gravely, continuing to stare at him. His eyes flickered.

"So are you." If his voice was just a bit thicker than before, she didn't notice it. She was too busy staring at that perfectly shaped mouth. She raised her hand to touch it. Beneath her fingers it was warm and surprisingly soft. He kissed her fingers, the gesture gentle. Amanda sighed with contentment, allowing her arms to slip around his neck.

"I do love you," she said, and her head nestled confidingly against his chest. Beneath her ear she could hear the heavy thud of his heart. She could have listened to the sound all night.

"You shouldn't say what you don't mean, Amanda." Despite the warmth of his arms around her, there was a faint hardness in his voice. Amanda frowned. What had she said? Oh, yes, that she loved him. But he knew that—she had told him so before. Again a niggling memory tugged at the edge of her consciousness, and again it slipped away.

"I *do* love you," she repeated for emphasis, tilting her head back against his chest as she stared up at him. Her eyes were like huge, cloudy amethysts as they met his. Her hair, dried now, framed her small face in thick swirls of silk. Against the deep blue of the robe, it gleamed like dark fire. Looking down at her, Matt thought that he had never seen a woman look lovelier, or more sweetly innocent. My red-haired angel, he thought with a pang. Then, remembering her perfidy, he hardened his heart against her. He might have been foolish enough to fall in love with her, but he was certainly not foolish enough to betray it.

"Come, I'll put you to bed." He was standing up, lifting her easily in his arms. His plans for the evening had gone awry, but he wasn't truly sorry. The kind of refined sexual torture he had had in mind for her tonight went against every dictate of his heart. What he wanted to do more than anything was to kiss her breathless, and make love to her until he died of it. But with his heart in its present uncertain state, that was better left undone. There was no telling what he might reveal under the heady influence of wine and passion.

"I thought you were going to make love to me." He had lowered her to the bed, but she continued to cling to his neck, refusing to release him. She was pouting, her mouth compressed in a lovely bee-stung bud that made him ache just to look at it. It cried out to be kissed . . .

"Not tonight, Amanda." He must be mad, to refuse the one thing he would have sold his soul for. But his emotions were in such a turmoil that he didn't dare risk it. If he made love to her now—she warm and sweet and pliant, he feeling the way he did—he would be lost for all eternity. She would own him, body and soul. Even if he could somehow arrange it so that he never saw her again, she would be emblazoned in his heart forever.

"Please, Matt. I want you to." If his blood had not been pulsing through his veins like a scalding tide, he would have laughed at the irony. The very words he had meant to force her to say, with his lips and hands, she had uttered without coercion. She wanted him, finally. And he wanted her. God, he wanted her.

"Let me go, Amanda. You will regret this in the morning." But his voice was thick, and his attempt to pull back was halfhearted at best. She looked delectable, lying back against the rough-woven blanket that covered his bunk, her hair a glittering nimbus against the brown cloth, her skin startlingly white against the gleaming blue silk of the robe. Through its thin folds he could see the outline of her body clearly. Her breasts strained against the material, seeming to cry out for his touch, her nipples aroused and clearly visible . . .

"Make love to me, Matt." She was seducing him, this chit of a girl, with her husky voice and luscious body, seducing him with every glance of her violet eyes, every movement of her lips—and he was helpless. He could no more have stopped himself from sitting on the edge of that bunk, from leaning forward and placing his lips against hers, than he could have stopped the pounding of his heart.

As she felt his lips against hers she sighed with satisfaction. Matt drank in the brandy-tinged sweetness of her breath and felt the last vestige of his resistance melt. Angel or devil, whatever she had done, she was his, and he would have her. And keep her.

Amanda accepted his kiss, conscious of a dreamy satisfaction as his mouth slanted with hungry passion across hers. He was no longer fighting her, but giving in to the desire that consumed them both. When his hands opened the robe and slid beneath it, she arched against their touch. She loved the feel of them on her breasts, loved the faint tremor that shook them as he touched her nipples with gentle fingers and then bent his mouth to them. At the touch of that hot, warm mouth, she moaned, and her arms came up to clutch his shoulders. He quivered in response, and Amanda rejoiced in her ability to make him react in such a way. Matt was so tall, so strong, so invincible. Neither deprivation nor torture nor the threat of death had managed to bow that proud black head. Yet now, beneath her hands, he was a trembling supplicant. The realization made her humble, and, at the same time, curiously proud.

The robe was open all the way now, exposing her body to his eyes and touch. Amanda felt no shame, only a fierce need to have him make her totally his.

She loved him, she belonged to him. It was right that he should claim her.

He kissed every inch of her skin, from the hollow beneath her ears to the soft instep of her feet. By the time he returned to her lips she was gasping. His mouth closed over hers, taking it with a savage hunger. Her arms locked around his neck, and she clung to him, blind and deaf to everything but her own spiraling desire.

The blue robe was removed and thrown aside. She was naked, but he was still fully dressed. Amanda felt the rough barrier of his clothes between them and writhed against him in silent protest. She wanted him naked, too. He was unbuttoning his shirt, his fingers clumsy, his eyes passionate as he looked down at her lying naked beneath him. Amanda stared into his eyes as her fingers moved to help him. Together they removed his shirt. As he tossed it to the floor, her eyes dropped from his to feast on his broad, muscled shoulders and powerful chest. His body was as beautiful as his face. The thick mat of black hair ran down his chest in a V, inviting her to run her fingers through it. And she did. He caught his breath as her nails scraped against his skin, pausing briefly to flick over the male nipples, which rose in quaking delight. Fascinated at this response that was so much like hers, she remembered how he had kissed her breasts—and lifted her head to press her lips to one of the flat brown nipples in its nest of dark hair.

"*God*, Amanda." The words were a groan. His hand tangled in her hair, and he pulled her head away from him to take her mouth in a smothering kiss. Amanda kissed him back wildly, feeling as if she were on fire. She wanted him so much she thought she would go mad.

He pushed her back against the bunk, his hands fumbling with his belt buckle while he continued to kiss her. Amanda's fingers clutched at his hair, stroked the broad back with its raised scars, dug into the wide shoulders. He tore his mouth away from hers only to jerk off his boots and then his pantaloons. Amanda watched him, her eyes openly admiring. His buttocks were firm and round, totally unlike her own soft posterior. The backs of his thighs and calves were muscled and strong-looking...Then he turned around. Her eyes went to the enormous thing that jutted between his legs. It was every bit as fearsome in appearance as before, but instead of being frightened she was intrigued. She wanted to touch it...

Standing beside the bunk looking down at her, he towered over her. Amanda half closed her eyes and lifted a tentative hand to touch the part of him that was still strange to her. He flinched as if her touch burned him. Her hand drew quickly away, and her eyes opened wide to stare at him. Had she hurt him? But the groan that issued from between his lips spoke more of pleasure than of pain. Before she could puzzle it out, he was beside her on the bed, one hand capturing hers and guiding it back to him. With his encouragement, she closed her hand around him, entranced as she felt it throb and seem to grow larger beneath her touch.

The feel of her soft little hand hesitantly holding him, learning to stroke and caress him, was both an ecstasy and a torment. Gritting his teeth, Matt tried to hold out, tried to stop himself from losing control as he had every other time he had made love to her. This time he wanted it to be right, for her as well as for him. He wanted her to experience the wonder of love as fully and gloriously as he would. But he couldn't wait. She was kissing his shoulder, her teeth nipping at his flesh, her hands learning all too quickly to give him pleasure with the motion he had taught her. If she didn't stop, he would explode in her hand. He groaned, catching her wrist and pulling her hand away from him. Her teeth sank into his shoulder in protest. Suddenly Matt knew he couldn't bear it any longer. He had to take her now, this instant, or spill his seed ignominiously on the blanket.

He rolled on top of her, his knees parting her thighs, his mouth coming down on hers in a kiss that rocked them both with its intensity. Her legs parted for him automatically, and he was slipping inside, driving home in her softness.

It was glorious. That was Amanda's last conscious thought as he took her, his hard body weaving a spell of unimagined rapture. Of their own volition, her legs came up to twine about his waist and her arms clung to his neck. Against her breasts she could feel his heart thud as though he were dying. Instinctively she arched her body to meet his thrusts, and her hips began to move in time with his rhythm. The tight little coil of pleasure that began in her belly spread out along her veins and then burst, flooding her with delight. She quivered with the unexpected joy of it, feeling herself caught up in a whirlwind of ecstasy so strong that it swept everything before it. She cried out his name once, twice—and the world went dark.

"I love you. Oh, God, I love you," Matt groaned against her throat in that final, earth-shattering moment. Then shuddering, he went limp.

He realized what he had said and stiffened, feeling her soft and yielding beneath him, knowing he had betrayed himself utterly. She would know that she had him where she wanted him at last. He hated to move, to face her, but it had to be done. Finally he lifted his head to look warily at her. Her eyes were closed; her lashes lay like thick black fans against her cheeks. He had to fight the cowardly impulse to slink off into the night. But he had to face the consequences of his loss of control.

"Amanda?" he whispered, dreading to see her triumphant smile. She didn't move, and he frowned and repeated her name. A gentle snore was his answer. She had fallen asleep. He was instinctively affronted. Then he thanked God she had not heard...

Matt was gone when Amanda awoke. Sunlight poured through the small porthole, mocking her. With a groan Amanda shut her eyes again, rolling away from the light and dragging the blanket over her head in protest. She felt dreadful—her head hurt and her mouth felt as if it were full of cotton. Then the most dreadful memories chose that moment to flit through her mind. Had she actually done those things? Told Matt she loved him—not once but several times—sat in his lap, kissed him, begged him to make love to her? She groaned as she remembered. He had promised her that she would beg him, and he had been right. But she had never suspected that he meant to get her drunk. That was despicable.

Her memory of the latter part of the evening was

far more hazy, for which she should probably be thankful, Amanda thought with a shudder. The impression that was indelibly imprinted on her brain was of a pleasure the likes of which she had never dreamed existed, but exactly how it had been achieved was better not examined too closely. It seemed to her that Matt had been as caught up in the maelstrom of passion as she, but, of course, he would be. Men were like that. He would get pleasure bedding a . . . a duck.

Amanda lay there for some little time longer, wishing that she could die and end it. When that didn't happen, and the pounding in her head subsided a bit, she decided to get up. If lying abed would cure what ailed her, she would have been well long since. She would wash and dress and go out on deck for air. Perhaps that would make her feel better.

She was sitting on the side of the bunk, stark naked, her hands propped beside her and her feet testing the surface of the floor, when the door opened and Matt walked in. Amanda jumped automatically, but when she saw who it was, she lifted a hand to her head and groaned. That sudden movement had made her head feel as though a fiery nail were being driven through it.

"How do you feel?" Matt eyed her rather warily, she thought, but she was too miserable to puzzle over the look in his eyes. She glared at him.

"Horrible. And it's all *your* fault. *Beast*."

Some of the wariness left his eyes, and he grinned unsympathetically.

"Now, now, no name-calling. What you're feeling is the result of too much punch, my girl. Of course, if

I'd known you were a secret drinker I wouldn't have mixed that punch, but how could I have known? From the look of you, you'd never touched a drop of liquor in your life."

"You know I hadn't," Amanda muttered resentfully. Then, glaring at him again, she added, "If you came to gloat, you can just go away again. I feel ghastly enough without your grinning at me."

"Is that what I'm doing?"

"Yes," Amanda said, and at that moment another pain attacked her head and she moaned.

Matt, still grinning, moved to the table and, picking up one of the bottles that littered it, began to slosh the contents into a glass. After a moment he turned to her, holding out a glass filled with a noxious-looking golden liquid. Amanda looked at it, then at him, with acute distaste.

"Is this the *coup de grâce?*" She was scowling, a fact that only made the laughter deepen in his eyes. He shook his head, continuing to hold out the glass to her.

"Drink it, Amanda, and I promise that you'll soon feel better. I speak from experience."

"I imagine so," Amanda said sourly, eyeing the glass. Then, with a fatalistic shrug, she took it, downing the contents in a series of quick gulps. This side of death, she didn't think she could feel any worse, and if it made her feel herself again, she would drink the filthy stuff five times over. But its taste on her tongue made her gag, and for one horrible moment after she swallowed the concoction, she was hideously afraid she would disgrace herself by being sick. Then she was sure of it. Her stomach growled warningly and with one killing look at Matt—he was laughing, the devil—she ran for the chamber pot in the corner and was violently ill.

"You *swine*," she said feelingly when she had finished. He was kneeling beside her, wiping her face with a damp cloth.

"Rinse your mouth," he instructed, passing her a glass of water. Amanda rinsed, spat, and drank the remainder thirstily. She had to admit that she did feel better.

"Come, get dressed. What you need now is some fresh air. And, a little later, breakfast."

Amanda shuddered.

"You'll be hungry shortly," Matt promised, and hauled her to her feet and over to the bunk, where he sat her down and proceeded to dress her as if she were a small child.

Strangely, Amanda did not feel the least embarrassment at his ministrations. She supposed it had something to do with the last vestiges of the stuff she had drunk, but it seemed perfectly natural for him to see her naked, to pull her chemise over her head, to help her into a clean pair of breeches—these were smaller and a much better fit; Amanda surmised that they must belong to Timmy, the cabin boy. When she was in a clean shirt, he ran a comb through her hair, and before she could mutter a grudging thank-you, he had swept her up in his arms and was carrying her from the cabin.

"Don't think that this makes up for what you did," Amanda told him resentfully as he crossed to the rail with her and sat her down on a coil of rope so that she could watch the play of sunlight on the smooth surface of the sea.

"What did I do?" He was leaning on the rail less than a foot away, his eyes crinkled against the sun as he looked down at her. Clad in severe black pantaloons and boots, his white shirt unbuttoned to the waist, he looked infuriatingly handsome. Amanda glared at him.

"You know what you did. You got me drunk deliberately so I would...beg you." The last two words were a furious mutter, and her cheeks glowed bright scarlet in embarrassment and rage. She had not meant to refer to what had taken place between them the night before, but shame was eating at her like a worm in an apple, and she had to make it clear to him that only strong drink—and his trickery—had made her behave the way she had.

"I did not get you drunk deliberately." He looked serious as he met her eyes. "That wasn't what I had in mind when I told you I'd make you beg. As for last night, you have nothing to be ashamed of, Amanda. That's the way it's meant to be between a man and a woman."

For a moment he looked so much like the earlier Matt, in the cave, that she stared at him wide-eyed. He was being kind to try to set her at ease, and that didn't accord with the character of the man she had come to know aboard ship. This was the Matt she had grown to love...She was overwhelmed with an urge to heal the breach between them, to try once more to convince him of the truth...

"Matt, I truly didn't turn you over to the authorities. Won't you believe me?" she said softly, rising and coming to stand beside him at the rail. The breeze blew her hair back from her face in a rippling mass of curls, and the sun caught it, bringing out glints of gold in the glorious deep red. Matt stared down at the small face turned up to his, at the perfectly modeled cheekbones and small, straight nose, at the decided chin and deep-rose mouth, at the amethyst eyes that looked up at him so pleadingly. His mouth tightened, and he turned to look out to sea.

"I understand how it happened," he said stiffly, as Amanda watched the dark profile silhouetted against the halcyon sky and deep blue sea. She felt a quick stirring of hope. "I said cruel things to you that night, and you were still shocked from finding out that lovemaking was not exactly what you'd been expecting. I know why you became angry, and, after having watched you in the throes of several temper tantrums, I understand what happened: you went to the constable and told him where to find me, but later you realized just what you'd done and came to warn me. That's what you were going to say, wasn't it, on the beach that morning?"

Amanda felt the hope that had been soaring inside her flutter and die. He wasn't going to believe her, not now, probably never.

"I did come to the beach to warn you, but I hadn't told anyone—not a living soul—that you were there. Matt, you're letting your judgment be colored by things that have nothing to do with us. I'm not your mother, and I didn't betray you." This last was a calculated gamble, a last, desperate attempt to break through the shell he had set around his heart. Amanda felt him stiffen beside her, saw dark color wash high into his cheekbones. His knuckles were white against the wooden railing as he gripped it hard; then he turned to look at her, his eyes a gleaming silver as cold and remote as the moon.

"Zeke has been telling tales out of school, has he?" His tone was grim. "I must compliment you, Amanda: you are remarkable. You managed to get around Zeke—who hated you before he ever laid eyes on you, by the way—in less than a week. And now? Will you take him to bed, too, so that you can watch while the two of us kill each other?"

The unexpected ferocity of his attack shook Amanda. She blanched, staring up at him disbelievingly while her eyes slowly darkened to huge purple pools. Then, as the full sense of his words penetrated, her mouth tightened and her eyes shot sparks at him. Without a word, she slowly drew back her hand and slapped him hard across the cheek.

"I feel sorry for you," she said contemptuously as he stared at her, one hand automatically coming up to touch the reddened cheek. Then, turning her back on him, she walked with quiet dignity across the deck to their cabin. She was so angry she was not even aware of the shocked stares of Zeke and the crew as their eyes swung between Matt's still figure and her own retreating back.

chapter twenty

Six weeks later the *Clorimunda* sailed into the Mississippi River port of New Orleans. Amanda stood at the rail of the quarterdeck, dressed in Timmy's breeches and shirt, the color high in her cheeks and her unbound hair streaming behind her like a crimson banner. Her eyes sparkled like jewels as she looked from the crowded harbor scene to Zeke, who stood beside her at the rail, a grin splitting his thin face as he answered her many eager questions. It was Zeke who had told her about Belle Terre, Matt's plantation on the shores of Lake Pontchartrain, where they would go after spending a few days in New Orleans. It was Zeke who laughed at her excitement as her eyes darted everywhere in an effort to take in the colorful port as the *Clorimunda* eased in expertly at the dock between two other tall ships. Matt was at the wheel, directing the crew, but even if he hadn't been needed there, Amanda would have preferred Zeke's company. Zeke had come to seem like a brother to her over the past few weeks, and she felt at ease with him as she no longer did with Matt, who had become a cold, distant stranger.

He had not touched her since she had slapped his face that day on deck. In fact, he had barely spoken to her. She was allowed the sole occupancy of the captain's cabin, and Matt bunked with Zeke in the first mate's. Where the first mate now slept, Amanda had no idea and had never asked.

Zeke, who had witnessed the confrontation, tried to serve as peacemaker and had earned the lash of his brother's tongue as a reward. Amanda, although grateful for Zeke's concern, was equally unresponsive to his efforts. If Matt's coldness hurt, she vowed he would never know. And she didn't think he was capable of feeling a thing.

The *Clorimunda*'s sails were lowered and furled, and the small boats that had towed her in had released their lines when Matt finally gave the order to drop anchor and lower the gangplank.

"Can we go ashore now?" Amanda demanded excitedly of Zeke. He smiled down at her, his expression indulgent. He had grown as fond of Amanda as she had of him, and strongly disapproved of his brother's treatment of her.

"I don't see—" he began, only to be interrupted as Matt appeared beside them.

"Not today," he said in answer to Amanda's question, and as she turned a disappointed, sulky face to him he added, "Zeke and I have business to attend to today. Tomorrow we'll take you ashore. You wouldn't be safe alone, and I don't trust any of the men enough to send them with you. You'd twist them around your little finger inside an hour."

Amanda glowered at him. He was just being contrary, she knew. If he had thought she didn't want to go ashore, he would have forced her to, if necessary. But now that he knew that such an excursion would give her pleasure, he had denied her out of sheer bloody-mindedness.

"Can't it wait until tomorrow?" Zeke asked his brother uneasily. Since he and Amanda had quarreled, Matt had grown moodier by the day. His once even-tempered, even jovial brother was now as likely as not to bite his head off at a wrong word. Indeed, the entire crew of the *Clorimunda* had felt the heat of his ill temper.

"No, it cannot," Matt replied brusquely, and turned away. Zeke stared after him, frowning. Then he looked down at Amanda.

"Sorry," he said with a grimace. "But I promise I'll take you ashore myself tomorrow, no matter what. I don't know what's got into Matt, but he's like a bear with a sore head. I'll have a talk with him."

"Please don't," Amanda said swiftly, and Zeke's mouth twisted as he looked at her.

"You're probably right." He shrugged, looking after Matt as he disappeared down the stairs to the main deck. "I've tried four times now, and the last time he damned near throttled me. Why don't you try, Amanda? Perhaps if you tried to make him see reason, he'd listen."

"As he did the last time?" Amanda's voice was bitter. "I'm not likely to try that again. Besides, I no

351

longer care what he thinks. He's stubborn and pig-headed, and I don't give a snap of my fingers for his opinion of me."

"Really," Zeke said dryly. Amanda scowled at him, knowing very well that he had a shrewd idea of the state of her feelings toward Matt. Well, she'd be damned if she'd wear her heart on her sleeve. Matt clearly didn't want to know, and she wasn't about to tell him.

"Yes, really," she said, defying him to say anything further. Zeke eyed her, clearly thinking about calling her bluff, and Amanda turned an impatient shoulder on him to stare out at the town.

"Oh, go with Matt, Zeke, before I quarrel with you, too. Then I really would be miserable."

"Would you?" He smiled down at her. "So would I. But I think I'd better go anyway. Big brother definitely does not like to be kept waiting."

Amanda hunched her shoulders as he left her, miserably aware of the excitement in the air. New Orleans appeared a thrilling place, and she wasn't going to see it—at least not today and, considering Matt's bloody-mindedness, perhaps never. Moodily she sniffed at the air, enjoying the tangy scent of citrus fruits and spices mingled with salt from the sea. How she wished she was on the dock to discover the source of the tantalizing aromas for herself. Out of the corner of her eye she caught a glimpse of the sun glinting off a familiar blue-black head, and turned to watch moodily as Matt and Zeke strode side by side down the gangplank and disappeared into the milling crowd on the wharf. She glowered at their retreating backs and felt a little better.

For a moment she toyed with the idea of going ashore herself, on her own. It shouldn't be too hard to sneak away and she would not stay long. She would be back before Matt, and he need never know she had disobeyed him. But then she studied some of the men on the quay and thought better of it. Swarthy men with bright scarves around their necks and gold rings glinting in their ears pushed carts full of oranges and other, less readily identifiable fruits through the mob, calling out in a language unknown to her to advertise their wares; ragged children darted in and out among the sea of long legs; sailors, some alone, some in pairs or groups, and some with women on their arms who looked no better than they should be, overflowed the nearby saloons to swill whiskey on the dock itself. Though she hated to admit it, Matt had been right when he said it would be dangerous for her to go ashore alone. As much as she relished the idea of defying him, she was not foolish enough to put herself at risk to do it.

Some hours later, after Amanda had retired disconsolately to her cabin, she heard a commotion on deck. Matt had left a skeleton crew aboard, with orders to keep an eye on everything, including, Amanda suspected, herself. Before she could leave the cabin to question one of the men, she was surprised to hear a brisk rap on the door. Opening it, Amanda blinked in astonishment at the figure who stared imperiously at her.

It was a lady—a very elegant lady. From the top of her plumed bonnet to the fashionable walking dress to the soles of her high-heeled buttoned shoes, she was the epitome of fashion. For a moment Amanda stared without speaking, too bemused to do more than blink while she wondered what possible business this woman could have on the *Clorimunda*. Then it came to her that the lady had knocked on the door of Matt's cabin, which meant that, more than likely, she was a friend of Matt's. Amanda's eyes narrowed and moved over the woman critically. Quite attractive, she thought, if one didn't mind that the lady was a trifle long in the tooth—and Matt apparently didn't.

"I'm sorry, but Captain Grayson is not here at the moment," Amanda said coldly, and made as if to close the door.

"Pooh, what has that to say to anything?" The woman shook her head, clearly scornful of such stupidity. "You are Lady Amanda?" She looked at Amanda with some suspicion, as if a lady could not possibly be found in a man's ill-fitting breeches and shirt, with her hair tousled and tumbling over her shoulders.

"Yes," Amanda admitted, eyeing the woman curiously. Who on earth was she, and how did she know her name?

"Then it is you I wish to see," the woman announced, and swept by Amanda with a haughty grace that would not have been out of place in a duchess. Surprised, Amanda turned to look at her, only to be even more astonished when two other, younger women, each dressed in a severe black gown and carrying a large valise, followed the first woman inside. She had been so bemused by her visitor's finery that she hadn't noticed her retinue.

Seeing nothing for it, Amanda turned to face her

uninvited guests, cautiously leaving the door open. "How may I help you?"

"It is *I* who will help *you*," her visitor sniffed, withdrawing a lethal-looking pin from her hat before removing the feathered concoction and placing it on the table. She eyed Amanda critically as she drew off her gloves. "I am Madame Duvalier, the most fashionable *modiste* in all of New Orleans. I was told that you need a complete wardrobe *tout de suite*." She favored Amanda's breeches with a disdainful glance. "And I can see that it is true. We will begin."

Amanda gaped as the two young women in black descended on her and began removing her clothes, making scornful noises at her unconventional attire all the while.

"These are my assistants, Rose"—the pretty brown-haired girl, who was helping Amanda off with her breeches, smiled shyly up at her—"and Marie." Marie had removed Amanda's shirt and was now opening one of the valises. She was not so pretty as Rose, Amanda saw, but her coloring—black hair and eyes and vivid red lips—was more striking. Madame Duvalier herself was a redhead, but Amanda suspected that the brassy tint owed more to artifice than to nature.

"But who sent you?" Amanda's voice was faint. She was standing in the center of the room, clad only in her much-laundered chemise, while Marie ran a tape measure around different parts of her anatomy, calling out the measurements in a businesslike tone to Rose, who jotted them down in a small notebook. Madame Duvalier herself had commandeered a chair and from it supervised the proceedings.

"Captain Grayson," Madame replied patiently, as if she were addressing a slightly backward child. Amanda would have taken exception to her tone if she hadn't been mulling over that most interesting bit of information. Matt ... Matt had ordered a dressmaker for her? He must not be so indifferent to her as she had supposed. At least he was concerned about her creature comforts. Then the sudden animation faded from her features as she considered the alternate possibility that Zeke was responsible for the modiste's presence. That seemed far more likely. Zeke would have known she needed clothes if she was to go ashore. Matt wouldn't have given the matter a single thought. Still, she would ask.

"Which Captain Grayson?" she asked carefully. Marie was putting away the tape measure while Rose extracted a book of fashions from the valise and carried it to Madame Duvalier. Madame accepted it without so much as a word of thanks and began to leaf through it, alternately looking at Amanda critically as she did so.

"That will do. Number three, Rose, in figured white muslin, I think. Very *jeune fille*. And number seven, in blue silk—"

"Madame," Amanda interrupted impatiently. Marie was pulling a garment over her head, so her words were briefly muffled.

"You do not know?" Madame looked surprised. "I would have thought only a very particular friend... But perhaps they both are that, as they are of mine. I have known both since they were boys. Matt is *très beau*, is he not? And Zeke is very attractive too, in his own way."

"But which one sent you to me?" Amanda had to know.

"I do not know," Madame answered, sending her hopes plummeting. "I received a note: 'Lady Amanda on *Clorimunda* needs complete new wardrobe. Bill to Captain Grayson.' Matt or Zeke, no matter. Either will pay."

"I see." Marie was pushing her this way and that as Rose pinned the garment. Looking down rather abstractedly, Amanda saw that it was a lovely dress of deep cream muslin, figured with tiny green flowers. The neckline, which bared her shoulders and the tops of her breasts, was edged with exquisite hand-made lace in the same deep cream as the dress. The hem of the full, fashionably short skirt—it just covered her ankles—was edged with more lace. The narrow waist was bound with a wide green satin sash that tied in the back in a ravishing bow. Looking down at herself, Amanda could not suppress a little thrill of pleasure. Except for the yellow silk dress that Matt had torn to shreds, she had never owned a garment so beautiful. She would be less than human if she did not relish the idea of wearing it in Matt's presence.

"A little tighter in the waist, Rose," Madame instructed as she eyed Amanda, her head cocked to one side like that of an inquisitive bird. "And just a tiny bit shorter in the skirt. There—*ravissante*. Is it not fortunate, Lady Amanda, that the family of one of my best customers was visited by a tragic loss? She had ordered this dress for her daughter, but with the family in mourning for six months, of course she had to cancel the order. I understood perfectly. *C'est la vie*. Besides," she added with a sudden smile and without her French accent, "she wouldn't dream of letting anyone else supply her and her daughter's mourning clothes. Her unpaid bill is too big."

Amanda smiled back, suddenly liking the woman. When she reverted to her true self, she was much nicer than when she assumed the role of the formidable Madame Duvalier.

"This dress you will have tomorrow early," Madame decreed, reverting to her original manner as Marie lifted the dress over Amanda's head, careful not to disturb the pins. "And accessories, of course. The others—one or two the next day. The rest—a week."

"Thank you for coming, Madame," Amanda said as she stepped back into her breeches and shirt, which the women eyed with severe disfavor. Rose had packed everything in the valises and they were ready to leave.

"It is my pleasure," Madame said formally. "For Matt or Zeke, which one it doesn't matter, I am always available. You will have the dress tomorrow," she repeated as she preceded her assistants out the door. Amanda stared bemusedly at the closed door for some little time after the trio had gone.

The prospect of new clothes relieved one of Amanda's nagging worries. She had been wondering how she was to get about in New Orleans clad in ill-fitting male attire. In England it would have been considered scandalous for a lady to appear in such garments, and she doubted that the New World was much different. But without a skirt to her name, she had had no choice. It was thoughtful of Zeke—or

Matt—to think of her difficulties and take steps to remedy them. Which brought her to another problem: it was less than respectable for either Matt or Zeke to pay for her clothes, but as she had no money, she didn't suppose that there was anything she could do about it. Besides, so much of what had happened to her since she had met Matt had been unconventional, to say the least, that she must now be quite outside the social pale. Losing her virginity had been dreadful, but no one but herself and Matt need ever have known of that. But she had been missing for nearly two months now, and she was sure that most of the people who mattered to her must be aware that the Duke of Brookshire's young half sister had disappeared. Even if no one had associated her disappearance with Matt—who, after all, was presumed dead—an unexplained absence of such length inevitably meant social ruin. And if it became known that she had spent the time with a company of men, one of whom had shared her bed . . . She shuddered; she would be lucky to find a convent that would take her in.

Amanda frowned. She was in a strange country, without friends or money, and with no place to go. She doubted that Matt would see her in want—indeed, he seemed to take it for granted that she would make her home with him and Zeke—but she could not allow him to support her for the rest of her life. The knowledge that she was now indebted to him for every morsel of bread flayed her pride. What would it be like in the future, when he had another woman and she was merely an object of charity living in his home? Unbearable, she thought with a grimace.

True, he was solely responsible for her presence—he had stolen her away from her school; she certainly hadn't begged him to take her with him—but that didn't alter by so much as a hair the situation in which she now found herself.

Painful as it was, it was time to face facts: socially she was ruined as thoroughly as ever Susan had been. No gentleman would marry her now. As she saw it, she was left with three choices: she could continue to live with Matt, labeling herself his mistress in the eyes of everyone and thereby cutting herself off forever from the respectable society of the wives and daughters of gentlemen; she could leave Matt's protection (if he would let her go, which was unlikely) and make a life for herself independent of him, which would undoubtedly include genteel starvation; or she could return to England, and eventually to Edward, whose family pride would at least ensure that she did not starve to death—if he did not plan a worse fate for her.

She was happier now than she had been since before her father died, she acknowledged. For the first time in years she felt alive, free; every day was an adventure. Matt's coldness was the only cloud in her newly blue sky. But with a sudden flash of insight, Amanda knew that she would rather be with Matt, coldly angry or not, than without him. He had become the focal point of her life—and that was something she hated to admit to herself. Damn the man, Amanda thought despairingly, and damn me, too, for being foolish enough to fall in love with him. But at least it solved her dilemma: feeling about him as she did, she could not bring herself to leave him.

It would be easier to live without her pride than without her heart.

It was long after dark when Matt and Zeke returned. Amanda was curled up on the bunk with a book when she heard Zeke's laughing voice and Matt's muted reply. They undoubtedly intended to go to their cabin without disturbing her, but Amanda was determined to resolve the matter of the clothes as soon as possible. She would be unable to sleep a wink if she did not.

She flew out on deck, a small, slender figure, with streaming red hair and clad in too-big men's clothes. The still-crowded dock was lit by flaming torches, which cast flickering shadows over the *Clorimunda's* deck; the ship herself was lit by a few strategically placed lanterns. The two sailors who were assigned to remain topside as officers of the watch were nowhere in sight. Presumably they were at either end of the ship to sound a warning if someone unauthorized tried to board her. Matt and Zeke were just coming aboard, with Zeke in the lead and Matt a pace behind. As they stepped into a golden pool of light Amanda noticed that they both looked oddly disheveled, Zeke more so than Matt. His brown hair was wildly tousled and his shirt collar was standing rakishly on end. Matt's black curls were untidy, too, but his clothes seemed to be in order. What struck Amanda was the dangerous glitter of his eyes.

Zeke saw her first. She had stopped, eyeing them suspiciously. The thought came to her that they had been drinking. Then Zeke spoke, and the faint slurring of his words told her all she needed to know.

"Good evening, Amanda," he cried, bowing so low

that he would have fallen flat on his face if Matt had not caught hold of his coattails. Zeke straightened, with the assistance of Matt's balancing hand, and looked at Amanda, frowning. "What, no new clothes? Didn't that pox of a woman come after all?"

Her question had been answered for her without her having to ask. Amanda swallowed an aching surge of disappointment that it hadn't been Matt, then summoned a smile for Zeke.

"Thank you, Zeke. As soon as Madame Duvalier told me why she had come, I knew that you were the only one thoughtful enough to have sent her. It was very nice of you." If those words had been selected with an eye to pricking Matt, Amanda wasn't admitting it. She didn't look at him as he stood a half pace behind Zeke, holding his brother unobtrusively upright. But she sensed his gleaming eyes boring into her.

"It *was* nice of me, wasn't it?" Zeke nodded, looking owlish and pleased with himself. Then he held out his arms to Amanda, grinning wickedly at her. "Won't you thank me properly?"

Ordinarily Amanda would have laughed at such a suggestion from Zeke. She knew it was made tongue-in-cheek, probably with a little-boyish desire to annoy his brother and shock her girlish sensibilities at one and the same time. But she, too, was conscious of Matt standing just behind Zeke's shoulder, watching her, his mouth and eyes sardonic. With a little toss of her head and nary a glance at Matt, she moved into Zeke's arms.

They closed about her enthusiastically, and if he looked surprised, it was just for a moment. Then he was bending his head and kissing her heartily. Amanda hoped that Matt, standing behind him, couldn't tell it was more the kind of kiss a brother might bestow on a beloved sister than a kiss between lovers. When Zeke let her go, stepping back from her with a lopsided grin, Amanda smiled at him, deliberately infusing as much warmth into that smile as she could.

"That was...very nice, Amanda," Zeke said, sounding faintly regretful. Amanda's brows began to knit at something in his tone. "But if that was a thank-you, you thanked the wrong man. It was big brother who sent Madame Duvalier to you."

Amanda's eyes widened and moved from Zeke's grinning face to Matt's dark countenance. He looked grim as he returned her stare, his eyes gleaming with mockery and something else she was afraid to try to define.

"Aren't you going to thank me with a kiss, too, Amanda?" His voice was very soft as he stepped out from behind Zeke and looked down at her. Dressed in a dark blue superfine coat, black breeches, and a white shirt and carelessly tied cravat, he looked very big and more than a little menacing. The silvery eyes glittered at her, and the lamplight painted a gilded nimbus around the halo of thick black curls. He had not shaved since early morning, and a faint black shadow roughened the lean lines of his jaw and chin. All in all, he looked so handsome that he nearly took Amanda's breath away—and he was holding out his arms to her as Zeke had done. Amanda could hardly think as she walked into them.

They closed about her so tightly that she feared he

must crack her ribs. Then his mouth came down on hers, tasting faintly of whiskey, and she couldn't think at all. He kissed her harshly, hungrily, as if he were starved for the taste of her mouth. He bent her back over his arm, his lips and tongue demanding and getting her total surrender. She clung to him helplessly, then, of her own volition, her arms were twining about his neck, drawing the black head closer, her nails embedding themselves in his nape. A sweet, wild trembling started somewhere deep in her belly and moved out along her limbs. She knew he had to feel it, holding her as closely as he was, just as she was totally conscious of every muscle and sinew of the hard male body enfolding hers—and of the growing arousal that he made no attempt to hide. Amanda forgot everything, their position on the open deck, where they were clearly visible to anyone who happened to glance their way, Zeke's interested gaze, even the differences between herself and Matt. All she was aware of was that this was her man, and she was in his arms again at last. Her only wish was that he never let her go.

He did, of course. His arms dropped away from her without warning. Amanda, lost in a kiss-induced dreamworld, tried to cling to him. He detached her arms from about his neck with brutal efficiency, holding them tightly for a moment as he stared down at her with a restless glitter in eyes that had become the color of smoke. Then, without a word, he released her, swinging on his heel and striding back the way he had come and off the ship. Amanda was left staring helplessly after him, tears filling her eyes. She felt as if she had just been kicked in the stomach.

chapter twenty-one

Three days later, Amanda was living in Matt's luxurious town house in New Orleans's exclusive Vieux Carré district. Matt and Zeke were out so much that Amanda barely set eyes on either of them. Matt had told Zeke to be ready to take another ship to England at the end of the week. The captain was ill, and the cargo—cotton destined for English mills—could not be delayed until his recovery. Amanda more than half suspected that Matt was exaggerating the urgency of the trip to remove Zeke from the scene, but if Zeke had similar suspicions, they didn't seem to trouble him. He seemed almost glad to be going.

Amanda, on the other hand, was despondent every time she thought of being left alone with Matt. Since the night he had kissed her, his attitude toward her had changed from cold civility to a hateful, biting mockery. He seemed to take positive joy in hurting her. And if she was unhappy during this brief period in New Orleans, with the shops and colorful street markets to entertain her, what would it be like when she and Matt were alone at Belle Terre? Because as soon as Zeke was gone, that was where he intended to take her.

The servants were another source of discomfort to her. Slavery was an accepted practice in New Orleans, but it made Amanda uncomfortable to be waited on by human beings that Matt actually owned, as he did a horse or a dog or a ship. And, what was worse, they seemed to disapprove of her. Lalanni, the coffee-skinned housemaid who Matt had assigned to accompany her whenever she set foot outdoors and to act as her personal maid at home, let slip in her soft creole voice that moral outrage was the reason for the servants' stiffness. In New Orleans, a gentleman did *not* have his mistress live with him. He bought his inamorata her own house, in a discreet section of town, and visited her at night. That was the way it was done, the way it had always been done, the right way. That Matt had set up his mistress in his own establishment was a scandalous breach of propriety.

The knowledge that all the servants considered her Matt's mistress humiliated Amanda. Never had she imagined she would be reduced to such a state. Even the fact that it wasn't strictly true was no consolation. Matt had given her her own room in the three-storied house, and he never entered it or laid a hand on her. But her mere presence—a young, unmarried, unprotected girl in a bachelor's household—was enough to cause a scandal. Amanda burned with the knowledge that she was no better than a fallen woman, and sometimes, when people stared at her in the streets, she wondered if her shame was so intense that it was somehow visible in her face.

She was, of course, totally cut off from any contact with New Orleans society. Her position in Matt's household made that inevitable. The world of afternoon barbecues and evening dances, mornings spent receiving and returning calls, elegant teas and all the other pleasant little activities that made up a lady's life was closed to her—she feared forever. Aside from Matt, Zeke, and the scarcely friendly servants, and an occasional word exchanged with a shopgirl or tradesman, she spoke to no one, and no one spoke to her. Sometimes when she wandered through the markets with Lalanni at her heels, she would encounter ladies who, under other circumstances, would have been Lady Amanda's social inferiors. They acted as though she didn't exist. After her first few tentative smiles were deliberately—and rudely—ignored, Amanda learned to treat them as they treated her, as if she were invisible. But, secretly shamed and hurt by such encounters, she took to staying within doors to avoid them. Used to Susan's easy friendship and to the camaraderie of the other girls at the convent, Amanda found it hard to be totally deprived of female companionship. She realized that until now, when it was lost to her, she had never truly appreciated the value of respectability.

One afternoon, when she was feeling particularly lonely, she gave in to a compelling urge to write to Susan. She thought it would be safe enough—the missive was carefully worded to reveal no hint of her whereabouts or whom she might be with. It said merely that she was well and happy. By the time she had sealed the envelope tears were coursing down her cheeks. She missed Susan terribly and knew that Susan must miss her just as much. It hurt to realize that, under the circumstances, she was unlikely ever to set eyes on her dearest friend again. But then she realized that, if she could choose to return to the convent, to the days before Matt had turned her life upside down, she would not. Dear as Susan was to her, Matt was far dearer. In the space of a few short weeks he had become the most important person in her world. But it was steadily being borne in upon her that she could not continue to occupy her present ignominious position in his life. Her self-respect would not permit it. Wiping her cheeks, she sniffed once and began anew to consider the alternatives.

As the days passed, and the time of Zeke's departure drew nearer, Amanda realized that she would have to confront Matt. Things simply could not go on this way. She was grateful for his care, for the food and shelter and truly lovely clothes he had provided, but she could not continue to live off his bounty. If she was ever to hold up her head again, she had to live within the conventions that governed the behavior of a lady. And that meant, at the very least, leaving Matt's protection and supporting herself.

She could work, Amanda thought, but what could she work at? Her needlework hardly qualified her to be a seamstress, and there was little other decent employment open to a lady. A post as a governess would probably be best, for she had had an excellent education thanks to the nuns, but to obtain such a post someone would have to recommend her, and the only people she knew in the whole of America were Matt and Zeke. And she hardly thought that a recommendation from either of those gentlemen would help her cause.

Still, there had to be something she could do. She would talk to Matt about it.

Amanda got her chance the next morning. Instead of sipping a cup of chocolate and nibbling a croissant in bed, as Lalanni seemed to expect her to do, she arose early with the intention of catching Matt at the breakfast table. She did—but only just. He was finishing a cup of coffee when she walked into the room. From the looks of the serving dishes, he had recently polished off a large plate of ham, eggs, and something the servants called johnnycakes. Amanda eyed his empty plate with some distaste, her stomach churning in revolt at the idea of consuming such a quantity of food so early in the morning. Why, the sun was barely up.

Matt's eyebrows rose as she came into the room, and his eyes moved over her. Amanda had dressed hastily, so she wasn't entirely comfortable under the insolent scrutiny. She didn't know that her full-skirted, tight-waisted morning gown of palest peach cambric made her skin glow like a pearl, or that the simplicity of her hair drawn back from her face with a peach satin ribbon gave her a young, untouched look that smote Matt's conscience. And was the reason for the sardonic curl of his lips.

"Back to impersonating an angel, I see," was his

greeting; he drained his cup and stood. "Rather wasted, under the circumstances, isn't it?"

Amanda felt her cheeks color angrily at the derision in his tone, but she was determined to say what she had come to say and she refused to let him sidetrack her. She crossed to stand at the end of the table, clutching the back of one of the graceful rosewood chairs for support.

"I want to talk to you, Matt."

"Oh? I was certain that all this finery so early in the morning was designed to dazzle my impressionable little brother. I'm honored that you went to so much effort for me."

"Will you please listen to me?" she demanded fiercely. His eyebrows rose again, and he subjected her to another of those unnerving looks. Amanda bit her lip. She would not allow this discussion to degenerate into an argument before she'd said what she had to say. Accordingly, her tone was milder when she continued. "I can't stay here, Matt."

"I fail to see why not." He looked over at her, sighed faintly, and pulled his chair away from the table again. "If we are going to discuss this subject, and I can see we are, I would appreciate it if you would sit down. I can hardly do so unless you do, you know."

Amanda was impatient at this bagatelle, but she sat down. So did Matt.

"Why can't you stay here? I am assuming you mean this house, not New Orleans in general."

"Yes." Now that the time had come, Amanda did not know quite how to phrase what was on her mind. "It . . . it isn't proper, Matt."

"Oh?"

He looked so unconcerned that Amanda had to restrain an urge to throw something at him. Of course the proprieties didn't matter to him—he was a man. Men were almost totally exempt from society's condemnation.

"Everybody thinks I'm your... your mistress. They think I'm a fallen woman."

Matt leaned back in his chair, one hand slipping inside the pocket of his pale gray pantaloons as he looked at her.

"Quite apart from the fact that both you and I know that isn't so—at least, not anymore—who is 'everyone'?"

Amanda shrugged. His nonchalance was annoying. "The servants... Lalanni—"

"Lalanni *dared* to say such a thing to you?" He looked angry. Amanda retreated hastily, not wanting to cause her maid trouble. Lalanni had merely been replying, reluctantly, to her questions.

"No. No, of course not. But I can tell—"

"If the servants have been anything less than respectful, I'll have a talk with them. That should settle the matter."

"Matt, it isn't only that." Amanda was maddened by his refusal to recognize her point. "I can't continue to live with you, and you can't go on supporting me. You *know* you can't."

"Why not? I'm reasonably wealthy, and though your clothes were rather expensive, you don't eat that much."

"Will you be serious?" Amanda glared at him, exasperated. He was deliberately making light of her difficulties. "You *know* what I mean."

He frowned faintly, picking up a knife from the table and toying with it. "Yes, I think I do. It bothers you that people think we're lovers. I can see your point, but I can't see what you expect me to do about it. Unless you're suggesting I turn you out into the streets."

"If you would help me find employment, I could be independent of you." She looked at him hopefully. He looked back at her, his expression thoughtful.

"And just what sort of work do you imagine you could do?"

"I could be a governess."

He snorted with derision. "At your age, and with your beauty? Your little charges' papa would take one look at you and be unable to think of anything thereafter except getting under your skirts, and his wife—if she hired you, which is doubtful—would discharge you without a character as soon as she caught the gleam in her husband's eye."

Amanda's cheeks burned, and her eyes were bright with indignation. "There is no need to be crude."

His lip curled. "Isn't there? Amanda, you must see that this discussion is ridiculous." He pushed his chair back and stood up. "I must go to the docks. Zeke's been there this hour and more and will be wondering what has become of me."

Amanda stood up, too, moving in front of him and catching at his arm. She could feel the hardness of his muscles through the dark blue coat.

"There must be *something* I can do."

His lips compressed, then his eyes began to glint

with amusement as he looked from her hand clutching his coat to her face.

"You are absolutely determined to earn your living?"

"Yes."

He smiled. "Then I think I know the perfect situation for you. You're a little short on experience, but the talent is there."

Something about his smile she disliked.

"What is it?" The words were wary, and her expression was more so. His smile widened, and his hand came up to catch her chin.

"You could be my mistress again, Amanda. Up to now it hasn't been lucrative, I know, but I'd be happy to remedy that in the future."

She jerked her chin from his hand, her eyes shooting violet daggers at him.

"How *dare* you," she gasped. He laughed, chucked her under her chin again, and headed for the door. Amanda stood glaring at his broad back. At the door, he turned to look over his shoulder at her.

"Think about it," he said softly, then, with another of those mocking smiles, left the room.

Amanda did think about it, all the rest of that day. Matt could have been teasing her, of course, but she had a feeling that, beneath the mocking amusement, he had been serious. She knew he found her desirable, and she knew, too, if she were honest, that she wouldn't truly dislike being his mistress. At least, not the physical side of it. She loved him, and if the truth were told, she had been first piqued and then annoyed, over the past weeks, when he had made no attempt to come to her bed. Which was shameful, she knew, but was the way she felt. What made it worse, and

373

made the idea of being Matt's mistress impossible, was the certainty that he didn't love her. Oh, he wanted her; he'd made that clear. But he didn't love her, didn't even trust her, and if she agreed to be his mistress, it would last only until he found someone else to amuse him. Amanda didn't delude herself that there would be any more to it than that.

With a wry smile, Amanda considered what the nuns and Susan and everyone else in her social circle would think if they knew she was even considering accepting a man's *carte blanche*. Before she had fallen in love with Matt, she would have been shocked and appalled herself. Like everyone else she knew, she had always thought that only a certain type of woman received such an offer, much less accepted it. Certainly she had never imagined that she, Lady Amanda Rose Culver, daughter of a duke, would ever receive such a proposition. Or that she would for a moment consider living with a man outside the sacred bonds of matrimony.

But she loved him, and there was the rub. Just the memory of that lean, handsome face, with its silvery eyes and chiseled mouth, was enough to send a thrill of pleasure down her spine. She loved everything about him, from the texture of his jaw when he had not shaved recently to the feel of his crisp black hair under her fingers. With Matt, no matter how angry he might be at her, she always felt safe and secure, protected. He made her feel as though she had come home.

Obviously he did not feel that way about her. His mother had made him wary of all women, and she had been unable to break the attitudes of a lifetime.

He wanted her, and at one time might have been falling a little bit in love with her. Then he decided she had betrayed him, on what seemed to her the flimsiest of evidence. Thinking about that, Amanda wondered with a quick flash of insight whether he might not have seized on the supposed betrayal as an excuse. He had been growing too fond of her, and he had panicked. What had happened that morning on the beach was a shield he could use to protect himself from becoming emotionally vulnerable to a woman again.

What she wanted, Amanda admitted to herself with a grimace, was for him to love her and ask her to marry him. The world could hold no greater happiness for her. It didn't matter that, as the illegitimate son of a prostitute, he was so far beneath her on the social scale that in theory such an alliance was laughable. It didn't matter that he was a convicted murderer who would certainly hang if he ever set foot in England. All that mattered was that she loved him. It was as simple as that.

He would never ask her to marry him. The knowledge was bitter, but it never did any good to blind oneself to the truth. She could be his mistress, in fact as well as in name, or she could leave him. Those were her choices, and both were painful.

Amanda was still considering the matter late that afternoon. She had just returned from accompanying Lalanni, who had bought fresh vegetables for dinner from the street vendor at the corner. New Orleans in July was stifling hot, a sticky, humid heat that curled the little tendrils that escaped from the simple knot in which she had dressed her hair, and caused dewy perspiration to moisten the pale skin at her temples. She had changed into a sleeveless, low-necked white muslin gown with only a lavender satin sash for ornament. Beneath it she wore only her chemise and a single petticoat. It was too hot for stays or for the two additional petticoats that convention required. In an effort to keep cool, she was sipping a large glass of mint-flavored iced tea and sitting on a chaise longue pulled up before the open French windows that looked out onto the walled garden. A book lay forgotten in her lap. She was more interested in watching the antics of a pair of hummingbirds as they flitted among the brilliantly colored flowers.

She had leaned her head against the soft upholstery of the chair, enjoying the lush perfume of the flowers and smiling faintly at the flight of the birds, when Lalanni tapped on the door. Amanda looked around, surprised. She was rarely disturbed in the back parlor at this time of day.

"Visitor, ma'am," Lalanni said after opening the door in response to Amanda's assent.

"Who?" Amanda sat up, swinging her legs over the side of the chaise longue and frowning slightly. She had not had a visitor before. Since the ladies of New Orleans were hardly likely to call under the circumstances, it had to be business of some sort. "The visitor asked for me, Lalanni? Not Captain Grayson?"

"Yes, ma'am. It's a gentleman. Wouldn't give his name, but he's a swell, from the look of him."

"Show him in, Lalanni," Amanda directed, lifting an abstracted hand to her hair as she stood up. She could not imagine a gentleman calling on *her*. More than likely, Lalanni was mistaken.

"Good afternoon, Amanda." The unmistakable clipped vowels of an upper-class English accent brought Amanda's eyes leaping to the man's face. She went so white that Lalanni started toward her in concern. Amanda waved her away, then recovered enough to say, "Thank you, Lalanni. That will be all. But stay within call, please."

"Yes, ma'am." By the time the girl curtsied and left the room Amanda had regained much of her poise. She was still shocked, but she was determined not to show it. Besides, what could he do to her now?

"Why are you here, Edward?" She made no effort to conceal the hostility in her voice. Her half brother smiled slightly, his cold eyes glittering with malicious amusement as they moved over her.

"Not a very sisterly greeting, Amanda, especially considering the trouble you've put me to."

"You must know I don't feel very sisterly toward you, any more than you feel brotherly toward me. I repeat, what are you doing here?"

"Why, I've come to take you home, of course. Did you think you could spoil my plans so easily?"

He was smiling at her with eyes like a barracuda's. Amanda almost shivered with fear before she remembered that she didn't have to be afraid any longer. She was no longer subject to Edward's authority. They were in America, not England. And there was Matt.

"You must know that I won't go back with you. If that's why you came, you've had a wasted trip."

"Oh, I don't think so." He strolled toward her, and she took an instinctive step backward. His smile widened.

"How did you find me?" She asked the question more to give herself time to think than from any real curiosity. Without Matt to protect her, there was nothing to stop Edward from physically forcing her to go with him. She doubted that the servants would come to her aid.

"That was easy. I had Jamison watching you, you know, from the time we had our little...disagreement. I was afraid you might do something foolish, like running away. Imagine my surprise when Jamison overheard you and a man in your bedroom—not nice, that, Amanda, especially not in a convent. A man you called Matt. With the description Jamison gave me after watching the fellow leave—in quite a temper, Jamison said; you must be somewhat lacking in the feminine arts, Amanda—I came to the horrifying conclusion that you were aiding and abetting—as well as bedding—the murderer all England was searching for. The next morning, it was a simple matter to notify the constable, then wait until you went to warn your lover. I sent the soldiers after you, Amanda. Your little ruse was quite easy to see through. And after Grayson was supposedly killed, I still had Jamison watch you. I wasn't convinced he was dead, you see. The soldiers aren't particularly good shots. He might have tried to contact you—or you might have tried to run away. I was taking no chances. Jamison followed you that night you went running along the edge of the cliff, and he saw everything that happened. He was even able to get the name of your abductors' ship. It was painted on the side of the boat they came ashore in—very careless, but I don't suppose they expected anyone to see them. With that information it was only a matter of checking the registry of the ship, which, I found, without much surprise, belonged to one Matthew Grayson of New Orleans. And here I am."

"I won't go with you, Edward." Amanda's voice was steady, and her eyes were calm and certain as they met his. Underneath, she was not nearly so confident. Edward, as she knew from experience, would have no compunction about using force. In fact, she thought he would enjoy it: he liked to inflict pain.

"Oh, I think you will."

"You can't carry me screaming through the streets of New Orleans. And I *would* scream."

"I could if it were necessary. After all, I am your legal guardian, Amanda. But I hardly think it will be necessary, once you've thought the matter over. Because there is obviously one aspect of it that you haven't considered."

Amanda looked at him in silent defiance, but her thoughts were churning. What could he mean?

"You haven't thought about your lover. If you don't come with me willingly, I will go to the British consul and tell him that an escaped murderer is here in New Orleans, living with my sister, whom he kidnapped. You would, of course, immediately be handed over to me, and your lover would undoubtedly be handed over to the proper authorities for extradition. Have you heard of extradition, Amanda?" When she continued to stare at him numbly, he explained it to her in loving detail.

"Why are you doing this, Edward? Lord Robert can't possibly want to marry me now." She was struggling to keep the despair out of her voice. But

Edward had won, and they both knew it: she would not be the cause of Matt's death.

"You're right, he doesn't. But he's willing to pay a good price to have you as his mistress, which is all you're fit for now. You should have considered that before you allowed yourself to be publicly disgraced, Amanda. No gentleman would marry you now. You'll end as a whore, like your mother, but without a husband to save your face." He smiled, clearly enjoying the prospect. "I've had to sell Brook House—because of you, you bitch—but I still need the money. And *you* need a lesson."

Amanda stared at him, fear and anger and desperation written plainly on her face. Edward's smile widened as he watched her. "Well, will you come with me?" he demanded silkily. Amanda swallowed, knowing there was only one reply she could give but unable to say the words. She would have to go with him, of course. She opened her mouth to tell him so. Then, to her mixed relief and dismay, there was a movement in the doorway. Matt stood there, his arms crossed over his chest, his wide shoulders leaning negligently against the jamb as he surveyed the scene before him. Dressed in the same pale gray pantaloons and dark blue coat he had worn at breakfast, his white shirt and elegantly tied cravat making his lean face seem even darker in contrast, he looked very big and very dangerous. Edward looked at him and stepped backward. Amanda had to fight an urge to run to Matt's side. His presence couldn't help her, of course; if anything, it merely complicated matters, because she doubted that Matt would easily agree to let her leave—especially with Edward. And if she didn't go with Edward, she had no doubt that her half brother would carry out his threat. But just looking at Matt made her feel infinitely better.

"Your half brother, I presume?" Matt asked Amanda softly. The sunlight glinted on his black hair as he turned his head in her direction. Amanda nodded, the movement jerky. The look Matt turned on Edward sent shivers down her spine; the smile that curved those handsome lips was tigerish.

chapter twenty-two

"A most unexpected pleasure." Matt's voice was so soft it was almost a purr. Amanda looked across at him, her eyes widening with alarm. She had never heard quite that note of deadly menace in Matt's voice, and it frightened her. At all costs, he must not be allowed to do Edward an injury. If he did, Edward would surely inform the authorities whether or not Amanda went back to England with him.

Swallowing, she crossed the room to catch at his arm. "Please, Matt, don't make any trouble," she whispered. He barely glanced down at her; all his attention was focused on Edward, who was staring back at him, his gaze measuring.

"You must be the murderer." Edward, evidently recollecting the sword he held over Matt's head, had recovered his aplomb. There was a barely disguised jeer in his voice. Amanda felt Matt's muscle tense beneath her hands, and she tightened her grip on his arm.

"Yes." Matt was still smiling, but it was the most ferocious-looking smile Amanda had ever seen. She cast a warning glance at Edward, who seemed unaware of his own danger. In a bottle-green coat and pale yellow breeches that showed his tall, slender figure to advantage, Edward looked the epitome of an elegant English nobleman.

"You were speaking to your sister when I came in, I believe. Would you care to repeat your words to me?"

Matt was going to kill him. Amanda could read his intention in his eyes, his voice, his very stance, which reminded her of nothing so much as a tiger poised to spring. And much as she would like Edward to get what he deserved, she couldn't allow Matt to do it. For his own sake.

"Edward was telling me that he has come to fetch me home," she put in hurriedly, before Edward could reply provocatively. "I . . . it would be best, Matt."

He looked down at her then, his eyes gentle for just a moment. Amanda was dazzled as she stared up into that lean, dark face. It had been a long time since he had looked at her like that.

"Never fear, Amanda. I heard what your half brother had to say—nearly every word, I imagine. And you're not going with him."

"If you think that, you must have missed one very important point, Grayson," Edward said, his narrow face insolent. "I shall go to the authorities and tell them where they can find you if Amanda doesn't do as I say."

Matt smiled that ferocious smile again. "No, I did hear that. And I meant what I said: Amanda isn't going anywhere."

"Matt, he *will* do it," Amanda said urgently. Her nails dug into his arm with the force of her agitation.

"I have no doubt that he will." Matt was looking down at her with that same dizzying expression in his eyes. "But it doesn't make any difference, actually. This morning I received an interesting message. Van Horn, the man I sent to England, found the necessary witness. And she's been persuaded to tell her story to the authorities there. The charges against me will, of course, be dropped."

"Oh, Matt, that's *wonderful*."

Matt smiled at her, then his attention moved back to Edward. "You owe your sister an apology." There was a steely edge to his voice, but Amanda was no longer worried. Matt wouldn't actually kill Edward, and Edward did deserve a thrashing.

"Apologize to Amanda?" Edward, realizing that his hold over Matt, and through him Amanda, was now substantially weakened, began to bluster. "Whatever for?"

"For threatening her." Matt's voice was mild. "And for calling her a whore. As well as for all the other insults."

"You *heard* all that?" Amanda couldn't believe her good fortune. If Matt had heard Edward's insults, he had also heard Edward boasting about being responsible for the soldiers on the beach that morning.

Which meant that Matt could no longer believe she had betrayed him...

"I heard." Matt looked at Edward. "Well, Culver?"

"And if I choose not to apologize?"

"I think you're too intelligent not to." Every word Matt had uttered had been perfectly civil, but Amanda could see that Edward was sweating. Perspiration beaded the high, pale forehead and dampened the edges of the fair hair.

"Very well." Edward gave in with poor grace. "Amanda, I apologize. Now, if you'll excuse me..."

He took a few tentative steps toward the door, then stopped when it became obvious that Matt had no intention of moving out of his way.

"There's just one point more." Matt's voice was still soft, but the gleam in his eyes was deadly as he straightened to balance on the balls of his feet. "Amanda, leave us, please."

She looked up at him, wide-eyed. "Why?"

"Because I told you to. Now, go on."

Amanda bit her lip. She did not want to leave the two men alone, but neither did she want to argue with Matt in front of Edward. Those silvery eyes flicked a warning look down at her. Reluctantly she went. But no farther than just outside the door, where she could hear everything that took place in the parlor.

There was a brief silence, as if Matt were waiting for her to be out of earshot.

"What do you want?" Edward sounded uneasy.

"As I said, we have one more thing to discuss: the matter of a very painful, swollen bruise you inflicted not so long ago on your sister's cheek."

"I never—"

"Oh, yes, you did. I saw her. And I mean to give it back to you—with interest."

There was a sudden flurry of movement, a cry, and then the sickening sound of a fist thudding into flesh. Amanda ran back into the room in time to see Matt deliver a hard blow to Edward's abdomen. Edward doubled over, gasping. Matt jerked him upright by his collar and held him that way just long enough to repeat the action.

Edward was groaning, his face pasty white beneath the blood from Matt's first punch. Matt grinned, a savage flash of white teeth in his dark face. Then his fist again slammed into Edward.

"Matt, *don't. No more.*" Despite her feelings toward Edward, Amanda was sickened by the violence, and the sight of blood dripping from Edward's nose onto the polished floor made her feel ill. Matt looked at her, clearly debating with himself, but when he saw her white face, he made a sound of disgust and let go of Edward's collar. Edward collapsed to the floor, his knees coming up to his chest as he gasped and groaned.

"I thought I told you to leave." Matt's voice still had an angry rasp.

"I did, but... oh, have you killed him?" This last came as Edward groaned loudly and tried unsuccessfully to lift his bloodied face from the floor. There was so much blood he was almost unrecognizable.

"No, I haven't killed him."

He looked up then, saw the small army of servants that had congregated in the doorway and beyond, and frowned.

"George, Malcolm," he said to the butler and

yardboy, "remove this man and take him to his hotel."

"Yes, sir." The two spoke in unison, and moved forward to catch Edward under the arms and hoist him upright.

"As for you," Matt said to Edward, the deadly edge back in his voice, "if I ever set eyes on you again, or if Amanda does, I shall finish the job. Do you understand?"

Edward managed to nod. Matt gestured to the men, and they carried out the still-groaning Edward.

"The rest of you, go back to work. Lalanni, bring me a bottle of brandy and two glasses."

The servants dispersed like leaves in a whirlwind. Lalanni brought the brandy and glasses, then left the room.

"Drink this." Matt poured a generous measure of brandy into a glass and held it out to Amanda. He had already seated her on the chaise longue. Standing beside her chair, looking down at her with an abstracted expression on his dark face, he seemed very remote.

"I don't like brandy."

"Drink it." He pushed the glass into her hand and watched as she drained it. He took the empty glass from her, set it on a nearby table, poured himself a large measure of brandy, then drank it in a single gulp. Having refilled the glass, he came to stand over her again.

"Feel better?"

"Yes." She smiled at him. He didn't smile back. His eyes were brooding as he stared out the window at the lush garden.

"Matt..."

"Amanda," he said at the same time. He paused, frowning down at her. She had no way of knowing how very beautiful she looked, with her cascades of hair confined in an elegantly simple knot on the top of her head while curling tendrils escaped to frame her small face in a cloud of ruby silk. She was very pale from shock, and her eyes were huge and almost purple beneath their frame of thick black lashes as she looked up at him. Her mouth was soft and defenseless, the color of the roses in the garden and twice as enchanting. Her skin was dewy, glowing like the finest pearl. The neckline of her dress was very low, allowing him, from his vantage point above her, to see the shadowy valley between the swelling mounds of her breasts. In the unadorned white dress she wore, she looked very young and very innocent. All at once the magnitude of what he had done to her struck Matt like a blow between the eyes, and he winced.

"Are you hurt?"

He shook his head, unsmiling. He seemed to want to say something, without quite being able to force the words past his lips.

"Edward didn't hit you, did he?" She looked at him anxiously. He had such a strange look on his face.

"Not likely." One side of his mouth twisted up sardonically. "I grew up in the toughest alleys in one of the toughest ports in the world. Your dandified brother didn't touch me."

"Your hand is bleeding," Amanda said suddenly, observing the hand raising the glass of brandy to his lips. He swallowed the liquid quickly, as if he needed it.

"Is it?" He sounded unconcerned as his eyes flicked indifferently over the smear of blood on his knuckles. Setting the glass on a nearby table, he extracted a handkerchief from his pocket and twisted it around the cut. "I must have caught his tooth."

Amanda eyed him, puzzled. He looked strange and he sounded strange, as if he had an unpleasant duty to perform and he was nerving himself for it. Matt didn't speak again for several minutes, merely stood beside her chair with his bandaged hand resting on the apple-green upholstery near her head as he stared out at the garden.

"I made your brother apologize to you," he said finally, looking down at her with a wry twist to his lips. "But I owe you an apology more than he did. I am sorry, Amanda. I should be shot at sunrise for what I've done to you."

She met his eyes with a faint smile in her own. He looked very handsome, with his black hair tousled as a result of his encounter with Edward and his silvery eyes almost the color of smoke. His mouth was held in a taut, straight line, as if he were afraid that she would fling his apology in his teeth. Apologizing was new to him, Amanda surmised.

"I never betrayed you," she said, looking at him steadily. She wanted to make sure that point was understood.

"I know . . . now." He looked away from her, spots of dark color rising to stain his high cheekbones. "I've been every sort of scoundrel. You told me and Zeke told me. I almost bloodied his nose for him, he kept after me so much. I thought he was just blinded by you—you're very blinding, Amanda," he added with a flicker of a wry smile, looking down at her briefly before looking away again. "But it was I who was blind. I didn't think it was possible for anyone to be as lovely and sweet and innocent as you seemed. I was wrong. And I'm sorry."

"I know, Matt." She spoke softly; there was a sudden lump in her throat.

"I always knew you were an angel," he said with a strangled laugh. Amanda smiled at him and reached up to touch the battered hand that rested beside her head. He caught her hand and lifted it to his mouth, pressing a kiss to the slender fingers. "Say you forgive me," he muttered against her fingers, the words almost an order. He was recovering his usual confidence, Amanda saw, noting the widening smile and the relaxing of his tense stance.

"You are an arrogant, pig-headed swine," she began severely, then smiled as his eyes narrowed. "But I forgive you."

Amanda moved her legs aside and patted the end of the chaise longue in silent invitation. Matt came around the chair and sat down, lifting her feet cozily into his lap. "I don't deserve you, Amanda," he said, his tone remorseful as he released her hand.

"No, you don't," she agreed with a smile. He smiled back, his eyes laughing.

"You don't have to agree with me," he complained.

"I'm a dreadful liar," Amanda reminded him demurely, and he laughed.

"Let me make it up to you, Amanda," he said, catching her hand and holding it tightly. "Marry me."

Amanda's eyes were as big as saucers as she searched his face. He was smiling at her, but his eyes were grave. He looked so handsome, so dear, that he caught at her heart. The one thing she had wanted more than anything else on earth had finally happened: he was asking her to be his wife. And she wanted to. She wanted to love him and have him love her for the rest of their lives. Then a tiny frown pleated her brow. He had said nothing of love—perhaps he was shy. At the thought of Matt being shy the frown vanished and she smiled deliciously. She would give him plenty of encouragement...

"You're looking at me as a hungry little cat looks at a canary." His smile widened. "Won't you give me your answer, Amanda?"

The tenderness of his voice was almost her undoing. She battled an urge to fling her arms around his neck and cry her acceptance to the world. But there was something she wanted to hear first.

"Why, Matt?" She looked at him through the veil of her lashes.

"Why?"

"Why do you want to marry me?"

His lips twisted, and her heart began to pound with hope. Now he would say it...

"It's the least I can do, under the circumstances—and as an *amende honorable*, if you will. What your brother said—though it enraged me at the time—is true. I *have* ruined your reputation, and with it your chances for the sort of life that is your due. I can't give it back to you, but I can give you the protection of my name. And I'll take good care of you, Amanda. You'll never want for anything as my wife."

Amanda felt deflated, like a punctured balloon. He would marry her only to salve his conscience. She had known almost from the beginning that he was an honorable man. Why, then, did she hurt so much now? She ought to have known that would be his reason for proposing. Perhaps if she had not raised her hopes, she would not now feel as if she wanted to cry and never stop.

"Well?" he demanded, impatient. From the look on his face, he was in no doubt of her answer. And she supposed he had every right to look that way. Under the circumstances, she was a fool not to jump at the chance.

"No," she said, lifting her legs from his lap and standing up. He stood, too, his face a study in contradictory emotions, and caught at her arm.

"What do you mean, no?" He sounded dumbfounded.

"No, I won't marry you." She tried to pull her arm from his grasp, but he refused to release her, his long fingers biting hurtfully into the soft flesh.

"Why the hell not?" He was both angry and affronted. Amanda reflected bitterly that it must be quite a jolt to nerve oneself to make a proposal of marriage that one really did not want to make and then have it thrown back in one's face. The sense of relief, she suspected, would come later.

"Because, to be frank, it doesn't sound like a very good proposition." Suddenly she was consumed with a need to hurt him as he had hurt her. Not that she could, of course. Her ridiculous love for him gave him an unfair advantage. But she could prick his vanity. She managed a silvery laugh. "You're very attractive, of course, but... *marriage*. When I marry, it will have to be to someone of my own social class. If I didn't, if I married someone like you, my father and all my ancestors would turn in their graves."

His face blanched. "Why, you snobbish little..."

Amanda smiled tauntingly as she watched him suffer. Not that anything could make up for the pain in her own heart.

"I'm sorry, Matt," she said very gently. "But I felt that it was best to be honest." He stared at her as she gently disengaged her arm from his slackened fingers. Then she turned on her heel and left the room.

"Where do you think you're going?" He was behind her, and he sounded ugly. Amanda smiled. She hoped that his damaged pride was paining him as much as her damaged heart was her. She cast a quick glance over her shoulder, surprised to find him so close.

"To my room. To pack. I'm leaving, Matt." They were in the front hall by then, and Amanda headed for the beautiful carved mahogany staircase that lifted gracefully into the upper regions of the house.

"The *hell* you are." He caught her arm again, swinging her around. Amanda glared at him, feeling fury flare and die as she saw his face. He looked half out of his mind. His mouth was contorted with rage, and his eyes glittered wildly down at her.

"You can't stop me, Matt," she said almost gently. He let out his breath with a sound like a snarl.

"Can't I, my fine lady?" He was looking at her as if he hated her. "We'll see about that."

Amanda turned away without replying, jerking her

arm from his grasp. Behind her she heard him swear violently. Glancing back over her shoulder, her eyes widened as she saw that he was coming up the stairs after her, vengeance in every line of that dark face.

chapter twenty-three

He caught her on the second-floor landing. Breathless, Amanda had picked up her skirts to run, hoping to reach her bedroom so that she could bolt her door against him. She didn't think that he would go so far as to burst through a locked door, not with the servants in the house. But Matt was too fast for her. Even as she had gathered up her skirts his hand closed over her arm roughly, swinging her around to face him. Amanda looked up at him, her heart pounding wildly at what she saw in his face. Then he bent and scooped her up in his arms, holding her struggling body hard against his chest as he strode down the hallway.

"Let me *go*, Matt." Suddenly he terrified her, this tall, dark man who was both lover and stranger. He looked like a man who had reached the end of his rope; his silver eyes burned with an unholy fire, and

397

that handsome mouth was set in a harsh, almost cruel line.

"Like hell." He looked down at her as he spoke. One corner of his mouth twisted up in a travesty of a smile, frightening Amanda almost more than the glitter of his eyes. Matt had shed his civilized skin like a snake, and she was left facing a primitive, untamed male.

"Matt..." She tried again to make him see reason, only to fall silent as he snarled.

"You always say my name so prettily." His tone was savage. "Do you do it deliberately, I wonder, or is it your feminine camouflage that gives you a voice like silk when underneath you're as hard and cold as a knife?"

"Matt, this won't stop me from leaving." She hoped to penetrate the angry bitterness that flamed so furiously in his eyes. As soon as she spoke, she knew that reminding him of her plans was a mistake. His jaw clenched, and his arms tightened around her, crushing her against his chest.

"Won't it?" He smiled down at her. Amanda shrank from the violence she saw in that smile. "I think it will. You're mine, Amanda, and this time I won't let you out of my bed until you know it, too. You belong to me—I'll never let you go."

"You're *insane*."

"If I am, you're the cause."

He had reached the end of the center hallway and now turned left along the corridor that led to his rooms. Lalanni came out of one of the bedrooms, a duster in her hand. Her eyes widened as she saw her master striding down the hall with a face like the devil's and Amanda struggling in his arms. The girl knew better than to say anything; Matt's face as he stalked past her told her that. She moved back into the bedroom, as if to make herself invisible. Amanda felt her face flame at being caught by her maid in such a humiliating position.

"Damn you, put me down." Embarrassment added fresh impetus to her struggles. Matt paid no heed to her efforts; he had reached the door to his bedroom and now shouldered through it. "Matt, I *won't* . . ."

Her voice trailed off and her face turned an even brighter shade of scarlet as she saw Lamb, Matt's valet, place a change of raiment on the bed. He regarded them incredulously.

"*Get out.*" Matt's voice was a snarl. Lamb, flushing, hurried to obey. When the door closed behind him, Matt strode to the bed, sweeping the carefully arranged clothes onto the floor with one hand before dropping Amanda onto the silk bedspread.

Amanda quickly rolled toward the edge of the bed and to her surprise, she wasn't stopped. Then she saw why. Matt stood between her and the door, a nasty, mocking smile on his face. As she watched he crossed to the door and turned the key in the lock. Then he came back to stand in the middle of the room. His eyes never left hers as he shrugged out of his coat and began to remove his cravat.

"This won't change anything, Matt," she warned, swallowing as she watched the lacy cravat fall to the floor and his fingers move to the buttons of his shirt.

"Won't it?" The last button came out of its hole; Matt pulled the shirttails from his pantaloons and shrugged out of the shirt. Amanda's mouth grew dry as she stared at the wide, bronzed shoulders and black-furred chest. If she were honest, she would have to admit that she had craved his lovemaking for weeks now. The last time he had taken her, he had introduced her to a range of pleasures that she had never imagined existed. Her cheeks colored at the memory of what he had done to her with his mouth and hands, and her heart began to beat faster. She wanted him—but she wanted him in love. Not like this, with anger and a desire to force her submission fueling his passion.

"If you do this, you'll regret it, Matt," she said softly. Standing in front of one of the two large, many-paned windows that stretched from floor to ceiling and let in a dazzling amount of sunlight, she could see every hair and pore on the bronzed skin while her face remained in shadow. Shirtless, he was magnificent: all hard muscle and rippling sinew, with a broad chest that could have been carved from teak and a flat, tautly muscled abdomen that she knew from experience was as unyielding as a board.

"I only regret not doing this weeks ago." He was bending to pull off his boots, then began to unfasten his pantaloons. "God knows why I didn't, but it doesn't matter. From now on I'll make love to you when, where, and how I please. And don't lie and pretend you'll find it a hardship. We both know that you enjoy the way I can make you feel—and we have only just begun."

"I won't be your mistress, Matt." He was sliding the pantaloons down over his legs, stepping out of them and letting them fall carelessly to the floor.

"I asked you to marry me." He straightened, looking

at her, his eyes suddenly keen. Amanda stared back at him, meeting his eyes calmly, determined not to let him know how affected she was by the sight of his nude body.

"I won't do that, either."

"Then, damn you to hell," he said, his voice suddenly thick. In two quick strides he was beside her. Amanda didn't try to run. There was no way she could escape him, and she knew it. As his arms came around her, pulling her hard against him, she knew that she didn't want to. She craved him as fiercely as he craved her.

When his mouth came down on hers, she met his kiss with a bitter passion that left him gasping. He didn't have to tell her what to do or force her response. Her arms twined about his neck, holding him tightly to her while her hands stroked the black head. She could feel the fine tremor in the hands that moved over her back, struggling with the myriad tiny hooks that closed her dress. She didn't notice when at last the dress fell open; her whole being focused on the kiss that threatened to steal her soul.

At first he had meant to hurt her. His mouth had been rough, insulting, as it had closed over hers. But when she opened her mouth to his without resistance, meeting his tongue with hers with a fierce joy, the kiss altered dramatically. It still throbbed with passion, but there was a tenderness in the chiseled mouth as it stroked over her lips that roused an ache deep in her belly. She wanted him—oh, God, she wanted him. More than she had wanted anything in her life.

She was hardly aware of what he was doing as his

hands brushed her clothes from her body. Finally she was naked in his arms, trembling as his hands found her breasts, the sun warm on her bare back and buttocks. Then his hands slid from her breasts down the front of her body and around to close over the curved flesh the sun had warmed. His big hands cupping her bottom, he lifted her, pulling her against him so that she was left in no doubt that she aroused him as much as he aroused her. Clinging to his neck, drowning in his kiss, she felt herself lifted off her feet, and then he was striding with her toward the bed.

It was a huge four-poster with a gold silk spread. Sunlight streaming in from the gold-curtained windows fell across it, warming the silk, which he didn't bother to pull aside. Achingly alive in every nerve, Amanda was aware of the sun-warmed silk against her bare back even as Matt came down beside her. Her hands moved restlessly over his shoulders, beseeching, as he kissed her deeply. She felt his hands in her hair as he withdrew the pins that secured her chignon. Then he was spreading her hair out against the silk, smoothing the thick waves. After a moment his mouth left hers and he buried his face in the soft fire of her hair.

"Matt..." she whispered in a low, aching voice as her hands ran over his shoulders and back. The contrast between the satiny skin of his shoulders and the rough mass of scars lower down twisted like a knife in her heart. She ran her fingers lightly, delicately over the raised surface. He shuddered against her. Amanda felt the movement of his big body with every centimeter of her skin. Then he moved on top of her, his mouth seeking and finding hers with a hungry eroticism that shook her to the depths of her being.

There was no hesitation—they wanted each other too much. Amanda twined her legs around his waist even as he settled himself between them, on fire for him, lifting her body in shameless need. He took her, fiercely, thrusting inside her with a flaming passion of his own. Amanda cried out, then cried out again as he repeated the movement. Then she was dissolving in a wave of bliss unlike anything she had known.

He was tireless. After that first time he took her again and again, in ways she had never dreamed a man could take a woman while the sun sank outside the windows and darkness stole over them like a velvet blanket. If she had been capable of conscious thought, she would have been shocked at some aspects of their lovemaking. But she was aware only of the volcanic heat of their passion, and how wildly she wanted him.

The moon had risen and was peering at them through the window when they both succumbed at last to an exhausted sleep.

Amanda awoke slowly, conscious of a penetrating warmth against her breasts and belly and thighs and around a narrow portion of her waist; her buttocks were cold. Frowning, she opened her eyes. Had she kicked the covers off half her body? She found herself staring directly at Matt's hard brown neck, and then she understood the reason for the mysterious disparity in temperature. He was holding her close against his chest, his arm around her waist and one muscular thigh thrown over both her legs. Everywhere he touched her, her body was toasty warm. But they were both naked, lying on top of the rumpled bedspread, and her buttocks were exposed to the night air.

The memory of what they had done, of her own wanton response, warmed her cheeks. He had treated her like something he owned, as if she had been bought and paid for, and she had reveled in it. How would she face him again without blushing? And then it came to her that she wouldn't, couldn't. Because she had refused his proposal of marriage, he had made her his mistress with a vengeance. But Amanda knew she couldn't live with either alternative—without love.

He had said many things in the heat of passion, but the word "love" had never passed his lips. And with good reason: he didn't love her. She doubted that he was capable of loving a woman. Oh, he wanted her; he had made that abundantly plain. But she needed more, much more. She needed to own him as he owned her, body and soul—and heart.

There was one other choice left to her. She could, as she had threatened earlier, leave him. Then she had been speaking in anger, and she doubted that, if he had persisted in his arguments, she would have acted on her threat. But now much more than anger was involved. Vividly she remembered that night in the cave, the first night he had kissed her, when he had warned her not to fall in love with him, warned her that he would break her heart. Well, she hadn't listened—and he hadn't lied. She had fallen in love with him as passionately as it was possible for a woman to love a man, and her heart felt as though it lay shattered in tiny, jagged shards inside her chest. She loved him—but he wanted only her body. That was the truth, however painful she might find it. She had to get away from him if she was ever to have a hope of repairing her fractured heart.

But where could she go? If she stayed in New Orleans, he would search for her, at least while his passion raged at its present white-hot intensity. Yes, she would have to leave New Orleans, but she was without funds or friends. Suddenly Mother Superior's kindly old face appeared in her mind's eye. If she returned to the convent, the sisters would take her in, she knew. The calm serenity of her days there beckoned to her. She needed peace now, whereas before she had craved adventure. Well, she had had her adventure, and it had been far more pain than pleasure. Suddenly she realized the answer to all her problems: she would return to the convent and, in time, perhaps take her vows. A life without pain or worry seemed infinitely appealing.

How would she get there? Amanda thought for a moment, and then the solution appeared. Zeke was leaving tomorrow—today—for England. If he would take her with him and deposit her at Lands End . . .

But first she had to get away from Matt. Her head was tucked cozily beneath his chin so that she couldn't see his face, but his deep, even breathing indicated he was still asleep. Even as she listened, a shallow snore confirmed her supposition. All she had to do was get out of the bed without waking him, dress, fling some clothes into a bag, and leave. But she had to hurry. If she knew aught about ships Zeke's would sail at dawn.

chapter twenty-four

It was a beautiful day, bright and sunny, the antithesis of Amanda's mood. The *Eloise* had been at sea for ten days; Amanda stood at the rail, staring glumly at the sparkling blue waves as they rolled and curled as far as the eye could see. She had achieved her goal: she had left Matt and was returning now to the convent. But she was miserable. And beginning to wonder if leaving Matt hadn't been a dreadful mistake.

Zeke had tried to talk her out of it. He had almost refused to take her with him, but at the end desperation had sent two big tears coursing down her cheeks, and, like his brother, Zeke was not proof against feminine tears. So he had allowed her on board, and the *Eloise* had sailed with the dawn. Since then, Zeke had grown progressively gloomier. He seemed to feel, like Amanda, that he had made a dreadful mistake.

To make matters worse, Amanda had been suffering from seasickness for almost the last week. Which was ridiculous, as the sea was as smooth as glass. But she was nauseated much of the time, unable to eat the shipboard fare. Zeke, becoming aware of her distress, had special dishes made up for her to tempt her appetite, but they suffered the same dismal fate as everything else she ate. Amanda supposed that her stomach must be reacting to her inner distress. It seemed that her whole body was rebelling against leaving Matt.

"Amanda." Zeke was coming down the stairs from the quarterdeck. Amanda turned to smile at him, unaware that she was so pale that she looked almost ghostly, and that her eyes were made even larger by the dark smudges beneath them. In the simple lavender-striped muslin day dress she wore, she looked almost fragile, her waist made tiny by the lavender sash, the dropped neckline revealing the delicate bones in her shoulders.

"You look ghastly," he said bluntly, crossing to stand beside her and looking down at her with concern. Amanda made a face at him.

"Thank you. You do know how to charm a lady."

He responded with a wry smile, reminding her so much of Matt that she felt a pang. She averted her eyes from his narrow face to stare again at the sea.

"Benson, the cook, tells me that you didn't eat anything again this morning."

"What is the use? You know as well as I that

whatever I eat will come right back up again. Besides, I wasn't hungry."

"If you don't eat, you'll make yourself ill."

"I'm ill now." That indisputable truth silenced him momentarily. Amanda knew he was genuinely concerned about her, and she appreciated it, but she was so miserable that she didn't want to talk about it. The state of her stomach was an annoyance, but it was not the worst of her distress. Her damaged heart was that.

"Amanda." Zeke's normally confident voice was oddly hesitant. It arrested Amanda's attention, and she turned to look at him, her brows lifted questioningly. She had not bothered to dress her hair that morning, had only run a brush through the thick waves and secured them back from her face with a lavender ribbon. The simple style made her look even younger than she was, and Zeke's frown deepened.

"Yes?" she said when it appeared that he wasn't going to say anything more. His eyes slid from her face to the sea, and he looked distinctly uncomfortable. Amanda's puzzlement grew.

"Amanda, forgive me for asking this, but... how long has it been since you've had your monthly time?" His face was scarlet as he put the question, and his eyes remained firmly fixed on the sea. Amanda blushed, too. A gentleman did not ask such a thing. Indeed, Amanda, like most of her sex, liked to think that men had almost no knowledge of a woman's bodily functions.

"I don't think that is your concern," she began

stiffly. He turned to look at her, his expression intent, although the embarrassed color remained in his face.

"Do think about it, Amanda," he said softly, looking grave. It had been a while, she remembered. Not since before Matt had had her dragooned aboard the *Clorimunda* . . .

"Oh, no," she whispered, appalled.

"My God," Zeke groaned, the color fading from his face. Apparently her horror-stricken voice was all the answer he needed. "I knew I should never have brought you with me. Matt will have my head on a platter when he finds out about this. You're carrying his child, and I'm taking you halfway around the world."

"It's nothing to do with him." Amanda raised her chin defiantly. Now was not the time to dwell on what she had discovered, to think what she would do now that she knew she was expecting a child. Under the circumstances, she could not even be sure that the convent would take her in. An unmarried girl who was with child—it was the ultimate in disgrace.

"You don't know much about it if you think that." Zeke's voice was dry. Amanda glared at him, blushed, and turned to stare back out to sea. "Well, there's no help for it. You won't be disembarking, my girl. You're coming back to New Orleans with me."

"No, I'm not."

"Oh, yes, you are. Like it or not, you're carrying my brother's child. That makes you my responsibility until you are safely back with Matt."

"I don't *want* to go back to Matt."

"But, you *will*." They glared at each other. Then Zeke's eyes gentled. "He'll marry you, Amanda,

410

you'll see. Matt wouldn't be Matt if he didn't do the honorable thing."

That flicked Amanda on a raw spot. She didn't *want* him to do the honorable thing. She wanted him to *love* her, damn it.

"I don't want him to do the honorable thing! He's already offered to, and I refused him."

"He asked you to marry him?" If possible, Zeke sounded more appalled than she had when the significance of her missed courses had become clear to her. "You didn't tell me that."

"You didn't ask me."

Zeke looked harassed. "Knowing Matt, it never occurred to me that he'd propose marriage to you— not without a compelling reason. He thinks marriage is a trap for fools—he's told me so times out of mind."

"Then I'm more glad than ever that I refused him," Amanda answered harshly.

Zeke groaned, rolling his eyes upward in a silent plea for strength before looking at Amanda again.

"I knew I should have steered clear of this. Damn it, Matt will have my hide, and I won't blame him. Why the hell didn't you tell me he wanted to marry you? I'd never have let you come aboard if I'd known. Instead you cried to get your own way." He sounded thoroughly disgusted.

"It worked, didn't it?" Amanda glared at him. His attitude infuriated her. Because she was carrying Matt's child, Zeke was ready to hand her over to Matt, lock, stock, and barrel. But she wasn't having any of that, thank you very much. Matt might be hard to defy, but she wasn't about to knuckle under to Zeke.

"God, I see now what my brother was up against.

I'm surprised he hasn't strangled you. I'm tempted to myself."

"Just you try, Zeke Grayson." Amanda tilted her chin at him belligerently.

Zeke stared down at her small, slender frame and had to laugh. "Matt told me you were a termagant, but I didn't believe him. Seems I've wronged him all around."

"I won't go back to him, Zeke." Amanda's anger had faded, and she spoke with quiet determination. Zeke's eyes turned serious, too, as they met hers.

"I thought you loved him." He spoke so quietly that Amanda wasn't prepared for the way the words stabbed at her heart. She turned away to look out to sea, not wanting him to see her face.

"Amanda?"

Amanda swallowed, then made an impatient gesture. "That's the problem—I do."

"God preserve me from women," Zeke muttered, putting his hands on her shoulders and turning her to face him. "Now, let me understand this: you love him, he wants to marry you, and that's the problem?"

Amanda met his steady gaze, and despite everything she could do, her lower lip quivered. "He doesn't love me," she explained softly.

Zeke's hands tightened on her shoulders, comforting her without words. "Are you sure?"

Amanda nodded miserably. Zeke started to say something, only to be interrupted by a cry from overhead.

"*Sail ho.*"

Immediately Zeke looked around, his expression changing dramatically.

"Where away?" he called back to the sailor high aloft in the crow's nest.

"Astern," came the answer, and unaccountably Zeke began to grin.

"Come," he said to Amanda, wrapping an arm around her waist and pulling her with him toward the quarterdeck. Once they were standing on the raised platform, Zeke let go of Amanda and seized a spyglass. Striding to the rail, he peered in the direction of the stern.

"Christ, it's too far away to be sure," he said disgustedly, lowering the glass.

"Be sure of what?" Amanda asked, mystified. Zeke waved an impatient hand at her.

"I'll tell you when I'm sure, which won't be for a couple of hours."

And despite her teasing, that was all he would say. It was rather more than a couple of hours before the ship came close enough so that Amanda could get an inkling of what he was talking about. She stayed on the quarterdeck for most of that time, scowling off and on at Zeke, who seemed oddly lighthearted. The ship behind them was at first no more than a tiny dot on the horizon, but gradually it grew until Amanda could see that it was much like the *Eloise* and the *Clorimunda*, a three-masted, high-prowed ship, elegant and graceful. Zeke seemed in no hurry to pull away from it, so Amanda deduced that he must know it for a friend. But he refused to answer any of her questions; instead he grinned maddeningly.

The sun was just beginning to sink below the horizon, bathing the sky and the sea and both ships with an orange glow, when the other ship pulled alongside. Watching, Amanda saw a sailor in the other ship's crow's nest wave two flags at them in a complicated pattern.

"Captain, he wants to come aboard," the sailor in the *Eloise*'s crow's nest called down to Zeke.

"He does, does he?" Zeke grinned. "Let's make him work for it. Tell him no, Darcy."

"Aye, sir." But the man sounded dubious. Amanda turned to Zeke, still puzzled. Then came an ear-splitting boom, and she turned back just in time to watch a round black missile arch over the *Eloise*'s prow. On the deck of the other ship, smoke billowed from the mouth of a small cannon.

"Zeke, they're *shooting* at us," Amanda exclaimed in horror.

Zeke grinned. "A warning shot over the bow only," he explained, his voice soothing. Then he grinned again. "He must be angry as hell."

"Who?" Amanda was still mystified. Zeke, shouting an order to heave to, didn't answer. She turned to look at the approaching ship again. *Rosimond* was the name on the prow. Thinking further about Zeke's odd reaction, she began now to have the faintest niggle of an alarming suspicion . . .

Zeke had left her side to see to the lowering of sails and anchor. Amanda turned back to watch as a small boat was lowered from the *Rosimond*'s deck. Three men climbed down a ladder from the deck to drop into the boat. Two began to row toward the *Eloise* while the other stood in the prow with one foot propped on the forward seat and his arms crossed over his chest. Even at that distance he looked furious—and familiar.

"Zeke, it's *Matt*." Zeke had come to stand beside her again. He was grinning, and at the horror in her voice his grin widened.

"It is," he said, sounding amused. "Come, let's meet him. Amanda, stay close to me, and allow me to do the talking. Agreed?"

Amanda looked at him. In that instant all her suspicions crystallized into certainty. "You knew he was coming, didn't you?" she said accusingly.

"Shall we say I hoped." Zeke slid his arm around her waist and propelled her with him toward the sailors who were lowering a ladder over the side.

Matt was the first one up the ladder. As he pulled himself up and over the side, Amanda stared at his face. It was black with temper. Instinctively she shrank against Zeke, who still had his arm fixed comfortingly around her waist. Matt looked up, saw them, and strode toward them.

"You son of a bitch," he roared at Zeke when he was still some paces away. "What the hell do you mean, sending me a message that you've run off with Amanda?"

chapter twenty-five

"It took you a long while to respond," Zeke replied mildly. The grin still played around the corners of his mouth. Matt glared at him, stalking across the deck until the two men stood eyeball to eyeball. Matt was some two inches taller than Zeke, and much broader and more muscular. Clad in a billowing white shirt and snug black breeches and boots, with his silvery eyes blazing murder and his mouth set in a hard, forbidding line, Matt looked capable of any violence. Standing slightly behind Zeke, ignored by Matt except for a single, searing glance, Amanda shivered. She was glad that all that fire and brimstone was not directed at herself.

"The only damned ship in port was being keelhauled," Matt growled. "Or I would have been here much sooner, I assure you. Damn it, Zeke, I should thrash you for all the trouble you've put me to."

"You didn't have to come," Zeke pointed out.

Matt snarled at him. "You knew damned well I would. Amanda is mine, and I don't share. Not even with you, brother."

One of Zeke's sandy eyebrows lifted in a quizzical gesture so reminiscent of Matt's that Amanda was struck again by the elusive resemblance. "Perhaps you should ask Amanda how she feels about that."

"I don't give a damn how Amanda feels. I've come to fetch her, and she's coming back with me. That's all there is to it."

At that blatant display of male arrogance, Amanda gasped indignantly. Stepping in front of Zeke despite his restraining arm, she glared up at Matt. Her eyes shot purple sparks at him while every inch of her small body shouted defiance.

"You don't *own* me, Matt. I'll stay with Zeke if I please."

"The *hell* you will." The fury in Matt's eyes blazed anew. Reaching out to grasp her roughly by the arm, he started to turn away, pulling the resisting Amanda behind him. She struggled, but her strength was as nothing compared to Matt's. He would have dragged her with him, willy-nilly, if Zeke had not stopped him with a hard hand on his shoulder.

"Wait, brother. Amanda is going nowhere she doesn't want to." Zeke's voice was calm, but something about the flat, even tone said that this time he was serious. Matt turned slowly back to look at him, not releasing his hold on Amanda's arm. She stopped struggling, looking from one man to the other with wide, alarmed eyes. There was no brotherly affection evident between them now; they were two hard-eyed men on the brink of doing battle.

"Take your hand off me, brother, and get out of my way." Matt spoke with a barely controlled menace.

"And if I do not?" To Amanda's horror Zeke seemed to be deliberately trying to rile Matt. They were glaring at each other as if they would come to blows at any moment—and relish the fight. Amanda bit her lip. Zeke was nearly as tall as Matt, with a wiry, whipcord strength, but he lacked Matt's power. In a fight between them, Amanda had little doubt about who would emerge the victor. And she knew that she couldn't bear it if she were to cause a rift between these two men who loved each other dearly, and whom she had come to love, each in a different way.

"Zeke, I'll go with him," she said softly before Matt could reply. Both men looked down at her, Matt's eyes as hard as the hand that still encircled her arm; Zeke was frowning.

"You don't have to, Amanda. He can't force you to."

"Can't I?" Matt's silky tone contained a threat. Zeke looked from Amanda's face to Matt's, his hazel eyes acquiring a steely gleam similar to his brother's.

"No," Zeke said with soft assurance. "I am captain here, and in command. Take a look around you, brother."

Matt glanced swiftly around, and so did Amanda. She was surprised to see the two men who had rowed Matt from the *Rosimond* planted squarely behind him while the entire thirty-man crew of the *Eloise* gathered around them in a loose circle. If the

Eloise's men decided to take Zeke's part, as he seemed to feel they would, Matt and his men would be easily overpowered. But she couldn't let it come to that. Zeke was dependent on his brother for his livelihood, and, besides, the affection that had always flowed between the two of them had been heartwarming. She couldn't destroy that, even if she wanted to stay with Zeke. Which she didn't. Angry or not, she longed to be back in the shelter of Matt's arms. If nothing else, her flight had taught her a hard-earned lesson: whether or not he loved her, she loved him. If his passion and his name were all she could have of him, she would take them and be grateful.

"Zeke, I will go with him. Please don't cause any trouble."

Zeke looked down at her. His mouth was still hard, but there was a gleam almost of laughter in the hazel eyes. She stared back at him, frowning. And then it occurred to her that the exchange between Zeke and Matt had been false from the start, at least on Zeke's part. Why, only a few hours before, he had been bound and determined to return her to Matt whether she would or not. What had caused the sudden reversal? Her eyes narrowed suspiciously.

"If you truly want to go, I won't stop you," Zeke said to her, still sounding grim. "But if I were you, Amanda, I wouldn't. At least not until I had the answers to a few questions. Why has he come hightailing it after you, and why is he so angry that you left? He never cared before when a woman left him. In fact, he usually showed her the door."

"Be quiet, Zeke," Matt growled warningly. Amanda's

eyes searched his lean, handsome face, surprised to see a tinge of dark color appear in the high cheekbones. He still looked furious—but also strangely ill at ease. He met her gaze briefly, then his hand tightened around her arm. "Come, Amanda. We're leaving."

She resisted, pulling back against the hand that urged her forward. "No," she said clearly. "Zeke is right. I won't leave until you answer the question. Why *did* you come after me, Matt?" She looked up at him steadily, her head slightly tilted so that her hair spilled down her back in gleaming red waves. The setting sun caught the silky strands, gilding them so that her small face seemed to be surrounded by a fiery nimbus. Her violet eyes were wide and questioning as his gaze met them almost unwillingly. She looked very small and fragile in the full-skirted dress striped with the color of her eyes—and so beautiful that she took his breath.

"I told you—you're mine." The words were gruff. "You knew I'd never let you go. I had made that clear before you left. Which is why, I suppose, you sneaked off like a thief in the night."

"But why *won't* you let her go, brother?" Zeke prodded mockingly. "You often shared a woman. Why, I remember three that you passed on to me."

Matt glared at him. "If you don't keep your mouth shut, I'll shut it for you with a great deal of pleasure. Especially if I find you've laid so much as a finger on Amanda. I haven't forgotten that night you kissed her, and it will never happen again."

"But what is so different about Amanda?" Zeke persisted. "You never minded sharing before—"

"Damn it, I *love* her," Matt growled, dark red color washing into his cheeks and his eyes staring furiously at his brother. Amanda stood transfixed. She couldn't believe what she had heard . . .

"Matt," she said softly, wonderingly. His hand dropped away from her arm and he turned on his heel, casting a furious glance at the grinning circle of men as he stalked toward the ladder. As Amanda started after him Zeke caught her arm.

"You'd best gather your things," he advised softly. "It's a long way back to New Orleans." Then he winked at her and grinned.

"Thank you, Zeke." Amanda's smile came from the heart. Then she hurried to her cabin, where she quickly stuffed her clothes and toilet things into her valise. Bright-colored tufts of several dresses and a tier of lace from a petticoat dangled from the valise when she dragged it on deck, but Amanda could not have cared less. She had a horrible fear that, having said what he had, Matt might actually leave without her. And at first she thought he had. Neither he nor his two men were on deck.

"*Zeke.*" She turned alarmed eyes on him as he walked to meet her.

"He's waiting—in the boat," Zeke reassured her, taking the valise from her hand and ushering her to the dangling ladder. Looking over the rail, Amanda saw the small boat bobbing below, with Matt in the prow and the two sailors ready at the oars. Matt looked up, scowling.

"Here, brother," Zeke called blithely down, and heaved Amanda's valise over the side. Matt caught it deftly and turned to set it aside. Then Zeke whispered to Amanda, "Be gentle with him. I think, for the first time in his life, he is feeling shy." And he grinned broadly.

"I will," Amanda promised, grinning back. Then, impulsively, she reached up to plant a soft kiss on his cheek. To her amusement Zeke actually blushed.

"I'm glad he's down there," he said, jerking his thumb at Matt, who was glaring up at them, his fists clenched in obvious anger. "Take care of yourself, Amanda, and my nephew or niece. And tell my cross-patch of a brother that I'll see him when I return."

"You take care, too, Zeke," Amanda said softly, and then he helped her over the side.

Matt caught her as she neared the end of the ladder, his big hands hard on her waist as he swung her into the boat. Amanda clutched at his forearms for balance, looking up at him as he settled her on the seat, searching vainly for some sign of softening in his face. His eyes were like flint, and his face could have been carved from stone. When she smiled at him, his answer was a cold glare. Still, Amanda was happy. He had said he loved her, and he wouldn't have unless he meant it. They could sort out whatever was troubling him as soon as they were alone.

When they reached the deck of the *Rosimond*, however, it became clear that Matt had no intention of giving her a chance to talk to him. He strode away from her, curtly instructing one of his men to show her to the captain's cabin. Amanda stared disappointedly at his retreating back. Then, suddenly, she had had enough.

"Matthew Grayson, you come *back* here," she yelled. He turned slowly, as if he couldn't believe his ears, to find her glaring at him, hands on hips as the temper that went with the color of her hair crackled from her eyes.

"*What* did you say?" The tone was ominous.

"You heard me." Oblivious of the gaping stares of the men as they looked from her slight figure to their captain's large form, she tilted her chin at him belligerently. His mouth tightened as he strode back to her.

"Have a care, my girl," he growled, grasping her upper arms and glaring down at her. "I have enough scores to settle with you."

"I want to talk to you," she said determinedly, ignoring his implied threat and matching him glare for glare. His eyes glittered as they met hers, and a tiny nerve began to jump at the corner of his mouth.

"I fail to see that we have anything to talk about."

Amanda's eyes blazed. "*Oh?*" She was quivering with temper. "In front of your brother and a whole ship's crew, you said that you loved me. And you don't think we have anything to talk about? Well, *I do.*"

The tips of his ears went red. His hands tightened on her arms, and there was a sudden vulnerability in his eyes that he tried to mask with an icy glare. He swore under his breath, and then he released one of her arms and began to pull her after him toward his cabin, nestled under the quarterdeck.

When they were alone, he let go of her, crossing to a cabinet and extracting a bottle of whiskey and a glass. Amanda leaned against the closed door, watching as he sloshed some of the golden liquid into the glass and bolted it back in a single swallow.

"Matt," she said softly. His back was rigid as he gripped the edges of the cabinet with both hands. Then he turned slowly to face her.

"How fond of my brother are you, Amanda?" he shot at her, the telltale nerve still leaping in his jaw.

Amanda smiled at him. "Very fond. Just as I would be if he were *my* brother. And very grateful to him, too. He arranged all this, you know, Matt."

"He ran off with you, you mean." He eyed her grimly.

"No." Amanda shook her head. "I begged him to take me. He didn't want to—but I cried. Neither one of you seems to have any resistance to tears. And he meant for you to come after us. He would have taken me back himself if you hadn't."

Matt's scowl wavered. "I must admit, I wondered about that message. He knew I'd come—and he's damned lucky I didn't throttle him. I went mad looking for you that morning. God knows what could have happened to you if you'd gone off on your own. I didn't get Zeke's message until that night—and by then I'd searched the whole town. He's lucky it took so long to reach your ship—I had time to remember that he is my brother." He hesitated, then shot her an uncertain look. "Why did you leave me, Amanda?" he suddenly asked in a softened tone.

She met his eyes with a tender gaze. "I couldn't bear it any longer. It was torture being with you, thinking that you didn't love me—when I love you."

"Is that the truth?" His voice was curiously unsteady.

"Cross my heart." She laughed a little, but there was a faint mist clouding her vision. He made a muffled sound deep in his throat, then held out his

425

arms to her. She ran into them with a little choked cry.

They closed around her, squeezing her so tightly she could hardly breathe. His face came down to rest on her soft hair, lightly kissing the sweet-smelling strands. Amanda's arms went around his waist, holding him close. He felt so hard and strong and solid against her. She knew, with a heart-quaking sense of wonder, that at last she had come home.

"I wanted you from the first moment I saw you on the beach," Matt whispered into her hair, his voice thick. "You were so small, and so exquisite. But then I found out that your heart was as beautiful as your face, and I was lost. I loved you, Amanda, when you cried over my scarred back, though I wouldn't admit it even to myself. And I loved you more the first night we made love. When you said you loved me... You don't know what you did to me, Amanda. I was yours from that night on. I wasn't going to abandon you to the machinations of that swinish brother of yours. When I left, I had already decided that you would come with me. I wanted to take care of you, spoil you a little, give you everything you didn't have."

"Oh, Matt..." That was all she could force through a throat that was suddenly tight. She had never dreamed that he loved her this much; it was everything she had ever wanted and more.

"I've been a swine to you," he muttered. "I know it. How *could* I have thought you had betrayed me?"

She pulled a little away from him then, smiling up at him mistily and placing silencing fingers over his mouth.

"Hush," she said softly. "We won't talk about that. I understand."

He smiled back at her, a crooked twist of his lips that said almost as much as the soft blaze in his eyes. "You're an angel," he said, catching her hand and pressing his lips into the palm. "My own red-haired angel. Marry me, Amanda."

Her eyes glowed. "Yes, darling," she answered, loving him with her voice as well as her eyes. His eyes flamed down into hers, and then he was swinging her off her feet, finding her mouth with his as he carried her to the bunk.

It was a long time later when she remembered to tell him about the baby.

epilogue

Zachary Peter Grayson made his entrance into the world on February 3, 1843, at half-past five in the morning. His father and uncle had been keeping vigil downstairs in Belle Terre's library since one o'clock the previous afternoon. Nervous as schoolboys, wincing at every cry from the bedroom above, they had mutually turned to strong drink for moral support. By the time Master Zack deigned to appear, the men were well past the stage commonly described as falling-down drunk. Amanda, upstairs in the master bedroom with two maids, a midwife, and a doctor in attendance, scarcely glanced at her son before falling into an exhausted sleep. Matt, when invited upstairs by the doctor to make the new arrival's acquaintance, showed even less interest. He ignored his son completely, heading straight for his wife's side, taking time only to press a gentle kiss on her brow and assure himself that she was indeed asleep and not dead before he passed out on the floor at her side.

Two months later, however, Master Zack's position in the household was very different. His doting mama and proud papa were eager to carry out his slightest wish (which they somehow divined from his various gurgles and smiles and coos), and his fond uncle brought him ridiculously unsuitable presents every time he returned from a voyage. In deference to Zack's existence, Matt had to all intents and purposes given up the sea, preferring to stay at home until Zack and Amanda could accompany him. He divided his time contentedly between overseeing Belle Terre's sugar crop and attending to his shipping business in New Orleans. Amanda was seldom far from his side.

"Doesn't he look like an angel?" Amanda asked fondly early one morning in April as she lay her sleeping son down in the hand-carved wooden cradle that stood in the place of honor at the foot of the bed in the master bedroom. Matt, having watched her nurse the child—Zack's greediness was a never-ending source of amazement to him—from the warm comfort of the big bed, smiled and stretched against the pillows.

"An imp of the devil, more like," he said, his voice gruff although his eyes were as fond as Amanda's as he studied the tiny, red-haired, thumb-sucking being who was his son.

"He is *not*." Amanda rounded on her husband, who grinned lazily at her. The sun was just beginning to peep over the horizon, sending golden rays into the room through the open windows. One touched

Amanda's unbound hair, bringing it to life in all its crimson glory. Newly slender, her face still flushed with the sleep that Zack had called her from, clad in a prim white nightgown, she looked scarcely more than a child herself; certainly not old enough to be the mother of a son.

"If he's an angel, then he must take after his mother." Matt's voice was indulgent. "Who is sweet as a kiss and heart-stoppingly beautiful. Aren't you coming back to bed?"

Amanda looked over at him, smiling. There was no mistaking the amorous note in his voice. The last months of her pregnancy and then her recovery from a difficult birth had forced a long period of abstinence on both of them. Since the doctor had pronounced her fit just two short weeks ago, Matt had been insatiable. Not that she minded, she thought with a grin. She had been insatiable herself.

"Don't you have to go to the fields?" She looked at him innocently through her lashes. Propped up against the pillows, his black hair tousled and his wide shoulders very bronze against the white linen, he was the epitome of the virile male. The sheet lay across the lower half of his body, leaving the broad, black-pelted chest bare to excite her imagination. As for his face—he was still the most breathtakingly handsome man she had ever seen.

"Later," he said, his voice thickening. "Come back to bed, Amanda."

She smiled at him, her eyes warming. Then she went back to bed.